RUN FOR YOUR LIFE

RUN FOR YOUR LIFE

A NOVEL

JEAN HOLBROOK MATHEWS

Covenant Communications, Inc.

Cover image: *Dark Park Alley* © Jan Kowalski; Shutterstock

Cover design copyright © 2014 by Covenant Communications, Inc.

Published by Covenant Communications, Inc.
American Fork, Utah

Printed in the United States of America
First Printing: January 2014

19 18 17 16 15 14   10 9 8 7 6 5 4 3 2 1

ISBN 978-1-62108-477-8

To Ken and Sue R. for continuing friendship, support, and expertise.

Chapter One

THE TALL, SLENDER YOUNG WOMAN with honey blonde curls moved gracefully around the room, checking floral centerpieces on the round tables that filled the back half of the big meeting room. As she did so, she unconsciously pushed a stray curl behind her right ear.

Things will be different this year after the announcement tonight—slower, quieter. I'm going to like that.

The news conference would begin in less than an hour. Her efforts for the entire week had been focused on arranging the details. This evening had been chosen so the story would make the Saturday night news broadcasts and Sunday edition of the paper. The meeting room at the Mesa Hilton just off Highway 60 was ready, and she expected that reporters from the local TV stations would begin arriving within the next thirty minutes to set up their cameras.

The royal-blue fabric of her dress reflected a slight sheen as she moved. It matched the blue ribbons on the red and white carnations that made up each centerpiece. Everything was ready, but something was bothering her. She hadn't heard from Craig since Tuesday.

What has kept him so busy? The ring of the cell phone in her pocket drew her attention.

She smiled broadly when she recognized Craig's number on the caller ID. "Hi, sweetheart, where have you been for the last four days? When you flew in from Washington with Uncle Max, I thought we were going to have some time together. When are you going to get here?"

His voice was tight with tension. "Mattie, I just left the district office. I needed to use the printer and the copy machine there. I'm headed to my car, so I should be at the hotel within the next twenty or twenty-five minutes."

"Be careful. The traffic is really—"

He cut her off. "Listen. That research paper I wanted to show your Uncle Max and Jeff Skidmore—the one on energy exploration—I've spent the better part of the last four days at the Ross Law Library at ASU verifying and expanding some of the information in it. I got most of the information from Ben Novak's younger brother, Theo. You remember Theo, don't you?" His words were coming fast.

Mattie knew Ben Novak well. She dealt with him by phone a couple of times a week. He was Max Southland's administrative assistant, usually referred to as an AA, the man who really ran the day-to-day operations of the Washington, D.C., congressional office and answered to her uncle.

"I've heard Ben speak of him—but I thought Uncle Max told you not to spend any more time on that energy research—that the matter isn't likely to be an issue in the election."

She could hear the crunch of gravel and the sound of passing vehicles as he walked to his car. "I know, Mattie, but I wanted to finish it because . . . well, I think when you read it, you'll see that the related legal matters Theo uncovered are critical on the national level, regardless of whether or not it's an election year. He discovered a hot law suit on the issue that's undoubtedly going to be appealed. What Theo discovered and what I've verified will impact the entire country. It involves the federal judiciary."

She heard him open his car door, slam it, and start the engine before he spoke again. "Theo e-mailed his research to me. He's a third year law student at the University of Texas in Austin, and he's done some terrific in-depth research. The right people need to know what he's found. He told me when we talked on the phone Tuesday that one of his law professors said the paper was good enough to be published. Theo's really proud of it, and frankly, I think it's every bit as important as his professor thinks it is."

"What's in it that's so important?"

"What no one else has looked for. They thought they had covered their tracks."

"They who?"

"You'll see when you read the report. I have copies of it with me—one for Skidmore, one for your uncle, and I'll put one in the mail for you tonight since I'm sure you'll be too busy to give it any immediate attention. If you want to see it tomorrow, you can read the copy I'll give your uncle." He paused. "I just feel that I need a backup copy somewhere safe, and the US Postal Service will have to do. You should get it early next week. Protect it. Put it in a locked file cabinet or a safe after you read it."

The worry in his voice was contagious. "Okay. I'm watching for you. Drive carefully." *What could possibly have him so worried?*

***

On the previous Monday morning, Professor Jurazski had actually rapped his knuckles on the lectern to begin his class on corporate law. That was sufficiently unusual that nearly half the surprised students sat up straight and looked directly at him. The twenty-two third-year law students were scattered in the small lecture hall made up of three elevated rows of desks. Most wore a look of passivity which said, "Got to have the credit, don't have to like the class."

Jurazski stood about five foot four in his stocking feet but compensated for his lack of height with an explosive temper which could be turned on students who were not giving him or the subject matter the respect he felt was merited. He was a rotund man of sixty with a receding hairline and a gray comb-over that accentuated his round, pink face. His long-sleeved white shirt looked as if he had slept in it. He had.

He pulled a sheet of paper from a folder which contained the syllabus for the course. He stated forcefully in his slightly nasal voice, "I spent the entire weekend reviewing the initial drafts of the formal paper you were each required to turn in last Friday. I'm sure you will remember that the assignment read: *A minimum of fifteen pages reflecting on or demonstrating the interaction of at least one major corporation and the governmental agencies which are charged with its oversight with a special focus on court cases growing out of that relationship. The completed paper will constitute one-third of your final grade.*"

He folded his arms and leaned on the lectern, looking from one student's upturned face to the next for several seconds before speaking.

"I realize that a first draft is not expected to be a finished product, but apparently only Mr. Novak took the assignment seriously. The vast majority of the papers were mediocre at best, and at worst, a few were at least partially plagiarized. To show you what this assignment should have been, we're going to spend the balance of the week discussing Mr. Novak's paper in detail." He pointed at Theo and, with a wave of his hand, signaled him to approach the lectern.

This development was a dream come true for Theo. He was what many of the other students at the University of Texas School of Law contemptuously called "a gunner." He was a serious student, the kind that never wasted a weekend partying. Instead, he spent every spare minute studying alone or in study groups with some of the other ambitious students on campus.

He consistently sat in the front row and raised his hand to respond to every question the professor asked. He could spit out the facts and holdings and concurrences and dissents and majority opinions of every case discussed. During each class period, he would ask at least one question others hadn't thought about or didn't remotely care about but which required an extensive and complex answer. He stroked, he polished, he curried the favor of every professor. He was known to suck up the class time like a black hole in space. Most of the professors liked him and responded positively to his search for learning—even if they suspected that he was playing every angle to graduate top of his class.

He had already decided that he would interview with every law firm that solicited his application, no matter how bad their reputation for overworking their new associates or how sleazy their client list might be. He had every intention of making partner before anyone else who graduated in his class even neared that coveted position.

As he stepped up to the platform, he colored slightly from the collar of his green plaid sport shirt up to his short, fiery red hair. He was sheepishly grinning with pleasure. He cleared his throat. "Where would you like me to begin, Professor?"

Though the collective groan was not audible, it was palpably felt by every student in the class.

"By introducing the corporations you researched and their specialties. Then we will take up their relationships with governmental oversight agencies."

***

After his last class was over that day, Theo hurried in a half trot to the law library and inserted a USB drive into one of the computers. He was grinning with satisfaction. He muttered to himself, "If it's good enough for Professor Jurazski, then it's good enough for Congressman Southland and his staff." He brought up the Internet, typed in Craig's e-mail address, and hit the send button with a smile of satisfaction.

As his brother had suggested in their most recent conversation, Theo e-mailed his paper to the attention of Craig Crittenden, Southland's senior research staffer, who would be at Southland's district office all week.

On Tuesday, when Theo continued the discussion of the paper, he said with a touch of poorly camouflaged pride, "I've e-mailed the paper to the head research staffer for Congressman Max Southland. I'm hoping that he will take an interest in it."

One of the other students, a young man by the name of Wilbur "Will" Wilcoxin III, had busily taken notes throughout class on Monday, notes that filled much of a thick tablet, which he opened again on Tuesday morning. He wrote nearly as fast as Theo talked. Since he was the only class member earnestly taking notes, it was something Theo couldn't miss. He was flattered. Though they had been in several classes together, Will had never so much as spoken to Theo previously.

Theo, the other students, and the professors knew Will as the eldest son of the senior partner in the long-established New York law firm Doty, Dotson, and Diller, which was listed in the *Martindale-Hubble Legal Directory* as having 430 attorneys in nine offices across the United States and Europe, including offices in London, Milan, and Moscow. Will was perceived as the natural heir to his father's birthright, a young man with a future of legal fame and fortune awaiting him. He normally associated only with other students whose pedigrees guaranteed similar success.

At the end of the class period Tuesday, the professor thanked Theo and stated, "Mr. Novak's paper is so much more than a simple legal brief. It's a fully researched paper worthy of publication in one of the university's legal publications, perhaps the *Journal of Oil, Gas, and Energy Law* or the *Environmental Law Journal*. When we've finished our discussion of it, with Theo's permission, I plan to send a copy of it to a friend who has recently been appointed to the post of regional director of the EPA in San Francisco. I'm sure he will find it of *great* interest." He turned to Theo and added, "It's evident that you have a great future ahead of you in the legal profession, Mr. Novak. This is sterling work." Theo couldn't help but color with pleasure again.

As the class members rose from their seats, there was polite, scattered applause.

Will waited in the hall. "Theo, if you have some time, I'd really like to learn more about your research. Could I take you to lunch somewhere?"

Now Theo was *really* flattered. "Yeah, uh, sure. Anywhere you want."

"Just leave your bike in the rack. I'll drive. Let's go to Gino's on Twenty-Sixth. Ever eat there?" Theo shook his head. On his budget, he usually skipped lunch and had a peanut butter sandwich for supper.

"I know Gino," Will bragged. "He's got great Italian food, and he'll take good care of us." Theo followed Will to a new black Cadillac Escalade in the parking lot.

Theo looked it over enviously. Before he climbed in, he reached out and touched it to verify that it was real.

They sat in the back booth of the little restaurant, which was not yet busy at eleven in the morning. When their food was set before them, Will started his questions. He didn't eat much, mainly breadsticks, but kept his questions coming. When Theo was finished with his plate of spaghetti, Will ordered another for the lanky young man.

Whenever Theo paused to put a forkful of food in his mouth, Will would stroke his ego. "This is really great research, Theo. I think you ought to interview with my dad's firm in New York when you graduate."

Theo managed to eat and answer questions at the same time with amazing thoroughness. By the time the meal was over, Will had a good grasp of the balance of the information contained in the paper.

***

After he had dropped Theo back on campus, Will watched him climb on his battered bike and ride away. He pulled out the tablet he had been writing in so industriously during class and added the additional information he had extracted from the naïve, well-intentioned young man. That took nearly an hour. When he finished, he put the car into gear and drove directly to the nearest FedEx establishment. There, he mailed the tablet overnight to his father at the New York office. The package was marked *Urgent. Open Immediately.*

***

Just before his midafternoon meeting on Wednesday, Wilbur Wilcoxin II made a call to the firm's most important client on a telephone line equipped with a scrambler. He explained to the person on the other end of the line that he had called a meeting of the partners at the earliest possible opportunity. The conversation lasted a full fifteen minutes—longer than usual.

***

As the four other senior partners and the head of security entered one of the smaller conference rooms in the extensive offices of Doty, Dotson, and Diller, they noted that the expression on the face of Wilbur Wilcoxin II was as humorless as a hatchet. He handed each one a stapled copy of the notes made by his son and pointed each to a chair. He continued to stand.

The firm filled four upper floors of one of the major office buildings on Park Avenue, where 248 of the attorneys were housed in addition to legal assistants and other staff. Their list of prestigious clients included chemical companies, shipping lines, insurance companies, airlines, banks, oil and gas corporations, as well as several governments who were not necessarily friendly to the United States. The list also included several large foreign shell corporations which sheltered activities that would be less than completely legal in the eyes of the IRS and treasury department if examined closely.

Wilcoxin had startled his secretary of twenty-five years when he had insisted on going to the copy room himself, not trusting the task to an underling. His male administrative assistant was assigned to sit outside the conference room door when the meeting began and had been told that short of a call from the White House, they were not to be disturbed.

Little was said as, page by page, the men pored over the notes, paying special attention to the areas highlighted by Wilcoxin. Finally, Howard Redwinn could keep his alarm pent up no longer. His words exploded into the room. "You say that the kid that wrote this is a student at U.T. Law? Where'd he get this much information?"

"He must have the sources footnoted in the full paper. What you've got in front of you is just notes taken from the lecture." Grim lines were evident around Wilcoxin's mouth like hard parentheses.

The man sitting across from Wilcoxin looked directly at him. "Will, you've got to know that we're in this . . . this mess because we took your advice and accepted that narcissistic egomaniac as a client when no other reputable firm was willing to deal with him."

"Look, Brody, you and I both know that's all water under the bridge." The words were terse. "With his worldwide corporations totaling a yearly gross income of more than thirteen billion, and our annual legal fees budgeted at 1 percent, *we all* felt it was worth the risk, and that included you. Now the issue is . . ." He paused for effect, "What are we going to do about it?" He looked grimly from one man to the next.

George Westfall, who was sitting next to Brody, loosened his three-hundred-dollar tie and put his head in his hands. "If this gets out, it will halt the entire process. The president won't even return my calls. My nomination will sink like a rock." His jaw tightened. "Why now?" He looked up and hit the table with a fist in frustration. "Now, when my name is on the short list?"

The question was rhetorical. He didn't expect an answer. He moved his frustrated gaze to Wilcoxin, whose dark, heavy eyebrows were pulled together like an overhanging ledge above his eyes.

"Maybe I'd better withdraw my name. I don't want this mess to impact the firm's reputation." His voice was saturated with bitterness. He put his head in his hands again.

"Pull yourself together, Westfall," Wilcoxin roared in contempt. He impaled the man with his stare. "You can't ask to have your name removed from consideration. Any nominee who does that will receive as much scrutiny as the final appointee. Remember the scandal a few years ago about potential cabinet appointees who hadn't paid their taxes?" Wilcoxin stood over the seated men like Thor, ready to throw a thunderbolt.

Unconvinced, Westfall slumped in his chair. Wilcoxin continued angrily. "We've *got* to have you on the bench when *Strategic Petroleum v. BLM* comes up on appeal." His voice moderated. "If you're not selected for *this* vacancy, we'll see that there are others. Our case won't reach the federal circuit for another two or three years, and between the costs of the original court case and our contributions to senatorial campaigns and the president's campaign, we've got millions invested in this."

Westfall's head flew up, and his face reddened. "But my wife will leave me and take my kids if this all comes out. If this makes the papers, the president will drop my name like a hot potato. The media will turn over every rock in my life as well as every controversial client or case the firm's ever handled. With this president in the White House and the Senate in the hands of the other party, even a whiff of our ties to Volos will stop my appointment like a freight train that's hit a mountain."

Wilcoxin paced at the head of the table. He poured himself a drink of water from the carafe on the table and swallowed most of it to relax his voice. "George, you're crossing bridges before we get to them. Right now, the damage is contained. My son said that the lecture group where this paper was presented paid little attention and took few notes. He feels that we don't need to worry about a bunch of green law students."

Westfall wouldn't be pacified. "But according to these notes, the professor announced that he's going to have the paper published in one of the U.T. law journals! He said that the Novak kid bragged about his plans to e-mail it to a researcher for Congressman Max Southland. Southland heads the International Relations Committee and is a senior member of the Ways and Means Committee. I told you we should've left Arizona out of the law suit. If he sees the paper, he's bound to get into the matter." His head went back down into his hands, and his fingers ruffled his thinning hair.

Wilcoxin tried again to ease the worried man's panic. "It's been rumored that Southland will be retiring at the end of the year. That means any influence he might have had will be seriously diluted, which is to our advantage." Wilcoxin put his hand on Westfall's shoulder, as if to lend his strength to the man.

"I've made the phone call and secured official authorization from our client to take whatever action is necessary." He paused and looked directly at the man who sat at the far end of the table.

A nonlawyer, Carlo Gulletti was known as a "clean-up man." He wore a gray pinstriped suit with a blue dress shirt and dark blue tie—all of which seemed to accentuate his swarthy appearance. He had been the bully in the schoolyard, and now he was in an executive job where he could dress in thousand-dollar Armani suits and get paid for doing what he loved. He had become the head of security for the entire firm and was believed to have contacts that reached from the Pentagon to organized crime. It was only when he addressed one of the senior partners of the firm who had the power to fire him that his usual smirk and rude undertone were suppressed. He was just the kind of man a mega-firm of lawyers occasionally needed.

"Carlo, you've got contacts in the Austin area?" The man leaned forward and nodded in response. "Then you have authority to use the full resources of the firm to handle the two problems there as swiftly and efficiently as possible."

"Full resources?" The stocky man leaned back with a poorly suppressed smile on his face and folded his hands across his middle. He'd waited a long time to handle a job as important as this.

Wilcoxin nodded. "And you'll need to nail down the location of this staffer who works for Southland. Congress is in recess right now. Call Southland's D.C. office and locate him. We've got to get ahold of every copy of that paper. Simply put, get a problem solver who can handle the situation in both the Austin and Phoenix areas. If it takes two, then handle it that way. And get it done before that paper is sent to the regional EPA director or is published."

"Yeah, I'll take care of it."

"Bring us a full report next Monday—Tuesday morning at the latest."

"That doesn't give me much time."

"That's why you have the full resources of the firm at your disposal."

Gulletti rose and left the room immediately. As the others shared a look of tense, white-faced concern, Wilcoxin exhaled. "This meeting never took place. Make sure all references to it are removed from your schedules. Understood?" The last word was a rigid demand.

Chapter Two

THE ASSASSIN RECEIVED A TEXT on his cell phone in a coded message less than thirty minutes after the meeting. He was finishing an early dinner on the veranda of his hotel suite. Gulletti knew him only as Lupo. *Deliver three packages this weekend. Speed essential. Contents may spoil. Your usual fee for each. Time sensitive.*

Lupo replied to the message with an affirmative answer and additional details followed. He left the dishes on the table. The girl who came twice a week to clean his rooms in the secluded hotel would find them. The Isla de Margarita was a possession of Venezuela, off the beaten path for tourists but with an airstrip where Lupo knew he could charter a small plane for the hop to Caracas. From there, it was only a few hours to the States.

He examined his dark beard critically in the mirror and then unlocked the safe hidden in the closet floor. He selected a Greek passport from among the dozen he possessed. He sorted through the other documents, locating a credit card in the same name. After locking the safe once more, he threw a few items in a small leather bag, took a heavily loaded key ring from a drawer, and after examining it closely, dropped it into the bag.

***

He arrived at the international concourse of the Dallas/Fort Worth International Airport at 2:10 Thursday afternoon. He'd paid heavily for the last seat available on the 747. His dark glasses, navy-blue turtle neck, charcoal-gray wool sport coat, and jeans told other curious passengers that he might be a university professor. There was so little gray in the beard, they would have guessed his age at about forty. His muscled frame stood at six foot two.

He was a handsome man in an indefinable way. Perhaps it was the way he carried himself. With the dark glasses on, his face was impossible to identify, a necessity for a man wanted in seven countries. Upon leaving the plane, he walked immediately to the domestic concourse with his leather carry-on. He passed the wait between flights pretending to read a newspaper while he studied the other passengers who gathered at the gate. He boarded the connecting flight and disembarked at Bergstrom airport in Austin just before five thirty that evening. He was met at the first luggage carousel by a man who carefully refrained from looking directly at him or offering a handshake. Lupo had furnished a description of his general appearance and apparel by e-mail. The assassin accepted an envelope from the man and a car key with an Avis tag. Written on the envelope was a note: *Short-term parking, slot B-15, dark blue Jeep 4x4.* Neither man said a word. They parted quickly, going in different directions.

Sitting in the Jeep, Lupo opened the large envelope. It contained a map of Austin with the location of the University of Texas marked in red. With it was an enlargement of a map of the campus with the law school and law library circled. The envelope also contained a credit card in the name of John Jackson of Hattiesburg, Mississippi, and a driver's license with a photo that was general enough to match almost any man with a heavy, dark beard. *Not a very original name*, he thought with a mental smile, but his Southern dialect was good. He spoke five languages and at least two dialects in each. A plastic room key was wrapped in a note which read, *Room 240, Longhorn Motel.*

He pocketed the motel key, reached in again, and pulled out several sheets of paper folded together. The first was a copy of a photo from a university yearbook. The youthful face looking back at him was of a redheaded young man of about twenty-two by the name of Theo Novak. The note with the photo listed his address and a few comments about his personal habits with mention of the Friday morning study group he never missed. Additionally, it stated the urgent need to locate a certain research paper. A bonus would be included if that were accomplished. Behind that were two more sheets of paper with photos attached. One was of a man of about sixty with a gray comb-over. He was identified as Professor Jan Jurazski. The notes on his movements listed his class schedule, his home address, and his office number on campus, and it stated, *Widower, often sleeps on campus in his office.*

The third photo was of a young blond man with an engaging grin identified as Craig Crittenden. The notes listed his personal habits, his position as the lead research staffer for Congressman Max Southland, the license number and description of the car he drove when in district, and the address of his temporary residence in Arizona, which was underlined. An additional statement read, *Temporarily resides in the home of the congressman for whom he works. Your activities should take place elsewhere to minimize the involvement of federal authorities. At this time, no action is to be taken against the congressman.*

The bearded man studied the photos and the additional information closely for several minutes. Then he tucked the photos and notes back into the envelope and lit it with the disposable Bic lighter that had been left in the glove box for his use. He had trained his mind to grasp details of this kind with unerring accuracy. His life often depended upon that well-developed memory.

He adjusted the envelope as it burned to avoid the flames and waited until it was nearly consumed before he dropped it through the window onto the pavement. Then he opened the door, stepped on the ashes, and twisted his foot to spread them into oblivion.

He started the vehicle and traveled the nine miles up I-35 to the campus, where he drove around until he had memorized the streets in relationship to the law school and library. He carefully studied the entrances and exits of the two buildings at the center of his assignment.

By ten o'clock, a few students were leaving night classes or were standing around in clusters after late study groups, chatting and laughing despite the dark and the chill in the February air. He located an empty parking space and walked determinedly to the law school, as if he had an appointment. No one noticed him. Though the lights were still on, the building was nearly deserted.

Once inside, he systematically walked the empty halls and noted the locations of the lecture halls, professors' offices, restrooms, and janitorial closets. He took special note of the third-floor office of

Professor Jurazski. The light was still on. As he wondered about the usual arrival time of the man in the morning, the light went out. *So he's sleeping here tonight.*

He considered breaking into the office and "delivering the package" swiftly, knowing that at that time of night, he would probably get away unnoticed, but he considered himself an artist, and his plan included the creation of a distraction that would camouflage the fate of both "packages."

He noted a janitorial closet near Jurazski's office. He tried the door. It was locked, so he dropped into a stoop and set a few coins on the floor within reach. Should someone approach him there in the hallway—unlikely because of the hour—he could always appear to be picking them up. He withdrew the ring of keys he had carried from Venezuela. The keys fit no particular locks but camouflaged the three small custom-made but illegal lock picks that hung between them.

He selected one of the lock picks and a small tension tool, removing them from the ring. He carefully inserted them into the lock. It released in less than three seconds. He stepped inside, closed the door, pulled the chain on the bare bulb hanging from the ceiling, and studied the contents of the storage room. Amid the large push brooms, the roll-around trash barrel, and containers of cleaning chemicals, there were three pairs of janitorial coveralls hanging from hooks on one wall. He looked each over then held the largest pair against his shoulders. It would do. He folded and wrapped it in his sport coat. Draping the now bulky coat over his left arm, he held it casually against his body. Then he noted with satisfaction an open toolbox on the floor, filled with several adjustable pipe wrenches, a hacksaw, pliers, vise grips, screwdrivers, and other useful items.

His lips formed a narrow, tight smile of satisfaction. He checked the hallway before he exited the closet, locking the door. He strolled out of the building to his car, noting that the parking lot was now empty except for his rented Jeep and one other vehicle, a red 1994 Olds Ciera, probably the professor's.

He spent a comfortable night at the Longhorn Motel and left the room at five thirty in the morning after wiping every surface to remove any possible fingerprints. He was fairly sure they were not identified in any country's automated fingerprint system, but there was always a very small chance that they were in a system somewhere from a previous crime but not yet identified.

After putting his leather bag into the backseat, he used the map to locate the residence of Jurazski, noting that the professor's carport was empty, which confirmed his conclusion that the professor had remained at his office the previous night. He parked a half block down the street and casually walked back toward the weathered frame house.

When he was sure that no one was watching, he made his way around the back of the house, which was screened by tall oleander shrubs, and within a half minute, he was able to open the lock on the back door. He pulled on a pair of latex gloves and made his way through rooms dusty with neglect. When he entered the professor's office, he noted a large manila envelope on the desk waiting for postage. It was addressed to the Director of the Environmental Protection Agency San Francisco Office. He opened it and smiled with satisfaction when he recognized a copy of what appeared to be the research paper he was seeking.

He exited the house the same way he had entered and pulled off the latex gloves. Stuffing them into his sport coat pocket, he made his way back to the Jeep.

He drove to the address of the redheaded young man, where he parked on the street a hundred feet past the tired-looking brick house built in the late 1940s, now evidently converted to multiple rental units evidenced by four mailboxes on the porch. At seven thirty, the unsuspecting young man climbed the exterior stairs from the basement apartment with a backpack hanging from his shoulders. He unlocked the chain that held a bicycle to a porch support post then mounted and rode toward campus.

Traffic was growing heavier, most of it drawn toward the campus four blocks away like iron filings toward a magnet. Lupo decided to utilize the morning forming the details of his plan. He located a visitor's parking space not far from where he had parked the previous evening. He entered the building, avoiding the elevator and climbing the two flights of stairs to the third floor. He entered the professor's office as if he had an appointment. A young woman with blue eye shadow and long fingernails painted a silvery blue looked up from her computer and smiled at the tall, dark stranger.

"May I help you?" she asked as she brushed a long strand of auburn hair out of her eyes.

"Is Professor Jurazski in? I was hoping to meet with him this morning." The Southern drawl was evident in Lupo's speech.

"No, he's in his eight o'clock class right now." She looked at the calendar on the desk and added, "Then he has two meetings that will keep him occupied until his faculty luncheon. He could see you this afternoon, I think, if you'd come back about one thirty." He was unresponsive, so she added after looking at the calendar again, "Or he's available Monday morning about eleven fifteen."

"I'll make every effort to get back here this afternoon. I'm just looking over the campus. I've come with a job offer from . . ." he paused conspiratorially, "from another institution, and I'm wondering if what I can offer him would have any advantages over what he has here." As he talked, he wandered around the little reception room. He opened a door with a louvered panel for circulation in the upper half. It was a large storage closet with a small natural gas furnace taking up a portion of the lower part. "How convenient. You have your own heating system."

"We don't need the furnace very often. Just occasionally this time of year, but it's nice to have."

He opened the door to the professor's office and noted a cot and a blanket behind the desk. He grinned at her and stated in a conspiratorial whisper, "I think we can offer him comparable quarters. We might even give him a hide-a-bed."

She didn't seem to appreciate his little joke. Instead, she was growing uncomfortable with his familiarity. "What university do you represent?"

"I'm sorry, that's confidential. I'm sure you can understand." He gave her his most charming smile. "I'll drop back about one thirty."

As he took his leave, she didn't look very happy. She was obviously not pleased at the possibility of losing her job if her boss was recruited by another university.

He sat outside in his car and, from the corner of the visitor's parking lot, watched for her and the professor. They left for lunch within ten minutes of each other. He reached into the backseat, grabbed the coveralls, pulled a fat, slow-burning candle and the Bic lighter from his leather bag, and put them in a brown paper bag, where they could pass for his lunch. He moved swiftly into the large building, which was quickly emptying since it was lunchtime on a Friday, and many students and staff were leaving for the weekend. He climbed the stairs, and when he reached the janitorial closet, he paused to look both directions before pulling out his lock picks. Inside, he pulled the coveralls over his own clothing and picked up two pipe wrenches from the toolbox and two stained towels from a shelf.

When he reached the office door, he tested it. It was locked, so he knocked, just in case someone else was there. When no one responded, he stooped and quickly opened the lock. He stepped inside, locking the door behind him, and opened the storage closet where the little furnace was located. He checked his watch. It was twelve forty-five.

In less than two minutes, he had loosened the connections on the natural gas line to the furnace. He licked the fingers on his left hand, and when he could feel and smell the steady seep of the gas, he pulled the candle from his pocket and placed it on a shelf of computer paper and ink cartridges well above the furnace. He lit it.

Experience told him that it would take about sixty minutes before the heavy gas would reach the candle flame. He put the two towels along the floor and closed the door against them to minimize any odor of gas that might escape into the room. Then he cracked the casement window in the other wall on the far side of the secretary's desk to allow some fresh air into the room to mitigate any suspicious odor.

He hurried back to the janitorial closet, passing two students in the hallway, neither of whom paid him any attention. He pulled off the coveralls and hung them on the hook, wiped the tools and the door-knob with his handkerchief, and casually walked out of the building. He was satisfied that the explosion was timed in such a way that being Friday afternoon, there would only be a few people still in the building. He regretted that the little secretary with the blue fingernails would probably be caught in it, but it was a mild regret. As he passed the bike rack, he took note that the bicycle Theo had ridden from his apartment that morning was still chained there.

He returned to his car and drove around the campus until he found a parking place a little more than a quarter of a mile from the law school building, where he could watch the building and the bicycle. He waited while most of the remaining students and faculty filtered away from campus for the afternoon, getting a jump on the weekend.

At one thirty, he saw Theo exit the library and unchain his bike. The young man mounted it and started pedaling away. Lupo started the Jeep and accelerated until he was about fifty feet behind the bicycle. The law school suddenly erupted in an explosion that shot up nearly two hundred fifty feet into the sky, like a fiery volcano. The impact shook the Jeep and knocked Theo off his bike. The young man pushed himself up from the pavement to turn and stare with amazement at the flames and confusion. Just before the impact, he lowered his gaze to the bearded man behind the wheel of the oncoming vehicle. His eyes widened in sudden terror as the rented Jeep struck him with such force that his body flew into the air, and a crack streaked across the tempered glass of the windshield.

Looking around, Lupo saw no witnesses. He pulled over and got out as if to render aid, again checking to see if anyone was looking his way. The three people within sight were staring at the debris and flames with their backs to him. He felt for a pulse. There was none. He knelt and looked inside the backpack. The laptop was there among several books and tablets. Searching the front pockets of the jeans the young man wore, Lupo found a USB drive. He slipped it into his pocket and threw the backpack and laptop into the backseat. He quickly drove a hundred fifty feet to the drive that connected to the parking lot behind the nearest building. He parked where the vehicle would be hidden from the street.

He wiped down the car for fingerprints, paying special attention to the back of the rearview mirror and the handle that adjusted the seat. After he removed the laptop, he searched the rest of the backpack and struck gold. A printed copy of the paper in question was in a manila envelope. He got out of the car with his bag and the backpack.

As if he were a professor headed home with a load of homework to attend to over the weekend, he walked to the cab stand he had spotted on his first reconnaissance of the campus. He watched the emergency vehicles pass in a stream of red-and-blue flashing lights. The promise of a fifty-dollar tip prompted the cabbie to hustle to the airport so his passenger wouldn't miss his plane.

"What happened back there?" the cabbie asked as another half dozen emergency vehicles passed with sirens and lights going.

"I've no idea. I wanted to stay to see what was going on, but I've got a flight to catch." While the cab weaved through traffic, Lupo stuffed the laptop, the USB drive, and the manila envelope into his leather bag beside the envelope from the professor's house.

When he arrived at the airport, the assassin dropped the backpack into a trash receptacle and went directly to the Delta ticket counter, where he paid for a seat on a flight that would leave in ninety minutes for the Phoenix area. While he waited, he watched the courtesy television screen while he ate a steak sandwich in the little pub near the concourse from which his flight would depart. A news crawler crossed the bottom of the screen. *News flash: Explosion on the campus of the University of Texas Law School kills three, injures four. Extensive damage to the law school and library.* No mention of the kid on the bike. That was fine with him.

When he had finished his sandwich, he sent a simple text message: *Two packages delivered. Prepare to pay bonus.*

He immediately sent another text message to a different number. *Meet me at airport at eight thirty by first carousel. Could not bring necessary items by air. L.*

***

At the luggage carousel at the Sky Harbor airport, he met the man who had received his text. The man handed Lupo a small brown paper bag. Feeling the objects inside, Lupo nodded at the man and each went in a different direction. He slid the brown bag into his sport coat pocket.

He sat in the Buick LeSabre he had rented and opened the paper bag. The .32 Smith and Wesson snub-nosed revolver and the cylindrical silencer would be adequate. He stuffed them into his pocket. Also in the paper bag was a file card with the address of Southland's district office. Satisfied, he turned to the map of the metro area and located the address. He drove into the northern business district of Scottsdale and took a room at the Marriott Camelback Inn. He preferred luxury hotels when he was traveling on business, as their staff was usually more discreet than those at the more economical establishments, and larger numbers of patrons granted increased anonymity.

***

After a leisurely breakfast the next morning, he located the congressional office. It was just another rented space in a strip shopping center, bookended between a beauty shop on the left and a sandwich shop on the right. Painted on the large glass window in an arch of silver words was "Congressional District Office of Congressman Max Southland." There was nothing pretentious about it. It couldn't have been much more than twelve hundred square feet in size. He parked in front of the sandwich shop on the far side of the car belonging to the man who was just opening up for the day.

He pretended to read a newspaper and occasionally checked his watch as if he were waiting for someone. Through the front window, he could see Craig in the office with two women who were apparently stuffing envelopes and answering the telephone. He watched them for a while then moved the Buick down the street to where he could unobtrusively observe Craig's Chevy Camaro. It was likely to be a long day, but Lupo was accustomed to long waits.

Chapter Three

AT TEN MINUTES AFTER SIX, Lupo watched as Craig left the office and locked the door behind the two women who had completed their task. He was talking on his cell phone as he walked to his car. The young man carried three 12 x 14–inch manila envelopes like the one Lupo had found in the professor's home.

As the Camaro entered traffic, the white Buick pulled away from the curb and followed. Several cars slipped in between, but the Chevy was never out of Lupo's sight. He watched as Craig parked in the Hilton hotel parking lot and walked toward the rear entrance. He parked, followed the tall, blond young man into the lobby, and watched as Craig crossed to the registration desk and handed one of the large envelopes to the desk clerk. After speaking briefly to the man in the hotel uniform, Craig turned, moved across the lobby to the elevator, and punched the up button.

Lupo approached the elevator and stood near Craig, where he pretended to study the poster which welcomed guests and media to Congressman Southland's news conference. When the elevator doors opened, both men stepped inside.

"You headed up to the press conference?" Lupo asked in his Mississippi drawl.

Craig answered in a preoccupied manner as he adjusted the remaining manila envelopes that were tucked under his elbow. "Yes, I'm one of Southland's staffers."

When the doors opened on the third floor, Craig started toward the double doors of the large conference room at the end of the hall. The bearded man pulled his weapon and quickly stepped behind him.

Maintaining the drawl, Lupo spoke. "That's a gun you're feelin' in your back. Unless you want a bunch of dead people at that press conference, you'll walk outside with me to the pool area."

Craig hesitated for a fraction of a second before he did what he was told.

They proceeded down a short hallway in the opposite direction of the meeting room, following the arrow on the sign that pointed to the rooftop pool area. Lupo nudged Craig with the gun until they had crossed the wide patio and halted at the far end of the pool, well out of the line of vision of anyone in the conference room. Only the lights under the water offered any illumination.

Lupo said quietly to Craig's back, "What have you got in those envelopes? Something important—important enough to rate a hand delivery?" He deliberately engaged Craig with questions while he screwed the silencer onto the threaded muzzle of the gun.

Craig swallowed hard and wet his lips. "Look, you can kill me, but this information is going to come out. You can't keep it under wraps indefinitely."

"Just turn around and hand me your cell phone and the envelopes."

Craig pulled the cell phone from his pocket as though he were going to comply but whirled, throwing the two envelopes and the phone at his assailant. The man dodged, and the envelopes and the cell skidded across the rough cement.

Lupo fired twice, hitting Craig in the chest. He was dead before he hit the water. Lupo removed the silencer and tucked it and the gun into separate pockets. He bent and picked up the thick envelopes and the cell, dropping the phone into his pocket next to the silencer. He broke open the envelope addressed to Congressman Southland and skimmed the first two pages. He nodded with satisfaction.

He reentered the hotel, located the stairs to avoid meeting anyone in the elevator, and descended to the lobby, where he approached the clerk at the desk.

Assuming the drawl again, he asked, "My friend—the young fella I rode up in the elevator with—he thinks he gave you the wrong envelope. Could I see the one he left with you?"

"I'm afraid I can't let you have it, sir. It was given to me with specific instructions to mail it right away."

"I'm not asking for you to give it to me. I just need to see it to make sure he didn't get them switched."

The clerk hesitated for a moment. "I guess that couldn't hurt anything," he said as he reached for the big manila envelope. It differed from the other two Lupo had taken from Craig only in that it had a different name and address and the words *Happy Birthday* written on it.

"Thanks. No problem. He got it right."

He strolled out to the rental car and found a different place to eat that evening. While he waited for his meal, he studied the call directory stored in Craig's phone. He noted that the last call the staffer had made was to someone listed as Mattie, the same name printed on the envelope given to the clerk. He memorized the number. Then he pulled the thick wad of papers out of the opened envelope and thumbed through them, pausing to read every few pages. He read the summary of the Strategic Petroleum case and smiled cynically. In the morning, he would FedEx both these envelopes and the ones he'd found in Austin to the address Gulletti had furnished him. He was satisfied that he had been worth his pay on this assignment.

As the server put his prime rib before him, Lupo sent another text message. *Third package delivered. Suggest potential fourth package be closely examined. May require disposal for safety of all concerned.*

The response came back before he'd finished eating. *Call me.*

***

Mattie dropped her cell phone back into her pocket as the first of the television news people came through the conference room door. She hurried to shake the hand of one of the easily recognizable anchor men who always read the local ten o'clock news. She greeted his heavily loaded camera man. The guests had begun to arrive.

Her uncle Max had served in Congress for twenty-three years, and tonight he was formally announcing his decision not to seek reelection. Just as importantly, he was introducing state senator Jeff Skidmore as the man he was endorsing to take his place. She moved to the door, and as more members of the media entered—identified by the lanyards and press tags around their necks—she greeted them and handed each a copy of the news release and Skidmore's résumé.

Cameras were set up, and notepads were held at attention by the time Congressman Southland and his wife entered with Jeff and Millie Skidmore close behind. There were more than a hundred present—a combination of friends, supporters, and media representatives. By eight thirty, the event was officially over, and the television and newspaper reporters had been forced by the clock to end their questions and hurry away to get their stories into print or prepared for the evening news broadcasts. Both men left the dais and were quickly surrounded by a crowd of old friends and supporters.

She had looked for Craig intermittently throughout the event and had concluded that something unforeseen had made him very late. She pushed the little niggling worry to the back of her mind and decided that she needed a few quiet minutes away from the crowd. She crossed the big meeting room to the sliding glass doors that opened to a concrete extension of the patio that surrounded the outdoor pool area.

She had become acquainted with Stan Stewart, the hotel security man, through the events her uncle had held there over the years. Stan was a big bear of a man with a shaved head and shoulders that would have looked good on a sumo wrestler. He had been watching the event from his position by the patio door. When she approached him, he looked at her with raised eyebrows. "You want to go out, Mattie? It's a bit chilly out there."

"I need a few minutes of quiet and fresh air, Stan."

He slid the door open. "I'll leave it unlocked so you can come back in when you're ready." He gave her a look that said that he thought the forty-five-degree February temperature would bring her back inside in a hurry.

She nodded her thanks and stepped outside into the muted glow that shimmered upward from the lights under the water of the large pool. The normal lighting on the large patio area had been turned off that evening as per her request so it wouldn't attract any polar bear–type swimmers who might distract the attendees at the news conference.

She breathed deeply and looked up at the sprinkling of stars whose light penetrated the night sky of the metro area. She wanted to take off her high heels, but the pool decking was of rough concrete, so she found a couple of deck chairs, sat down in one and pulled up the other so it would serve as a footrest. From there, she looked at the lights of the city through the Plexiglas panels that allowed the swimmers to look down on the traffic that swept past the entrance of the hotel two flights below.

She turned when she heard the sliding glass door open again and watched Brad Lowe step out and wave at her. "I needed a few quiet minutes too," he said as he approached her. "Hope you don't mind if I join you out here."

Brad was a tall guy in his forties with a ski slope of a nose and a long, lanky body like a skinny teenager. The lid of one eye drooped a little, so he was not handsome enough to be a candidate in the media-driven political environment, but Mattie knew he loved politics and was always up to his elbows in the campaign end of things. He had headed Max Southland's four most recent reelection campaigns. Mattie had known his wife since she was a university student. Now he was making the lateral move over to the Skidmore campaign.

"This may be the only quiet time I'll have for the rest of the year." He chuckled.

She pointed at a deck chair about four feet from the ones she was using. "Glad to have you. I just needed a few minutes away from the noise." From where they sat, the deck chairs and the tables with their folded umbrellas hid much of the large pool. She rubbed her arms. The chill breeze had penetrated the lightweight voile sleeves of her dress. He noticed and offered her his suit coat. She gladly accepted.

As she draped the coat over her shoulders, he asked, "How long have you been managing your uncle's district office? It seems that I've known you for quite a while, but you aren't all that old."

"I'm flattered—I think," she responded with a grin. "I've been in the local office nearly six years." When he said no more, she continued, "After I graduated from the university, Uncle Max asked me to fill in for his office manager when she had a baby. I had served an eighteen-month humanitarian mission for my church in Taiwan at twenty-one, so I was twenty-three, a bit older than some of the other graduates. Within a few months, I was managing the office, handling constituent requests, that kind of stuff. With him retiring, I'm going to have to find some 'honest' work by the end of the year." They both laughed at the old joke.

Brad stretched his long legs out in front of his chair. "Why *is* he leaving public service? I know officially he says he wants time to write a book about his experiences, but is that the *real* reason?" His eyebrows were raised as he searched her face.

"My aunt Cecelia had a minor stroke about five months ago. She kept it quiet. Though she's recovered well, it made him face mortality—both hers and his. He'll turn seventy-two this year. They plan to take a cruise and spend a lot of time together to make up for the time his position has taken."

She stood and straightened her back, made stiff by the long day. He followed her example, and they began to walk toward the raised, curving peninsula in the concrete that pushed out into the pool, turning it into a very large kidney shape. That protrusion gently rose to about eighteen inches above the rest of the patio area, and on two sides, tiled stairs led down into the water. During the heat of summer, the children of hotel guests would run squealing and laughing to leap into the pool from that spot.

They walked in a relaxed manner around the far end of the large pool toward the eight-story wall of rooms with small balconies that towered over them at the far end of the patio area. About half the windows were lit, but no draperies were open.

Brad looked intently at the pool. "The water is an unusual color tonight. Have you noticed? Do you think the hotel is going to color the water to match the season? My wife reminded me today that Valentine's Day is tomorrow. She's hoping for something special."

"You won't fail her, will you?"

He murmured a noncommittal answer. Mattie grinned, remembering the past two Valentine's Days and how Craig had made each so special. *But he's been so busy this year. Maybe he hasn't had time to plan anything special.*

She took a couple more steps and paused to look at the water. "You're right. The water is pink. Maybe they'll tint it green for St. Patrick's Day." As they took a few more steps her chuckle stopped. "There's something in the pool on the other side of the stairs."

"You're right. Maybe someone left a towel in the water?"

Somehow they both suspected that it was more than that. They took several hurried steps, and Mattie grew very cold but not due to the temperature. It was a man's body, rocking facedown in the gentle current.

She took a deep breath and smothered the impulse to scream. She spoke through a tight throat. "I'll get Chief Jepson if he's still here. If he's left, I'll call 911." Her voice sounded a little squeaky, even to her own ears. Because he was a good friend of her uncle's, Jepson had chosen to attend the event as part of the security.

Brad had kicked off his shoes and was pulling off his socks. "I'll try to get him out of the water," he said as he started rolling up his pant legs.

She ran back to the sliding glass door. Stan saw her coming and pulled it open.

"Stan, do you know if Chief Jepson's still here?" she asked breathlessly.

He pointed. "He's over there talking to your uncle."

She made a major effort not to appear panicked as she hurried through the remaining people standing around in clusters. Her smile was stiff and strained. She stepped up to the police chief and laid her hand on his sleeve to get his attention. He was a man of about fifty, best described as "bulky," like a farmer who worked out of doors. He was wearing a dark gray suit and a red tie that appeared to reflect its color against his ruddy face. His hair was prematurely gray, and he had tired eyes.

Mattie spoke to her uncle. "Uncle Max, I need to borrow Chief Jepson." Both men looked at her closely, and one of her uncle's eyebrows rose. He could see from her white face that something had upset her.

He nodded. "I'll let him go, but bring me up to speed on why he's needed—when you can." He turned and began to speak with the couple standing near him, deliberately avoiding a show of alarm.

"Follow me." She waved at Jepson and hurried toward the doorway. She spoke to the security man. "Stan, we'll need you too. Please come with us."

She ran toward the pool, making the men behind her break into a trot to keep up. Brad was sitting on a patio chair, pulling his socks over wet feet. He stood and pushed his feet into his shoes as they arrived. He pointed to the body that he had managed to pull partially from the water. It lay faceup on the stairs.

"I couldn't get him out of the water. He's too heavy. I pulled him out as far as I could with that thing over there." He pointed to the extension pole with the long, curving loop—a shepherd's crook that the law required to be part of the easily accessible equipment at each public pool.

He turned from Jepson to Mattie. He looked grim. "I'm sorry, Mattie. I know you and he were . . ." He paused and then added softly, "good friends."

Not grasping what he meant, she took a few steps closer and looked carefully at the body. It took a full second in the muted light to recognize him. Before, he had just been a silhouette against the luminous water of the pool.

Her heart seemed to plunge like an elevator in free fall. It was Craig. He might have been looking at the stars in a relaxed manner. His wet blond hair was dark, and his open eyes gave his face an innocent, slightly startled expression.

She wavered a little, and a strangled sound escaped her throat. Brad grabbed her arm and pulled her back from the water. Stan looked at Jepson, and receiving a slight suggestion of a nod, the younger man pulled his feet out of his shoes, stepped into the water, and scooped Craig up in his arms like a child. He laid the body on the patio decking and closed Craig's eyes with a gentle hand.

Jepson took his cell from his pocket and hit the speed dial for Mesa police headquarters. He was no longer the relaxed friend at a social event; he had suddenly become a cop—all business.

"Who's on duty tonight in homicide?" he said in clipped tones. "A gang shooting? Where? How many dead?" He ran his hand through his thinning hair as he listened. "Anything else?" Pause. "How many hostages? Is SWAT on the scene?" He exhaled a long, tired sigh as the dispatcher continued to talk. "Was anyone killed?" Under his breath, he muttered, "You'd think there was a full moon tonight." In a normal tone he added, "No, no. I wasn't talking to you."

After a deep inhale, he continued. "Since we're spread so thin, call DPS." After a patient pause, "Are you new?" Then he explained tiredly, "DPS is the Department of Public Safety. Call and talk to the head of CIU, the Criminal Investigation Unit. Get him out of bed if need be, and tell him to send Jack Summers. Tell him Chief Jepson wants Summers." His voice was solid and unchallengeable. "He was my best man until they enticed him away, and for this investigation, I want him back. I want him and the medical examiner at the Hilton off Highway 60 five minutes ago—at the pool area outside the third-floor meeting room. It's a homicide."

He ended the call, turned, and looked at her. "You know him, Mattie?" He gestured toward Craig's body.

The knot in her throat wouldn't let any words come out. She just nodded stiffly. Brad spoke for her. "Chief, it's Craig Crittenden, the chief researcher on the congressman's Washington staff. He and Mattie were good friends."

"How good?" Jepson questioned. She still couldn't talk, so Brad answered again. "Very good. I'd heard that it was getting serious."

Mattie nodded again, as stiffly as a marionette. Finally, she was able to form some words, but they came slowly. "We hadn't made it public yet . . . but we were unofficially . . . engaged. We thought we might get married after the election . . . maybe Thanksgiving weekend." Still white-faced, she turned and looked into Brad's eyes and then back to the police chief. "Who would do this?" Her voice was hardly audible, and a tear traced the contours of her cheek.

Jepson put his hand on her shoulder, led her to a patio chair, and gently pushed her down into it. His manner and voice softened. "We'll find out, Mattie. Just give us some time, and we'll find out." He dropped into a stoop beside her chair. "I'm sorry, but I'll need you to answer some questions as soon as the DPS detectives get here."

He stood and turned to look at Craig's body. He systematically went through each pocket. He examined the wallet and its contents. "About sixty dollars here, so it wasn't robbery." He examined the credit cards, driver's license, and the other miscellaneous cards, then returned them to the wallet and slipped it back into the pocket. Other than a set of car keys, some loose change, a handkerchief, and a roll of dissolving mints, there wasn't anything else.

As he bent over to remove the pen from Craig's shirt pocket, he looked closer and waved Stan over. "What do you make of this?"

They were bending over, blocking Mattie's line of vision, but she heard the security man speak. "Two in the heart. Looks like a professional hit. Why would a pro take out a congressional staffer?"

He hadn't expected an answer, but Jepson responded thoughtfully. "That's the key question." He turned to Brad. "Maybe you'd better take

Mattie inside and have someone bring her something hot to drink. We'll talk with her as soon as we can."

He turned to her. "Go inside with Mr. Lowe, get warm, and try to think of anyone who would want Mr. Crittenden dead. Will you do that?"

She nodded stiffly. Brad led her through the doorway. The sudden realization as to why the water in the pool was pink made her dizzy. It wasn't for Valentine's Day. It was Craig's blood.

She broke away from Brad and rushed to the ladies' room at the opposite end of the conference room. The small handful of people who were still talking to Southland and Skidmore turned and watched in surprise. Once inside, she pushed the door closed and leaned on it, sliding to the floor as though her tears were so heavy they pulled her down. She felt as if she were breaking apart inside, so she hugged her knees hard, leaning her forehead against them, and sobbed, trying to hold herself together.

Chapter Four

AFTER A FEW MINUTES, SHE became conscious of her uncle's voice calling her name. He was knocking, his voice muffled through the door. "Mattie, let us in. Chief Jepson told us what happened. You're worrying your aunt. Let us in." His voice was firm and insistent.

She managed to stand and pull a paper towel from the dispenser by the sink to wipe her tears. "I'm all right," she said as she opened the door. "I'm sorry if I worried you, Aunt Cecelia." She put her arms around her short aunt, who returned the embrace to offer what comfort she could.

"Mattie, come with me. I'll get you some hot cocoa. Come and sit down. The police want to talk to all of us. Can you answer some questions?"

"Of course, if it'll help." She dabbed at her eyes with the crumpled paper towel as she was led to one of the round tables. Through the sliding doors, everyone could see that the exterior lights on the patio area had been turned on, and uniformed officers had arrived. Two men in white from the medical examiner's office were briefly visible. Noting the direction of her eyes, the congressman gently led her to the other side of the table, where she wouldn't be looking outside.

When the server set the mug of hot cocoa in front of her, Mattie wrapped her hands around the cup, suddenly aware that she was chilled and shaking.

Max, Cecelia, and Brad Lowe sat at the table with her. Skidmore and his wife stood behind Southland, wondering what could be said under the circumstances. Mattie's face was white with distress. The other guests had been encouraged to take their leave after Jepson had acquired their names and addresses and had determined that they knew nothing of the events at the pool.

Her hands shook as she picked up the mug.

***

When Jack Summers received the phone call from his boss, he had been getting ready to turn off the television and go to bed. It had been a long day. Every day had been a long day since he'd been assigned to the Arizona DPS Criminal Investigation Unit and promoted to sergeant. For the eight years he'd been a cop, he had been called to investigate everything from domestic murders to violent deaths of gang bangers because someone had taken offense to the color the kid had been wearing. But this was the first time he had gotten a call to investigate a murder at the scene of a political event.

He had immediately called his partner, Dexter Barstow, and told him they'd meet at the Hilton. "It's going to be a long night."

When he entered the meeting room, he was greeted warmly by Chief Jepson. "Jack, sorry about the call. I hope the folks at DPS fully appreciate the fact that they took one of my best men." Barstow arrived while Jepson and Jack were talking.

Jepson explained the matter quickly. "An aid to Congressman Southland was found dead in the pool, shot twice. The young woman in the blue dress and the fellow sitting by her found the body. And of course, no one saw anything; no one heard anything." His voice reflected his cynicism.

He and Barstow followed Chief Jepson to the table where the small group was gathered.

Jepson introduced them. "This is Sergeant Jack Summers of the Criminal Investigation Unit of the Department of Public Safety and his partner, Detective Dexter Barstow. We're spread thin tonight, so I've called on DPS to give us some help. I'm sure you'll give them your full cooperation."

Summers was about six feet tall and, apparently, in his early thirties. Aside from a small scar on his left cheek near his ear, he had even features with strong cheekbones and a broad forehead. His dark brown hair was moderately short and lay neatly to the left. He evidently worked out regularly as his muscular shoulders filled the brown-and-tan tweed sport coat he wore. He had no sign of the thickening around the waist that was so common in cops who spent their days behind a desk or a steering wheel. His dress shirt was dark gold, and he had a chocolate brown tie that matched his head of thick hair and his brown eyes. His badge was displayed on his coat breast pocket. His build and stride were full of natural confidence.

As Summers approached Mattie, he looked her over swiftly with practiced eyes. She was a long-stemmed beauty with an ivory face set off by a mass of blonde curls. Her strong cheekbones were highlighted with blush; her mouth was shaded in soft pink.

But it was her eyes that caught the attention of most people. They were large and blue—as blue as a still, deep lake. Her mascara was light but slightly smudged. It was evident she had been wiping away tears.

Summers looked around the table before he spoke. "We need to talk to each one of you, but we'll begin with the folks who found the body. If the rest of you will find a place to sit over there"—he nodded toward the far side of the room—"we'll get to you in turn."

Everyone except Brad and Mattie moved across the meeting room, where they sat in the remaining chairs the hotel staff had not yet collected. Brad rose when Barstow gave him a wave of his hand, and the two moved to another table while Mattie remained where she was seated, holding the warm cup. Summers sat down and took a small tablet from his inside pocket. He took Mattie's full name, address, and telephone number.

"I understand that you found the body and that you were a friend of the victim. Did you know him well enough to give me his full name and address?"

"His full name is—" A catch in her throat interrupted her words. She took a deep breath and continued, "was Craig Steven Crittenden. He lived in Arlington, Virginia. He worked for my uncle in the Washington office as chief researcher and often traveled with Uncle Max when a staffer was needed."

"Uncle Max? Do you mean Congressman Southland?"

She nodded before she continued. "For the last two years, whenever my uncle came home from Washington, D.C., he had Craig travel with him to handle e-mails, text messages, telephone calls, research, and any other business that might arise."

"Where did Mr. Crittenden stay when he traveled with your uncle?"

"He used one of the spare bedrooms at the house. He had his own key and came and went as he needed."

"The house?"

"My uncle and aunt's home. I live there too, in the guest quarters."

"Did he own a car?"

"About a year ago he bought a four-year-old Chevy Camaro that he kept at the house."

"Do you know where the car is right now?"

"No. He was on his way to the hotel when we last talked."

"You were with someone else when you found the body?" She nodded. "Tell me how that happened."

"After the media had left and the crowd was beginning to thin out—"

"The media?"

"The news conference was to announce that Uncle Max was not seeking reelection and that he was endorsing Jeff Skidmore to replace him." She sat quietly for a moment, looking at her hands.

In her mind, she was still seeing Craig's body in the water. She shuddered before she continued. "When it was over, I needed a breath of fresh air, so I stepped out onto the patio through the sliding glass doors. I sat down to relax a bit when Brad, er, Mr. Lowe followed me out. He said he needed some quiet time too. We sat for a few minutes, and then we started to walk around the pool while we chatted."

"How does Mr. Lowe fit into the situation? Is he a friend of yours or the congressman's?"

"Both. He's run several of Uncle Max's campaigns in the past, and he's going to be running Skidmore's election campaign."

As he took notes, she continued. "We were talking as we walked when we saw something in the water on the other side of that rise where the steps go down into the water. When we got closer, we could see it was a body. I rushed back to the group to find Chief Jepson while Brad tried to pull him from the water."

"Did you recognize the body?"

"No, not at first." Her throat closed off for a few seconds. She had to swallow several times before she could continue. "It was just a silhouette against the lights under the water. I'd been looking for Craig the whole evening. He'd called me at about six and said he was on his way, but I never saw him arrive." Her composure was weakening fast, so she pressed a hand over her mouth.

"Do you have any idea why anyone would want him dead?" She shook her head.

The paper towel had disintegrated, so she wiped her tears with the back of her hand. "He's a good man, a fine man—at least he was." She whispered the last four words. "He always gave 100 percent to whatever was asked of him. There's just no reason for anyone to do something like this." Her last words ended in a choked sob.

Summers closed the notebook. "I'll be in touch with more questions as the investigation continues. I've got to talk to a lot of other people, but here's my card in case you think of anything else."

As he stood to leave, Mattie rose, suddenly feeling dizzy and ill. She walked slowly across the room and sat by her aunt, who put her hand over hers and squeezed it. Then she leaned over and whispered to her niece, "I don't want you driving home alone. You'll ride with us, and after a warm bath and a cup of hot milk, you'll be able to sleep."

At that moment, Mattie felt that she would never sleep again.

***

While she rode in the backseat of her aunt's silver-gray Town & Country minivan, chosen for its inconspicuousness, she closed her eyes. As her alertness faded from physical and emotional exhaustion, she slipped into a dream of the night she and Craig sat in a little Chinese restaurant while they ate and talked about the future. She had been so proud of him. He'd graduated from the Chicago School of Law at the top of his class with a special focus in international business and trade law. He had turned down offers from several top law firms so he could work as a researcher for her uncle in the D.C. office. She had just begun to plan the wedding . . .

The sound of the wrought iron entry gate sliding open at the Southland estate brought her back to reality. Mattie had been living in the guest quarters of the brick Tudor mansion in Paradise Valley for the previous five years. She had moved there after her mother had passed from a long and difficult battle with cancer. Mattie became her aunt's companion when her uncle traveled or was in Washington, D.C.

Her aunt and uncle accompanied her into the little living room of the guest quarters next to the rear-facing garages. Her aunt shooed Max away. While Mattie soaked in a hot tub full of the bubble bath her aunt insisted on adding, Cecelia fixed a glass of hot milk. After Mattie dutifully drank it, she was literally tucked into bed.

"Should I turn off the light, or do you want me to leave it on?" Cecelia asked from the bedroom doorway.

"Please leave it on. Thank you for everything, Aunt Cecelia."

"You'll be all right? I can stay if you don't want to be alone."

"I'll be okay. You can go to bed."

Cecelia closed the door and moved into the main portion of the house without making a sound.

Mattie lay with her arm bent over her eyes to block out the light she didn't want turned off, and she tried to sleep. Whenever she would begin to drift off, she would see his body gently moving in the pool or remember the plans for the wedding that would never take place. *My life has been totally altered in one night . . .*

She finally got out of bed about two o'clock in the morning and moved to the living room, where she turned on the television. The anchor man on the "all news all the time" cable channel mentioned the fact that Congressman Max Southland had announced his retirement and had endorsed state senator Jeff Skidmore to take his place in Congress. There was no mention of Craig's death. His body had been discovered too late to make the evening news. For that she was grateful. After a while, she returned to her bed, curled up into a fetal position, and quietly wept until the pillow was soaked under her cheek.

There were events that marked a life. Afterward, everything was divided into what went before and what followed. Mattie knew that Craig's death was one of those events.

Chapter Five

At nine o'clock the next morning, Cecelia knocked on the door that connected the living room of the guest quarters to a hall that led into the main part of the house. She opened it. Hoping not to wake her niece if she were still sleeping, Cecelia said quietly, "Mattie, are you awake?"

"I'm awake, Aunt Cecelia. Please come in." She had dressed in a pair of white jeans and a dark blue turtleneck sweater, and had tried—unsuccessfully—to powder away the dark circles under her eyes.

"I've fixed breakfast, dear. Will you join us?"

"I'm not very hungry." Noting the look of disappointment on her aunt's face, she added, "But I'll join you."

In the kitchen, Max was sitting at the table, reading the paper. Max Southland was the kind of man that inspired trust and usually deserved it. He was tall and athletic for a man in his early seventies. He stood five eleven with a shock of white hair that made him stand out in any group. His blue eyes were marked by smile lines. His self-depreciatory manner made strangers and even politicos who disagreed with him genuinely like him.

He put the paper down and asked sympathetically, "How are you feeling, Mattie?"

"I'm still stunned—I actually feel ill, as though someone hit me in the stomach." She sat down across from him, and Cecelia put a plate of bacon, eggs, and toast in front of her.

"Uncle Max, did you see Craig at all last night?" She halfheartedly pushed some scrambled eggs around with her fork.

"No, I didn't. Why? Did you or anyone else see him?"

She shook her head. "He called me before the news conference began and said he was bringing copies of a research paper on energy exploration for you and Jeff Skidmore. He told me that it was really important for both of you to read it because some related matters could become national issues."

"I wonder why he would think that in a state that has as little natural gas and oil as we have."

"Evidently it isn't the actual *focus* of the paper that's important but something that relates to it. If you didn't see him last night, then you couldn't have seen the paper." She wondered aloud, "Maybe we need to tell Sergeant Summers about the paper."

"You think it might have something to do with . . . with what happened?" Max was choosing his words carefully.

"I don't know, but I can't help but wonder."

As Cecelia cleared away the dishes, she looked at Mattie's plate with disappointment. Her niece had hardly touched the food. "Would you like to attend church this morning, dear? We still have an hour to get ready." She was trying hard to be cheerful and keep things normal.

Mattie shook her head. "I'm just not emotionally ready to face people yet. I'm sure some of them will have learned about Craig's death—it probably made the morning news—and many won't have heard. I don't know which group will be more difficult to face—those who know or those who don't. I think I'll just try to get some rest." Her head suddenly flew up. "Uncle Max, we've got to notify Craig's parents. They need to hear it from us rather than in a news story."

"I called them this morning, Mattie. It was nine o'clock in Virginia. The police here had already arranged for them to be notified. I wanted to break it to them gently, but they'd already been told. They'll notify my office in D.C. about the plans for the services."

"Thank you, Uncle Max." She rose from the table. "If you'll excuse me, I think I'll go lie down." They both made sympathetic noises as she left the kitchen.

She walked down the hall toward the guest quarters like someone carrying a heavy load, but out of habit, she paused at the doorway of her uncle's den-turned-office. She not only managed his district office but also served as his local scheduler. She entered the room and picked up his desk calendar. Some weeks earlier, she had made a note about a speaking engagement for Monday evening. She pulled a file card from the drawer and listed the who, what, and where of the event so her uncle would have the information he needed to prepare.

As she hurried back toward the kitchen, she could hear the conversation. Her aunt was saying, "I don't really know what to say to make it easier for her. He was such a fine young man . . ."

As Mattie entered, her aunt looked up with a guilty expression, not because of what she'd said but because she and her husband were sharing a large frosted cinnamon roll. Aunt Cecelia had been diagnosed as mildly diabetic a few months earlier and knew she shouldn't indulge in such pleasures.

Mattie ignored the cinnamon roll, crossed the kitchen, and for a fraction of a second, froze as she handed the file card to her uncle. There was a beautiful valentine sitting by her aunt's plate. It was evident that her uncle had waited until Mattie had left to present it to his wife.

In a cold, revealing flash of recognition, Mattie remembered that it was Valentine's Day. The awareness squeezed her chest so hard that it physically hurt. *Never another card or thoughtful act or smile from Craig . . .*

She forced herself to take a deep breath to push the pain away. She didn't want her aunt and uncle to have their special moment ruined because of her hurt. She tried to smile. "With everything that happened last night, I almost forgot to check your calendar. Since Congress is in recess this week, you agreed to speak to a group sponsored by the Metro Interfaith Council tomorrow night at six. They want you to discuss recent Supreme Court decisions that deal with governmental encroachment on religious freedoms."

He took the information and looked at it. "Now that you mention it, I remember agreeing to speak to the group. What do you suppose they mean by 'recent decisions'?"

"I'm sure that will be up to you—and they invited Aunt Cecelia to attend with you."

He looked at his wife of forty-five years with a tender smile. "Well, my dear, do you want to come and listen to me expound on federal court decisions?"

"I'd love to, Max, but I don't think I should leave Mattie alone so soon after . . . after last night."

Mattie responded firmly, "Aunt Cecelia, I won't tell the doctor about the cinnamon roll if you'll go with Uncle Max tomorrow night. I'll be fine. Please don't worry about me."

"Well, if you're sure, then I'll go." Her voice was a bit chagrined.

Mattie spent the balance of the day in her room, trying to rest but repeatedly rising to pace. She remembered her mother's death and the depth of the grief that had engulfed her at that time. After her mother's passing, Mattie learned from a grief counselor that the heart needs a brief and intense period of mourning before it can move to the next stage. He explained that if she refused to give in, the grief would sneak up on her at unexpected moments for years to come, manifesting itself in painful reactions to difficult situations. He warned that the pain would continue, but the stages of regret and, finally, acceptance would be more subdued. He had promised that eventually she would let go and move on with life. She had found that he was right as she grieved for her mother, but she had only just begun the grieving process for Craig.

With the door to the main portion of the house closed, she wept—sometimes silently, the tears running down her face, but other times, when the feeling of the unfairness of it all overwhelmed her, sobs shook her body, and she felt that her grief would drown her. The future she had planned was gone, and the weight of that knowledge was too heavy to carry. Her heart actually hurt. She was angry but didn't know where to focus that anger. She wanted someone to pay for Craig's death, and she wanted everyone to know that the world had lost a good man who would have made it a better place.

She lay down on the couch at about four o'clock and drifted into a fitful sleep. When she awoke with a start an hour later, she was struck with a sudden sensation of how impossible the situation was. She sat up in the room darkening with winter twilight. *This has all just been a bad dream.* She rose, flipped on the light, hurried down the connecting hall to the main house, and paused outside the bedroom Craig used. *He'll be here. All of this nightmare will be over.*

She knocked gently with the knuckle of one finger and carefully turned the doorknob. Opening the door, she reached in and turned on the light. Her heart stopped when she saw the empty room. She stood unmoving for several seconds. *Anytime now, I'll wake up and find the switch to light the dark place I'm in. The phone will ring, and it will be Craig.* But she understood now that she was deceiving herself. Craig was dead, and she was grasping at straws.

As she turned to leave the room, she noted a square white envelope sitting on his dresser. She stepped closer. It had her name on it in his handwriting. Moving slowly, as if sleepwalking, she crossed the room and picked it up. It wasn't sealed.

With great deliberateness, she opened it. It was a valentine, and he had written a note inside. "Mattie, I'm sorry we've had so little time together the last few days. I promise I'll make it up to you. Let's go out to dinner and make wedding plans. I love you, Craig."

By dark, she sat unmoving on the couch in her little living room trying to determine how she was going to get through the rest of her life without him, something she had never considered since their second date. She remembered something her father had told her when she was about ten. Her beloved dog Dixie had died, and he explained that emotional pain had a positive side to it. "Your pain proves you're alive. If you can't feel anything, you might as well be dead." But right at that moment, she wished she were. When she fell asleep from exhaustion, she felt that a living and vital part of her was totally lost, forever beyond recall.

***

By Sunday morning, the doctor allowed police to question Professor Jurazski's secretary. She'd been late getting back to his office after her lunch with friends. When the explosion erupted, she had been getting out of her car in the parking lot, so she'd suffered only a concussion from being blown against the car, first and second degree burns, and a broken ankle.

Her memory of the day was hazy, but she did remember the visit of the bearded man and that he'd said he would return about one-thirty that afternoon. The fire department and rescue dogs searched the rubble but found no unaccounted-for bodies.

***

Gulletti found a note on his computer message board when he arrived in the office Monday morning at seven thirty. It was a command: *My office, ASAP.* Signed, *W.*

He shook his head in irritation. He was sick of being treated like lower level office staff, of no more importance than a secretary, simply because he wasn't an attorney. In his mind, his skills had never been fully appreciated. *Trust Wilcoxin to want a report before I'm even required to be at my desk,* he thought grimly.

To prove that he was his own man, he waited until eight before entering the outer office of the senior partner. Wilcoxin's secretary, an attractive woman of fifty in a gray business suit with her salt-and-pepper hair pulled neatly into a bun at the base of her neck, looked up at him and smiled pleasantly. "Let me tell him you're here," she said as she picked up the telephone receiver and pressed the intercom button. "Mr. Gulletti's here, sir."

Gulletti didn't return the smile. He had pushed his way through the imposing solid walnut, soundproofed double doors before she had finished speaking.

Wilcoxin was standing, chewing the stub of an unlit cigar. He simply pointed with it toward the chair that sat squarely before his six-foot walnut desk. The senior partner had unbuttoned his top shirt button and loosened his tie. His sleeves were rolled up to his elbows, something Gulletti had never seen him do. The black mood of the senior partner was as palpable as a heavy San Francisco fog.

"Give me a report," Wilcoxin demanded in clipped words.

Gulletti was satisfied with the report he was about to give. "The two packages in Austin have been delivered. One was a simple hit-and-run, and the other was a natural gas explosion that will, in all likelihood, be ruled an accident. The third has—"

Wilcoxin cut him off. "Yes, I saw the news report on CNN. I figured that the footage of the explosion and fire was related to your 'delivery man' and his work."

Gulletti hadn't yet realized that Wilcoxin was not offering praise. "Yes, I thought that was a nice touch. No likelihood of any suspicion of foul play. It really was a work of art."

Wilcoxin's face grew scarlet with rage. "You idiot!" He threw his cigar into the waste basket for emphasis. "Did you forget that my son is a law student on that campus? Your man might have killed him too. Couldn't he have made a neat, surgical strike? No," his voice cut like a knife, "he had to take out a student and a secretary in addition to the target, according to the most recent report. The FBI and the ATF are all over the place down there. What kind of moron did you hire?"

Now Gulletti's temper was rising. "He's not a moron. He's the best in his field. There's no one better . . . sir," he added belatedly.

"Then who's to blame for the mess in Austin? What kind of orders did you give him?"

Gulletti knew Wilcoxin had him there. He had never ordered that collateral damage was to be kept to a minimum. The how of the task had been left entirely up to the assassin.

His jaw tightened. All he could do was throw himself on Wilcoxin's mercy—if he had any. The senior partner was not a man to try to fool. "I'm sorry that I didn't give him more specific information, sir. I'm entirely to blame." He felt as if he had just laid his head on the chopping block, hoping that the executioner might have some pity.

Wilcoxin put his hands flat on his desktop, leaned forward, and stared at his security man with narrow, angry eyes. His voice was low. "Consider yourself *very* lucky. If my son had been killed or injured . . ." He let the sentence hang in the air for at least three seconds before he straightened. "Was the third package delivered?"

"Yes, sir. No witnesses. It was an efficient delivery on Saturday night. When my man notified me, he said that there was another potential package."

"Get your man out of the country," he said irritably. "Just get all the information about the situation before he leaves. If there's another delivery to be made, make sure your next man won't make such a production of it. We don't need any more Hollywood-type special effects drawing the attention of the Feds."

"Yes, sir." Wilcoxin waved him out of the office. It took every ounce of Gulletti's self-control to turn and walk out at a normal speed.

Back in his own office, Gulletti picked up the telephone and called a seldom-used number. "I may need a delivery man in your area. Who would you recommend?" He wrote down the name, phone number, and e-mail address.

His next text message went to Lupo. *Call me,* followed by a disposable cellular telephone number.

It took a half hour to get a response. When the disposable phone in his pocket rang, Gulletti answered simply, "It's me."

"Why the phone call? Wouldn't a text or e-mail do?" Lupo's voice was curious.

"Too many questions. There are some people very unhappy with the situation in Austin. ATF and FBI are crawling all over the place. Too much collateral damage. All the attention it's receiving is making certain people very uncomfortable."

"But the Feds won't find anything suspicious. It'll be up to the gas company to handle the lawsuits." The voice was full of satisfaction.

"What about the other potential package you mentioned? Have you had it under surveillance?"

"Yes."

"What is your gut feeling in the matter?"

"Recommend that the package be delivered."

"Tell me about it." Gulletti picked up a pen.

"She manages the district office for the congressman. Package number three mailed her a copy of the paper. She could have it as early as tomorrow."

"What about the congressman? Do you think he needs to be delivered?"

"At this point, I don't think he's had the opportunity to view the information. If you move fast, it won't even get to him."

"Describe the girl."

Lupo described Mattie, giving her full name, home and office addresses, telephone number, car description, and license plate number. Gulletti made notes.

"The payment has been wired to your account. You're released from any further duties. I'll use another delivery man for this package. Recommend you get out of the country." Gulletti's voice was hard. His pulse had finally slowed to normal.

Lupo was glad to leave. The payment for the three deliveries would free him from the need to take another contract for a year or longer.

Gulletti ended the call and pulled out his iPod. He sent an e-mail to the number given him by his contact. Within thirty minutes, the arrangements for locating and delivering the next package had been made.

Chapter Six

On Monday morning, Mattie's cell phone rang at eleven. It was Summers. Her eyelids felt like lead as she answered groggily.

"I have a few more questions," he told her. "Can you talk with me this morning?"

"Yes, of course." Her voice was scratchy. "Are you coming here?"

"I thought maybe you could come down to headquarters."

"If you come here, both my aunt and uncle will be available if you have questions for them."

He thought about it for a moment and then agreed. When Mattie told her aunt, Cecelia responded, "Well, he'll just have to join us for lunch. I'm not going to try to keep it warm while he asks a lot of questions."

Within forty minutes, the intercom buzzed in the kitchen, and Jack identified himself. Mattie pressed the button that opened the entry gate. When the bell at the front door rang, Mattie and her aunt both hurried to answer it. Jack had left his car in front of the house in the curved driveway. He had driven a dark blue, unmarked Crown Victoria, an official police vehicle.

Mattie opened the door, and her aunt invited Summers in as she dried her hands on her apron. "Come in, come in. I've set another plate at the table so we can have lunch together."

He raised his hand in polite refusal. "This is an official call, Mrs. Southland. I don't want to interfere with your meal. I just have a few questions for Mattie—and maybe a few for you and your husband."

Cecelia was only five foot two, but she could be formidable. "Of course you'll join us. I won't take no for an answer." She turned on her heel and headed back to the kitchen.

Jack noted the dark circles under Mattie's eyes as she gave him a crooked, halfhearted smile. "You'll get your questions answered much faster if you give in." She led him to the large kitchen with its stainless steel appliances and a large island. The floor of black marble tiles matched the marble countertops and the table at the end of the room, where Cecelia had set four places.

She placed the large square dish of lasagna and a large bowl of tossed green salad in the middle of the table. Mattie's uncle shook Summers's hand and pointed to a seat at the end of the table. The detective removed his gray tweed coat and hung it on the back of the chair. This morning he was wearing a white dress shirt, a deep blue tie, and black slacks.

They sat down, and Max offered grace. The plates were passed to Cecelia, and she dished up the lasagna. As she handed Summers a cruet of salad dressing, she stated firmly, "Now you can ask your questions." Max tried to hide a smile behind his napkin.

The detective pulled a pen and a small notebook from his shirt pocket. After opening the notepad, he put it on the table near his plate. "I appreciate your hospitality," he said in a slightly apologetic manner. He cleared his throat and sampled the salad. Mattie pushed her food around her plate halfheartedly, and the other three noted her lack of appetite.

Her aunt leaned over and whispered, "Please try to eat, Mattie. You're much too thin as it is."

Summers put his fork down and picked up his pen. "Now that you've had some time to think about it, have any of you thought of any possible reason someone would kill Mr. Crittenden?"

"This was a senseless death," Southland responded. "I've never met a finer young man. I think it had to be a case of mistaken identity. I can't see any other explanation." Cecelia nodded in agreement.

Summers looked at Mattie and waited for her to respond. She shook her head slightly. She had no answers.

"At Chief Jepson's request, the Criminal Investigation Unit of the state DPS will be assisting the local authorities. We're interviewing every guest and staff member at the hotel. So far, no one saw anything out of the ordinary."

Mattie sat up straighter and looked directly at Summers as something occurred to her. "I asked the hotel management to lock the doors that opened onto the pool area to keep distractions to a minimum during the news conference. You can't see the pool from the meeting room, but sometimes the swimmers are visible on the end of the patio." She slowed her words. "If the doors were locked, how did the killer get Craig's body into the pool?"

"What time were the doors supposed to be locked?"

"Six thirty, the same time I asked for the outside lights to be turned off."

The detective pulled his cell from his pocket and punched a speed dial button. "Barstow, are you still interviewing the hotel staff?" He paused. "Did you ask about the time the lights were turned off and the doors to the pool locked?" A pause. "Have you learned anything new?" Another pause. "Okay, keep at it."

He responded to Mattie's expectant look. "The lights were turned off at the central electrical box about six fifteen by the hotel maintenance man, and a staff person was supposed to lock the doors at six thirty. That man doesn't come on duty until four this afternoon, so we haven't verified that. If the doors were locked at six thirty, then that helps us fix the time of death between six, when he called you, and six thirty, when the doors were locked. The only hotel staff person that remembers anything else about Saturday evening described a man with a black beard asking about an envelope Craig had left at the front desk to have mailed."

"Did it get mailed?" Mattie interjected.

Summers nodded. "He said he mailed it at a post office drop box with some letters from a couple of other guests on his way home from work that evening about eight—before Mr. Crittenden's body was discovered. He remembered that the manila envelope had *Happy Birthday* written on it. As of yet, no one has anything else to add to the little we know right now. Perhaps the autopsy will tell us more. It should be done tomorrow."

Mattie visibly blanched at the word *autopsy* and put down her fork. Summers looked at her and tried to soften his manner. "I'm sorry for mentioning it, Miss Mathis. I know that was the last thing you needed to hear about." He cleared his throat uncomfortably.

"Just call me Mattie, please," she answered mechanically, her voice a near whisper.

"Then call me Jack." He looked around the table and added, "We may all know each other very well by the time this investigation is over."

She nodded, looking at her plate of untouched food. "I can't think of anything unusual except a research paper he'd been working on that seemed especially important to him. He told me on the phone that he was bringing copies to the news conference, one for Uncle Max and one for Jeff Skidmore. I don't know what happened to those copies." She looked directly at Summers. "Has anyone located his car? Maybe that's where they are."

"Late Saturday night, I had the license plate of every car in the hotel parking lot and on the street around the hotel run through DMV. We identified Craig's car then and searched it, but there wasn't anything of use to us." He looked at her with his eyebrows raised. "You haven't mentioned the paper before."

"I didn't think of it at the hotel. I hardly knew my own name after we found him." There was a sheen of tears in her eyes.

"What's the paper about?"

Mattie rubbed her right temple for a moment to ease a developing headache, and Southland took the opportunity to answer the question. "Craig had been researching oil and natural gas exploration, more specifically retorting and hydrofracking, which are processes very much on the mind of many members of Congress right now."

Jack's eyebrows went up with a look that asked for further explanation.

"They're processes used for energy exploration, and both are somewhat controversial. Hydrofracking uses deep drilling—often as deep as two miles or more—to force the rock layers of the earth to widen preexisting fractures so the gas, oil, and in some cases, ground water, can be more readily extracted. The water is mixed with sand or ceramic particles to hold the fractures open while the oil, gas, or ground water is harvested. Retorting is a method used to extract oil from shale. As much as the nation needs more oil, these processes have some potentially serious environmental impacts."

When Max paused to take a bite of salad, Mattie spoke. "Craig didn't say anything specific about why this paper was so important, but he told me that he'd gotten some information from Theo Novak, the younger brother of Uncle Max's administrative assistant in Washington. He said I'd understand when I read it. He was going to put a copy in the mail to me, since he figured I'd be too busy or too tired to read it after the news conference. Maybe that was the envelope he left at the registration desk. He didn't seem to think that the issue of energy exploration was likely to become an issue in Skidmore's campaign but thought some related issues might draw national attention. He didn't tell me what those issues were."

Summers put down his fork. "So if we don't find a copy of the paper, we won't know what was so important that it might have gotten him killed."

Mattie sat up straighter as a thought struck her. "We might be able to find the paper on the computer at the district office. Craig was working on it there before we talked on the phone."

"Can we check that computer right now?" Summers dropped his napkin on the table and hurriedly pushed back his chair.

"Yes, we can. You'll excuse us, won't you, Aunt Cecelia? Uncle Max?" Before either had responded, she stood and bent to give her aunt a peck on the cheek. "I'll tell you what we find when we get back. Thanks for lunch." She turned to Summers. "Wait a minute. I've got to get my bag."

She quickly returned with a gray leather bag chosen for its capacity and noticed that Summers had picked up his notepad, pen, and cell phone and was tucking them into various pockets. She led him to the front door, where she paused long enough to get a jacket from the closet. She shrugged it on as the detective opened the door. They hurried across the lawn to his unmarked sedan, and he had the engine running before she had even pulled her door closed. With an astounding adroitness, he backed the car down the driveway and out the gate.

He followed Mattie's directions to the congressional district office and parked in front. She was the first out of the car with the keys in her hand, but as she went to put the key in the lock, the door moved under her hand. Summers pulled her back with his left hand while he withdrew a .45 automatic from his shoulder holster.

"Step back," he quietly ordered.

While she waited outside, he moved through the office, checking the reception room, Mattie's office, the meeting room, the kitchenette, and the restroom. He returned to the front door. "Come on in. It looks like someone has trashed the place."

She looked around in alarm at the half-open drawers of file cabinets and the files that had been dumped on the floor. She dashed to her office. "The computer's gone. So's the external drive."

"What else is missing?"

While Mattie moved from room to room, evaluating damages, Summers called headquarters and asked Chief Jepson to send someone from the robbery division as well as a crime scene technician. Mattie returned to the reception room and, with her hands on her hips, looked at the mess again. "Jack," she used his first name tentatively, "I can't tell if any of the files are gone because they're scattered all over."

"Without the computer, is there any way we might get a copy of what was in it?"

"We can try Uncle Max's AA in Washington. Maybe he has a copy of at least part of it. Help me find the Washington congressional directory. It's a blue phone book."

They both started looking for it, gathering up the papers scattered around the room as they went. She finally found the directory nearly completely behind a file cabinet. "Here it is. It's got office, home, and personal cell phone numbers." She thumbed through it until she located Congressman Southland's staff listings. She took the phone out of the charging cradle and started to dial Ben Novak's number. Summers took it out of her hand.

"Just a minute." He pushed the back panel off the phone and examined the inside. He slipped it back together and replaced it. Then he put a finger in front of his lips to signal her to silence. "I need to use the restroom. Just give me a minute." He nodded his head toward the restroom at the rear of the office, and she followed him. When they were both inside, he closed the door and whispered into her ear, "It's bugged—and not just phone calls, but it will pick up everything in the office."

"Can't you take it out?" she whispered back.

"Then they'll know we're on to them—whoever they are. Can you follow my lead?" She nodded.

He flushed the toilet for effect, and they returned to the reception area, where they began a conversation for the benefit of the listener.

"How much do you estimate the computer and the external drive are worth?" he asked.

"Less than a thousand dollars. I can't place a value on the information I've lost, but I think donor records and constituent requests and that kind of thing can be copied from the Washington office. It's just going to be a major inconvenience."

"Did you see anything else stolen or broken?"

"The copy machine looks like it might be damaged, and I can't tell if the fax is okay. They may need to be replaced."

"Will you be able to get some help to clean up the place tomorrow?"

"I can probably get a couple of volunteers to come in."

Two police vehicles pulled into the parking lot while they were talking—an unmarked, dark green Crown Victoria, and a CSI van. "After the boys from robbery have finished with the place, I'll take you home so you can let your uncle know what's happened. Let's get out of their way." He stepped through the front door and met them outside, where he said quietly, "The place is bugged, so watch what you say. Keep it all business." Eyebrows went up, and the men nodded before entering the office.

While the office was photographed and dusted for fingerprints, Mattie and Jack sat in his car. "What made you suspect that the phone was tapped?" she asked, a vertical worry line forming between her eyebrows.

"It was sitting on the desk apparently undisturbed in an office that had been turned upside down." He changed the direction of the conversation. "If Crittenden worked for your uncle in the D.C. office, how did you get to know him so well?"

"The first time he came from D.C. with Uncle Max, he was put up at home. We hit it off immediately. Aunt Cecelia had been interested in getting me married off for the last several years, so she noticed. She got Uncle Max to throw us together whenever possible. Perhaps Craig traveled back here more often than was absolutely necessary because of that." She swallowed hard to control the quaver that had crept into her voice.

"When was the last time you saw him alive?"

"Aunt Cecelia fixed breakfast for the four of us last Wednesday. He told us he was headed to the law library at ASU to do some additional research. He didn't know how much time it would take, and I didn't worry because the law library is open until ten. I tried to call him a couple times, but his cell was off. I knew he was working on something important, or he would've called me. His phone call from the office Saturday was the first time I'd heard from him since then. He must have been coming home so late each evening that I didn't see or hear him, but then the bedroom he was using is in the main part of the house, and I live in the guest rooms behind the garages."

"I think you need to give the staffer whose brother produced that research paper a call. What's his name?"

"Benjamin Novak."

"Give Mr. Novak a call. We really need a copy of that paper." She had left her bag in the office, so he handed her his phone.

She searched the congressional directory she was still holding and located the personal cell number for Ben. His phone went to voice mail.

"Ben, it's Mattie Mathis from the district office. Call me. It's really important."

Next, she located the number listed as his home and dialed it. After five rings, a man's muffled voice answered, "Novak residence."

"I'm calling for Ben. Is he in?"

After a slight hesitation, the voice asked, "Who is this?"

"This is Mattie Mathis. I manage Congressman Southland's district office, and I need to talk to Ben, if I can."

"Oh, Miss Mathis. He's mentioned you. This is his father. Since my wife died, I've been living with Benny. I'm sorry he isn't here." His voice broke. "He's in Austin, Texas, making arrangements to bring his brother's body home."

"Theo's dead?" Mattie's voice rose, and her head swiveled to face Summers with alarm.

"Yes. Did you know him?"

"We had never met, but Ben talked about him. He was very proud of his brother."

The man's voice quivered with emotion. "We all were."

"How did it happen?"

"He was riding his bike on campus"—he was struggling to keep his composure—"when a car hit him. There was an explosion in the law school about the same time that distracted everyone, so no witnesses have come forward." His voice trailed off.

"I'm so sorry, Mr. Novak. I'm so very sorry. What a terrible loss. How bad was the blast? Were others injured or killed?"

"Benny said that one of Theo's law professors was killed."

"That's strange." She paused before adding, "Please tell Ben to call me or Congressman Southland if there is anything, *anything* we can do."

"Thank you," he murmured before he disconnected the call.

Mattie turned to Summers. "They killed them too." The color had left her face, and her voice was a tight whisper.

As he took the cell from her hand, he urged her, "Don't jump to conclusions. Maybe there's no connection. Tell me what happened."

She repeated the information Ben's father had given her and added insistently, "Theo produced much of the information in that paper. Now he and his professor are both dead. Craig spent four days confirming Theo's information and probably expanding on it, and he felt their research was important enough to bring to the attention of my uncle and Jeff Skidmore. There has to be a connection. Will you call the Austin police or the police department at the university, whoever will have jurisdiction in a case like this, and see if they've discovered anything?"

Summers hesitated for only a fraction of a second before he nodded. After a couple of attempts, he had the desk sergeant in Austin on the line.

When he ended the call, he said grimly, "The campus police called the city PD because of the serious nature of the hit-and-run. They're leaning toward calling it an accidental death, but I'm beginning to think you may be right. I'm not a believer in coincidences. I hate to admit it, but all of this may be connected." He slipped his cell into a pocket and looked at her intently. "Mattie, who else would have seen that research paper?"

"Craig told me on the phone that Theo's law professor said it was worthy of publication in one of the U.T. law school journals. Theo had been so excited that he e-mailed the paper to Craig and said that his professor was considering sending a copy to an old friend who's the regional director of the EPA in San Francisco."

"How soon can your uncle contact someone at that regional office? Maybe we're overreacting, but that director needs to be warned." She nodded. He continued, "Try calling Ben's cell again. If he's got a copy of that paper, we need it."

Mattie left another message. "Ben, call me. This is Mattie. It's really important. You can call me on this line or my cell or home number. I'm sure you have them."

Jack was shaking his head. He whispered, "Not your personal cell or home phone."

She hesitated and then spoke into the phone once more. "No, scratch that. Use the number of the cell I'm calling on. You can talk to me or to Jack Summers, if he answers. Please, Ben, it's really important." While she talked, Summers watched through the front window as the CSI technician pulled off his latex gloves and put his equipment back into its case. It was apparent that the man from the robbery division was finished as well.

No one paid any attention to the scruffy-looking man with the longish hair and ragged beard that walked behind the cars parked in front of the office. He dropped some change when he pulled his dirty handkerchief out of his pocket to blow his nose. He stooped behind Jack's departmental Ford to pick up the coins. No one saw him slip the magnetized tracking chip into the rear wheel well of the car.

Chapter Seven

As THE TECHNICIAN AND THE detective exited the office, Summers stepped out of the car to speak to them. The CSI tech was not encouraging. "The place has been wiped down thoroughly. We found a few prints in the kitchenette on the microwave and a couple on the mirror in the restroom, but I suspect they belong to the staff. This was done by a professional and made to look like an amateur job."

"You're probably right, but thanks for your time. Get back to me if anything turns up." Summers shook the hands of both men before they left.

Mattie locked the office door, though it seemed pointless. As Summers steered the car toward the exit of the parking lot, she asked, "Can you take me to the hotel so I can pick up my car?"

He was slow to answer. "Okay, but I'm going to follow you home and talk to your uncle. I want to put a man at your uncle's home tonight."

"So you agree that the deaths are connected." It was a statement, not a question. "Won't someone sitting in a police car outside the gate be a bit obvious—and potentially useless on a six-acre estate?"

"I'll put him inside and have him do a check of the grounds each hour."

After a thoughtful minute, Mattie stated, "I'm going to have my sister Cora's husband bring their dog over. Butch is an eight-year-old German shepherd, and he's the best watchdog in the state. If you insist on putting an officer at the house, I'll have my brother-in-law tell Butch to obey him."

"If that will make you feel safer, it's fine with me."

"Just have the department send out a man who likes dogs. Butch can tell if you don't feel at ease around him."

As Jack pulled into the hotel parking lot, Mattie pointed to her red 2010 Mazda convertible parked near the rear hotel entrance. "That's my car."

As he pulled behind her vehicle, his cell phone rang. "Summers here." After a pause, he handed it to Mattie. "It's Ben Novak."

"Ben, thanks so much for getting back to me. Your dad said that Theo was hit by a car on campus and killed. I'm so sorry."

"Yeah, I've had my phone off while I've been at the mortuary arranging to have his body shipped home. Oh, Mattie, this is so senseless." His last statement sounded like a wail of grief.

"When was he killed?"

"We got the phone call late Friday evening, and I grabbed the first plane to Texas that I could get on Saturday. This has been really hard on my dad."

She was quiet for a second before she asked in a tight voice, "Have you heard about Craig?"

"No, has something happened to Craig?" His voice rose in alarm.

"Saturday night, someone shot and killed him." She bit her lip to steady her quivering chin for a moment. "I'm so sorry to add to your grief. I know you two were good friends."

There was silence on the line for two or three seconds. "Mattie, how? Why?" He took a deep breath. "Why would anyone kill Craig? Oh, Mattie, I'm so sorry for you. I know that you and Craig were close—that you were planning to get married. Craig let me in on it before he left Washington."

She swallowed hard to regain control of her voice. "I think his death may have something to do with the research paper Theo sent him, but I don't know how it's related because we don't have a copy of it. Do you have one?"

"No, I don't. All I know was that when Craig talked to me Tuesday night after he received it, he said he was going to spend some time verifying and adding to what Theo had sent him."

"When you get back to the office in D.C., will you go through the files on the office computer and see if Theo sent you any part of it? We need to know what was in it."

"Yeah. I'll do that as soon as I can."

"Ben, be careful. Be very careful. Keep up your guard."

"I'll be careful, Mattie. You be careful too."

***

On the drive home in her own car, Mattie's thoughts were wheels within wheels as she tried to make sense of the three deaths. When she looked behind her, she began to wonder if she was being paranoid. Jack followed her in his departmental car, but behind him, a Honda motorcycle made every turn the two of them did. It finally disappeared when they reached Valhalla Drive, where the Southlands lived.

She punched in the numbers to open the gate, and as she drove in, she put her arm out of the window and waved at him to follow her. They drove in tandem up the long curved driveway. He followed her around to the rear concrete pad behind the two double garage doors. When he got out of his car, she asked, "Did you see the motorcycle following us? And please don't tell me I'm just being paranoid."

"Yes, I saw it, and no, I don't think you're being paranoid."

As Mattie put her key in the door, she noticed Summers looking the rear of the house over. He was taking in the three chimneys, nearly six acres of rolling lawns, pool, and tennis courts.

As she pushed the door open, she answered the look on his face. "No, Uncle Max doesn't make enough as a member of congress to possess a home like this. He inherited it when his older brother, Ed, passed away about nine or ten years ago. Ed had made a fortune in the Silicon Valley microchip industry. He'd married late in life and was widowed a few years later, so he had no children of his own. If he hadn't left a trust to go with it, Uncle Max might not be able to pay the taxes and upkeep on it. And yes, the architecture is unusual for this part of the country. It was built before the residential zoning codes demanded a Southwestern style. It really stands out like a white elephant."

He smiled at her easy recognition of his thoughts as they walked down the hallway to the main portion of the house.

Summers stayed at the mansion until the congressman and his wife arrived home from his speaking engagement. Within a few minutes of their return, Bob Curtis, an out-of-uniform Mesa police officer, arrived. Mattie fixed ham sandwiches for everyone and served them with some of Cecelia's barbecued beans and potato salad. Mattie's brother-in-law, Sam, sat down and joined the impromptu meal when he arrived with the dog. As Mattie put the food on the table she thought, *It's like a picnic, a picnic in February brought on by three deaths.* She shivered slightly at the thought.

Butch was introduced to Bob, and their friendship was sealed by a portion of Bob's sandwich.

When they had finished eating, Sam told the dog, "On guard, Butch." The dog quickly stood, fully alert. As Sam was putting on his jacket, he turned to Bob, "Don't give him any instructions you don't want him to follow. He does what he's told. My brother brought him back from Afghanistan about a year ago after Butch was wounded by an IED. The army didn't want him back, so he needed a home. When he's in the yard, needless to say, I don't worry about my girls."

Max retired to his office and tried to call the regional director of the EPA but couldn't raise anyone that evening. He left a message on the answering machine that he wanted to speak to Director Donohue as soon as possible the next day. He said quietly to Mattie, "I'll try again in the morning."

Mattie eventually fell asleep that night knowing that once an hour, Butch and Bob would make the rounds of the house and grounds, but dreams of Craig woke her repeatedly and brought renewed tears.

***

In the morning, after Bob had been thanked, fed, and had taken his leave, Butch remained behind. Against her aunt's objections, Mattie insisted on going in to the district office. She called two women who enjoyed working as volunteers, arranging to meet them there at ten.

As the gate slid open at the end of the driveway, she saw the mailman. She waited while he halted his truck and got out. They had greeted each other many times in the years she had lived with Max and Cecelia, so he took the large envelope and the other mail in his arms and handed it all to her. As he did so, he said, "Happy Birthday."

She looked up at him in surprise, and he responded, "I noticed the package is addressed to you and it says happy birthday. Many happy returns. By the way, at my last stop, I had to chase a homeless guy out of the truck. He apparently wanted your mail. Maybe it's his birthday too." He laughed at his own joke and climbed back into his truck. With a wave, he headed down the street.

She took note of her sister's name in the return address. *It's not my birthday.* She also noted that it was not her sister's handwriting. It was Craig's. *What had Jack said about a bearded man asking about a package at the Hilton, one that the clerk said had* Happy Birthday *written on it? Was this Craig's attempt to camouflage it?*

She pulled open the flap on the envelope and looked inside. It was a stack of computer-printer paper. When she slid it partially out, she found a note clipped to the top sheet. In Craig's handwriting, it read: *Mattie, I have a bad feeling about this. There are too many people who will try to prevent this from becoming public, so I'm mailing this copy to you in case—well, just in case. Craig.*

She had to hold her breath and wipe away two tears before she regained her self-control. Then she stuffed the other mail into the mailbox and hurried back to her car, where she fumbled in her bag for her cell phone. Summers's cell went to voice mail.

"Jack, it's Mattie. I need to see you ASAP. Call me right away. I'm headed in to the office."

As she drove toward the office on Highway 202, her cell rang. "Mattie, it's Jack. You wanted to talk to me, but it's better if we don't do it by phone. I'm headed for your office and should be there within twenty minutes. See you then."

The rest of the way, she kept a watch in her rearview mirror. Once or twice she saw a motorcyclist with a dark helmet who seemed determined to stay within a hundred feet of her car, no matter what lane she was traveling in. She breathed a sigh of relief when she reached the office and he disappeared.

Jack arrived a few minutes after her two volunteers had begun reassembling scattered files and straightening the rooms. Remembering the bug in the telephone, she introduced Jack as a friend, rather than as a police officer. One of the women extended her sympathy on Craig's death, having no idea of how deeply the death had touched Mattie.

Jack greeted each woman and then pulled Mattie outside. "What did you want to talk to me about?" Neither of them took note of the man on the motorcycle sitting against the curb about two hundred feet down the street under the shade of a tree.

She had the manila envelope pinned against her body by her left arm. She pointed at it with her right hand. "This. It's a copy of the research paper. The mailman brought it this morning. He said that some homeless guy had gotten into his truck, apparently trying to get it."

"Can you leave one of these ladies with a key so they can lock up when they're done?"

"Why?"

"Because I'm taking you somewhere safe so we can read the paper. You might not be here when they're finished."

They stepped back inside. "Betty, if I give you the spare key, will you lock up if I'm not back when you're done?"

"Sure, Mattie. And I'll come in tomorrow morning to finish anything else that needs to be done and to answer the telephone."

"You're an angel, and so are you, Sadie." As they left the office, she asked, "What about my car? Should I leave it here?"

"It should be okay. It's in a very visible spot. I doubt that anyone would try anything."

After they got into Jack's car, Mattie voiced what had been on her mind since she had opened the big envelope. "Jack, shouldn't we go directly to the FBI with this paper?"

"Not until we've read it. If we give them our only copy, it might disappear into a black hole of federal red tape. The bureau is not known for its willingness to share information with local authorities. They like to run things themselves, and I'm not going to get shut out of the investigation. Besides, at this point, it's still a local matter."

"Where are we going?"

"As soon as I can be sure that we aren't being followed, we're going to a certain pizza place. We'll order a pizza and read this paper."

The pizza shop was nearly empty, as it was an hour too early for the lunch crowd. Its wood floors were sanded smooth by the feet of fifty years of pizza-loving customers. Each booth had a cloudy mirror and cracked-and-split red imitation leather seat covers on the banquettes which formed a U around each warn and stained wooden table. Summers led her to a booth in the back corner where he could still see the front door and window.

With her pad and pencil poised, the waitress asked Jack, "Whatilitbe?" He ordered a supreme pizza—at Mattie's request—and two sodas.

While they waited, Mattie pulled the paper from the envelope. After she read each page, she handed it to him. They read for the twenty minutes it took for the pizza to be ready. After the server set the pizza in front of them, she smiled broadly. "Can I getcha anythin' else?"

They both shook their heads, impatient to get back to the paper.

She put the bill upside down on the tabletop and moved away.

They had skimmed much of the paper when Jack stopped reading. He took the pages Mattie had in her hands and stuffed them back into the envelope. He called to the woman who had brought the pizza, "We need to take this with us. Can you bring us a box?"

He pulled some cash from his wallet and laid the money on the table. When the pizza was boxed, Summers urged Mattie to follow him quickly. He took the manila envelope and gave her the pizza box to carry. "If someone tries to take the envelope, I'm bigger than you. Now that I've seen it, I think it *could* be the cause of the death of three men. We're going somewhere more secure." He nodded toward his car and looked around thoroughly as they made their way toward it.

When the car merged with traffic, Mattie spoke quietly. "If what we suspect is correct, now that I have a copy of the paper, they won't hesitate to kill me." She looked around as he drove. "Where are we going?"

"Do you have any cash with you?"

"Not much, maybe twenty-five dollars. If I'm going to need cash, I'll need to stop at the nearest branch of First National and make a withdrawal."

After twenty minutes of darting through narrow streets and parking lots until he was sure they weren't being followed, he stopped at a Radio Shack in a small strip mall. "Put the pizza in the backseat. We're going to buy you a phone." He was moving so fast she couldn't slow him down enough to ask why.

They left the store with a twenty-dollar phone with seventy-five dollars' worth of prepaid minutes loaded in it. She had paid for it with a credit card. "That's the last purchase you make with a credit card. You understand?" His jaw was set, and his eyes held a don't-mess-with-me look. "Anyone with real clout can get a credit card traced."

"Then let's get to the bank so I can get some cash."

"We're playing in the big leagues now." He continued as though he hadn't heard her. "Your iPod has a GPS chip in it, and its location can be traced by people with the right connections. By the way, make sure it's turned off. "

She pulled it from her purse and pressed the off button. Jack reached out and took it from her, slipping it into the inside pocket of his sport coat. In response to the startled look on her face, he responded, "Just in case you're tempted to use it." The hardness of his words was softened by his look of concern.

When they pulled up under the portico at the bank's drive-up window, she started to make out a withdrawal slip for $500, but Jack stopped her. "Make it more than that if you can. Going underground can be expensive. You'll need a change or two of clothes as well as personal items, and you'll need to pay for meals and rooms, at least until we decide whether or not we can bring the FBI in on this."

"But you said this is still a local matter."

"If we get to the point that we can prove that the information in this paper links the murders, it could become federal in a hurry."

Chapter Eight

Within thirty minutes, Summers flashed his badge at the clerk behind the registration desk of the Jardin Hotel. It was one of the older hotels of the area. The interior was updated and quietly elegant, but the hotel's greatest attraction was the fact that it wasn't excessively expensive. The yellow brick structure had been constructed in the twenties as an office building. Each floor was marked with a row of symmetrical casement windows, below which was a decorative granite frieze that wrapped the building and was topped by a twelve-inch wide ledge, a perfect location for pigeons.

When Mattie couldn't produce any ID in the name they had selected, Janice M. Smith, Jack pulled out his badge and told the clerk, "I'm her verification." When the clerk told her the cost for the night was $200, Jack looked at him and stated firmly, "Give her the government rate. What is it?"

The clerk responded hesitantly and in a slightly embarrassed manner, "The government rate is $95 per night, sir."

She paid for one night with cash. The room she was given was on the sixth floor overlooking the parking lot of a four-story office building next door. Only a driveway separated them.

Once they had been shown to the room, she examined the scene from the window. Jack pulled the large upholstered chair to the desk, which was on the far side of the bed. He motioned Mattie to sit down. He sat on the desk chair. While Mattie opened the pizza box, Jack pulled the research paper out of the large brown envelope. They both took a piece and started to read again, this time much more closely.

It was comprised of about forty-five sheets of paper, all double-spaced with narrow margins and size ten typeface. The words *For more information contact Craig Crittenden* and his address and phone number were printed at the top. It was a bit erudite with long sentences full of legalese, but any reader would find it genuinely fascinating reading if they could get past the lawyer talk.

The first part of the paper dealt with methods of increasing oil and natural gas production in the western United States through hydrofracking and retorting. Mattie skimmed much of the technical jargon looking for the information that Craig had felt was so vital. When she came to the discussion of a major lawsuit, she noticed Craig's handwriting in the margin. He had written, "Very important!"

The lawsuit had tied up several dozen attorneys for four years in an expensive, bitter warfare in the United States Court of Federal Claims, where the verdict came down against a group of energy companies that had sued the Bureau of Land Management. The outcome was not certain despite the lower court verdict because of the appeals process.

Mattie gave her full attention to the list of fifteen plaintiffs. The research had been so thorough that it included the names of members of the boards of directors, CEOs, and CFOs from the corporate annual reports. The names of major stockholders of the publicly traded companies had been listed. One particular name appeared as a major stockholder in each publicly held company. Craig had written, "Big player!" where the name Gregorovich Volos first appeared. It had been underlined wherever it occurred thereafter. From diagrams Craig had drawn on the back of pages thirty-two and thirty-three, it was evident that many of this man's investments were protected by a cadre of holding companies, a firewall that had probably taken Theo weeks of research to penetrate. The name Volos was the link that tied all the plaintiffs in the case together.

Craig had summarized the legal maneuverings that laid the groundwork for a potential appeal. The plaintiffs claimed that the verdict against them had been purchased or in some other way illegally obtained. Accusations and counteraccusations, as well as requests from the plaintiffs that the judge recuse himself because of perceived bias, had generated many more legal documents. Theo or Craig had listed requests for sanctions and fines to and from both sides that must have kept dozens of associate attorneys in the back rooms of the powerful firm Doty, Dotson, and Diller trying to intimidate government witnesses by the hour.

She suddenly remembered something Craig had said on the phone on Saturday night. She spoke, interrupting Jack's reading. "Craig said this information was 'what no one else has looked for. They thought they had covered their tracks.'"

Jack was stumped. He rose and paced for a couple of minutes before responding. "Why would this information be suppressed with so much violence if it could come out sometime in the future?"

She turned the matter over in her mind for a few seconds before she spoke. "The only reason I can think of is that it's time sensitive. Somehow, if the information came out now, it would be a problem that it might not be in the future."

"You know more about the functions of the federal government than I do. What could be affected now that might not be in the future, if the information came out later?"

Mattie rose from the couch and paced for a minute. "Federal appointments are often time sensitive, but a federal appointee can be encouraged—or forced—to resign if some scandal comes to light that might embarrass the administration."

She suddenly whirled and pointed at Jack with her face alight. "The exception to that rule is the federal judicial bench. Federal judges are appointed for life. They're nearly impossible to impeach once the appointment has been confirmed by the Senate. Maybe that's it. If it is, we need to notify the FBI." Her voice was urgent.

Her hand flew up and covered her mouth in alarm for a moment. "Wait, wait, wait," she said to give herself a moment to think. Her eyes narrowed thoughtfully. "This is getting complicated."

"Why?"

"If this really does have to do with a federal appointment to the bench, there will be senators on the judiciary committee who will be involved in the appointment. The senator from the home state of the nominee will have to sponsor him or her.

"With a formal request, a senator can be privy to just about anything the FBI, ICE, IRS, DOD, or almost any other federal law enforcement agency is working on that falls under the jurisdiction of the committee he sits on. The only intelligence agencies which members of the Senate can't easily access would be the CIA and NSA. Even judiciary committee members would have to fill out a bushel of forms to try to access what either of those agencies are doing, and even then it might take a very long time and come up redacted beyond recognition."

"You'd know how to find out what senators sit on which committees that could access the bureau files? Can you do that with a phone call?"

"Do you think the phones into my uncle's office in Washington, D.C., might be bugged?"

"Don't know. It wouldn't be difficult since the public has access to the office. Since we know the one in the local office is, we'll go on the assumption that the others are as well. Can you get that information some other way?"

"I'll call the congressional operator and have her connect me with one of the other congressional offices. I'll have a staffer there fax us a list of senatorial committee assignments and a copy of all pending federal appointments to the bench. Will you call the hotel operator and get the fax number here while I call D.C.?" Jack nodded.

She pulled out her prepaid cell, and within a minute, she had a staffer on the phone in the office of the congressman whose district adjoined Southland's. "Hi, Sally, it's Mattie Mathis in the Southland district office. I'm out of the office right now, but I need a copy of the committee assignments for the Senate. Can you fax that to me?" She paused and then added, "And by any chance do you have a list of pending appointments to the federal bench?" She thanked the young woman on the other end of the line and read off the hotel fax number that Jack had written on a napkin and put in front of her. She hung up the phone and looked at Jack. "She'll fax that info to us right away."

Jack picked up the hotel phone again and called the desk. "You'll be getting a fax from Washington, D.C. It may be several pages." He hesitated for a fraction of a second while he tried to remember the name Mattie had used when she checked in. "It's for Janice Smith in room 620. Will you call us when it comes in? We need it ASAP."

Chapter Nine

BY THE TIME THEY HAD finished the pizza, the front desk had called. Jack pushed himself up from the couch and gathered up the papers. He organized them, tapping the pile on the desk until the edges were aligned. Then he put the report into the manila envelope. "I'm going to go downstairs and get the fax. At the same time, I'll request that they make two copies of the paper. Keep the chain on the door and don't open it for anyone but me."

He returned to the room with the fax in his hand within a few minutes. "It's going to take them a few minutes to get the paper copied. They've got a busload of folks trying to check in."

While they waited for the desk clerk to produce the copies of the research paper, they looked the fax over thoroughly.

Mattie circled a list of names with a hotel pen. "Here are the names of the senators who sit on the Senate Judiciary Committee. Frankly, there's only three or four that I think might allow themselves to be used by a man like Volos." She sat quietly for a moment before she added, "If we try to bring the FBI in on this, we may be giving those interested parties a pipeline to what we're doing."

With a crooked smile, Jack asked, "What *are* we doing?"

"I wish I knew." She slowly shook her head.

They looked over the names on the list of potential federal bench appointees. They meant nothing to Mattie. In another fifteen minutes, the desk called to tell them that the copies were ready.

Jack instructed her, "Like I said before, keep the chain on the door and don't open it for anyone but me."

While she waited, she stood by the window and watched the traffic moving past the hotel and in and out of the nearby parking lot. She noted a motorcyclist wearing a dark helmet, a black suit, and a tie that was flapping over his shoulder as he entered the parking lot below. It left her feeling uneasy.

It was nearly three, and she suddenly felt exhausted. She kicked off her shoes and lay down on the bed while she waited for Jack to return.

***

When the man on the motorcycle had parked behind the adjoining building, he sent a quick text to Gulletti. *Located the package. Will notify you when delivery is made.* Leaving his helmet on the handlebar, he walked into the rear entrance of the hotel and made his way to the lobby. There, he approached the desk.

He pulled out an authentic-looking badge, though he did not give the clerk time to examine it. "You recently had a young woman check in, tall with curly blonde hair. She was with a man who said he was a policeman. What room is she registered in?" His tone revealed an Eastern European accent.

Summers had instructed the clerk not to give out any information about Mattie, but the swarthy man in the dark, poorly fitted suit grabbed him by the lapels. "What room is she in?" The ferocity in his voice established his determination. When the clerk was slow to answer, he demanded, "Do you want to be charged with obstructing justice?"

The clerk was thoroughly intimidated. He stuttered, "Room 620, sir."

"You don't touch that phone," the man yelled as he moved across the lobby to the elevator. The frightened employee hurried to the office behind the registration desk where the other desk clerk was putting each of the copies of the research paper into separate manila envelopes while Jack waited.

"Officer, a man just demanded to know what room the lady with you was registered in. He showed me a badge. I thought you should know."

Forgetting the copies, Jack ran to the elevator, where he punched the button repeatedly. Realizing that it might be headed up to higher floors, he dashed for the stairs and took them two at a time.

***

Mattie was awakened by a hard knock on the door. "Miss, this is hotel security. I have a message for you."

She sat up. Jack had told her not to open the door for anyone else. She slid off the bed and, in her stocking feet, moved to the door to look through the peephole. She could see a man's shoulder in a black suit but he was half turned away, nearly hiding his face. Something about that bothered her. She nervously stepped away from the door.

He knocked again more forcefully. "Hotel security, Miss Mathis. Please open the door. There's been an accident involving your uncle and aunt." Her heart nearly stopped: *How would he know my name or who my aunt and uncle are?*

Her bloodstream was quickly filling with adrenaline because she didn't know where to go. It was making her heart pound so hard in her chest that it hurt. *If he forces his way in, I have nowhere to hide but the bathroom—no help there.* She picked up the telephone and punched zero for the hotel operator. "There's a man pounding on my door. I don't know him." Her voice was filled with panic. "Please, tell Sergeant Summers to hurry. He went down there to pick up some papers the clerk was copying for him."

As she returned the receiver to its cradle, she could hear a quiet snicking sound as the man began to work at the lock. She stepped into her shoes and, in one swift motion, slipped her jacket on. She put her purse over her shoulder and rushed to the window. *Will it open?*

The casement window hadn't been opened in a long while. She twisted the lock on the window sash and struggled with the lower half. It finally began to move. It took her an adrenaline-filled minute to inch it up far enough to allow her to kick off the screen. She stuck her head out and noted the decorative ledge under the windows around the entire sixth floor. She could still hear the man at the door working at the lock.

She pushed her bag around to her back and stuck her head out of the window. She could see a fire escape about twenty feet to the right. *Why couldn't they have put me in that room?* She squeezed under the window and put her knee on the ledge. It had been home to several thousand pigeons during the life of the building. She carefully stood, grasping the rough brick. Facing the wall, she took a cautious side step. The recessed mortar would have allowed the bricks to offer a good finger hold if it weren't for the fact that the exhaust of thousands of cars had deposited a dusty layer of soot. Inch by unsteady inch, she slid her feet cautiously toward the fire escape.

The sound of the door bursting open and the safety chain clattering against the wall startled her. Immediately after that, she heard the sound of a man's voice—Jack's voice—yelling breathlessly, "Police. Drop the gun. Put your hands up."

The man with the slight accent answered, "Hotel security."

"Put the gun down, or I'll shoot."

"Hotel security," she heard the man insist.

Another voice, deep, angry, and also out of breath responded, "*I'm* hotel security."

Two gunshots scared her so badly that her right foot slipped off the ledge. She pressed herself against the wall, where the bricks scratched her cheek. She carefully put her foot back on the ledge, took a breath to steady herself, and continued her slow progress toward the fire escape.

She could hear sirens but didn't dare look down. Her whole focus was on inching toward that fire escape. As she reached it and lifted her leg over the railing, Jack's head appeared out of the window of the room she had left. He called to her, "Stay there, Mattie. The security man will open that room, and I'll come and get you."

His head disappeared back inside. His promise did not bring much comfort. *They found me. I don't know how, but somehow they found me. If Jack comes to get me, they'll find me again. What to do, what to do, what to do?* The words pounded through her mind.

As if in answer to her indecision, a voice spoke clearly in her mind. *"Hide, Mattie. Find yourself a place to hide and go underground."*

She started down the fire escape ladder, slipping and falling the last half of the distance from the fourth floor to the third. She ducked down the next ladder, and when she reached the lowest one that should have extended nearly to the ground under her weight, she found that it was locked in its retractable position. She tried to unlatch it, but it had rusted in place. In frustration, she rattled it, but it wouldn't budge. Under her, she could see an open Dumpster almost nearly full of cardboard boxes and restaurant garbage. Hanging by both hands, she swung from the bottom step of the unmoving ladder and dropped into it.

"Mattie, what're you doing?" Jack's alarmed voice reached her from where he had climbed out on the fire escape six floors above her. "Mattie, don't run. They'll find you."

She climbed out of the dumpster and dropped to the ground. *Not if I can help it!* She looked up at him briefly and gave an almost imperceptible shake of her head. *Jack, I want your help, but right now, I think I'm better off alone.* Despite the bruises from the drop into the dumpster and the fear that made her legs feel as if each weighed a hundred pounds, she turned and started to run.

He bellowed her name. "Mattie!"

***

He was frustrated and angry. He couldn't go after her. He had to wait for the ambulance to take away the man in the poor-fitting black suit. He watched as the CSI techs finally finished their work, his jaw set hard as a rock and his guts twisted with worry. His heart pounded as he thought of her out there alone while he was stuck at the crime scene. He pulled his cell from his pocket and dialed her number. No answer.

When the on-site investigation was complete, Jack collected two of the three copies of the paper from the office. On an impulse, he asked the clerk to keep one copy in the hotel safe. Then, dreading what he had to do, he headed for headquarters to report to Chief Jepson.

***

He knocked on the office door, and a curt voice responded, "Come." He stepped in, knowing there would be much to explain. Jepson continued to work on the papers on his desk for an additional minute without looking up, leaving Jack to stand before him without an invitation to sit.

After Jack had been made to feel sufficiently uncomfortable, Jepson put down his pen. His voice was as inviting and friendly as the inside of a freezer. "Tell me what happened."

Jack knew any incident ending in the shooting of the suspect reflected badly on him, the Mesa PD, and DPS. To make matters worse, the potential victim had disappeared. Every squad car in the department and every law enforcement agency in the state had been given her description with a photo and instructions to apprehend her for her own safety.

Jack explained, and Jepson responded tiredly, "I wish I could hand you back to DPS for the internal affairs investigation, but you're assigned to my department at my request, so you're my problem. Give me your badge and gun. Until IA makes a decision, you'll be on desk duty." Jack quietly followed his instructions. "Now get out of here. I've got to explain to Congressman Southland that his niece is missing." He picked up the telephone receiver. "And get your car checked out by a CSI tech. Somehow that hit man located the two of you all too easily."

Jack was nearly overwhelmed with internalized anger at his own stupidity when the CSI tech found the GPS locator under his rear wheel well. He was still smoldering when he sat down at a desk in the office at headquarters and was immediately handed a four-inch pile of reports that needed to be put into the computer. He turned the screen toward him and began the process while his mind worked on the problem of Mattie's whereabouts and safety. His thoughts were churning, his stomach full of rocks. *Where did she go? Where is she now? If they find her, it will be entirely my fault.*

***

As harsh as Jepson had been with Summers, he knew the situation was not something Jack could have foreseen. He hit a button on the phone that rang in the internal affairs department. When the voice on the other end answered, he identified himself and stated firmly, "Get this matter of the shooting at the Jardin Hotel evaluated ASAP. I need Summers back on the job right away. That report needs to be completed within forty-eight hours. Can you handle that?"

The answer on the other end was noncommittal, but Jepson felt that he had done all he could to light a fire under IA.

Chapter Ten

MATTIE RAN ACROSS THE PARKING lot behind the office building next door, stumbling over the uneven and broken asphalt. She paused and looked over her shoulder before she moved down an alley between two buildings and reached the sidewalk on the opposite side of the block. She paused a fraction of a second to look both ways. *I've got to hide until I can figure out what to do.* She began to run in the direction of the Walmart she had seen when they had driven to the Jardin.

The new cell phone rang. She knew it was Summers. She pulled it out of her bag and turned it off.

After three blocks, she finally saw the giant superstore. As she ran, a plan was forming in her mind. She darted through the parking lot and grabbed a cart inside the entrance. In the women's department, she took a pair of black jeans and a wine-colored sweater off the racks. She grabbed a big, black purse, a hat with a floppy brim, and a reversible bomber-style jacket of microfiber.

What else do I need? What else do I need? She hurriedly pushed the cart to another department and picked up a tooth brush, toothpaste, a hair brush, hair dye, hair gel, and finally located scissors in the fabric department. She moved to the food section and dropped a package of frosted cinnamon rolls in the basket, thinking of her Aunt Cecelia with regret for the worry she'd be feeling. She added a six pack of small cans of V8, two apples, a small bag of corn chips, and a sixteen-ounce bottle of vitamin-infused water.

She hoped that she hadn't forgotten anything important enough to force her to go out again that evening. She entered the lane at a check-out counter, and as she waited, she visually scanned both entrances to see if Jack—or anyone else—had discovered her whereabouts.

She paid with cash and hurried through the parking lot to the sidewalk, where she crossed the street and darted up another alley which took her farther from the hotel. Two more trips through alleys, and she found herself in an older part of town where almost all the buildings were alike in their Spanish architecture and peeling paint. Nearly a quarter of them were empty. The fact that it would be dark in less than an hour filled her with urgency. *I've got to find some place to stay for the night.*

After two more blocks of hurried walking, sporadic jogging, and regularly looking over her shoulder, she spotted the Cactus Motor Court. Had her situation not been so dire, she would have smiled. It was a page out of times past. She stepped into the doorway of a closed coffee shop and stood for nearly five minutes, waiting for her heart to slow while she watched for anyone who could be following. The sidewalks were empty.

She crossed the street fifty feet before the driveway that turned into the old motel. She studied it as she approached. It was probably built in the late forties. The paint on the neon sign, which advertized private baths and single rooms at twenty-nine dollars per night, was faded and peeling. The motel ran deep into the block like a giant L, and each unit claimed its own carport. She stepped nervously into the office.

The elderly manager was asleep behind the counter in a battered recliner in front of an old television that she thought was loud enough to be heard by every living human being for a half mile in any direction.

She cleared her throat, but he didn't move. His wispy gray hair lay across the stripped pillow beneath his head. She couldn't help but note that he needed a haircut. She cleared her throat again. He was of an age where he probably slept more hours than he was awake, so she looked around for a tactful way to wake him. She found a bell on the far end of the counter. She hit it with her palm. No response. She hit it hard three times. He stirred and opened his eyes.

She raised her voice above the sound of the TV. "Sir, I'm sorry to disturb you, but I need a room tonight. Do you have a vacancy?" She tried to smile, but her lips felt so stiff from tension that she thought they might crack.

He picked up the remote and silenced the television. He laboriously pushed himself out of the chair. As he stood, Mattie noted his rounded back and hunched shoulders, and she had a sudden impulse to rush out to the nearest pharmacy and buy him a bottle of calcium tablets. Under different circumstances, she might have followed that impulse. His glasses rested on his head, and his striped overalls would have been more appropriate on a Missouri farmer. "My goodness gracious, I've got a whole raft of rooms. You kin take yer pick."

"Something in the back where it's quiet would be nice."

"You got it. You got it. Including tax, that'll be $32.80. I can take cash or put it on a credit card." He pushed a registration card toward her. "Do ya have a car?"

"Not tonight. It's . . . not tonight," she said weakly. She pushed three tens and a five toward him, and he pushed a registration card to her.

"Well, jus' fill this out with yer name and home address and show me yer driver's license."

She filled in the name Mae Matthews. It was close to her own, and with his glasses still on his head, she hoped he might not notice the difference. She put down the address of the house where she and her sister had been raised as children. When she held up her driver's license, her finger partially over the name, he squinted at the photo and nodded. "That's jus' fine. Here's a key to number 10 in the back. It ain't been used in a while, so you might wanna open the window and let it air out a bit. You stayin' more 'un one night?"

She paused and looked around. "I'm not sure; maybe. Just in case, let me pay for a second night." She gave him another thirty-five dollars. Even if she changed her mind and found another place, she felt it would be good to have this place as a backup.

"Oh, that's great. That's wonderful. Wait till I git yer change."

"No, you've been so kind; you keep it."

His smile brightened his face. "Well, I won't argue with that." He handed her a key attached to a plastic rectangle that advertized Smitty's Auto Repair. "You have a good night."

The room was located in the short leg of the L almost as far from the office as possible. From there, she could see the traffic on the street if she looked out the window. The manager was right. From the musty smell, she guessed that the room probably hadn't been used in at least a year. She opened the old window a few inches, pulled the curtains closed, and washed the corpse of a dead spider down the drain of the old porcelain sink in the little bathroom. It had a shower that had dripped water onto the old tile until it was stained orange. It was not the Jardin, nor even an EconoLodge, but it was safe—hopefully.

She turned the television volume on low then ate a cinnamon roll and drank a can of V8 while she watched the news on channel twelve. Nothing mentioned about the shooting at the Jardin. She shuddered, remembering the climb out onto the ledge. *That story may make the ten o'clock news.* As she washed the frosting from her fingers in the bathroom, she heard steps in the gravel in front of her door and then a knock. She suddenly felt a dark, strangling fear. Her light was on, so she couldn't pretend no one was there.

She tried to lower her voice. "Who is it?"

"It's jes' me, miss. I thought I'd see how you like the room." It was the old man from the office.

"It's fine, just fine, thank you."

"I'm glad. I'm gonna turn the lights on in a few of the other rooms so it looks like the place has some visitors. I do that every night. You enjoy yer stay."

She heard his steps as he walked away. She moved to the front window and watched as he entered one of the units across the potholed parking area. The light went on. He stepped out and locked the door. He did that three more times, making the courtyard almost cheery with the light from the empty rooms. She closed the window and dumped the things from the Walmart shopping bag on the bed.

She knew what she needed to do. She picked up the box of hair dye and the scissors. It took an hour, but when she was done, she was a brunette with short, spiky hair. As she examined herself in the mirror, the thought briefly crossed her mind that she looked cute—in a junior high kind of way. She flushed the remnants of her curls, feeling a little sad as she watched them circle the bowl before disappearing. She put the white jeans and her gray leather handbag into the shopping bag. She planned to wear her gold sweatshirt to bed. After brushing her teeth, everything else went into the new, oversized purse—except the clothing she was going to wear in the morning.

She picked up the prepaid cell phone and called her aunt and uncle. "Aunt Cecelia, please don't worry about me. I can't come home right now. I'm safe for tonight, but—"

Her aunt broke in on her words. "Mattie, you come home right now. Sergeant Summers is here, and he's very upset with you." Her tone was accusatory.

"Let me talk to him."

"Summers here. Mattie, where are you?" His voice was tight and angry.

"Jack, I'm fine for now. If whoever is behind this is as powerful as you have said, then that line you are on could be tapped. I'm not telling you where I am. I'm safer on my own for the time being. Don't try to coerce me; don't try to control me. Right now I have to do what I think is best." Her voice was a mix of anger and fear. "They found me. Even though I was with you, they found me. If you want to contact me, get a prepaid phone." She hit the end button before he could respond, and she immediately turned off the cell.

***

Jack looked at the cell phone and took several deep breaths to ease his tension. *What is the matter with the woman?*

Cecelia Southland wrung her hands, and her husband demanded, "Are you going to call the FBI in on this? It's well past time, isn't it?"

Jack nodded and punched a familiar number into his cell. "Special Agent Davis Jeffries, please."

He waited while the call was transferred.

"Jeffries here."

"Dave, this is Jack Summers. I need to have an off-the-record talk with you to pick your brain—right away."

"I'm just about out of the door right now, headed home. Do you want to come to my office tomorrow?"

"No. Somewhere private."

"You know where I live. Come out tonight. My wife, her sister, and my daughters are having a girls' night out. I'll put the boys to bed a little early, and we can talk without interruption."

"Sounds good. See you right away." When Jack reached the front door, he turned to Max and Cecelia. "I'll let you know if anything new develops."

Jack decided to suppress his police identity and make it tougher to tail him. He drove to the DPS impound lot and parked the department car. There, he exchanged his official car for a 1992 blue Mustang. He put his signature on the sign-out sheet and thanked the manager. Then he stuffed both of the thick envelopes containing copies of Theo's research paper under the front seat, folded the fax from Washington, and stuffed it into his jacket pocket.

With a 5.0-liter engine, a five-speed manual transmission, and a supercharger, the car had been the pride and joy of an underage drunken dragster who had been arrested six weeks earlier. He'd put all his money into the vehicle and then lost his job because of his arrest, so he didn't have any money to pay the ninety-dollar-a-day storage fee. The rumor had gone around that he had actually cried when he signed the car over to the state. It had a 500-horsepower engine in it and could do zero to eighty in less than ten seconds. At least six members of the department had expressed plans to bid on it at the next DPS auction.

Jack grinned to himself as he took it out on Highway 60 and covered the thirty miles to Jeffries home with ease in twenty minutes. Maybe he'd bid on it himself.

As he ushered Jack into the front room, Jefferies asked, "When are you going to find a good woman and get married again, Jack? You need some little guys like mine running around your house." It was the same question he had asked several times before.

He received the same answer, always delivered with a grin. "When the right woman comes along." Jack's tone quickly changed, becoming much more serious. "Are you sure your place isn't bugged?"

Davis looked startled at the question. "Yeah, I'm pretty sure. What's so confidential?"

"Perhaps I'm just being paranoid, but I'd feel better if we talked outside." Jeffries shrugged on a sport coat, and they settled themselves on lawn chairs in the light on the porch that splashed through the french doors leading out of the dining room.

Jack handed a copy of the research paper to his friend. "You can skim the first twenty pages, but read the balance of the paper carefully." Neither spoke for the nearly twenty-five minutes it took for Jeffries to read the paper. Several times he flipped back and reread certain pages.

When the FBI man put the paper down on the chair next to him, he simply said, "Whew."

Jack explained the suspicions he and Mattie shared about the connections between the paper and the three murders.

"It makes fascinating reading, Jack. And it may be entirely accurate, but if you've come to get the bureau involved, I've got to tell you it's entirely circumstantial. And you know the bureau can't get involved in murder cases unless we're officially requested."

Jack took a few seconds to respond. After a long exhale, he spoke. "I understand your position, and that's why I'm here talking off the record. I wanted you to be aware of the details in case it breaks in such a way that it becomes a matter for the bureau. I didn't want to discuss it at your office as we're a little leery that a request for information in the matter could come from a Senate office."

"Yeah, in something like this you're smart to cover yourself. Most of us who've spent any time working out of the D.C. office know that this guy Volos"—he tapped his knuckle on the paper—"is a big friend of the president and has the private telephone number of several powerful members in the Senate and the House."

Jack looked him in the eyes. "Do you think Volos has any influence over Congressman Max Southland?" This was a matter that had been bothering him since he had read the paper.

"Not as far as those of us at the bureau are concerned. I'm not aware that Southland has ever taken money from any of the political action committees or corporations controlled by Volos. I think Southland's a straight arrow—you know there are a few of those in public office." He grinned at his attempt at humor.

That response eased some of Jack's worries but at the same time added a concern that Southland might also become a target.

***

Mattie lay down and listened to the television. When the national ten o'clock news came on, the commentator led with a follow-up story on the explosion at the University of Texas Law School. The camera cut to a news reporter from the Austin affiliate standing before the blackened ruins. "The police have released very little information, insisting that the investigation is in the early stages, but our news crew noted that agents from both the FBI and the Bureau of Alcohol, Tobacco,

Firearms, and Explosives are involved as well. As we uncover additional information, we will pass it along."

The national network reclaimed the broadcast. When the station went to the local news, the shooting at the Jardin hotel was given twenty-five seconds as the lead story. The suave, smooth-faced anchorman—who Mattie recognized from Southland's news conference—stated, "The wounded man has not been identified, and we have learned that he has refused to cooperate with authorities. The officer involved in the shooting has been placed on administrative duty."

No wonder Jack was in a foul mood when we talked.

She stared at the ceiling until midnight, her mind wandering through the murky waters of the who, how, and why of the three deaths. Again, she wondered if she were just being paranoid. Then she remembered that the man who had pounded on the door in the hotel had known too much about her. She fell asleep thinking, *Oh, Craig, it's all so unfair. I miss you so much, and I'm scared, really scared.*

She woke in the morning at five thirty to *I Love Lucy* reruns. At seven o'clock, she rose, dressed in her Walmart purchases, and stuffed her sweatshirt into the shopping bag. She sat down and finished the last two cinnamon rolls and another can of V8 before she left the room with the heavy purse over her shoulder. She put the hat on so the brim hung low, almost covering half her face, and walked briskly past the office. On the street, she looked both directions, hoping for a bus or a cab. When none was evident, she started walking toward the main business district about four miles to the north.

She needed to find a place to get rid of the Walmart bag and the things in it. After another block, she noted a blue deposit box for the Boys and Girls Clubs of Greater Phoenix sitting in the parking lot of a large grocery store. She stuffed the bag into it. She had gone about a mile when she saw a cab letting a fare out at the curb in front of an insurance office. She waved and ran to it. The driver turned as she got in and said, "Lady, I'm a dispatch cab. You gotta call the office. I don't pick up fares off the street."

She pulled out her telephone and said, "What's the number. I'll call for you."

He shook his head and said on a heavy exhale, "Okay, okay. Where do you want to go?" He dropped the flag to start the meter running.

"The Ross-Blakely Law Library at ASU. Do you know where it is?"

"I can get you to the campus. Can you point it out to me from there?"

"Yes. Thanks. I really appreciate this." She leaned back in the seat and closed her eyes to gather her thoughts.

Chapter Eleven

SHE CLIMBED OUT AT THE library and handed the cabbie the fare and a five dollar tip. She hurried to the entrance and waited for fifteen minutes, hoping a couple of male law students would soon arrive. When two did, they pulled out their student IDs to show to the uniformed guard at the inside desk. She stepped in behind them, taking the arm of the one with the long, uncut hair.

She waved her driver's license as if it were a university ID and asked the flattered kid, "Are you in corporate law this semester?" The guard returned to reading his newspaper.

They both shook their heads, and the long-haired one responded, "Nah, that's on the fall schedule for me."

"Oh, so you wouldn't know where I might find the required reading for that class?"

"Wouldn't have any idea."

At that, she unlinked her arm and separated from them, moving behind the stacks, leaving both of the young men looking disappointed. She had been in the law library only one other time about eighteen months earlier, when Craig and she had come as staff members of Congressman Southland and had been treated with great courtesy, but circumstances were different now. Craig had shown her how to look up legal cases on Westlaw and Lexis-Nexis. It was her intent to access those online law libraries to look up the background of the case mentioned in Theo's paper. She deeply regretted having made no notes as she read it. She would probably be duplicating the research Theo and Craig had done.

Recalling Craig's bar number, she used it to log on to one of the available computers. She remembered that the case had been titled *Strategic Petroleum vs. United States Bureau of Land Management (BLM)*. The summary in Westlaw stated that Strategic Petroleum and fourteen other corporate plaintiffs had initiated the lawsuit opposing a change of policy which had radically impacted a contract the corporations had obtained from the BLM six years earlier. The final verdict went against the plaintiffs. She wanted more information on the case, so she asked the librarian behind the main desk how to get the motions and pleadings.

"You'll need to contact the actual district court where the case was heard. They keep individual files of their cases for a number of years. The documents are public records, and the clerk of the court can fax or mail copies upon request and payment of a fee. I can help you do that if you'll give me your university ID or your bar number."

She gave the woman Craig's bar number. "I'll cover the cost when I pick it up." As the librarian filled out the form, Mattie asked, "Could you please put a rush request on this? Please explain that Congressman Max Southland's office needs this information right away. Our fax is down, so please have it faxed here to the attention of Mae."

The woman was cooperative, and when the request had been sent, she stated, "I think it may come back as soon as tomorrow, since a member of Congress has requested it. I'll have it held it for you here at the desk."

Mattie returned to her research, and by two thirty her head ached and her stomach had begun to growl, so she slipped into the ladies room and drank another can of V8 and ate the package of corn chips.

She returned to the table behind the rear stacks and reread the notes she had made in her neat, tight handwriting on both sides of more than thirty sheets of the computer paper she had taken from the printer. She added the stack of printouts she had from the online research services.

She turned her attention from the court case to a search on Gregorovich Volos. She systematically entered that name in every available search engine on the library computer. In a list of important financial figures of the past hundred years, he was simply identified as a New York hedge fund manager.

She located a biography of this hazy figure and read that he'd been born of Hungarian parents, but upon the death of his mother when he was five, his father had taken him to Germany two years before the invasion of Poland. His father had been thoroughly indoctrinated in fascism and taught his son to be grateful for a powerful, controlling government, as it would bring order out of chaos, even at the cost of individual rights.

Leaving war-torn Central Europe, he immigrated to England and graduated from the London School of Economics. Thereafter, he was hired by one of the largest brokerage firms in London. His specialty was arbitrage, which he defined as buying stocks and bonds in one country and selling them in another at a profit.

Bits and pieces of information were available from many magazine articles and newspaper interviews, but a landslide of facts poured from the voluminous quotes taken from the three books he had published between twenty and twenty-five years earlier.

In his book titled *The Magic of Investing*, published in 1989, he stated that as Germany collapsed in the final years of World War II, he had concluded that no god would have allowed such a great nation as Germany to be defeated by capitalistic America. Thus, it was apparent to him that there was no God.

Before the age of thirty, he immigrated to America, where he joined a prominent New York brokerage firm. There, he made even greater profits. In his book, he reaffirmed his belief that the only god worthy of worship was money—that money did, indeed, make the world go round. He concluded that with sufficient money, he could accomplish anything he desired.

In his second book, *Reshaping the World*, a close associate was quoted as saying that Volos was "a man with a messianic complex" and that it was "power and the wielding of it that fascinated him." This acquaintance went on to say that he believed that Volos saw himself as "the god of the Old Testament; invisible, powerful, all-seeing, the conscience of the world, willing to bankroll organizations and causes he deemed worthwhile" in his desire to reshape civilization. Other progressive political figures called him "a new founding father."

He acquired a Panamanian bank with an unrestricted banking license, putting up the requisite one million US dollars as paid-in capital. With a bank among his assets, he could issue letters of credit to himself and write his own references, all with complete privacy, feeding his personal fortune.

His primary guiding philosophy was that any belief system or individual claiming to be in possession of "ultimate truth" was an enemy of his ideal "open society." He viewed all knowledge as conjectural rather than certain, as evolving rather than fixed. As she read this, a quote from the New Testament slipped unbidden into her mind: *Ever learning and never able to come to the knowledge of the truth.*

By extension, he did not share the American Founders' confident assertion that certain truths were "self-evident," and he scoffed at the idea that certain rights such as the right to "life, liberty, and the pursuit of happiness" were unalienable simply because they had been granted by the ultimate authority, the "Creator."

In the third book, he stated that his role was to bring about government action that would equalize society through governmental redistribution of wealth. One particular quote from that book left Mattie wondering if she'd slipped through the looking glass into a nightmare wonderland. Volos had written, "In this new industrial age, the people simply aren't fit to rule themselves as the misguided Founders envisioned." He further likened himself to a shepherd and the masses to his helpless flock. He explained that he was meant to become their guide and leader by whatever means necessary. "It is the responsibility of the elites in society to manipulate the general public into decisions they aren't smart enough to make on their own, by whatever means necessary."

She continued to read, ignoring the clock, her hands damp with nervous perspiration. *This man's vision for this country is a great nanny state, where every citizen will be spoon-fed in every aspect of what would become his or her simple, dreary life. He wants to show them how to vote, what to eat, what to love or hate, what to think, and when to think it.*

She continued to read the writings of this powerful man. He expressed contempt for American political figures who displayed unshakable confidence in their own cultural nobility and who held that the tenets of the Declaration of Independence and the US Constitution were timeless, immutable truths. Instead, he held that "ultimate truth remains permanently beyond our reach." *In other words, at any point in time, truth is whatever he wants it to be. What a convenient, self-serving philosophy.*

He bragged about contributing millions to the most "progressive" politicians in government at both national and state levels. In one book, he admitted that "because of my extraordinary wealth, major political figures suddenly became interested in me." Through these connections, he was appointed by President Clinton to travel to the former Soviet Union to help Premier Boris Yeltsin move from a socialized society to a privatized one. Never a man to pass up an opportunity, he borrowed $200 million and purchased one-third of the natural gas and oil industry in Russia. From the time he had emigrated from England until now, he had accumulated a fortune of $13 billion, as he combined his Russian oil and gas holdings with his preexisting resources, which had come largely from his firm, Volos Fund Management. With this massive fortune, he became one of the most powerful men in America, if not the world.

One of the magazine articles stated that his fortune was estimated to have grown so large that it had been stowed in banks from Panama to Switzerland and that he had homes in Venezuela and Switzerland as well as in the United States.

In an interview for an article in *Forbes* magazine, Volos explained with pride that he had used much of his vast fortune to destabilize and overturn several small- and medium-sized governments around the world by funding sometimes violent and sometimes quiet revolutions. He had been quick to help fund the so-called Arab Spring in Egypt. "All part of my decision to remake the world," he had told the journalist. Another quote slipped unbidden into her memory: *wars and rumors of wars.*

When the interviewer asked him if money was the most important thing in the world, he'd responded, "With money, you can buy anything: power, comfort, convenience, security, loyalty, respect. What else is there?" It was evident that even though he lived the good life of a Western capitalist, enjoying the personal liberties that this form of government offered, he believed that a select and brilliant few should make the decisions for all others and that it could only be accomplished through selectively and efficiently applied power.

In the last chapter of his third book, *Reforming Society*, he advocated legalizing all illicit drugs, opening the borders, and granting immigrants all available social benefits and the right to vote. He expressed a fierce opposition to the "war on terror," which he believed had grown out of America's unwillingness to share its wealth with the impoverished countries around the world, especially those in the Middle East. He was referred to by those who admired him as "the most progressive individual in America."

He had dedicated his third book to someone by the name of Manuel Heiselman. Mattie googled that name and discovered that he had been a founder and active member of several radical organizations in the 1960s and 70s, including the old SDS and the bomb-planting, now-defunct Weather Underground. Heiselman was the executive director of Volos's tax-exempt organization, the Open Society Foundation. The purpose of the foundation was to make America into a copy of the European Union's widespread socialism.

Mattie rubbed her forehead. She was perplexed. *Why imitate Europe considering the unstable economies of many of the nations there? Why would he want do that? There are so many enormous problems in the world such as two billion people who desperately need clean, drinkable water. Why not spend his millions that way?*

Her exhaustion had almost forced her to call it a day when she came across an article in the *Wall Street Journal* which listed the names of four individuals, including Volos, who were believed to have made massive fortunes in the near collapse of the Greek economy. They had cherry-picked the best assets of corporations on the verge of collapse, buying them for pennies on the dollar. They thwarted certain debt restructures that the European Union had offered in an attempt to solve the crisis, knowing that the EU and America would never permit Greece to go under because of the resulting consequences to the world stock markets. When Greece was finally bailed out of its financial crisis, the stock purchases made by Volos and the other investors swiftly increased a hundredfold.

She sat back and rubbed her eyes. *Was any of this what Theo had uncovered, and if so, how did it bear on the court case and his death—and that of his professor—and Craig? Why Craig? None of this information was secret, but good people are apparently being killed to suppress it.*

She stretched again and yawned. *Perhaps I'm mixing apples and oranges. Maybe Craig's death has nothing to do with this man or this court case. Perhaps Uncle Max was right and it was just a case of mistaken identity.*

She put her head in her hands for a full minute before she looked at her watch. It was nearly eight o'clock. The library would be open for two more hours, but she was exhausted and had one more thing to do before she found someplace to eat.

She looked up the name of the legal firm that had represented the corporations in the *Strategic Petroleum* suit—Doty, Dotson, and Diller. The name meant nothing to her. She checked the *Martindale-Hubble Legal Directory*, which listed the senior partners and associates. She printed a copy of that page and put it with her other notes folded and stuffed in her purse.

As she left the building, she evaluated her situation. Should she try for a cab? As she reached the street, she saw the Valley-Metro bus coming. She ran toward it, waving her arms above her head. The driver pulled over and opened the doors.

"Hey, lady, the bus stop is a half block ahead. In the future, you need to wait for me there."

"Thanks. I'm new to the area, so I wasn't sure where you stopped." She took a seat at the front of the nearly empty bus. "Is there a cab stand on this route?"

"Yeah, sure. There's one up on University Drive. Want to get off there?"

"Yes, please."

When she climbed off the bus, she nervously looked up and down the street before dialing the number on the cab advertisement. *I don't know why I'm so jumpy. I've got to get my nerves under control.*

A cab pulled up about ten minutes later. As she climbed in, she said, "Take me to the Walmart on Elliot. Do you know where it is?"

"Sure." He dropped the flag, and the meter began to click.

She stopped long enough at the big store to buy sunglasses, a pair of soft, faded blue jeans, and a white turtleneck sweater. Then she grabbed a Big Mac at the in-store McDonalds. She ate it sitting at the back of the little restaurant, watching everyone who came in after her. After she had finished her soda, she hurried across the parking lot and, with a combination of running and walking, made it to the Cactus Motor Court in twenty minutes.

When she'd locked the door of her room, she sat on the tired chenille bedspread and took several deep breaths. She pulled the cell phone from her purse and checked to see if there was a message from Jack. There were six messages, each the same: "Mattie, call me." Each message that followed was in a sterner, more agitated voice. The last message was almost shouted. "MATTIE, CALL ME!"

She noted his number. It was the same prefix as her disposable phone, so she was sure it was one like hers, probably bought at the same store. She dialed the number, and he answered on the first ring.

His worry and frustration came across as anger. "Why haven't you had your cell on? I've called you a half dozen times. Where are you? Are you okay?"

"I'm all right." Her voice was so tight that he probably doubted her statement, but he wasn't going to waste time by arguing.

"Why did you run away? I'm here to help you. Your uncle and aunt are worried sick, and I ended up in deep trouble with Chief Jepson." He stopped for a second and took a deep breath, bringing his tone of voice somewhere near normal. "But more importantly, you've put yourself in real danger with no immediate help nearby." His worry was obvious. "I *need* to know where you are."

"Jack, they found me last time. I don't know how, but somehow they found me."

"I'm sorry, Mattie." His voice was suddenly contrite. "That whole episode at the Jardin Hotel was my fault. I had the car checked over by a CSI tech after we finished the investigation at the scene, and he found a tracking bug inside a wheel well. I didn't anticipate that they would have moved so fast."

"Well, it doesn't do any good to agonize over it now. You got the guy. At least that's what I thought the gunshots meant." Her nerves had made her snap at him.

"Yes, I got him."

"Do you know who he is?"

"Some hired hit man from Eastern Europe from the looks of his dental work—apparently in the country illegally. He's hanging on by a thread. Are you sure you're okay?"

She paused before she admitted, "I'm scared, Jack. I'm alone, but that's the way it's got to be right now." She took a deep breath and held it to steady her voice.

"Why can't I meet you somewhere?"

"One reason is that I have a burning desire to see my twenty-ninth birthday. I'd even like to see my thirtieth. Walking around with you at my elbow is like waving a red flag to the bad guys."

"We need to talk, Mattie, not just for a few minutes on these ten-cents-a-minute phones." His frustration was showing.

"I'll sleep on it. Maybe I'll call you tomorrow. But you can do one thing for me right now. Give me Ben Novak's cell phone number from when I called him yesterday."

She copied it down as he read it to her. "Thanks."

"What are you going to call him about?"

"I want him to do some research for me." She ended the call without giving him time to say any more.

She dialed Ben's personal cell number, and when he answered, without introducing herself, she stated, "Ben, grab a pencil. I need some information right away. Can you put a staffer or a volunteer to work tomorrow looking up the campaign contribution records of several senators?"

"Yeah, I can do that. What's this all about?"

"No time to explain right now; I'm on a prepaid phone." She read him the list of senators who sat on the judiciary committee and the names of the corporations in which Volos had a substantial interest. "Oh, and see if any received money from a donor named Gregorovich Volos."

"Spell it."

She did and added, "I don't think you'll find his name, as his political contributions probably all pass through funds from his corporations and PACs, but try to trace the political action committee donations, if you can."

"How soon do you need it?"

"Yesterday."

"Has he given large amounts?"

"Vast amounts, I'm sure."

"Does this have something to do with Craig's or Theo's deaths?"

"If I'm right, it has a great deal to do with them."

"I'll put two interns and a staffer on it. You'll have your information tomorrow afternoon."

"Thanks, and make sure that they understand that this is all on the QT. Give my best to your father. I'm sure you and he are both still mourning Theo."

"Yeah, I will. He's pretty broken up about it. And Mattie, I'm so sorry about Craig."

"Thanks, Ben," she whispered. "So am I."

She ended the call and tried to push her grief out of her mind as best she could. She turned on the television and stretched out on the bed, putting three limp pillows behind her head. She pulled her notes from her purse and started to read the information on Doty, Dotson, and Diller that she had been carrying in her purse. Their client list was as varied and prominent as she had expected. She paused as she read the names of the partners. She sat straight up. *George Westfall—why did that name sound familiar?*

She'd been forced to leave the research paper and the faxes from D.C. at the Jardin when she bolted, so she couldn't really remember if that name had been in the material still in Jack's hands. She picked up the phone and called him again.

Without a greeting, she asked, "Jack, do you have a copy of the fax from D.C. with you?"

"Yes, why?"

"Check it. See if the name George Westfall is on the list of potential appointments to the federal bench."

After a minute, he responded, "Yes, that name's here. It's at the head of the short list for appointment to the Court of Appeals for the Federal Circuit."

"I think that may be it!"

"What do you mean?"

"I think that's the reason they're trying to suppress the research paper. If it becomes public knowledge that he's a partner in the firm that does legal work for Gregorovich Volos—if the media finds out—his appointment may become so controversial that the president would be forced to pass him over. Jack, we may have discovered the link, the motive."

"Are federal judgeships so valuable that people will kill for them?"

"In a word, yes. Doty, Dotson, and Diller represented every one of the corporations in that law suit that Theo researched. They sued the

BLM for altering the provisions of a contract they were given five or six years ago. Volos either founded every one of those corporations or he holds a large percentage of stock in them. That decision is sure to be appealed, and when it is, it will come before the Court of Appeals for the Federal Circuit sometime in the next two or three years. If they could get someone like Westfall appointed to that circuit bench, he would be in a great place to influence the outcome of that appeal." Another thought thrust itself into her mind. "Jack, maybe they've already influenced other appointments to the federal bench." The thought made her grow cold.

"How could the FBI have overlooked something like this when they vetted Westfall?"

Mattie was thoughtful for a moment. "Maybe his name was never directly connected to the actual litigation against the BLM. It may have been handled by the other partners. If he was kept at arm's length by the firm, maybe the case wouldn't have come to the attention of the bureau."

"So you're saying that if they get Westfall appointed to the appellate circuit bench, they'd have a real chance of getting the lower court decision overturned on appeal." Jack's voice was somber.

"Overturned, possibly, but the appellate court could do any of several things. It could affirm the verdict, reverse the verdict, or find enough error to send the whole thing back for a new trial. They could also affirm *part* of the verdict, reverse part, or remand part of it back to the lower court."

"Wouldn't any involvement by Westfall in such an appeal be a serious conflict of interest?"

"Yes, technically. But it's nearly impossible to impeach a federal judge. I only know of two cases of impeachment in the past hundred years."

"But what happens if, in the face of all this maneuvering, the verdict of the lower court is upheld?"

"Then the fun would really begin. Either side can appeal the case to the Supreme Court."

"But the Supreme Court picks and chooses the cases it hears. What happens if the Volos corporations lose at the appellate level, and the Supreme Court refuses to hear the case?"

"Volos has enough money to keep an army of lawyers churning the issues until they find something else to take them back to square one and file another lawsuit—but I think those who want the original verdict overturned would do almost anything to get what they want at the appellate level."

"Including the murder of anyone with information that might halt that appointment." Jack's voice was quiet and worried. "Now that we're getting this figured out, I'm really nervous about your being alone. Let me come and get you."

"No, I've got some more research to do tomorrow." She ended the call and turned off the cell phone.

As she lay in bed that night, her mind ran like a computer with no off button. She didn't get much sleep.

Chapter Twelve

At two o'clock, Gulletti stared at his watch and drummed his fingers as he sat at his desk. His man should have called with a report by now. Something must have happened to prevent the delivery of the last package. That left him in a bad place, as Wilcoxin would demand a report right away.

He pulled a prepaid cell from his pocket and called another contact in the Metro Phoenix area. "Gulletti here. I had a man assigned to carry out a job there yesterday, but I haven't heard anything from him. Can you find out if anything might have screwed up the task—maybe call someone at a local newspaper or TV station?"

The voice came back at him. "I'm watching the noon news right now, and the leading story is about a cop taking down some Eastern European yesterday at the Jardin Hotel. Do you think he's your man?"

"Yeah, sounds like it." Gulletti shook his head angrily. "I need a replacement. How would you like a job?"

"Depends. What d'ya need?"

"I need a package delivered, if you know what I mean."

"Tell me about it."

Gulletti pulled a tablet from his shirt pocket and relayed everything he had on Mattie Mathis, including physical description, employment, and home address. "I'll double your usual fee if the delivery is clean, fast, and untraceable. Give me your e-mail address, and I'll get a photo to you."

The man's voice had risen as his interest increased. "How fast do you need delivery?"

"Right away, before she can go public with the information in her hands."

"Where do you think she's likely to be?"

"She's undoubtedly on the run. You've gotta handle the situation before she can go to the FBI."

"You're sure she hasn't?"

"I'm sure I would've heard something if she had, but I'm going to do some checking. You just get the job done quickly and quietly."

"Can you tell me what this is about so I have some idea where to start looking?"

"It's about a research paper with too much information about a certain lawsuit. We're sure it came into her hands, but if the information in the paper had been made public or had reached certain individuals in government, there would have been repercussions by now."

"Where do you suggest I start looking?"

Gulletti rubbed his forehead as if it would help him think. "I recommend that you check out the local office where she works. She may show up there, if she thinks the coast is clear. Check any law libraries in the area. She may be trying to find additional information before going public—and watch the major newspaper office in your area if you can. She must have left a trail. Find a way to follow it."

"I'll get a couple of guys to help me with the surveillance. My fee—half now and half when the delivery is made."

"Same bank as before—the one in Panama?"

"You got it."

After the call had ended, Gulletti simply wrote down the name *Harden* in his pocket tablet with the words *one mil* beside it. He picked up the phone, called the HBSC bank, and ordered that half the money be transferred. Then he sat back and permitted himself a cynical grin. He'd held back the payment for the Albanian assassin, so the failure had cost nothing, making one bright spot in an otherwise dismal situation.

***

After the report from Gulletti, Wilcoxin picked up the telephone. He flipped on the scrambler and dialed a number from memory. He did not identify himself but simply stated, "We've neutralized three problems that might potentially impact the appointment. We're in damage control mode."

"You've taken care of them?"

"Yes, sir. One other individual may need to be . . . handled. She'll be dealt with soon. So far, we have heard of no leaks, but a discreet call from you to some of the senators on the judiciary committee requesting any reports the bureau may have received mentioning either the BLM case or your name would be . . . ah, wise."

"That will be done in the morning. How hard will it be to handle the situation involving the woman?"

"She's picked up a cop as a bodyguard. He may get in the way."

"There's no way to get to him and call him off?"

"Not that we can see. We checked him out. He's got a reputation for being clean and stubborn."

"That's the trouble with young, idealistic cops. They've got to be taught who to listen to. Take him out as well. Just get it done before it messes up the appointment."

The call ended before Wilcoxin could respond.

***

Mattie slept fitfully that night in the lumpy bed at the Cactus Motor Court. Before she dressed the next morning, she called a cab company, telling the dispatcher to have a cab pick her up in front of Walmart in thirty minutes.

She was dropped off at the law library again, and using the same approach as the previous day, she entered the building on the arm of a very flattered male law student.

Hoping that the fax would be there, she approached the librarian, a different woman than the previous day. When she asked if the fax for Mae from Congressmen Southland's office had come in, she was handed a stack of sheets nearly three inches thick.

"You really ought to request that this kind of thing be sent to the congressman's office. It tied up our fax machine this morning for nearly two hours." Mattie couldn't have obtained more brusque or impersonal attention at the local DMV.

"I'm sorry. I had no idea it would be so extensive. Thank you so very much for your help. What do I owe you?"

"Ten cents a page."

Looking at the stack the woman placed on the counter, Mattie handed her forty dollars and received eighty cents back in change.

She tucked the heavy pages into her big purse and made her way to one of the computer stations. She clicked on the website of the Court of Appeals for the Federal Circuit and located the category of vacancies and pending nominations on the drop-down menu. She found what she expected.

The press release byline was Washington, D.C., yesterday. It read: *The White House has announced that New York attorney George Westfall has been nominated to serve as a judge of the United States Court of Appeals for the Federal Circuit. If confirmed by the Senate, Mr. Westfall will fill the judgeship left vacant when Circuit Judge Stephen Samuelson was killed by a hit-and-run driver on December 15 of last year. Mr. Westfall is a litigation partner in the New York firm of Doty, Dotson, and Diller. He brings extensive experience to the position, as his practice focuses primarily on appellate litigation in state and federal courts. His name has been placed before the Senate Judiciary Committee. It is expected to go before the full Senate for confirmation as soon as Congress reconvenes next week.*

The press release then listed the credentials and experience of the nominee. Her suspicions were not only confirmed, they were deepened.

Samuelson killed by a hit-and-run driver a few weeks earlier? Was this just another coincidence?

She moved from the computer station to a table in the back of the library, where she started to read the motions and pleadings that had come by fax. She read fast and discovered that the case centered around the fact that the BLM had contracted with the fifteen plaintiff companies to experimentally apply two processes—retorting and hydrofracking—to extract oil on governmental lands in North and South Dakota, Montana, Wyoming, Colorado, Utah, New Mexico, and Arizona. The lawsuit had been triggered by the unilateral decision of the BLM to alter the contract, which was done under threat of cancellation, based on evidence that the processes being used had proven to be excessively damaging to the environment. Furthermore, both processes were strongly opposed by the Native American tribes in those states.

She continued to read, discovering that retorting required mining the shale and hauling it to a processing facility that crushed it into small chunks, thus extracting a substance called kerogen. The kerogen was then put through the heating process of hydrogenation, a process that required vast amounts of water, a valuable resource that was limited in many of those states. The kerogen was then refined into gasoline or jet fuel. The volume of desiccated shale that had to be disposed of at the end of the process was greater than its initially mined volume.

The EPA had informed the BLM that the remaining waste would be rife with low levels of heavy metal residue and other toxic waste that could leach out and contaminate water sources in the area.

The retorting process had previously been used by Exxon in western Colorado, but that effort had been terminated in May 1982, as the corporation had found the process and legal challenges to be too expensive. Despite the problems faced by Exxon, Strategic Petroleum and its related companies were willing to try again in light of higher gas prices and with hope of a more economic outcome.

Strategic Petroleum and its partners were contesting the claims of damage to the environment and were demanding that the provisions of the contract be honored. Furthermore, they argued that the corporations had poured massive amounts of money into the hydrofracking and retorting processes, the diversion of water sources, transportation equipment, and efforts to meet environmental compliance, and those efforts should be respected and the companies allowed to proceed with the processes as per the original contract.

In an attempt to strengthen their arguments, they pointed to mega-corporations including Chevron Shale Oil Company, Shell Frontier Oil and Gas, Kennecott Exploration Company, and EGL Resources of Midland Texas—all of which had recently applied to the BLM to establish pilot programs in shale-extraction technologies. These efforts were interpreted by officers of Strategic Petroleum and its partners as attempts to shut them out.

But now the BLM was demanding that Strategic Petroleum and its partners alter their process completely and use a newer technology called "in situ" mining, which heats the shale while it's still in the ground to the point where the oil leaches from the rock. This in-situ conversion process, or ICP, had been recently used on private property in western Colorado and had produced over fourteen hundred barrels of light oil plus natural gas from a small test plot.

The attorneys for the plaintiffs argued that converting to the newer process was prohibitively expensive and not required by the original contract. When the case had been brought before the US Court of Federal Claims, the decision had come down against Strategic Petroleum and its partners. The decision was expected to be appealed to the Court of Appeals for the Federal Circuit.

Mattie put her head in her hands. *Here we are—fully involved—when Arizona is the least likely to be affected by this lawsuit or these exploration processes. But Craig and Theo understood what it's all really about—the manipulation of the federal bench.*

***

The offices of Doty, Dotson, and Diller were cheerful—even smug—as congratulations were passed from partner to partner, office to office, staff member to staff member. Copies of the White House news release announcing the nomination of George Westfall to the Court of Appeals for the Federal Circuit had been circulated through the inner-office mail with an invitation to all members of the firm and their staff to attend the lunch reception in the main conference room.

As the associate partners and staff crowded around Westfall and shook his hand, most did not note his stiff, self-conscious smile. The few who did attributed it to nervous excitement. Only Wilcoxin and the other senior partners realized that much could yet be lost in the Senate.

***

After finishing his phone conversation with Gulletti, the man known as Harden donned a black sweat suit and jogging shoes, and located a small but expensive digital camera that would fit in a pocket. He could pass for a businessman trying to keep in shape. His salt-and-pepper hair had the tidy look of a business executive—nothing threatening about his appearance. But he didn't leave his apartment. He made himself comfortable with his feet on a chair, where he watched television for two hours, checking his bank account from his laptop every thirty minutes. When it finally registered the receipt of a six-figure deposit, he got serious about the assignment.

He opened the e-mail from Gulletti, which contained a photo of Mattie. He transferred the photo to his iPod. Then he googled area newspapers and Arizona law schools. He wrote down the address of the major daily newspaper.

He searched further and determined that one of the law schools was in Tucson, so that was scratched off his list. There were two others: one on the ASU campus in Tempe and another in Phoenix. He called on two associates and sent one to watch the local newspaper office and another to watch the congressional district office.

He spent the balance of the afternoon standing outside the law library at ASU, moving from one spot to another but always keeping the main entrance in view.

***

At five o'clock, Mattie decided it was time to consider her information search done. She was bone tired. She gathered up the thick fax and the computer printouts, stuffing them in the big purse. She had plenty of reading material.

Though it was dusk, she slipped on the sunglasses, put the heavy bag over her shoulder, and pushed her way through the doors. Something in her mind said, *Heads up, Mattie. Be alert.* She had only taken a few steps toward South McAllister Avenue when she saw a man in a dark sweat suit putting something in his pocket. It was apparent that he'd been leaning against the wall of the physical education building, watching the front of the library. Even though he was about fifty feet from her, the way he straightened up upon seeing her caught her eye. A chill climbed her spine, and the hair on her arms began to rise. She plopped the big hat with the floppy brim on her head. When he started in her direction, she increased her walking speed to a near sprint. The voice in her mind said, *Run!* She did.

So did he. She reached the street and saw a bus coming. She ran for it as she had the night before, waving her arms.

He was a different driver, but as she climbed on, he told her much the same thing she had been told the night before. "The bus stop is a half a block ahead. That's where you should catch the bus."

"I'm sorry for the inconvenience, but there was a man following me," she explained breathlessly.

The driver shrugged as if he had heard that excuse before. He closed the doors and pulled away from the curb.

Mattie turned before she sat down and saw the man in the sweat suit standing with his fists on his hips, watching the Route 40 bus.

She sat behind the driver and asked, "Where would you suggest that I get off to find a clean but inexpensive motel? I'm not familiar with this area."

"If you want cheap, get off on Power at Main. There are several within easy walking distance along there."

She climbed off at Main, and after walking about six blocks past the Desert Villa apartments, an oil change station, a window screen security door business, a Motel 6, an older Travelodge, a taco fast food establishment, and a large Goodwill, she settled on the Palm Winds Motel, which looked like the management needed the business and might not be too fussy about identification.

A fifty dollar bill pushed across the counter to a young man whose arms were covered with tattoos got her a room on the ground floor facing away from the street. He smiled knowingly when she explained that she'd lost her driver's license. The room wasn't exactly seedy, but it was in need of a new coat of paint, and the orange shag rug had surrendered to the feet of many guests years earlier. The draperies didn't quite close completely, so someone had used a big safety pin to hold them together about a foot below the curtain rod.

She sat on the bed and noticed that it crackled due to the plastic sheet over the mattress. She stretched some of the kinks out of her neck with a wide roll of her head. A headache weighed on her head like a heavy hat.

Her stomach growled. Despite the tension of her situation, she was hungry. She decided that she was hungry enough for pizza again. She pulled the dog-eared phone book out and looked up a pizza delivery. After she placed her order, she lay down and tried to rest, but the wheels in her head had started again. *Who was he? What would he have done if he had grabbed me? Should I call Jack?*

The arrival of the pizza delivery boy was a nice distraction. She tipped him a five, and as she ate, she started to reread everything she'd gathered from her two days at the library. She felt that she was beginning to put the pieces together. It was time to test her theory. She located a number in the Yellow Pages and picked up the telephone.

A cheerful voice answered. "*Arizona Morning Star*, a member of the Granite News Media family. How may I help you?"

"I need to speak to the managing editor."

The line clicked, and another female voice answered. "Don Williamson's office."

"May I speak to Mr. Williamson?"

"Mr. Williamson's in conference. May I tell him who's calling?"

"Yes, please. Have him call Mattie Mathis at . . ." She looked at the prepaid phone and had to take a moment to remember the number. She recited the number and added, "Tell him this is *very* important."

"Yes, Miss Mathis. I'll tell him."

She lay back down on the bed and tried to put together the facts as she knew them in a succinct way. Within ten minutes, the little cell phone rang.

Williamson was as pleasant as she remembered from when she'd taken him a press release about legislation her uncle had introduced in the House. "Mattie, it's good to hear from you. How are things going? I hope you saw the Sunday edition with the story on Max's endorsement of Skidmore for his congressional seat, and the Monday edition, where we covered the death of that young man at the hotel after the press conference . . . What was his name?"

"Craig. Craig Crittenden." He didn't hear the catch in her throat.

"Yes, I remember now. He was a staffer for your uncle's D.C. office. We made every effort to separate the stories and minimized his connection to your uncle."

"I haven't had the opportunity to see either paper, Don. Events have, uh . . . let's just say events have interfered. When I get the chance, I'll read both stories." She hurriedly continued. "I called because I've come across something that you may want to put your best investigative writer on. It could win your paper a Pulitzer."

"Can you give it to me in a nutshell?"

"I'll try. A student at the University of Texas Law School spent weeks putting together a research paper connecting several large energy companies that are the plaintiffs in a suit against the Bureau of Land

Management. They lost the case in the lower court, so it's sure to be appealed. One of the partners in the law firm that represents these companies is the nominee who is awaiting Senate confirmation to the Court of Appeals for the Federal Circuit, which will hear any appeal of the case in question. Those companies are largely controlled by a man by the name of Volos, Gregorovich Volos. The more I've investigated—"

Williamson cut her off. "Mattie, hold it. I don't want to hear any more."

She was stunned at his response. "What do you mean? This is a big story, and I have an enormous amount of documentation." Her voice rose in frustration. "All your writer would need to do is verify it. That could be done in an afternoon."

"Mattie, as much as we deny it, even the press has constraints. Let's just say that Granite Media is a publicly traded corporation. I hate to admit it, but that fact influences the way we handle certain stories. I can't say anything more. Just let me wish you good luck with getting your story to the public." At that, he hung up.

Mattie sat looking at the cell phone in her hand as if it were a viper. She laid it down for a few seconds before she grabbed it again and dialed Jack's number.

Chapter Thirteen

THE MAN IN THE BLACK running suit had watched with narrowed eyes as the bus pulled away. *Where will it take her? Where will she go to ground?* He waited for fifty minutes, until another bus on the same route arrived. By that time, he'd decided that she was likely looking for a place to stay.

He climbed on and sat behind the driver. "Are there any good motels around here—not too expensive?"

The driver nodded. "There are several on Main. I'm sure you can find something there to your liking."

The streetlights lit the intersection where he left the bus. He moved down the street, locating and approaching each motel office where he produced an official-looking badge. He showed each clerk the picture on his iPod as well as the picture from the yearbook and asked, "Have you seen this woman? She's changed her hair color. We think she may have registered here in the last few hours."

Each one shook his or her head and responded similarly. "No, what'd she do?"

"Suspected of embezzlement and fraud. You're sure you haven't seen her."

By the time Harden reached the Palm Winds Motel, he had decided that the show of some cash might get some more positive answers. As he showed the picture with his left hand, with his right, he withdrew a wad of twenties from his pocket.

"I don't think I've seen her." The clerk's voice was a little hesitant, and his eyes strayed to the money in Harden's hand.

"You're sure?"

His eyes were still on the money. "I don't *think* so."

"Look again." He peeled off one of the twenties and pushed it across to the young man.

"Well, there was one woman who checked in about two hours ago."

Harden peeled off another twenty and pushed it across the counter. "Was it her?"

The clerk picked up both bills and nodded. "Yes, sir, I think it mighta been."

"What room's she in?"

"Well, I'm not supposed to give out that kind of information. You could call her room, and she can tell you if she wants to."

A fifty was pushed across the counter, but Harden kept his hand on it. "It's important that she doesn't know the law is on to her. And I need you to put a picture from my camera into your computer and let me send it to a friend."

"That's my personal computer, mister. I don't . . ."

Harden let go of the fifty.

"Yeah, yeah, I can do that. Where do you want it e-mailed?"

Harden wrote the e-mail address for Gulletti on a piece of paper, and the clerk connected the camera to the laptop.

He asked, "Anything you want to say to go along with the picture?" Harden thought for a moment and then shook his head. Gulletti would know what it was all about.

When he was done, the clerk stepped over to the counter and looked at the office computer screen. "She's in 26, 'round back." As the desk clerk pocketed the bills next to the fifty Mattie had given him, he couldn't help but think that it had been a profitable afternoon.

"Give me the room next to hers."

"That'll be sixty dollars for one night, and I need to see some ID, sir."

This kid was getting the hang of it. Harden's lips twisted in a half smile; he pushed three twenties across to the clerk. "For the room." Then he pushed another two toward him and added, "There's my ID."

The clerk handed him a key for room 27. "Hey, you ain't gonna have a big to-do with a lot of police cars and sirens and all, are you? That's really bad for business."

"No, no, this will all be handled quietly," Harden reassured the clerk, who had no idea that part of the plan was to see that *he* was not left alive to speak to the police after Mattie had been "delivered."

***

When Gulletti received the unexplained e-mail of the picture of Mattie, he studied it for a moment before he pulled the picture from her yearbook out of his desk drawer. *Yes, it's the same woman.* He forwarded it with a brief message to the only e-mail address he had for Volos: *Most recent photo. My man has located the package. Delivery soon to follow.*

***

When Jack answered his cell, Mattie asked, "Are you still on administrative leave?" He smothered an impulse to ask her where she was. He had concluded that she would tell him when she was ready. Pushing only made her resist.

"How'd you hear about that?"

"In the TV news report of the shooting."

"I'm back to being official now. Chief Jepson pushed internal affairs to rule on the shooting right away so I could get back on full duty"

"Good. It's time we talked. Can you meet me now?"

Jack had been sitting at his desk at headquarters, where he had been searching criminal records on the computer for any way of identifying the man he had shot at the Jardin. "I'll be there as quick as I can."

"Don't come in an official car. Drive something that doesn't scream 'police.'"

"I've got just the thing. It won't take me long." Now he could ask. "Where are you?" He grabbed a piece of paper and a pen.

"Palm Winds Motel, 6388 East Main, number 26, around in back." She paused for a moment.

His voice rose. "Is something the matter?"

"I heard something. I think someone just checked into the room next door."

"Keep your door locked and don't answer it until I get there. Listen for the TV in the next room."

"Why?"

"If it goes on, you probably don't have anything to worry about."

When the call ended, she rose and pushed a straight-backed chair under the doorknob. She didn't hear the TV next door.

While she waited for Jack, she checked the telephone book and placed another call, this one to her stockbroker. She didn't have much invested, but a couple thousand dollars of Apple stock gave her access to someone who was a good source of information on the market.

He picked up. "Mr. Landon, this is Mattie Mathis. You handle my stock account. Do you remember me?" She remembered him as about thirty with an owlish expression exaggerated by heavy horn-rimmed glasses of the same brown as his hair.

"Sure. Are you ready to buy some more stock? The market's been up for several days."

"Today, I need some information. Could you look up a publicly traded company and tell me if the major stockholders can be identified?"

"That's not hard. What's the name of the company?"

"Granite Media."

"That's a big one. Hang on while I do some digging. It may take a few minutes."

"Can you call me back as soon as you know? I'm on a prepaid phone, and I don't have a lot of minutes."

"Will do."

While she waited for the return call, she turned on the fifteen-year-old television, keeping the volume low. She ate another slice of pizza, and as she was washing the sauce off her hands, the phone rang. She turned off the TV before answering.

Without a greeting, Landon said, "OK, here's the info you wanted. The three major stockholders are a major railroad company—do you need the specifics on that?"

"No, keep going."

"The next is something called the Orion Information Corporation out of Bern, Switzerland. I'd never heard of it, so I took the time to look it up. It's publicly traded as well. Its major stockholder is a man named Gregorovich Volos. He owns about 51 percent of Orion. The other big stock holder in Granite is—"

"That's what I needed to know, Mr. Landon."

"Hey, when am I going to get you to call me Russell . . . or even better, Russ?"

"Okay, Russ. Thanks for your help."

"How about lunch sometime? We can talk about the stock market, and I can deduct it as a business expense."

"Maybe. But right now, I've got my hands full." She hung up feeling minimally flattered to learn that she was viewed as both a desirable lunch date and a legitimate business expense.

She stretched out on the bed and watched the dust motes dance in the dawn-to-dusk light that fell between the draperies.

***

Jack was as good as his word. He knocked twenty minutes later. When he stepped into the room, he took one look at her. "What have you done to your hair?" His voice rose in shock.

"I thought it was a good idea to change the way I looked."

"You sure did." There was no approval in his voice. He looked around at the room. "Couldn't you find something a little less . . . uh, rustic?"

"The selection is limited when you can't produce ID or a credit card."

"Have you heard anything more from the next room?"

"No. Maybe I just imagined the noise there." Jack did not look reassured.

"I'd feel better if your neighbor was watching television." He stepped over to her TV, turning the volume up. To erase the worry lines in her face, he smiled and added, "Just a precaution so we won't be overheard."

She sat on the bed and nodded at the chair she'd pulled out from under the doorknob. "Have you had anything to eat?" He shook his head, so she pointed at the pizza. He picked up a slice, sat down, and put his ankle over his knee.

"You called me here. Now tell me why." He took a bite.

"Jack, it's time to go public. Where should we begin? I tried my contact at the Arizona Morning Star. In the past, he's always been pleased to be given any good story, especially if it involved members of the House or Senate from Arizona, but he turned me down flat. He wouldn't even listen to what I had to tell him. The moment I mentioned the name Volos, he shut me down. I called my stockbroker, and he looked up the company that owns the Star, an outfit called Granite Media. He identified Gregorovich Volos as a major stockholder in the umbrella company that owns Granite—something called Orion Information Corporation. No way is he going to risk his job and the jobs of others at the newspaper by breaking the story. I don't know where to turn. I don't know if we can put off going to the FBI."

"I wish I had better news there. I had a long and unofficial talk with *my* contact—an agent named Jeffries—and he said that considering the sensitivity of the case and the fact that it's totally circumstantial, he recommend that I not make any kind of official contact with the bureau. That way there can't be any leaks."

Her expression demonstrated her disappointment. She took a deep breath and whispered, "So there's no hope there, at least not yet. I don't know what else to do."

He leaned forward and patted her hand. "We'll come up with something." His touch felt reassuring, calming. She gave him a weak smile as a thank-you.

He leaned back, finished the last piece of pizza, and wiped his hands on a paper napkin. "Let's get you out of here. I'll take you to the Westin and check you in as my wife. I'll feel better if you're in a more reputable place."

Mechanically, she stood, and he held her jacket while she slipped into it. She picked up her purse as he switched off the television then held the door for her. The Mustang was parked parallel, the passenger side squarely in front of the unit within four steps of the front door; it was taking up most of three parking places in the otherwise empty lot. As Jack opened the passenger side door and Mattie slid in, the door to room 27 opened.

Harden stepped out and, seeing Mattie, reached under his coat. He pulled out a Beretta .45 caliber handgun. As he pointed it at them, Jack tossed the car keys to her and yelled, "Get out of here." Then he threw himself at Harden, knocking the gunman off his feet. Both men rolled inside the room, a tangle of arms and legs. The man's gun flipped out of his hand and slid across the floor.

As both men struggled to rise, Jack pulled his weapon from his shoulder holster and yelled again, "Mattie, get out of here!" His voice was a command. "Now!"

As Harden clambered his feet, Jack jammed him against the wall with his shoulder. Harden dropped and twisted between Jack's legs, tipping the cop backward and forcing him off balance. He hit the floor hard. Harden stretched, reaching for the gun he had dropped.

Mattie slid behind the wheel and, with shaking hands, turned the key. When Harden heard the engine start, he looked away from Jack, pointed the gun out of the door, and fired twice, putting two bullets through the passenger side window and the windshield. Jack threw himself at the man again, pinning him against the wall.

As the glass in the passenger door window shattered, Jack yelled again, "Get out of here!"

The wheels spun in the gravel of the parking area, and the car fishtailed out of the lot and onto Main, narrowly missing a delivery truck.

Jack stepped back and pointed his gun at Harden. "Drop your weapon."

Harden's eyes narrowed, and Jack recognized the expression. He dropped into a stoop as Harden fired twice. Jack felt something hot hit his ear and returned fire. The shot caught the hired killer full in the chest. He dropped like a sack of cement. Jack rose and, putting his hand to his ear, kicked the man's gun away.

Harden lay on the floor, breathing heavily, the front of his shirt wet with blood.

Jack pulled out his department cell and called headquarters. He identified himself then ordered, "Send an ambulance to the Palm Winds Motel. Shots fired. Man down."

The ambulance arrived in seven minutes. The attendant caught Jack's eye as the gurney was pushed inside. The EMT shook his head. Harden's skin was the color of putty.

Jack rode back to headquarters with the responding officers. There, he was told that Chief Jepson was waiting for him. The normally stoic man was pacing when Jack entered the office. Without any kind of greeting, he demanded, "What the devil happened, Summers? Where's Mattie? Max Southland is more than a little upset that I *still* can't tell him where she is."

Jack looked at him and said truthfully, "Frankly, I have no idea."

"You know the routine. Give me your badge and gun. I've notified DPS that I'm suspending you. *This* incident is not going to be dismissed as swiftly as the shooting at the Jardin."

Jack said nothing as he laid his badge and gun on the chief's desk, but his lips formed a thin, tight line.

"I don't dare handle this any other way, Jack. Two shootings in three days doesn't look good, no matter how justified." Jack just nodded, trying to be rational, but it didn't work. He was upset. The administrative leave after the first shooting was bad enough, but he'd never had a full-blown suspension on his record.

"If there's nothing more, I'll get out from underfoot." Jack's voice was edgy.

Jepson's voice softened. "Jack, your supervisor at DPS agreed with the way I'm handling this, but I'm not saying that you can't keep looking for Mattie as a private citizen. We certainly can't stop a friend from looking for another friend. Just remember that for the present, you're not working in an official capacity." His smile was cynical as he added, "Get your report written, and then make yourself useful in an *unofficial* capacity."

Jack's shoulders relaxed, and he gave a rueful smile before heading out of the chief's office. After he finished his written report, he told the property clerk that his department car was at the impound lot with the keys in the ignition.

After leaving the building, he stood for a moment outside headquarters, wondering where he was going to get another vehicle.

Barstow had followed him out of the building. "For two men who are supposed to be partners, we sure haven't seen much of one another the last few days." He didn't expect a response. "You need a ride somewhere?"

Jack looked at him and grinned mischievously. "Will you take me over to the impound lot? I left a department car over there."

"You can't drive a departmental car while you're on suspension."

"But it's a great excuse to have you drive me over there so I can get a car that isn't a departmental vehicle." Barstow returned his grin.

Barstow officially checked out the big black Lincoln that had been confiscated from a drug dealer two months earlier. They walked back to the rear of the impound lot, and Barstow handed the keys to Jack. "Drive carefully. It's in my name."

Jack slapped him on the back and climbed in. He drove home and hung up his sport coat. After taking off his empty shoulder holster, he put on a pair of jeans and a long-sleeved, blue plaid shirt. He pulled his personal holster from a drawer. It was a paddle holster with the plastic extension that slipped over the belt at his right hip, his preference for carrying his personal weapon, a .9 mm Ruger. With a jacket, the weapon was fully concealable. He slid the gun into the holster and slipped on a light gray wool jacket. He looked in the mirror. *Jack Summers, private citizen*, he thought with some bitterness.

He got back into the Lincoln and headed for the Southland mansion.

Chapter Fourteen

MATTIE FOUND HERSELF DOING 120 as soon as she hit Highway 202. Her heart was slamming against her chest, her hands and arms shaking with the electricity of fear. It was all she could do in her adrenaline-pumped condition to pull her speed down to eighty. She realized the car was taking the curves too fast, but her right foot felt like lead. She made herself lift her foot until the speedometer dropped to seventy-five.

This is the second time Jack has intervened and saved me, but I don't even know if he's still alive. The sound of gunfire echoed in her memory, and she couldn't get a frightening picture of his body lying in the motel parking lot from her mind.

Even in all the excitement, she had recognized Harden as the man she'd seen following her on the ASU campus earlier that day. *How did he find me?* She'd probably never know. *Where to go? What to do?* She forced herself to take three long, deep breaths as she pushed herself back against the seat with stiff arms. *Empty your mind*, she told herself. *Just empty your mind. An answer will come.*

She rode for three more miles, deliberately trying to keep her mind blank. Finally, that voice gave her the answer. *The cabin. Go to your grandfather's cabin up beyond Strawberry.*

She hadn't visited the cabin in several years. It held too many memories, but it had been used by cousins and their families, who had often invited her to join them. It was probably in good shape. The rules for using it had been simple: leave it clean with a few groceries for the folks who follow you. *Can I find it?* When she was young, she and her sister, Cora, had usually slept on the way there while her parents chatted in the front seat. She did remember that they had always taken Highway 87.

As Mattie followed the winding highway north, the wind whipped in the broken window, and even with the heater on high, she was only warm below the knees. She was deeply grateful for the jacket she had bought less than three days earlier. After a few more miles of driving, her cheeks were stiff with the cold.

The metro area fell behind her as she passed the wide fields of the Mohave-Apache Indian reservation. The highway rose steadily, until patches of snow were visible glowing in the moonlight between the pine trees. Her headlights cut the darkness like bright blades. After another few miles, the patches united in a ground cover of snow under the ponderosa and piñon pines. Snowflakes began to swirl past her headlights. She finally recognized the little town of Pine, and about fifteen minutes later, she zipped through the darkened community of Strawberry. The winter months had stripped the RV parks and campgrounds of their usual inhabitants, leaving them looking as lonely as an empty playground.

She slowed to make the hairpin turn that took her northeast, toward Winslow. As the cold wind pushed dead leaves and pine cones across the road, she began to look for the old café that was near the turnoff to the cabin. It had been run by the same couple for many years, the two of them happily growing old as they fixed waffles and donuts for truckers and local year-round folks. She fervently hoped the place was still there and open.

She slowed even more. *Where is it?* Her white-knuckled grip on the steering wheel eased a little when her headlights flashed across the front of the Mountain Café. She recognized the red gingham curtains at the twelve-paned windows on each side of the door. The worn-frame building gave the same impression as the curtains, faded but clean. The handwritten poster taped to the window read, "Breakfast served all day." The lights were still on. At least something had gone right that day.

It was nearly eight o'clock when she parked next to a battered pickup truck in the gravel that served as a parking lot. As she climbed out of the car and started for the café, the wind kicked up a cloud of snow, stinging her face.

As she entered, the bell on the door jingled, and the heat in the room wrapped her in palpable warmth and familiarity. The Formica-topped tables and chrome chairs were the same as she remembered. Even the floor of chipped red-and-white ceramic tile was the same. Both the lone customer at the counter and the man in the white apron behind the counter looked up. The man in the apron was about as wide as he was tall, and his bald head, ringed with a fringe of gray hair, was moist with perspiration from the heat of the kitchen. He used a corner of the apron to mop at it as he looked at the large clock on the wall.

"Good thing you got here when you did, young lady. I'm gonna close up in about ten minutes. What can I get for you so late tonight?"

"I would love a stack of pancakes with maple syrup and a *huge* glass of milk. Would that be too much trouble?"

"No trouble at all," he responded. "That's a specialty of the house." He turned and entered the kitchen.

The customer she had taken for a rancher put his fork down and turned toward her on the old swivel stool. "You look mighty cold, miss. You been thumbin'?"

"No, the heater in my car is just . . . inadequate for the cold." She sat on a chrome chair with a torn plastic seat at one of the tables about fifteen feet to the left of the door in case someone opened it and let in more cold air.

"You live around here or are you jus' passin' through?"

His questions were just meant as friendly conversation, but they made her uncomfortable. "Just passing through. I haven't been here in a long time. I had forgotten how cold it can get up here in the mountains." Putting the conversation ball in his court, she asked, "Do you live around here?"

"Yeah, I own a few acres down the highway about five miles. My wife died last fall, so I've been eating three squares a day here with Al and his missus. She works the kitchen."

Learning of the man's loss, Mattie was quickly overwhelmed with thoughts of Craig and ashamed that she had hardly thought of him that day. "It's hard to lose someone you love." Her voice was low.

"Yeah, at my age you finally figure out that life doesn't usually deliver everything ya order when yer young. Yer really blessed if ya get even a few of the things that really matter."

The man in the apron exited the kitchen and set a plate of five, eight-inch pancakes in front of her. He had sliced a banana on the top of the stack. The glass he sat next to it must have held twenty ounces of cold milk. He unscrewed the cap on the syrup bottle he had tucked under his arm, putting it in front of her with a little flourish as if he were serving a special guest.

"Oh, thank you. I'm famished."

The rancher slid off the stool and put on his battered hat. "Have a good evenin', Al. Nice knowin' ya." He nodded at her before he sauntered out. She heard the old pickup truck engine turn over and the crunch of gravel as he drove away.

She had eaten about half the pancakes by the time the wife of the big man in the apron entered the dining room. She paused to pull off her hairnet, and standing in front of a faded mirror on the back wall, she patted her gray hair back into shape. She couldn't have been more than five feet tall and was as thin as her husband was broad. He had been wiping down the tables and sweeping the floor.

She turned and looked at Mattie. "Oh, I forgot we still had a customer. Don't let me hurry you, hon. There's no rush. All me and Al will do when we get home is turn on the TV and fall asleep in our recliners."

"Where do you live? If you have a long drive, I don't want to keep you."

"No, hon, it's just down the road about two hundred feet on the other side. You can see our mailbox from here." She crossed over and sat down on the opposite side of the table from Mattie. "You look kinda familiar. You ever live around here?"

Mattie wondered if she should continue to present herself as new to the area, but the thought occurred to her that it might be useful to have a friend or two. "I used to come up here every summer when my folks were alive. My grandpa owned a cabin back up in the woods on Old Sawmill Road not far from here. I'd come up and ride his horses, and he'd teach me and my cousins to fish in the Blue Ridge Reservoir."

The rotund man quit sweeping and moved over to listen to the two women talk. He scratched his scalp. "Your grandpa named George Mathis?" She smiled and nodded as she put another forkful of pancake in her mouth.

Al sat down and laughed. "Well, if it ain't a small world. Don't you agree, Lil?"

Lil agreed and said so. "Which one of the grandkids 're you?"

For a fraction of a second, she wondered if it would hurt anything if she told them who she was. She postponed answering with another question. "Do you remember all the grandkids?"

"We remember that there were a whole bunch of 'em. Let's see, there was Billy, young Georgie, Brian, Stanley, Mazie, and . . . and the twins, Martha Mae and Coral . . . or was that Cora?" Lil's head lifted in triumph. "You have got to be Martha Mae, the one they called Mattie. I remember your sister was short . . . and plumper." The last word was added carefully, as if to state the obvious tactfully, hoping not to offend. "I remembered you as being a curly-headed blonde kid. You sure got your sister's dark hair now."

That answered Mattie's question. She didn't need to give her name; they already knew it.

"What brings you up here in this weather? Isn't your grandpa's cabin closed for the season?" Al asked.

"Yes, I'm sure it is, but I needed a place to do some quiet thinking." She put her fork down, her hunger finally satisfied.

"Well, the cabin is a good place to do it. But if you plan on goin' up there tonight, you'll find it hard to get the place heated up with nothin' but the cold, damp wood from the woodpile. I doubt you can get the propane goin' by yerself. You could stay with us tonight if you want to. We got a good couch."

Mattie was warmed by his spontaneous hospitality. "I appreciate your offer, but I think I'll be okay." She pulled her prepaid cell from her purse and hit the on button. The screen read, *Out of service area*. "I do need to make a phone call. Do you have a land line I can use?"

"Sure. Nobody uses cell phones in this area. No dependable reception." He pointed to the ancient wall phone with the rotary dial near the kitchen door. The folks in the area come in to use the phone here pretty regular."

Mattie pulled out her wallet and laid a ten on the table.

"Oh, hon, that's too much, and the cash register has been locked up for the night." Al protested.

"Those were the best pancakes I've ever eaten and worth every penny. Consider this my thank-you for your kindness and for good food on a cold night."

"The next time you come in, you can order anythin' you want, and it won't cost ya a penny." Al's voice was firm.

"You're both wonderful folks. If I can just make my phone call, I won't keep you any longer."

Chapter Fifteen

She hurried to the phone and dialed Jack's prepaid cell number. He picked up immediately.

She didn't give him any time to speak and kept her voice low. "Jack, I'm okay. How are you? I've been worried sick that he might have shot you."

"I'm fine, but he isn't. Another shooting was too much for Chief Jepson. I'm suspended until everything is worked out with internal affairs."

"I'm sorry about that, but I'm so glad that you were there. Without you, I'd be dead." Before he could respond, she added, "I'm up beyond Strawberry. I'm going to stay in my grandpa's cabin for a while. I'll be safe here. No one knows about it except family."

"Mattie, your uncle and aunt are really worried. Your uncle is concerned about the strain on your aunt's health. Is it okay if I tell them where you are so they won't worry?"

"I'm sorry I've worried them. I should've realized Aunt Cecelia couldn't handle the stress. Tell them not to worry. I'll be all right here."

"Mattie, I don't like the fact that you're alone. Tell me how to find you."

She was quiet for a few moments. She knew that she would feel better with him close by. She had to trust him. There was really no one else.

"Can you get another car that isn't registered as an official police vehicle? I don't mean just unmarked; I mean untraceable."

Jack knew she was remembering the vehicle that had led the hired gun to the Jardin. "I went back to the impound lot, so I'm prepared. How's that Mustang running?"

"It runs great. It's just a bit cold without the window."

"I'll bet. Give me directions so I can find you."

She turned and called out to Al and Lil, who were still sitting at the table she had used. "Do you have a street address so a friend can put it in his GPS?"

"Nah, we're just a PO box, but if he comes north on Highway 87 and passes through Strawberry, he just needs to watch for the café and make the turn onto Old Sawmill Road. Tell him if he reaches the little place called Long Valley, he's gone too far."

She repeated Al's instructions and added, "When you get to the little café, turn right on the dirt road about fifty feet beyond and follow it about a mile through the trees. The cabin's at the end of the road. You'll pass a couple of other cabins on the way, but they'll be closed for the winter. Grandpa's cabin has green shutters and a green roof."

"Got it. See you as quick as I can get there." He ended the call.

Al waited for her to get her purse before he started turning out the lights. She thanked them again for their kindness and took a deep breath before going out into the cold. The gray-haired, living example of a reverse Jack Sprat and his wife locked the door and started up the road with a wave. She waved back then climbed into the very cold Mustang.

The road to the cabin was narrow and would have been almost indiscernible except for the space between the pine trees where it rose and fell. The Mustang jounced over the potholes, and she had to keep it in low to avoid spinning the tires on the upward slopes. The five-inch-deep snow was crusted and smooth, disturbed only by the footprints of wildlife. Occasionally, she could see the brief red reflection from a rabbit's eyes. The last half of the distance grew steeper, and her tires churned through the deeper drifts, occasionally spinning.

When she finally saw the cabin in the headlights, she unconsciously exhaled a sigh of relief. It was constructed of great varnished logs, and the ivy of the summer months hung along the edge of the green metal roof like frozen lace, waiting for the warmth of summer to coax it into new growth.

It appeared to be in good repair, but now she had a new concern. *What if the key isn't there?* She parked on the lea side of the cabin, where a more recent extension of the roof made a casual but not entirely adequate carport. She climbed out, and by the ambient illumination of the moon, she walked through the crusted snow to the woodpile behind the house. She turned on the Maglite on her key chain and moved the beam across the ground, finding no footprints, no disturbed snow, except where it had slid off the steep roof and piled itself in heaps along the rear of the building. The snow got into her running shoes, chilling her feet, and it soaked her jeans halfway to her knees.

She examined the woodpile, digging through the crusted snow with her cold fingers. The key was always in the crevice between the bottom log and the wall of the cabin. *Please, please, please, let it be there now.*

It was! She laughed aloud in relief. She stiffly stood and hurried to the front door, remembering that the rear door had a dead bolt that was always pushed into place when anyone closed up the cabin. Her hands were so cold she could hardly get the key into the lock. The key finally turned, and she pushed the door open. When she turned on the ceiling light, the living room proved that time could stop. The inside of the cabin looked just as it had every summer for so many years when she had come to visit her grandparents. Just seeing it again made her miss them intensely. Her grandfather's big laugh and broad smile had always made her feel that the world was a safe place.

She walked through the cabin, visiting each room. It was a large rustic home in the style of the 1950s with open beams supporting the high ceiling and knotty pine walls. The floors were well worn. Mattie's grandfather had loved the mountains, and for the solitude this place had offered him after retirement, he had been willing to drive many miles to get groceries or to attend church and his beloved Lions Club meetings. And wherever and whenever Grandpa was happy, Grandma was happy too.

They had passed within a year of each other. She had gone first, after a bad fall off a horse.

He had not been content to live without her and had slipped away ten months later of no apparent cause. The cabin became part of the family trust.

She noted that the furniture was a little dusty, and the square green shag carpet in the middle of the wood floor was a bit more tired looking, but the matches and tinder were in the hinged box on the hearth. Whoever had used the cabin last had even left a stack of logs in the fireplace, ready to light. It must have been Brian. He and his wife were such careful, thorough people. The newspaper under the logs was dated the previous October.

The kitchen was clean and tidy. She opened one of the cupboard doors. *Hmm, pork and beans, beef stew, a package of spaghetti and a bottle of spaghetti sauce, a package of pancake mix, and a bottle of syrup. I won't starve for a few days.* She opened the freezer. *Let's see . . . some frozen trout and a couple of pounds of hamburger.* Now she was sure the last residents of the cabin had been Brian and his wife, Sarah. If it had been any of the other cousins or even her sister Cora Sue and her family, Mattie would have been lucky to find two cans of pork and beans.

She stepped into the master bedroom and turned on the light. The double-wedding-ring pattern in the quilt Grandma had made leaped out at her, and a knot rose in her throat. She stepped over and touched the fabric gently and reverently. She remembered her grandmother's stiff fingers carefully sewing those little pieces of color together.

She checked the second bedroom, furnished with two sets of rustic bunk beds so several grandkids could visit at once. Handmade quilts covered those beds as well.

She shook off the memories and reminded herself that she was there seeking a refuge not a walk down memory lane. She returned to the living room and stooped to light the fire. After it was going well, she pulled up a straight-backed chair and sat near the flames, trying to warm herself and dry her jeans.

She sat staring at the flames that licked and twisted around the logs; the smell of pine filled the air while the moisture in the wood hissed and popped. The fire appealed to her sense of smell, hearing, and sight. It was nearly hypnotizing.

After ten minutes, she shook herself, returning to an increased alertness. She noted that there was no kindling piled near the fireplace. She dreaded going out in the cold again but rose and went out the kitchen door to the woodpile. Loading her arms, she shouldered her way back into the cabin. She did that two more times, wanting enough wood to last until morning.

She located the propane tank outside under the kitchen window, and after she brushed the snow off it, she could see that it was still about half full, enough to meet her needs. Her hands were too cold to open the valve. She'd try again in the morning.

As she moved into the kitchen, she checked her watch and noted that it was nearly ten. *Probably another two hours before Jack can get here.*

She took two quilts from a set of bunk beds and carried them into the living room, which was growing warmer. Another twenty degrees and she could take off her coat. She wrapped them around herself and, fully dressed, lay down on the long, lumpy couch facing the fire. She drifted off into a nightmare-filled sleep, a sleep that offered no real rest.

***

Jack drove rapidly to the Southlands' home. When he rang the bell at the gate, the voice of Mattie's uncle came through the intercom. "Who is it?"

"It's me, Jack Summers. I need to talk to you and your wife for a few minutes." The gate slid open.

When Cecelia answered the door, her normally cheerful countenance was strained with worry. An officer in plain clothes stood behind her. Jack looked at him with a question in his eyes.

Max Southland walked in, noting the unspoken exchange and answering the unasked question. "Chief Jepson seemed to feel that under the circumstances it might be good to keep a man here. Come in, Jack. This is Officer Bert Shields. Where's Mattie? Chief Jepson called to say that she had disappeared again. Cecelia and I . . . and Mattie's sister, Cora Sue, are so worried. For the sake of Mattie's safety, we haven't told any of the other family members what's going on. The fewer who know about it, the better."

As Max had entered the room, the German shepherd had followed him, his tail wagging as he recognized Jack.

"I'm glad to see that Butch is still here." The dog pushed his head under Jack's hand. He scratched Butch behind the ears and spoke. "Mattie called me a little while ago to say that she's at her grandfather's cabin up near Strawberry. I thought you ought to know, but it's important that you tell no one. Do you understand?" Max nodded.

Cecelia's relief was immediately evident. She sat down for a moment but quickly rose and excused herself. "Forgive me, but I've got to get an aspirin. It's been such a stressful time."

After she found the aspirin bottle in the master bathroom, she returned to the bedroom and quietly made a phone call. "Cora Sue, it's Aunt Cecelia. We just learned that your sister is up at the cabin near Strawberry, so you don't need to worry anymore. I thought you'd like to know. Don't tell anyone except Sam."

Max and Jack had continued to talk. "Jack, I received a phone call telling me that the funeral for Craig is scheduled for the day after tomorrow. His body has been released and shipped back to Virginia."

Jack nodded. "I'll let Mattie know, but I came to tell you that I think it would be a good idea if you and your wife took a trip out of town as soon as possible, somewhere other than D.C."

"But Congress reconvenes next Monday. You think we may be in danger?" Southland's brow was furrowed.

Jack nodded. "Very likely."

"What makes you think that?"

"The individuals who have tried to kill Mattie probably believe that by now you are privy to the information in Theo's paper."

Max was suddenly very subdued. "I see."

"Will you do that?"

Max cleared his throat. "Yes, if you feel it's necessary. I can use Cecelia's health as a reason to miss a few days of the session, if necessary."

Jack looked at the officer who had been assigned to guard them and added, "Glad you're here. The congressman and his wife will be going on a trip, and I hope you'll drive them to the airport." The officer nodded.

Cecelia reentered the room. "Jack, won't you take off your coat?"

"No, I'm headed up to the cabin. I want you to know that I'll do everything I can to keep Mattie safe."

"We know you will, Jack. I want you to take Butch with you. If you're going to do guard duty, he could be helpful." She patted the dog's head.

The congressman made reservations for Fort Lauderdale, Florida, for the next day as Jack led Butch out to the car. The big dog looked a little disappointed when Jack insisted he ride in the backseat.

***

The van had been painted to look as if it belonged to the telephone company. It sat two blocks from the Southlands' mansion. When its bored occupant heard the click of the connection with Cora's phone line, he turned on the tape recorder. It was connected to the wire tap equipment which trailed over to the underground utility box near the sidewalk. When the call ended, he placed one of his own to Gulletti in New York. He was glad to have something to report for the many hours he had been sitting in the van.

***

Grateful for the update, Gulletti immediately placed a call to a private investigator of questionable reputation in the Phoenix area, waking him.

Gulletti's voice was hard and sharp. "I've got a job for you. In the morning, get down to the hall of records or wherever they keep public land records out there, and check out the property deeds in the area around a place called Strawberry. I need you to locate a cabin."

They had never personally met before, but if they had, Gulletti would have noted that the bags under the man's eyes were more likely caused by a dissolute life rather than a lack of sleep.

The man scratched his head as if to stimulate his thinking. "Which county?"

"I've got no idea. The fastest way is to check the tax rolls. Check every county, if you have to. You're looking for property probably held in the name of Southland or Mathis. Get on this first thing in the morning."

"Usual rates?"

"You get the info to me by noon, and I'll double your rates."

"I'm on it."

***

After leaving the Southland home, Jack stopped at an all-night grocery store and picked up a bag of dog food, a gallon of milk, some butter, eggs, bacon, and a loaf of bread. *At least we'll have a good breakfast tomorrow.* As he neared the checkout counter, he remembered he'd need some additional things. He detoured to the personal items aisle and picked up a disposable razor, shave cream, two toothbrushes, a tube of toothpaste, and aftershave. With his purchases, he climbed back into the black, four-year-old Lincoln with the crumpled rear fender, and began looking for an open gas station.

After filling the tank, he moved onto Highway 202 and watched the speedometer needle pass eighty. He almost missed the exit onto Highway 87. He pressed the big car to ninety whenever the road conditions permitted.

As he drove, he scolded himself. Why had his thoughts become so monopolized by this young woman? It was affecting his thinking. In the years since his wife's death, he had lived like a monk, suppressing all interest in other women, focusing all attention and interest on his work. His feelings for Mattie provoked a sensation of guilt. Surely, his feelings were inappropriate; he felt he was being disloyal to his wife's memory. *When this mess is over and I'm free to take a little time, I'll take some flowers to Abby's grave and tell her how much I miss her.*

It was eleven by the time he slowed down to pass through Payson. When he had passed the dark and quiet community of Strawberry, he started to watch for the Mountain Café and Old Sawmill Road.

***

The slam of a car door woke Mattie. She checked her watch in the fire-light. It was after midnight. She struggled out of the quilts and got to the door as she heard three quick raps. She pulled the drape aside enough to recognize Jack's silhouette in the moonglow radiating from the snow.

She opened the door, feeling the frigid air swoosh in, bringing a flurry of snowflakes that scattered like glitter across the carpet. Butch pushed past Jack and almost knocked Mattie over. "Jack, I'm so glad you brought Butch."

"Your aunt insisted. I think she felt that my efforts as a bodyguard needed to be augmented." A bit of a beard was showing on his chin and jaws, and a scab had formed on the upper edge of his left ear.

"Hey, what's wrong with your ear?"

"Nothing serious. I just didn't move fast enough when the bullets were flying at the Palm Winds Motel. It isn't bleeding anymore.

"I am so glad you're okay." Her relief showed on her face. "All the way up here, in my mind I could see your body lying in the parking lot." She patted the dog's head as he nuzzled her leg. "Hey, put everything there on the couch. Did anyone follow you?" She knew he was too careful to let that happen again, but she had to ask.

He shook his head. He put the bag of groceries and the gallon of milk down and looked around. "Hey, this is great. Why didn't you come up here sooner instead of hiding out in some old motel?"

"Because I didn't think of it sooner."

He removed his coat. As she took it from him, she couldn't help but notice the side holster and his Ruger.

"I haven't been here in nearly ten years. All the other cousins use the place, but they have families—you know, spouses and kids. I had planned to arrange a big family reunion this summer and have Craig come up here to meet everyone, but"—she looked around as if seeing everything for the first time—"that won't happen now." Her expression darkened briefly.

Jack suddenly recognized how deeply wounded Mattie was, hurting like a young widow who had dreamed that she would grow old with the love of her life but then had suddenly lost him. The depth of her hurt was evidently as great as his had been when his wife had been killed. He was instantly ashamed of his insensitivity, but just keeping her alive had taken up all his focus.

She straightened her shoulders and looked up at him. "Did you have anything to eat before you came?" He nodded. "Do you want to keep your coat on for a while?"

"No, I'm fine. It really feels great in here." At his words, she took his coat and hung it in the living room closet, releasing a wave of cold air when she opened the door.

"Where should I put the groceries?" He hefted the bag and the milk.

She led him to the kitchen, where they emptied the bag, putting the perishables in the thirty-year-old refrigerator. They returned to the living room, and she walked over to the fire to add another log. Standing and facing him, she asked, "What's new, if anything?" Without waiting for a response, she asked another question. "Do you have a copy of Theo's paper with you—and the fax from D.C.?"

"There's a copy of the paper under the front seat of the Mustang. The fax is in my coat pocket. I also left one of the copies of the paper with your uncle without your aunt knowing it. When your aunt stepped into the other room for a moment, I told Max to get it into a safe after he read it. The third copy is still being held in the safe at the Jardin Hotel. I thought that was as good a place as any."

"Good, I want to read it again in the morning." She sat on the rug in front of the fireplace to be close to the warmth. "Jack, how did that man find me in that motel?"

He stood and paced the room, pausing and stooping to put another piece of kindling on the fire. "I've been thinking about that. He had an iPod with a photo of you and must have been working the area, checking at every motel registration desk with an official-looking badge. We found one in his pocket before he was hauled to the hospital."

"He's still alive?"

"He was for a couple of hours. After I completed my written report and the interview, handed in my badge and gun—again—and received my official suspension, I called the hospital to check on his condition. He went to his grave without saying a word."

"So you're not on administrative duty? You're officially suspended?" Her voice rose in surprise and alarm. "Why? You saved my life."

"Two shootings in three days needs to be treated seriously—you can imagine what the newspapers could do with that if I hadn't been."

"So you're here as a private citizen."

"I have the chief's unofficial approval to act on your behalf—out of friendship and as a private citizen, as he put it."

"So he knows you're here?"

"No, I haven't told him where you are."

"It looks like we're no better off than before—except that there's another body to add to the count." She looked at him, her face pinched with worry. "You know better than anyone that there are some powerful people determined not to let me tell anyone what I know. I hope I haven't exposed Uncle Max and Aunt Cecelia to the same danger."

"After my visit to your aunt and uncle, they're both much less worried and grateful to know that you're okay. I told them that you were here."

"I hope that wasn't a mistake. I know my aunt shouldn't be under any more stress than necessary, but sometimes she can hold information about as well as a sieve holds water."

"They needed to know for their own peace of mind. I made them promise that they wouldn't tell anyone. I also made them promise to get a couple of plane tickets and leave the area as soon as possible—to take a trip somewhere besides Washington, D.C. The cop Jepson has stationed there looking out for them will drive them to the airport and see them on the plane."

"Thank you." Mattie was suddenly almost overwhelmed with exhaustion. With Jack and Butch near, she felt she could let go and get some real sleep. "Let me show you the cabin. There's a bedroom you can use if the bunk beds aren't too short."

"I think I'll sleep here on the couch. It's long enough. That way I can keep the fire going." What he didn't say was that in the living room he would be in a better position to hear anything that happened outside.

"Well, let me show you where the bathroom is. You're going to have to let the water run long enough to clear the pipes of rust if you want to brush your teeth or shower. It runs off a well, and in the fall it's shut off to keep the pipes from freezing."

He followed her through the rooms, and she opened the back door so he could see the woodpile and the propane tank. "To fix breakfast in the morning and to heat the water for a shower, we'll need to turn on the propane."

"I can do that right now." He stepped over to the tank and, using both hands, opened the valve. When they went back into the house, she led him to the bathroom and pointed behind the fabric skirt that fell from the old pedestal sink. He bent and opened the water valves. Then she took him into the kitchen, where she pointed at the shut-off valves under the sink. When he opened the faucets, the water poured out rusty orange, but it ran clear within a minute.

"Thanks, Jack. Now, if you'll forgive my lack of sociability, I'm going to warm up my bed and crawl into it. I'll shower and brush my teeth tomorrow."

She returned to the living room and removed what Jack had thought was an antique wall decoration. She took a pair of tongs from the hinged box on the hearth, opened the metal warming pan, and filled it with glowing coals. Then she carried it into the master bedroom, threw back the quilts, and ran the pan over the sheets as if she were ironing them, thus driving out the winter mountain moisture. Then she returned to the fireplace, where she dumped the coals and hung the warming pan up.

"I'm glad you're here. Good night." With that brief comment, she returned to the bedroom and closed the door. She stepped out of her shoes, tossed her coat on the rocker, slipped out of her damp jeans, and climbed into the bed.

She was asleep in two minutes, but soon dreams of a man forcing his way into the Jardin Hotel room filled her mind. Suddenly, she felt herself falling from that fire escape. She started, waking with a cold sweat that made her neck and hands clammy. She sat up and looked around in the darkness, afraid to call out, afraid not to. After a long moment, her heart rate slowed as she remembered where she was—that Jack and Butch were in the next room. She lay down, and eventually sleep came again.

Chapter Sixteen

THE SMELL AND SOUNDS OF breakfast woke Mattie. It was nearly nine by her watch. She stretched and called, "Do I have time for a hot shower?"

"Sure. Breakfast will be ready in about ten minutes."

With her short, dark hair still wet, she dressed and entered the kitchen, where the smells told her that Jack had made pancakes, eggs, and bacon. Butch lay under the table, not begging, but certainly hoping for a few scraps.

***

By ten that morning, Reggie Howland—formerly a licensed private investigator in the state of California but now a self-employed jack-of-all-trades willing to take on any assignment for seventy-five bucks an hour—had spent three hours on the Internet searching the property records in each county in the northern half of the state. He finally located the record of twenty-seven-and-a-half acres purchased by one George Mathis and wife Evelyn in 1947 in Coconino County. The improvements listed on the property records included a cabin and a five-hundred-foot-deep well. The title had been changed six years earlier to read, *Mathis Family Trust, Brian Mathis, trustee.*

Reggie noted the longitude and latitude of the plot, and utilizing an Internet mapping program, he located the area. He hit the print button and soon had his locator map in hand. Looking it over, he nodded with satisfaction.

Next, he pulled out his cell and called Gulletti. It was only eleven thirty. When Gulletti answered, all Reggie said was, "Got it. Make that check out for double my usual fee."

Gulletti's brain began to process the actions he needed to take. In no way did he feel that he could trust such a sensitive case to Howland, but he was running out of contacts in that area.

He made a decision. "I'll get out there in the company plane tonight. What's the best airport to fly into near the property?"

"Flagstaff. It's big enough for a jet. That'll serve your purpose, won't it? Want me to meet you?"

"Yes. Get to Flagstaff, and I'll call you an hour before the plane lands."

After he ended the call, Gulletti hurried to Wilcoxin's office. The senior partner was out. The secretary could see that Gulletti was upset about something, so she gave him her full, thousand-watt smile. "He's meeting an important client for lunch, Mr. Gulletti. Can I have him call you when he gets back?"

"Yeah, tell him it's important. I'll be in my office—waiting."

It was one thirty before Wilcoxin returned the call. He asked tersely, "Something new?"

"Yeah, my man has located the Mathis woman."

"Good. Did you ever hear from the man you hired when that Romanian or Albanian or whatever he was botched the case?"

"No, but not to worry. I've got everything under control. We know where she is, and I plan to fly out and take care of the situation personally. Is the company plane available?"

"Yes. Get out there, and get the situation under control." Wilcoxin's voice was as hard as flint on stone. "I've had confirmation that the Senate committee hearings are expected to begin on Monday. I've got the necessary votes to bring it out in four days, so we need to keep this quiet until Thursday. Considering that most committee hearings take two to three weeks, that's the best we can hope for. If things go well, the appointment should be on the president's desk a couple days after that." Wilcoxin's speech slowed to a deliberate speed. "Don't mess this up." Gulletti did not miss the threat in his voice.

***

As Mattie sat down at the kitchen table, Jack noted that she still looked tired. He scooped eggs and bacon onto her plate. She smiled. "This is a real treat. I haven't had anyone besides Aunt Cecelia serve me breakfast in a very long time—and she doesn't do it very often."

He took the plate of warm pancakes from the oven and laid it on the battered pine table before he sat down across from her and responded with a serious expression. "Your uncle told me that Craig's family has scheduled services for him in Arlington tomorrow. Max said that he would send the entire office staff. He and your aunt will have to miss it, but he said they'll send flowers and condolences in your name as well as theirs."

Mattie looked down at her food. "Thanks for letting me know," she whispered.

Seeing her subdued reaction, he changed the subject. "I spent most of the night trying to determine where we go from here." As he poured syrup over his pancakes, he shared his thoughts. "Let's sum up what we know. We're both sure that the deaths are related to Theo's research paper and that the information is time sensitive because Westfall, a partner in the law firm that represents Gregorovich Volos, is up for a federal court appointment. At this point, we need to confirm that Volos is a big donor to key senators on the judiciary committee as well as to the president. If he is, then we can be sure that he has the power to sway that appointment. If any of those senators who are beholden to Volos can pick up the telephone and get a report from the FBI on an ongoing investigation, then we're right not to seek help from the bureau. So, I repeat my question. Where do we go from here?" His question was rhetorical. It hung in the air while he chewed.

Mattie put her fork down on her plate and, elbows on the table, folded her hands together to support her chin. "I called Ben yesterday and asked him to have someone in the D.C. office look up the political contributions to the senators on the judiciary committee as well as the president. Since we're out of cell phone range here, I could call him this afternoon from the café and see what he's uncovered. I don't think he'll have the information before then."

"We'll do that."

The day passed quietly. While Jack rebuilt the fire that had nearly gone out, Mattie climbed back into bed. Having Jack there made her feel secure enough to catch up on some sleep.

She awoke about eleven. Jack asked, "Do you want to eat my cooking again for lunch?"

She gave him another smile, this one not quite so weak. "I'll bet that between the two of us, we could make a pretty good meal."

He was glad to see that she was beginning to relax. Though they only fixed spaghetti and meatballs, the joint effort was pleasurable. For the rest of the afternoon, they talked, learning about each other while Butch slept on the carpet in front of the fire.

Jack explained that he had served a mission in Monterrey, Mexico. When he returned home, he'd married his high school sweetheart and completed a college degree. He started teaching high school history, and the future looked good. On Thanksgiving Day at his parents' home in Sedona, Abby had announced that she was pregnant. They had just celebrated their first anniversary. On their way home that night, Abigail had been killed in a rollover. Jack had been at the wheel. He admitted that his guilt had never left.

"I've always felt it was my fault. We hit black ice on the highway during a snowstorm, and I lost control of the car." She could see by the faraway look in his eyes that he was somewhere else as he talked. In a whisper that was meant more for himself than for Mattie, he added, "I suppose that may be why I've never seriously considered a second marriage. Twelve to fifteen hours of work a day is easier to deal with."

"I'm glad to know that you're LDS. Surely that must give you comfort to know that you'll see her again—that life continues. I'm LDS too, and that has helped me deal with Craig's death—more on some days than others," she added in a whisper.

The silence hung between them for a few minutes before she spoke again, trying to change the subject. "Why did you become a cop?" Mattie's question brought him back to the present.

"One of the state highway patrol officers who arrived at the scene of the crash was so compassionate and caring. I've always felt that I would have lost it if he hadn't been there. After the funeral, I enlisted and spent three years in the army, and when I got out, I decided to apply to the police academy. I felt that if I could become as fine a cop as he was, I could make the world a better place—and somehow make up in some small way for the loss of Abby . . . and the baby."

During the silence that followed, Mattie began to think seriously about his occupation. Cops were much like emergency room physicians. They worked long, hard hours, often in blood, and didn't always get to go home at five o'clock. She wondered what sights Jack had seen, what images of violence were stored in his memory. He regularly witnessed the stuff of nightmares and had learned to live with it.

When she spoke, it brought him back to the present. "It sounds like you haven't ever considered doing anything else with your life."

He visibly shook his head as if to rid himself of the painful memories. "I suppose if I were to marry again, I could be talked into looking at another profession. I could go back to teaching. I've been through the FBI training program for local law enforcement at Quantico, Virginia. I suppose I could apply for the FBI. I'm not too old for that yet. Or I could go into corporate security. But I'm good at what I do, and I think I make a difference."

"Is Jack your real name? In my experience, it's usually a nickname."

He grinned at her. "My given name is John, but for the first four years, while I was in uniform, I built a reputation as a man that followed the rules. I don't smoke or drink. I don't cuss—at least not very often—and while I was assigned to vice, I was even polite to the 'ladies of the night.' The other guys started calling me Saint John behind my back. When I grabbed a man hiding in an attic after he had killed his wife, they started calling me John the Revelator. When I pulled a woman and her seven-year-old daughter out of a car in a flooded drainage canal, you can guess what they called me."

Mattie smiled. "John the Baptist?"

He nodded and grinned. "You got it. Those nicknames weren't meant to be flattering, but in a way, I suppose they were. When I passed the detective's exam and went into homicide, I insisted that the guys I worked with call me Jack. Since I took the job with the DPS, the harassment has been considerably lighter." He changed the subject. "What are you going to do when your uncle leaves Congress?"

"I have no idea. I'm not worried. Something will come up."

At about three, it started to snow, the flakes driven by a hard wind. By the time the early winter twilight wrapped the cabin, the flakes were falling more gently. Nature had laid a heavy blanket over the landscape.

She stood at the window and whispered, "It's beautiful, just beautiful here. I finally feel safe."

***

At five fifteen, they drove carefully back to the café over the rough road and through the drifted snow.

"Just grab a chair, and I'll be right with you," Al called to them as they entered.

"It smells wonderful, Al, but we're just here to use your telephone."

"Sure." He nodded toward it and returned to wiping down the tables that were still covered with remnants of the meals of earlier diners who had braved the storm.

Mattie dialed Ben's cell number, and when he answered, she asked in a low voice, "Ben, have you been able to get that information I requested on the names and contributions to those senators?"

"I've got it right here. The report is at least three inches thick. It took half a day on the part of both the interns and my best staffer over at the Federal Elections Commission to check on the donors and then four more hours for them to sort through the donations to the president, but they learned enough to make it worth their while. They looked up the names of the corporations you gave me, and it looks like money flowed to those individuals through a variety of super PACs connected to those corporations. If, as you said, they're controlled by this guy Volos, he must have all sorts of lawyers who've figured out how to spread money all over the place. I think it's all legal, but when you include the money given to the president, it amounts to millions. Can I fax or mail this information to you?"

"No, not right now. Put it somewhere safe, and I'll find a way to get my hands on it. You're great, Ben. Give my best to your dad."

After she had hung up, Jack placed a call to the private cell phone of Chief Jepson. He said simply, "I've located my 'friend' in a family cabin up near Strawberry. So far, everything's okay. We can hole up here for several days or a week, if necessary."

Jepson responded simply, "Good to know."

Mattie pulled a five-dollar bill from her pocket and paused near Al, where he was carrying a tray of dirty dishes toward the kitchen. She poked it into the breast pocket of his apron. "I just called Washington, D.C. This should cover it."

"Glad to be of service. Are you still workin' for that congressman uncle of yours?"

She nodded.

"Well, you tell him to straighten up the mess that's in Washington." With a wave of her hand, she and Jack headed for the door. "Hey, you should stay and have dinner."

"Maybe tomorrow night," she responded.

When they slid into the front seat, it was apparent that Butch, who was sitting in the back, was hoping for something that tasted as good as they both smelled, but he was disappointed. They drove carefully back up the long, rutted road, following their own tire tracks.

"We were right about the big donations. I think we're right about the entire matter," Mattie said quietly while they were hanging up their jackets in the living room closet.

After a simple supper, they talked and watched the fire until Mattie started to doze. She shook herself awake. "I think it's time for bed." She paused at the door to the bedroom and turned. "Jack, thank you for your—for everything." At that, she closed the door and climbed into bed. That night the nightmares left her alone.

Chapter Seventeen

GULLETTI HAD CALLED HOWLAND AT four, after his talk with Wilcoxen. "I'll be coming in on the company plane tomorrow about noon. I couldn't get out of here today. The pilot said that the weather is too bad to get into Flagstaff tonight. Get to a hardware store and pick up two large bags of nitrogen fertilizer and a couple five-gallon cans of gas. Then meet me at the airport tomorrow with a rental car or, even better, a truck or a Jeep."

Howland met Gulletti at the airport with the requested items in the back of a rented Jeep Cherokee. After Gulletti's leather duffel bag and briefcase had been tossed in, the two men sat in the front seat and studied the area on the map.

With Howland driving, they headed south on I-17, watching for the turnoff onto State Highway 260, which would take them to Highway 87.

***

Al took the order from the two men when they sat down in the café.

While their orders were prepared, Gulletti said quietly to Howland, "Stay put." He rose, and pulling the picture of Mattie from his inside coat pocket, he approached the three other customers eating lunch.

"We're looking for this young woman, and we hear she may be staying in the area. You ever see her?"

The first two just shook their heads and turned back to their food. The third one looked at his questioner and asked, "Why'd you want to know?"

Gulletti recited his cover story quickly. "My friend and I are working for a New York law firm that's handling the estate of her father. They've been estranged for a few years, but he left everything to her in his will. It's my job to find her."

Al had been listening as he set the food down in front of the customer. He straightened up, and after wiping his hands on his broad apron, he put out his hand. "Let me see it. If she's in the area, I probably know her."

He recognized Mattie immediately, but the story the man had given didn't sit right with him, not at all. He knew her father had died nearly eight years earlier, and they had never been "estranged."

He studied the photo as if trying to remember but finally handed it back. "Nope. Doesn't look like anyone I've seen."

The third customer also shook his head, in a hurry to eat the hot meal Al had put before him. Lil called from the kitchen, "Order up, Al. Two meat loaves."

Gulletti looked at Al and said, "Would you mind if I ask your kitchen help if they've ever seen her?"

Al said with a disapproving edge in is voice, "That's my wife, mister, not the 'kitchen help.'"

"Yeah, sorry. I need to show her the picture."

Al called out, "Lil, this man has a picture he wants to show ya. He *says* he's lookin' for somebody." There was a warning in his tone.

Lil pushed through the swinging kitchen door, wiping her hand on her apron. "What's this all about, Al?"

"This man says he's from some big New York law firm lookin' for some woman who's inherited a fortune from her dead father. He *says* he's supposed to find her." Al's voice conveyed his skepticism.

Lil took the picture, and her eyes widened. She looked quickly up at Al, and Gulletti saw the look that passed between them. Hesitantly, she spoke as she handed the picture back to Gulletti. "No, I guess I haven't seen anyone that looks like that."

Gulletti took the picture and said with a synthetic smile, "Well, thanks anyway." He returned to the table where Howland had been watching the scene. Al hurried the two meat loaf orders to the table. With an artificially jovial voice, he said as he set them down, "The best meat loaf in the state."

"I'm sure it is." Gulletti's voice was also unduly cheerful as he picked up his fork.

Having learned what he wanted to know from the look that passed between Al and Lil, he was no longer in a hurry. He ordered a slice of Lil's apple pie for both of them.

After the two men paid their bill, Al stepped over to the window and watched them get into the black Jeep, wondering what kind of trouble they could mean for Mattie.

***

Gulletti ordered Howland, "Drive down the road and find a spot to park where we won't be noticed, where we can wait until it's dark."

About two miles south at a wide spot where a large snow-covered earth mover sat, Gulletti pointed, "Pull around to the other side where we won't likely be seen. This Jeep has four-wheel drive, doesn't it?"

"Yeah, I made sure it did."

They sat with the engine running and the heater on. Gulletti leaned his seat back and closed his eyes.

After an hour, he sat up abruptly. "This is the program. I'll put the longitude and latitude of the Mathis property in the GPS on my cell phone. We shouldn't have any problem locating the cabin." He reached into the back for the briefcase he had brought with him. "In an hour, when it's good and dark, we'll park nearer and carry the fertilizer and the gas cans up to the cabin. If we're lucky, we'll be able to stay in the trees and keep out of sight. When we have everything positioned, you're going to find a place where you can hit the gas cans with a well-aimed shot—you brought a weapon, didn't you?" Howland nodded and patted his shoulder holster under his left arm.

Gulletti continued. "I'll make my way around to the side or front, wherever I can find a good place to pick off anyone exiting the cabin. "When I'm ready for you, I'll fire one shot. You'll shoot one of the cans, and that'll set up the fertilizer to explode. If anyone leaves the cabin on your side, take 'em out."

Howland was glad to finally know the plan. He put the Jeep in gear, and following the GPS, they made their way past the café, where they turned up Old Sawmill Road. It was only faintly visible where the snow had nearly covered the ruts of the day before.

After they had covered three-quarters of a mile, Gulletti said, "Stop right here."

"Right here? What if someone comes and sees the car?"

"Not likely. But the Mathis woman might try to drive away from the cabin. If so, we've got her blocked."

They climbed out of the Jeep and made their way farther along the rutted roadway, trying to avoid turning an ankle on something hidden under the snow. The road crested a rise, and looking over it, they could see the cabin. Lights were on, and smoke rose from the fireplace chimney.

"We've got her." Gulletti's whisper was exultant. He took a full minute to thoroughly look over the area. The cabin sat in a clearing that extended about fifty feet in every direction as a firebreak. They were looking at the cabin from the front. "Let's get the fertilizer. We've got enough light from the moon to see what we're doing."

They followed their own footprints back to the Jeep, where they each put a forty-pound bag of nitrogen over one shoulder and picked up a gas can. By the time they'd made their way through the trees, stumbling over roots and fallen branches, they were perspiring heavily.

The moon made the shadows nearly as defined as they would have been in the daylight. On Gulletti's signal, they crept around to the rear of the cabin, quietly placing the bags of fertilizer against the propane tank. They bookended the bags with the cans full of gasoline.

They didn't hear the low, throaty growl in Butch's throat as they started back toward the tree line.

Howland found a place where he had an easy shot at the closest gas can, and Gulletti made his way through the trees to the Jeep, where he sat in the dark and assembled the rifle he had carried from New York in the briefcase. When he was finished, he climbed out of the vehicle and up the gentle rise that visually separated it from the cabin. There, he found a place about twenty feet into the trees where he could steady the barrel of the gun on a fallen tree trunk with a good view of the front door.

Chapter Eighteen

BUTCH'S LOW GROWL WOKE JACK. The dog was standing motionless where he had previously been sleeping by the dying fire. "Something happening, boy?" he asked as he threw off the quilts. He reached for his gun and slid the holster over his belt. He hurried down the hall with the dog following on his heels. In the dark kitchen, he pulled back the curtains at the window. In the moonlight, he spotted a man's silhouette darting into the trees. "Butch, wake Mattie."

Jack grabbed a plastic pitcher from the cabinet and filled it with water while Butch pushed his nose into the crack of the bedroom door, forcing it open. He padded over to the bed and licked Mattie's hand.

Mattie roused enough to turn over. "Go 'way, Butch. I'm trying to sleep." The dog pulled at the quilt with his teeth, and then he stood on his hind legs and put his paws on her. Realizing that something had agitated the dog, she roused enough to sit up. "Butch, what is it?" She quickly got out of bed, pulled on her jeans, and slipped her feet into her shoes.

As Jack passed the bedroom doorway headed back to the living room carrying the pitcher, he said quietly, "Mattie, get your coat. We have company—and keep the lights off."

Her heart plummeted and turned to a lump of ice as she grabbed her coat from the rocker by the bed. *They found us? But how?* She put the coat on in one swift motion, draped her big purse over her shoulder, and followed him to the living room. There, she watched as he knelt on the hearth and poured water over the coals.

"What are you doing?"

"It looks like we're going out the front door, and I don't want any light behind us when we do."

"What's happening?"

"Butch warned me that someone's out there. I saw a man from the kitchen window."

He pulled on his coat and grabbed her right arm tightly. "Keep up with me. We're going to run—and fast." As he pulled the front door open, they heard the crack of a rifle shot followed immediately by a second shot from another gun somewhere behind the cabin.

The sound of three more quick rifle shots rang in the little valley, and simultaneous thuds hit the logs near the front door as they dashed out. Jack pulled Mattie toward the darkness of the trees. They heard two more shots from behind the cabin just before an explosion rocked the building. As they reached the trees, a second, greater explosion and a giant fireball colored the world around them, throwing them both to the ground, where Jack tried to cover her body with his. Butch crouched near them.

***

Gulletti had been caught off guard. He had no way of knowing about the dog, so he expected that they would still be sleeping. When they burst out the front door, he took fast but inaccurate aim and pulled the trigger three times, but they were in the woods before the explosion of the propane tank blew the cabin apart like a set of Lincoln Logs. Great sheets of the green metal roof peeled open and upward like a sardine can, and the logs rose in the air like missiles, decapitating trees at the fifteen- to twenty-foot height for a hundred feet into the woods.

***

After the fragmented portions of the cabin had quit falling from the sky, Jack spoke to the dog and pointed in the direction where he thought some of the shots had originated. "Butch, take him down." The dog didn't need any more instructions. He was gone, moving silently in a crouch through the snow, every instinct honed in Afghanistan fully alert.

Jack pulled Mattie to her feet. She looked through the decimated trees toward the cabin and could see both cars burning brightly.

"Stay close," Jack whispered, "and stay low. He's out there with a sniper rifle. Butch may get him, but until then we've got to keep moving."

They stumbled toward the highway over a mile to the west. When they heard Gulletti's scream—a sound that chilled Mattie's blood—Jack said simply, "Butch got him. I saw another man behind the cabin, and there might be others. We've got to keep moving."

By the time they had gone another half mile, Butch had caught up with them. His sleek form slid up behind Jack, and he made a quiet "rowrrr" in his throat to say that he had followed orders.

"Good dog. Follow, on guard." They continued in the general direction of the highway.

"Shouldn't we send Butch after the other man you saw behind the cabin?" she asked breathlessly.

"I don't want to give him a command that could get the wrong person killed. We don't know where the other man is by now. Give me your hand." He helped her over a fallen log.

When their way was blocked by a gully nearly six feet deep, they were forced to change direction. Mattie's shoes were soaked, and she was shaking with fear and cold.

He tried to encourage her. "We'll reach Old Sawmill Road soon, and then we'll follow it to the highway. We just have to keep out of sight."

She just nodded, too chilled to speak.

***

When the initial gunshots and the first explosion sounded across the little valley, Al had been sitting in his recliner by the front room window, unable to sleep because of leg cramps. He turned his head in time to see the great orange ball of the second explosion light up the area, the sound echoing for five miles in every direction. As he heard more rifle shots, he sprang out of the recliner—something he hadn't done in twenty years—and rushed to the bedroom.

Lil was sitting up in bed. "Land o' Goshen, Al. What was that noise?"

"Get yerself dressed and down to the café. Call the sheriff and the forestry service from there. It looks like the Mathis cabin just exploded.

I'm goin' over there to see if anyone survived." He could have won a gold medal at the getting-dressed olympics. He pulled his pants over his pajamas and slipped on his shoes without socks. He reached into the closet and pulled out his twelve gauge shotgun with one hand and the box of magnum buckshot shells with the other. He rushed to the front door, where he reached into the coat closet and threw on a jacket. He was out the door and into his old truck faster than he had moved in decades. He had to coax it to start, but it finally chugged to life and he hurried it past the café and onto Old Sawmill Road.

He bumped over the potholes, noticing the tire tracks made by the Jeep. The way was made nearly as bright as day by the flames that rose above the treetops. "This is bad. This is real bad," he muttered aloud.

When he reached the Jeep Cherokee where it still blocked the road, he muttered again. "I knew those guys were up to no good." He loaded shells into the shotgun and racked one into the chamber before he climbed out of the cab of his truck. He paused and looked into the rented vehicle. The keys were in the ignition. He opened the door and pocketed them. "You guys ain't gonna get away if I kin help it."

***

The sound of Gulletti's scream unnerved Howland. He had been in Vietnam years earlier and remembered hearing that kind of sound only one other time. He knew he was now likely on his own, so he started to make his way through the remaining trees around the cabin and toward the Jeep. Even if it cost him his fee, he was getting out of there. *If Gulletti's hurt, tough for him.* Even in the light from the flames, Howland had a difficult time making his way through the felled trees and debris from the cabin. By the time he could see the vehicle, he was panting from the effort.

He paused and examined the situation. He was no more than thirty feet from the Jeep and could see someone moving around it, but it wasn't Gulletti. It was the big bald guy from the café that everyone had called Al. Howland pulled the Glock out of his shoulder holster and fired. The bullet hit the side door within inches of the man. Al sprinted around to the other side. Howland sprinted closer and took aim again. But before Howland could pull the trigger, Al straightened up to his full height and fired the shotgun directly at the approaching man. The shock wave of air spread out from the muzzle, and the barrel whipped upward with the recoil. Howland was literally blown off his feet. An acrid smell permeated the air.

***

The sound of the Glock followed by the sound of a shotgun made Jack and Mattie freeze. Jack's nerves sizzled like exposed wires.

Butch stood without so much as a quiver, awaiting orders. Mattie looked up at Jack and whispered, "They wouldn't be shooting at each other if Butch got one of them. What's going on?"

"Don't know. You wait here. Butch, stay." With the dog guarding Mattie, Jack started toward the sound of the gunfire.

She sat motionless, trying to fight a rush of panicky tears. She tried to stiffen her spine and square her shoulders. She knew she couldn't fight her enemies by falling apart. As she listened for anything that could give her a clue as to what was happening, thoughts of her parents slipped unbidden into her mind. For the first time in her life, she was almost glad they were both gone—not there to be experiencing the anguish and worry that she was putting her uncle and aunt through. *Everything is such a horrific mess! The cabin's gone and everything in it.* She put her head in her hands.

***

When he reached Old Sawmill Road, Jack could see two sets of tire tracks. He followed them back toward where the cabin had stood and saw one man standing above the other, holding a shotgun. Jack pulled his Ruger and yelled, "Freeze. I've got you covered."

The form didn't freeze. He turned and looked at Jack with wide, shocked eyes. "I didn't mean to kill him, but he was shootin' at me."

"Al, is that you?"

"Yeah, it's me. Who're you?"

"I'm Jack Summers, Mattie's friend." He holstered his gun. "If you hadn't come when you did, he might have killed us and gotten away."

Al was still stunned. "I ain't shot anybody since 'Nam. I really didn't want to kill 'im."

Jack took the shotgun and gently shook Al's left shoulder. "It's okay. You were acting in self-defense. Can you get back to the café and call the sheriff's office?"

"Already told the wife to do that."

"Then wait here and keep your eyes open—we don't know how many of them there are. Get in your truck and stay warm." Jack examined the body to see if the man on the ground was as dead as he looked. He was. He straightened up. "I'll go get Mattie."

Mattie was sitting on a fallen tree trunk holding on to Butch, shivering with cold and tension. She had been trying to distract herself by studying the moon, which seemed to be caught like a prisoner in the branches of the tree she was sitting under.

"Mattie, follow me back to the road. Al's there with his truck. He'll help you get warm."

They made their way to the old truck, and Mattie stopped to stare at Howland's body before Jack motioned her into the truck's passenger side door. The old heater was doing its best to keep the cold at bay.

He asked Al, "Do you have a flashlight? I need to search the area to see if there's anyone else out there." He was also going to look for Gulletti's body but didn't want to say so.

Al reached under the front seat and handed over a four-battery flashlight. Jack walked toward the burning remains of the cabin, looking for footprints that might belong to anyone other than the two men who lay dead. He found Gulletti's body but didn't need to feel for a pulse to know that he was dead. He found no other footprints. By the time he had returned to the truck, he could hear sirens in the distance.

He climbed into the truck, pinning Mattie between himself and Al. She was still shivering. "Did you find anything?" Her words were distorted by her chattering teeth. "W . . . were . . . were there others?"

"No, I didn't see any sign of anyone other than those two, and I can hear the sirens so help is on the way." He cleared his throat. "Al, tell me about your sheriff. Is he a competent lawman?"

"Not 'specially. There ain't much crime around here. Walt Watson's just well liked, so he can always get reelected."

The red-and-blue bar lights on the roof of the sheriff's patrol car turned the trees into dark silhouettes. Jack climbed out of the cramped cab of the truck. "Mattie, come out here. I need to talk to you for a minute."

When she was out of the cab, he led her about ten feet past the Jeep. "We don't know these men. We don't know why they did this. All we could do is guess, and it's better to keep our guesses and speculation to ourselves. Our best bet is to just insist that it must be a case of mistaken identity. Don't share your suspicions."

She nodded. "Okay." There was no time for her to ask for an explanation. That would have to come later.

***

Al, Jack, Mattie, and the sheriff spent the balance of the night sitting in the café, where Jack spent nearly forty minutes answering questions. Then it was Al's turn to answer questions about the death of Howland. Mattie huddled in the corner, trying to get warm. Her jeans were wet to the knees, and her running shoes were like wet sponges. The events of the night left her sagging against the wall next to the table where she sat fighting to maintain her composure. She was gripping the table so hard her knuckles were white.

"Hon, you must be starved and freezing. Here's a waffle and some hot cocoa." Lil set the cup and plate before her. Mattie gratefully picked up the warm cup and took a sip.

The sheriff finally got around to Mattie, but he was inclined to discount her as anything more than a spectator. That was fine with her. She was weary and worried and just wanted to go home.

Lil bustled about making waffles and hot chocolate for everybody. Watson's two deputies had arrived and were sent to investigate the scene while they waited for the tow truck to haul the Jeep away. The county coroner probably wouldn't get there until daylight. A man from the US Forestry Service arrived and went to look at the burned cabin and the smoldering hulks of the cars. When he came back to the café, Lil put a plate of waffles in front of him.

Al remembered that he had the keys for the Jeep in his pocket. "Thanks, Al," Watson said as he took the keys. "It'll be towed to Flagstaff, where the CSI technicians will go over it in the morning and try to identify any fingerprints. We need to know who those guys were." Howland had not carried any legitimate ID, and the sheriff was dubious about Gulletti's business cards and driver's license.

He was also very interested in the photo of a young woman with short curly blonde hair that he found in Gulletti's pocket. He held it up and studied Mattie's face. "Sure looks a lot like you, Miss Mathis. What've you got to say about that?"

Mattie took the picture and noted that it was a photocopy of her university yearbook picture. "Well, she looks a little like me, but she's younger and very blonde. Maybe that created a mistaken identity problem." Watson didn't look entirely convinced. He slipped the photo into his shirt pocket.

When Jack was interrogated, he insisted that he was just a close friend of Mattie's who did "security work" for a living, and they had come to the cabin to "discuss their relationship."

The response from the sheriff made him smile. "Well, the two of you better be discussing marriage, as far as I'm concerned. And what about that dog? I saw what he did to that man's throat." Sheriff Watson's voice grew hard and his eyes narrowed.

Mattie stood with more energy than she felt and responded forcefully. "He belongs to my sister and her husband. He was trained by the army and acts on command. He isn't a danger to anyone unless he's ordered to attack. He took down that man on Jack's command. If he hadn't, we'd both be dead."

"Well, Miss Mathis, he may still have to be put down."

Her sense of righteous indignation propelled her to within a foot of his face. She stated vigorously, "No, he won't! He's a decorated Afghanistan hero. The army won't let that happen, and neither will my uncle." The determination in her voice equaled his.

"We'll see. Who's your uncle?"

Mattie answered in a more controlled tone of voice. "My uncle is Congressman Max Southland, and I run his district office." Mattie didn't like using her uncle's position to gain favor in the eyes of others, but to save Butch, she was willing to use any advantage her relationship to her uncle afforded.

That got the sheriff's attention and an increased amount of curiosity. "But you think that this might just be a case of mistaken identity?"

"Why would anyone take an interest in me or try to kill us? I just run a district congressional office and answer constituent requests. Maybe you need to check out the owners of the other cabins in the area. Maybe they mistook us for one of them." It was a thin story, but she was tired and just wanted to get the questions over with. She returned to her chair.

"We'll look into that possibility. In the meantime, I want the dog to stay here."

Mattie looked at Jack, hoping he would rise to the dog's defense.

Jack looked at Butch and simply said, "Lay." The dog spread out under the table on his side near Mattie's feet.

The questions finally stopped, and the sheriff turned to talk to the man from the US Forestry Service about any remaining potential for fire danger. In the meantime, a highway patrol officer had arrived. Lil promptly put a plate of waffles in front of him.

Mattie rose and stepped over to Jack, "When are we going to get out of here?" she asked quietly.

Al saw her concern and heard the question. His arms were filled with dirty dishes, but he stepped over to Jack and lowered his voice. "I can get the two of you out of here in my truck. You need to get back to the Phoenix area?" Jack nodded. "Can the dog ride in the back?" Jack nodded.

Still holding the dishes, he stepped over to the sheriff. "Hey, Walt, my wife will stay here long enough to see that everybody gets all they want to eat. Stay as long as you need. In the meantime, if you've got no objections, I'll drive these folks back to the Phoenix area so neither of your men will need to leave the crime scene. I know you got lots to do here." Nodding at Jack and Mattie, he added, "I'm sure you got their phone numbers if you need 'em agin."

"Thanks, Al. We appreciate your hospitality." Walt and the forester returned to their conversation.

Al stepped into the kitchen to deposit the armload of dishes and then stepped back to push open the swinging door. He gave a short jerk of his head to Jack and Mattie in the direction of the kitchen as a signal for them to follow him. As Jack stepped past Al's bulky form in the doorway, Al whispered, "Can you git the dog in here quiet like?"

Jack turned and looked at Butch, who had rolled over and was watching him alertly. He patted his leg. The dog rose and quietly made his way into the kitchen, drawing only a glance from the highway patrol officer. From there, Al led them out the back door and around to the old truck. Al dropped the tailgate, and Jack motioned Butch into the truck bed. He said, "Down," and the dog lay down so he couldn't be seen. Al carefully and quietly closed the tailgate before he climbed behind the wheel.

After Mattie was tightly pinned between the two men, Al stated, "Now it's pretty crowded in here, so when I put in the clutch and say 'shift,' you'll have to put it in gear. You know how to shift a standard transmission?"

"Yes. My dad taught me." She was sitting so close to Al that she was straddling the floor-mounted gearshift.

Al turned on the ignition, coaxing the engine to life. The tappets sounded like a hard rain on a metal roof. He raised his voice. "Now put it in reverse."

The gears ground a little, but when he raised the clutch, the truck backed up. "Now put it in low." She firmly but gently shifted into low, and the old pickup moved out onto the highway.

***

As the old truck rumbled away, the forest ranger looked around and asked Watson, "Hey, Walt, they took the dog. Do you want to send someone after them?"

Watson shook his head. "I'm not takin' on a congressman over a dog. It's his problem now."

They returned to their conversation.

***

After a couple seconds, Al pressed the clutch and said, "Second." When he said, "Third," the truck had nearly reached its maximum speed. All the way down the highway, even though the altitude dropped rapidly, the truck never went over forty.

"Can't go much more than forty without maybe throwin' a rod," he said by way of apology.

Thinking of Butch in the open back with the cold wind, Mattie raised her voice and answered, "That's fine with me, and I'm sure it's okay with Butch."

Jack finally spoke. "Al, we really appreciate your help. I think we need to go by Mattie's uncle's place. If it looks like it's free and clear, we may stay there for the time being."

"What do ya' mean 'free and clear'?"

"I'm sure you've figured out by now that those two men were trying to kill us."

"Yep, I figured as much, but if you weren't goin' to tell the sheriff, I didn't feel it my place to say anythin'. I imagine Mattie's uncle has enough connections that he don't need the input of some county sheriff."

"In a nutshell, there are men who're prepared to kill to keep Mattie from sharing what she knows with the right people in Washington. I've asked her uncle and aunt to get out of town, and hopefully, they're gone by now. The information is important, but we can't seem to find the right folks to help us. The FBI is likely to leak to the wrong people—not deliberately, but big organizations are . . . well, porous, if you know what I mean."

"You said you told the congressman and his wife to get out of town? How did you do that?" Al took his eyes off the road and looked at Jack in amazement.

"I'm a DPS cop, and right now I'm Mattie's protection. If, when we get to her uncle's home, there's someone watching the place, we'll have another problem."

"Well, as I ain't a walkin', breathin' GPS, you better give me some directions."

Chapter Nineteen

By the time Al reached Paradise Valley, their clothing was nearly dry and Mattie had quit shivering despite the weak heater in the old truck.

Jack told him to turn onto Valhalla Drive. "Drive the full length of the street so I can see if anyone is watching the house."

As Al turned the corner, the three of them could see a black Chevy Suburban sitting up the street about two hundred feet from the gate to the Southland estate.

"Keep going," Jack urged Al. "Don't slow down."

As they passed the vehicle and noted the man sitting inside, Jack said, "We've got a watcher. Mattie, can we get into the estate any other way without being seen?"

"If Al will turn left at the next corner, past the next house on the left you'll see the rear wall of my uncle's estate. It's a decorative privacy wall painted beige. Al can pull up next to it, and if we stand in the back of the truck, we can climb over the wall there."

As they turned the corner, she pointed to where the wall ran along the residential street behind the corner house. When Al had pulled up onto the sidewalk, she leaned over and gave him a peck on the cheek. "That's for you and Lil. You're really special folks. Give her my love." He grinned broadly.

At that, Jack opened the door, and they both slid out. The two of them moved around to the back of the truck, and Jack lowered the tailgate. Butch's tail thumped with gratitude at the sight of them, but he didn't stand until Jack told him, "Up, Butch."

Jack lifted Mattie up so she was sitting on the tailgate and then made a one legged leap into the truck bed. He jumped up to the top of the eight-inch-wide wall, put his hand out, and helped her up.

"Butch, come." She steadied her balance, and the dog leaped with ease to the top of the wall. "It's a six-foot drop from here, but if you walk toward the corner," she pointed, "where the wall makes a right angle, the lawn slopes up, and it's only about a four-foot drop. It'll be easier for us."

They walked single file along the top of the wall where a hedge of oleanders rose four feet above it. In Al's headlights, they looked a bit like kids and a dog having fun balancing on the top rail of a fence. At the corner, Jack parted the oleanders and dropped to the lawn, followed by Butch. As he helped Mattie down, she said, "Follow me."

They heard Al's old truck drive away as the three of them hurried about four hundred feet across the velvet green lawn toward the rear of the house in the weak, early morning dawn. She pulled a key chain from her bag and opened the door to the guest quarters. When they were inside, she closed door and punched the code into the security system to rearm it.

She took a deep breath. "We made it. If we don't turn on any lights in the front of the house, no one will know we're here. I'm sure Aunt Cecelia put some of the lamps on timers. They may give us sufficient light in some rooms."

Jack was looking around while she talked. "Stay here while I check the house," he whispered. He put his finger against his lips and pulled his weapon. It took him nearly five minutes to carefully check every room. When he returned, he had holstered his gun and looked considerably more relaxed. "Everything looks okay. I suggest we get some sleep."

"There are a couple of bedrooms down the hall into the main house, across from my uncle's office."

"I'll find one. Don't worry about me. Butch is going to be on duty. If you hear the water running, don't let it bother you. I may take a shower, if that's okay with you."

"I'm going to fall into bed and sleep for about a hundred hours. It would take more than running water to wake me."

***

The pilot felt that he had waited long enough. It was Saturday midmorning, so he called the emergency number he had never previously needed to use.

It rang five times and then went to voice mail. A voice said, "Leave your message and we will get back to you, if necessary."

"This is Scarlotti, pilot number one. Gulletti had me fly out here to Arizona in the company plane on Friday and said I was to wait until I heard from him. He didn't expect to be off the grid for more than a few hours, but it's been a lot longer than that. I haven't heard from him. What do you want me to do?" He hung up to wait for a return call.

Wilcoxin's administrative aid had heard the cell phone as it vibrated on his desk. The rule was to allow calls on that number to go to record and then check the message. After he listened to the message, he called Wilcoxin's private number, interrupting his lunch at an Arlington Country Club with two prominent members of the Senate Judiciary Committee.

Wilcoxin pulled the phone from his pocket and said simply, "Yes?" His voice was terse.

His aide repeated the pilot's message and asked, "What should I tell him?"

"Tell him to give it until eight tonight. If he hasn't heard anything by then, have him come on in."

***

Gregorovich Volos had been waiting for the call from Wilcoxin much longer than he felt was justified. He was irritated. Even though it was late Saturday afternoon, he dialed Wilcoxin's office, and after several audible indications of a scrambler on the line, the phone began to ring.

When Wilcoxin answered, Volos did not offer any of the pleasantries that usually open a telephone call. His voice may have reflected age but did not hide a rock-hard determination to win every challenge and contest and to reach every goal, no matter what or who was in the way. "Has the problem been handled?"

Wilcoxin cleared his throat. "We're working on it."

"What does that mean?" The blue veins on Volos's gnarled hand stood out prominently as it gripped the receiver.

"I'm waiting for a call from the man who went out to Arizona a . . . a few hours ago to take care of it personally."

"Get back to me when it's done."

"Yes, sir," but the call had been terminated.

***

Jack slept for four hours before a dream awakened him that made his heart beat so hard and fast that he knew he wouldn't be able to get back to sleep. The dream alarmed him. In it, a stranger had attacked Mattie, and Jack had his hands around the throat of the man and was squeezing the life out of him. It left him with a dark, heavy feeling.

He rose and located a change of clothes in the closet of the room he was using. He figured that it had been the room Craig had used. The clothing fit him well.

Locating the gun-cleaning equipment he had spotted in Max and Cecelia's large walk-in closet, Jack sat down in the living room and began the process of cleaning his Ruger. He needed to put his hands to work so his mind could deal with their situation.

As he worked, he tried to free himself from the dark feeling that the dream had caused. He tried to remember some advice from his father that would offer some emotional calm.

He smiled as he remembered the lecture he had received after a dustup on the baseball diamond when, as a teenager, Jack believed he'd been deliberately hit in the head by a pitch.

"Jack, let it go. You've got to understand that hate destroys the person that holds it. You've got to forgive that kid."

"But Dad, he meant to hit me, and that was his third try in one game. I don't know what he's got against me, but I'm going to make him stop." Jack had been ready to deck the pitcher.

"Jack, listen to me. When you're full of hate, you lose clarity of mind. It interferes with clear thinking. It's a waste of energy that could be better used in constructive ways. That pitcher knows if he gets you angry enough, you'll do something stupid and get yourself thrown out of the game." He could see his father's face and feel his firm hands on his shoulder. "Son, take a deep breath, and let it go."

Okay, Dad, I'll try to follow your advice.

***

When Mattie awoke, it was nearly noon. She sat up and looked at her watch in confusion until she remembered the events of the night before. She had slept in her clothes, so she slipped on her shoes and hurried down the hall that connected the guest quarters to the main house.

"Jack . . . Jack," she called out in excitement. "I've finally figured out how to make this story go public. If we can't get a newspaper to run with it, then we'll publish it ourselves—on the Internet." When she reached the living room, her face was flushed with her enthusiasm, but she stopped in the doorway, her throat suddenly tight.

She saw him sitting on the couch in a maroon sport shirt and a pair of jeans that had belonged to Craig. The pieces of his gun were spread out on the coffee table. The dog was lying at his feet. He looked up at her, surprised by her sudden silence.

"I noticed the gun cleaning equipment in your uncle's closet when I searched the house. I hope he won't mind my using it."

"No, no, of course not. It's just that for a moment I thought you were Craig. I gave him that shirt for his last birthday." She turned away, struggling to fight off the dark, soul-wounding sense of loss that nearly overwhelmed her again.

He rose, and his expression grew apologetic. Without thinking, he turned her to face him and put his arms around her. He spoke quietly into her ear. "I'm sorry if I took too much for granted. I've been wearing the same clothes for about three days and needed a change. His clothes seemed to fit me fine. I'm sorry it upset you. It was thoughtless of me."

She pushed herself away, noting the pleasant but faint smell of his aftershave. With a stiff smile she brushed away his embarrassed explanation. She was determined that he would not see her as a frail, weepy woman—even if she had been acting like it.

"Of course it's all right." She cleared her throat and moved across the room to sit across from him. She cleared her throat again. "I had an idea as I was waking up. Remember the 'Fast and Furious' scandal a few years ago? The ATF permitted hundreds of weapons to be smuggled into Mexico in an attempt to trace them to the drug cartels, and two of the guns were used to kill a US border guard? The ATF whistle-blowers couldn't get the Justice Department to admit to what was going on, and no one in Congress would look into it. When the information leaked online, there was enough public attention to force members of Congress to act. The site asked everyone to e-mail or call several key congressmen and demand that action be taken."

Jack was looking perplexed.

"Don't you see? When we get a copy of the research paper in hand, we can put everything on the Internet with all the sources listed for corroboration. We can embarrass them into halting Westfall's confirmation and force the FBI to investigate—not just Westfall and his law firm but Volos as well."

Jack looked skeptical. "I'm not a computer whiz. It sounds like grasping at straws."

"More people will see it on Facebook than would read it any single newspaper." Her intensity grew. "Jack, I'm really serious. If we put what we know about Westfall and Doty, Dotson, and Diller on a site, surely we can get enough attention to stop Westfall's confirmation and trigger an investigation. Don't you see? We'll e-mail it to every member of the judiciary committee," she paused before adding, "and the FBI and a few select newspapers. Surely that kind of exposure will prompt a front-page story from some paper that Volos doesn't control and will break this can of worms wide open. That will embarrass the FBI into initiating an investigation."

"How will we get the members of Congress to take the e-mail seriously?"

"I'll send out an abbreviated version, kind of a summary that can be digested in one sitting. Then I'll call Ben and have him put his staff on the telephones calling every office that we send it to. If he uses Uncle Max's name, most of them will give it some attention."

"Will your uncle allow his name to be used in this way? You don't want to endanger him or your aunt."

"I think he'll go along with it. I need to talk to him. You said you talked him into taking Aunt Cecelia on a trip to get away from here. If he read the research paper before they left, he'll go along with our plan—I hope," she added quietly.

"Do you have a cell number where you can reach him?"

She nodded and hurried to locate her cell. When the phone on the other end of her call went to voice mail, she left a message. "Uncle Max, I must talk to you. Please call me on this number as soon as possible. This is really important." She looked at Jack after she ended the call. "Now all we can do is wait. How about something to eat?"

"That's just what I've been thinking."

***

Mattie's prepaid phone rang at six that evening. It was Southland. "Mattie, I just got your message. We're in Florida visiting my sister Emily and her husband. What's wrong? Your message alarmed your aunt."

"Uncle Max, did you read the research paper before you left?"

"Yes, I did. That information about the court case and the judicial appointment was worrisome. Are you sure Theo and Craig got it right?"

"Very sure. I'm also sure that it cost Theo, his professor, and Craig their lives—and that it's the cause for the attempts on my life."

"*Attempts* on your life? More than one?"

"Last night someone tried again to kill me—again."

"I thought you were up at the cabin where you were safe."

"Somehow two men found out where I was and came after me. I'm so sorry, Uncle Max, but the cabin was burned down. Jack and I just barely got away. One of the men had my photo and a business card from the law firm in New York that represents Gregorovich Volos and his corporations. That seems to confirm that he's connected to all this. We need your help in going public with enough information to halt the Westfall confirmation and trigger an investigation. We need to use the power of your office to get some attention." Mattie paused and held her breath while she waited for him to respond.

It took about two seconds for him to cautiously answer. "How?"

"We need to e-mail this information to every senator on the judiciary committee and others who might be sympathetic to the matter, as well as to the White House," she paused to get a good breath. "And to some of the major newspapers across the country. If they put the story in print and on their websites, it'll grow legs and really take off."

"But Mattie, most senators get so much e-mail from constituents that yours may not be read for days and not taken seriously, even then."

"We'll send a summary by e-mail and tell them to read the entire paper online. We'll post it right away. I need your permission to have Ben and the office staff call everyone who will receive the e-mail and use your name to urge them to read it in its entirely and, more importantly, to act on it."

"I don't know how much pull my name has anymore now that I've announced my retirement, but go ahead if you think it will help." He sounded resigned.

"Is it okay if we use your computer here at the house to send the e-mails? The people who don't want this information made public might be able to trace the IP address here."

"You might as well, since it looks like I'm going to be tied to it three ways from Saturday, as the saying goes. What a way to end a political career." There was a mix of mild humor and deep regret in his voice.

"Thank you, Uncle Max—and this is the best way in the world for you to conclude an honorable career. What is more important than getting public attention focused on the lawsuit, the wide-reaching power and influence of Volos, and the murders of three good men? In the past, you've told me that sometimes you just have to come face-to-face with your fears to measure your courage and your human value."

"You're right, Mattie. It's just that as I've aged, I've developed an aversion to confrontation and controversy."

"But this time, being in the right means everything."

"Mattie, just remember that great wealth makes it possible for evil to keep coming. Going public with this information is no guarantee that Volos will be stopped. All too often, evil just changes its face or its name, but it keeps on coming. You're opening a Pandora's box with this effort."

She was quiet for a second before she answered, "I know that, Uncle Max. But for Craig—and Theo, I've got to do it. Give my best to Aunt Cecelia."

***

When the call was ended, Max turned to his wife. "I'm sorry to give you bad news, my dear, but Mattie says that two men found her and Jack at the cabin and tried to kill them." To calm her sudden look of alarm, he added, "They're all right, but she said the cabin was burned to the ground."

Cecelia's face blanched. "Someone found her at the cabin? Oh, Max," she wailed as she sat on the bed, "it's my fault. It's all my fault. I called Cora Sue to tell her where Mattie was so she wouldn't worry. She must have told someone else."

Max shook his head. "I doubt that Cora would tell anyone and endanger Mattie's life. I think Jack was right when he told us our telephone line might be tapped."

"I forgot. Good heavens, this is all my fault," she repeated. "She could have been killed." She put her hand over her mouth and rocked back and forth in consternation while her husband sat by her and put his arm around her shoulders to calm her agitation.

Chapter Twenty

JACK STOOD AT THE WINDOW behind the sheer curtains that offered some privacy in the darkened room and watched the black Suburban where it sat on the street. He grinned to himself and pulled his prepaid cell from his pocket. When the dispatcher answered, he said, "There's a big, black car sitting on our street. It's been there for a couple of days, and I think the driver is planning a robbery or something. He doesn't belong in our neighborhood. Will you send a police officer around to check on it?" He gave the location and hung up without identifying himself.

Another half hour passed before a squad car pulled onto Valhalla Drive. As it parked behind the big Chevy, the red-and-blue light bar came alive, winking its warning for the neighborhood to see. The uniformed officer approached the big car and, within ten minutes, found sufficient reason to put the driver into the squad car.

As the black-and-white pulled away, Jack called to Mattie, "I'm going to the Jardin to get that copy of the research paper so you can get started on the e-mail and post the paper online. Our watcher is gone, so at least for a while, we can come and go without anyone taking notice. Can I use one of your uncle's cars?"

"Yes, I'll get the keys to my aunt's minivan. I'm coming with you."

***

Mattie stood next to Jack at the registration desk at the Jardin while he showed his driver's license to collect the copy of the research paper that had been left in the hotel safe.

When they arrived back at the Southland mansion, they both took note of the empty van still sitting on the street. Once inside the house, Mattie sat down at her uncle's computer and called Ben's cell.

"Ben, I'll be sending you an e-mail shortly which I need you to forward in broadcast mode to every member of the Senate Judiciary Committee, the White House, and the other members of the Senate whose names will be on the list I send. I'll summarize the information we're going to put online regarding the pending appointment of a man named Westfall to the court of appeals. I need you to get your staff to call every recipient of the e-mail on Monday morning and urge them to read the expanded information on the blog. Can you do that?"

"Sure, we'll do it."

"I also want the e-mail sent to several newspapers across the country, and we'll need you to initiate a follow-up call to them as well."

"We'll get on it Monday morning."

***

Mattie spent an hour at the computer putting together the list of those who should receive the e-mail, including the director of the FBI. She sent it immediately to Southland's D.C. office, marked to Ben's attention.

Next, she outlined the information that was to go in the e-mail. That included the lawsuit against the BLM and the fact that the corporate plaintiffs' legal representation was the firm of Doty, Dodson, and Diller. The second paragraph discussed the hearing on Westfall's appointment before the Senate Judiciary Committee and his connections to that law firm.

She was about to mention the connection of Volos to the lawsuit but paused with her fingers over the keyboard. *We need our ducks in a row before we take on that man. If I mention him now, I may be showing our hand too soon. One thing at a time. Let's stop the Westfall appointment first.*

She closed the e-mail with a plea to all members of the Senate, the editors of the newspapers that would receive the e-mail, and all others on the list to go to the blog for greater details. It was ten o'clock when she finally hit Send and the information was on its way to the D.C. office for distribution.

By this time, Jack had stopped reading over her shoulder and had gone to the kitchen to rummage though the Southlands' refrigerator. He managed to throw together a couple of omelets and a tossed green salad. As Mattie sat back and tried to loosen the stiffness in her neck and shoulders, he said from the doorway, "You've made a good start. Come and eat something before you collapse for lack of food."

As they ate, Mattie seemed to disassociate herself with their immediate situation and philosophized, "Jack, I've come to the conclusion that life is a lot like a bus route." Jack looked a bit nonplussed at the comment. She continued to muse. "We plan our route through life but find ourselves forced to get off at unplanned stops along the way. We chart our itinerary, but then all we can do is hope and pray that God agrees with it—but in my recent experience, He often has other plans."

Jack grinned and teased, "That's pretty deep, Mattie. If you keep it up, I'll need hip boots." He took a bite, turning thoughtful as he chewed. He swallowed and asked, "Why didn't you mention Volos in the e-mail?"

"He's a man with unlimited amounts of money at his disposal. That makes him dangerous and powerful. My uncle pointed out that with money, evil can keep coming at you." He nodded in agreement. "I want to sneak up on him somehow—if possible."

After they had eaten every scrap of food on the table, Jack took over the kitchen cleanup, and Mattie returned to format the blog. She began with the details of the lawsuit and, for the next four hours, typed steadily, revising repeatedly to fit the length constraints of the site and the patience of her potential readers. Jack came in after the kitchen was clean and stood behind her. He read and made suggestions as she typed.

It was nearly 1:15 a.m. when she felt she had input all the necessary and available information in a concise manner. As she rolled her head, she realized that the muscles in her neck and shoulders had the tautness of a bowstring.

"We need to reread everything I put in here to make sure we haven't overlooked anything important. I haven't mentioned the attempts on my life. I haven't even mentioned that Gregorovich Volos is a major stockholder in the plaintiff companies that are publicly traded or that he has contributed to the campaigns of key senators and the president.

Hopefully, what I have included won't spook him into leaving the country. Let's not wake the sleeping giant—yet."

At 2:10, she completed proofing the entry and checked the word *public* in the drop-down list that determined how the site would be accessed.

"Now it's up to Ben and the staff in D.C. to get the right people to read this stuff." She leaned back in her chair, thoroughly exhausted.

"You didn't send this information to any television stations. Is there a reason for that?"

"I didn't include the TV stations because their news broadcasts seldom cover anything in depth. Their average story runs about fourteen seconds. Twenty-eight seconds is about as in depth as they ever get."

"And the average Joe thinks he's getting all the news from the talking heads at six and ten o'clock." Jack's laugh was cynical.

"It's even worse when you realize that the three national mainstream news networks take their cue from the front page of the *New York Times* as to what stories to report, with very few exceptions. When we watch the news or read a newspaper, it's little more than a second reporting of the *New York Times*."

"I hope that paper was on your e-mail list."

"It was. We'll see if they show any interest. Who knows how much influence Volos has there."

***

The Suburban had been towed, but by Monday morning it was back. This time it was under an overhanging tree closer to the Southlands' gate.

"I knew he wouldn't be behind bars very long." Jack shook his head. "He's undoubtedly working for someone who got an expensive lawyer for him."

"Jack, we can't let him or whoever he works for keep us prisoners here at the house," Mattie said.

"When we need to leave, I'll make another phone call."

***

Late Monday afternoon, Ben called. "Mattie, I think we've stirred a hornet's nest. I hope your uncle's ready for this."

"What's going on?" *A hornet's nest is what we want, isn't it?* she thought.

"I've received about a dozen calls today, five from the AAs in the offices of members of the judiciary committee. I hadn't even had time to call them yet. They all answered with the same statement, nearly *verbatim*: 'The senator is busy with the Westfall confirmation hearing, but when he has the opportunity, he'll read the e-mail and look into the site.' It's obvious that they compared notes and decided on that particular response. That means that they're stalling for time.

"Now here's the important part—your uncle says he will handle any members of the Senate who may be frothing at the mouth. But for the media, the official story is that he's in Hawaii for his wife's health, so he's authorized you to handle the in-depth interviews for the time being."

"Have you heard from any papers?" Mattie's feelings were a mixture of satisfaction and nervousness.

Ben continued. "Wire service journalists for the *St. Louis Post-Dispatch* and the *L.A. Times* have called."

"I think Jack and I should get to D.C. right away, Ben. Will you arrange a news conference for Wednesday morning? That ought to give us the time to get there and get prepared."

"Yeah, sure, if you think that's the way to handle the situation. Where do you want it—in the office here?"

"No, let's go for broke and hold it outside. Security for anything inside the Capitol Building is too stringent. It will limit attendance. Outside, perhaps we can draw some members of the public. Let's use the landing between the upper and lower stairs on the west side of the Capitol. That will give us a wonderful backdrop for the cameras. Send an e-mail to each network affiliate as well as to everyone on the original list."

"That will take some doing to get permission from the Capitol police. Since 9-11, they have been pretty leery about outdoor events like this. Is your uncle going to be there? We need his presence to give the matter real credibility. Needless to say, a press conference held by a congressional AA and the district office manager won't carry much weight."

"I'll call him and let him know our plans. He can probably get there in time."

After she hung up, Mattie immediately called Southland, waking him. "Uncle Max, we need you in D.C. Can you get there by tomorrow? We're scheduling a news conference for Wednesday to deal with the media interest, but it's imperative that you're there when it's held. Jack and I are flying in to D.C. as soon as we can get a flight."

"I'll book a flight out of here as soon as I can." He sounded resigned to the fact that it was going to happen.

"I'll call Ben and tell him it's on for Wednesday, noon. Try to get there well before then so we can put our heads together."

"Look, Mattie, don't endanger yourself over this matter. We don't want anything to happen to you. This whole thing might get out of hand. Please be careful."

"I will, Uncle Max. See you soon."

When she hung up, Jack grasped both of Mattie's upper arms and looked into her eyes. "Mattie, think this through. You will be vulnerable at a public news conference. Is this wise?"

"Jack, timing is vital. This is the best way to get the news out. I don't see that we have any choice."

Jack still looked worried.

Next, she dialed Ben's cell. "It's Mattie. I've just spoken with my uncle, and he'll get here in time for the news conference at noon on Wednesday. Will that work? The vote on Westfall's confirmation shouldn't come before then."

"We'll make it work. I'll tell all interested parties the time and place for the news conference. That may pacify them. If it doesn't, they can run with a story from the information you posted online."

When they ended the call, she looked at Jack. "We need to get our watcher out of the way—again—and get to Washington, D.C., as quickly as we can. I'll book a flight while you get that observer out on the street removed long enough for us to get out of here without a tail."

She had the tickets reserved within twenty minutes, paying a high price for the last two seats on the Delta flight leaving that morning at 8:40. "Do you think we have time to go to your place and pack you a bag?" she asked him.

"No, let's not chance it. There could be someone watching my place, just like here. They're going to be watching for us anywhere they think we might show up."

"I think you'll need to pack some of Craig's clothes. They seem to fit you fine. His suitcase should be in his closet, and he has—" She took a deep breath and started again. "He had a suit or two that will probably fit." After he had packed enough of Craig's clothing for several days, he unloaded his Ruger and packed it in the suitcase as well, hoping there would be no problems at the airport if he checked the bag.

Mattie packed a suitcase and included a dressy suit and a pair of heels for the news conference. She had packed so many times in the previous five years that her bag of cosmetics was sitting in a drawer, ready to go. Then Jack called the police dispatcher and urged the department to send a patrol car to check on the suspicious man sitting in the black car watching the houses on Valhalla Drive.

The patrol car came at 6:30 a.m., and the driver was put in the backseat and returned to headquarters. Jack and Mattie immediately set the security system, locked up the house, and put Butch in Cecelia's minivan. They drove to Cora and Sam's home thirty minutes south. As they opened the gate, Jack noted that the yard looked like an example of a Toys"R"Us wheeled inventory. They urged Butch inside the fence.

"Stay," Jack told him. The dog pulled his brows together in a look of disappointment. He walked dejectedly over to the front door and laid down on the stoop with his chin on his front paws.

From there, they hurried to Sky Harbor Airport, where they parked in long-term parking. By seven thirty, they had checked their bags. Jack had quietly stated that he was transporting an unloaded weapon in the checked bag and showed his police ID card. The ticket agent put a green sticker on the suitcase. They walked down the concourse to a sandwich machine and bought two stale croissants; then they moved to the gate to wait for their flight.

While they waited to board, Jack's mind was working. He pulled his prepaid phone from his pocket and called his partner, Dexter Barstow.

"Hey, Jack, you've been off the grid for a while. I know that Jepson suspended you, but a man should keep his partner in the loop to let him know what's going on. I've left about six messages on your cell."

"Look, Dex, I'm caught up in something that has me working under the radar right now—with Jepson's unofficial approval. I need you to do something for me. I need you to call on every contact you ever established while you were army intelligence and see if you can find the whereabouts of a man by the name of Gregorovich Volos. It looks like he's behind three murders and three attempts on the life of Mattie Mathis, Congressman Southland's niece. Keeping her alive has become full-time work for me." He took a breath. "I've been told that he has a home in Bern, Switzerland, another in Venezuela, and one somewhere in the U.S., probably in New York State. I think he's in the U.S. right now, because he's pressing his attorneys to file an appeal in a lawsuit against the BLM and is actively seeking the appointment of one of his lawyers to the federal bench."

"The BLM?"

"Bureau of Land Management. This appeal may determine whether or not some of his corporations will obtain a lucrative contract for the extraction of oil and natural gas on government land."

"So there's big money involved?"

"Potentially millions—perhaps even billions."

Barstow chuckled cynically. "Where there's big money, there's big temptations—and usually big sins."

"Your help will be appreciated. And use this phone number, not my department phone."

"Will do. I'll get back to you when I have something."

As Jack disconnected, Mattie asked, "Who was that?"

"Dex Barstow, my partner," he said as he dropped the cell into his jacket pocket. "I've been wondering where we go from here. We can't run from a man like Volos forever, and if our interference costs him the Westfall appointment and potentially the appeal in the BLM case, he's likely to carry a very big grudge."

"You're right, but what can we do?"

"That's why I called Barstow and asked him to find as much information on the whereabouts of Volos as he can. It's time we stopped running and started pursuing—very carefully."

Chapter Twenty-One

VOLOS'S VOICE WAS A LOW hiss, like pressure released from a leaking tire. "Wilcoxin, can't you get anything right? The CEO of Strategic Petroleum received a call from some newspaper reporter asking if I had manipulated Westfall's nomination." The pause that followed was as difficult to bear as the words had been. "You have not improved the situation. How many problems do we *still* have out there who have firsthand knowledge of that research paper?"

Wilcoxin struggled to keep the nervousness out of his reply. "Gulletti told me before he left that he was fairly sure that the woman—the niece of Southland who runs his district office—is in possession of it, and the cop who's been shadowing her is probably privy to its contents, so he arranged to fly out to Arizona to locate them both." Wilcoxin paused to swallow the nervous bile that was gathering at the back of his throat. "Yesterday, I received a telephone call from a sheriff out there who asked if we had an employee named Gulletti. He was calling to tell me that his body had been found near a burning cabin in the mountains. Of course, I denied knowing him, but at some point, if this sheriff isn't a total fool, he'll figure out who Gulletti was. We can probably stonewall him for a few weeks. Eventually he'll get a warrant for our employee records, but by then the confirmation is sure to be completed."

"Anything else I need to know?" The sarcasm in the words stung.

He hesitated for a moment before admitting, "There's an additional problem, sir. Much of the information linking Westfall to our firm and our firm to the Strategic Petroleum case has been put on the Internet. Apparently, Southland's staff is behind it—probably that niece."

Volos responded forcefully. "We'll put on a hard press to discredit anything that appears on the Internet. Needless to say, it's becoming more important than ever that we neutralize anyone with firsthand knowledge of the paper. Who else would that include?"

"Probably Southland and maybe his wife by now. At least we need to assume that's the case." Wilcoxin's voice was uneasy.

"You've made a thorough hash of this, Wilcoxin. I'm going to have to straighten out the mess." The threat in the words was plain. "As my attorney, you do not want to know my intentions. As for the present, I plan to continue to retain your firm—but that could change."

***

Volos disconnected without another word then immediately dialed another number, a number with a European prefix. The voice on the other end was colored with a faint German accent. "Futura Energy Incorporated. How may I help you, Mr. Volos?"

"Connect me with Holst in corporate security."

The next voice stated, "Gustave Holst. How may I help you, Mr. Volos?"

"Get yourself to Ottawa, Canada. Use a corporate jet, and get here within the next eighteen hours. Bring a dependable man with you. Herman Stitz might be best. Contact me when you have your arrival time. I'll have someone meet you."

***

Jack and Mattie collected their checked bags at Reagan National, and she led him to the metro station that was just a few hundred feet from the terminal. They rode the metro to the stop nearest the Longworth Building on Capitol Hill, something she had done several times in past years.

At the main entrance to the big congressional office building, they were required to pass through a metal detector and have Mattie's handbag searched. Her congressional staff ID made the process perfunctory until Jack's pistol was spotted in the X-ray of his suitcase. The attention of the two guards was piqued. They insisted that the weapon and both suitcases be left at the guard station.

Jack took a quick look at everything as Mattie led him through wide marble halls to the second-floor office. "Is it always this busy around here?"

She laughed. "Yes! Congress officially ended its President's Day recess yesterday. Everyone's coming back to work."

Door after door was marked as the office of one congressman after another. At the heavy mahogany door of the office of Congressman Max Southland, there was a flag mounted on each side; one was a US flag and the other, the state flag of Arizona with the central star and radiating beams.

The outer office was about fifteen by twenty feet with the receptionist's desk centered in front of the partition that separated it from Southland's private office. The walls were paneled in deep, rich walnut that matched the large desk. On one wall was a painting of a desert sunset with a saguaro cactus silhouetted before it. On the other wall hung a very large print of the Arnold Friberg painting of George Washington kneeling in the snow, bowed in prayer next to his horse. The plaque on it read, "Washington at Valley Forge." Comfortable chairs sat in the corners of the room near end tables with trailing ivy plants and decorative lamps, and that gave the room a warm glow.

A new receptionist sitting at the front desk looked startlingly like Mattie. The young woman's black hair was also cut short, and she stood about the same height. The two women looked at each other and, seeing the resemblance, smiled broadly. Mattie hadn't met her before.

"I do have a twin sister, but I didn't expect to find her here." Mattie put out her hand to shake the hand of the younger woman, whose nameplate said she was Jane Johanson. "Ben is in, isn't he? He's expecting us. I'm Mattie Mathis, Congressman Southland's niece. This is Jack Summers." She offered no further explanation for Jack's presence.

Miss Johanson punched a button on the telephone and spoke into the receiver. "Those visitors you've been expecting are here, Mr. Novak. Should I bring them back?"

"You don't need to. I know where his office is," Mattie said with a big smile. She signaled Jack to follow her.

When she led Jack past the open door of Southland's personal office, he could see that it was as tastefully decorated as the outer office but was much larger.

"I take it that all this luxury is at taxpayers' expense?"

"Perhaps in most of the offices it is, but my Uncle Max's furnishings were a gift from Aunt Cecelia. She selected them herself. He can take them with him when he retires, but I suspect that he'll leave a lot of it for Skidmore . . . if he wins."

When they reached the little office, Ben was trying to eat a stale sandwich at his desk. His office was more the size of a large closet and was filled with file cabinets almost covered by stacks of file folders. Proposed legislation in thick loose-leaf binders cluttered the desk.

He stood up as if to greet strangers before he recognized Mattie. "Good grief, Mattie. What have you done to your hair?" Mattie laughed at his stunned expression.

"Just a change of appearance, not that it seems to have done much good. The bad guys have still been able to find me. If it hadn't been for this man," she nodded at Jack, "they would have succeeded in their attempts to kill me. Let me introduce Sergeant Jack Summers. He's presently serving as my unofficial but very competent bodyguard through the good graces of Chief Jepson of the Mesa PD."

The men shook hands, and Ben pointed the pair toward the two wingback chairs that faced the desk and crowded the little room. "Excuse the mess. There's always too much to do." He sat. "I saw to it that the press release about the news conference was sent to everyone on the e-mail list, like you asked, with the addition of the television network affiliates, including CNN and Fox. I took care of it myself because Frank is in the hospital in Vail, Colorado, with a badly broken leg. His skiing vacation turned nasty. Hope my efforts meet with your approval."

By way of explanation for Jack's benefit, Mattie explained, "Frank is Uncle Max's press secretary." She turned back to Ben. "Ben, you're a whiz. We'll manage without him. Have you heard from Uncle Max? Is he going to get here in time?"

"He and your aunt are coming in tomorrow morning to Reagan National. The heat's turned on in the apartment in Georgetown, so it's ready for them. Where are the two of you going to be staying?"

"Can you get us a couple of rooms at the Holiday Inn on the Hill, two in the block of rooms they keep for folks making official visits to Washington who want reasonable rates?"

"Sure." He picked up the phone and buzzed Jane in the front office.

"Make sure they're adjoining rooms," Jack instructed. "I have had my hands full trying to keep this woman alive."

"Janie, call the Holiday Inn on the Hill—you know, the one where we usually put guests—and reserve two rooms, adjoining rooms. They'll call it a suite. Have it put on the office account." Ben hung up. "Now we can get down to nuts and bolts."

The balance of the afternoon was spent drafting a rough outline of the statement that Southland would read at the news conference. They were ready for an early dinner by the time they had agreed to the content of the statement and the best answers for the anticipated questions.

Ben stood up and stretched. "Let's get out of here and get something to eat. I'm starved. How about you? There's a really great new restaurant on DuPont Circle. If I drive, are you game?"

Over dinner, the conversation became very serious as Jack and Mattie told Ben what had happened at the cabin. His fork paused in the air. "Wow, you must have had angels watching over you." His voice dropped as he added, "I wish Theo had."

"Ben, did you ever have someone check the telephone lines in the office for bugs?" Jack's expression was serious.

"After you told me about Craig's death, I had one of the Capitol police look at the phones. He found a bug that had been slipped into the receiver. It was pretty simple equipment. He took it out, but two days later, I found another one. I've asked Jane to see that the reception desk is never unattended, but when groups of people are visiting and requesting to see the congressman, it's hard to do."

"You don't have any idea who might have placed them in the phones?"

Ben shook his head. "Nearly impossible to tell as there're so many people constantly in and out."

***

After they pulled up in the front drive of the Holiday Inn on the Hill, Ben lifted Mattie's suitcase from the trunk of his car and asked, "Can you catch the metro in to the office tomorrow, or do you need me to pick you up?"

"Metro's fine. Thanks. We'll see you in the morning."

As soon as the bellhop had shown them to the adjoining rooms and unlocked the door between them, Mattie suddenly felt like a balloon with the air nearly gone. Exhaustion had crept up on her. She handed the man a tip and said, "You can leave the connecting door closed." He looked confused. "Unlocked but closed," she clarified.

"Yes, ma'am."

After Jack was settled in his room, he opened the door between and said simply, "Everything look okay?"

She nodded wearily. "Everything's fine. I'm going to shower, shampoo my hair, and climb into bed. I'll see you at eight in the morning."

"Leave the door unlocked. By the way, I've got a thought. Maybe we need to get you a blonde wig for the press conference. You don't look much like yourself right now."

"We'll do that. G'night." She waved him away, and he closed the door.

Jack didn't go to bed right away. He checked the minutes on his phone and noted that he had sixty-five left. *That ought to do it.* He dialed Barstow. When his partner answered, Jack asked, "Do you have anything?"

"I had a good talk with an old army intel buddy by the name of Jeremy Logan. He's been CIA for the last five years. He says Volos is hard to nail down. He has several planes and a couple helicopters. He keeps at least two personal jets and one helicopter at his New York compound. His home is in the Adirondacks and has a landing strip that will accommodate a personal jet. It's about four hundred acres with a bunker for a residence: ten-foot walls, electronic security, and armed guards who make six figures a year. Jerry knows this because another of our mutual army buddies, a guy by the name of Don Price, sold out to the dark side and went to work for Volos a couple years ago. Jerry talks with him about twice a year. He said that Don has gone so far as to suggest that Jerry and I and anyone else who was army intel apply for a job." He snorted with disgust. "I will admit that some days I might be tempted. Is this the kind of info you wanted?"

"Yes, this is exactly what I need."

"So your special assignment involves Volos?

"In a big way. Can you get me specific directions to his compound?"

"I *might* be able to talk Jerry into that." He sounded dubious. "You ought to know that the CIA is *very* interested in Volos. Jerry said—and remember all this is technically off the record—that he's suspected of having connections to Russian organized crime. He made a big oil buy a few years back, supposedly about a third of all the oil reserves in Russia. Since then, he's evidently been using the Russian Mafia to protect his investments over there. He's increased his profit margin by jacking up the price of the oil that's shipped to Europe. How did he attract your attention?"

"It started with a research paper by a law student about the oil and natural gas industry. He sent his paper to the primary researcher for Congressman Max Southland because Southland's AA was his brother. He thought it was important enough for someone at the federal level to know about."

"You said he 'was' the brother of Southland's AA?"

"He's dead now. We think Volos—or someone working for him— had a hand in it. Southland's primary researcher picked up where the student left off and dug around and found enough information to expose the fact that one of the partners of the law firm that represents Volos and a bunch of his companies is awaiting confirmation to the federal appellate bench. This law firm is a big donor to the president, as are several PACs with ties to Volos.

"The appeal of a case involving several of the companies controlled by Volos will likely reach the Court of Appeals for the Federal Circuit sometime in the next two or three years. If the president's appointee is confirmed, he will be in a position to sway that decision. Without a doubt, the FBI did a mighty superficial job vetting this guy, possibly because he and the other partners of the firm are tight with the president."

"Oh man, oh man, oh man," Dex muttered. "Jerry and his CIA friends are gonna want to see that paper. Can that be arranged?"

"Sure."

"I suspect that you'll be hearing from him. When is too late?"

"Never too late. I'm not going anywhere tonight."

Chapter Twenty-Two

JACK HAD BEEN WATCHING THE national news with the volume low. His cell rang at twenty minutes after ten. "Summers, here."

"Sergeant Summers, this is Jeremy Logan, a friend of Dex Barstow. Dex told me that you and I share a common interest in a particular individual. Could an associate and I visit you this evening?"

"Fine with me. I'm in room 321 at—"

"Barstow told us where you are. We'll see you in about a half hour."

***

At ten fifty, Jack heard the knock. When he opened the door, he saw two men wearing London Fog–type overcoats. One said simply, "I'm Dex's friend, Jerry. This is Curt Giles. Can we come in?"

Jack stood aside and motioned for them to enter. No one said anything else until the door was closed. "You have some credentials, I hope."

They both pulled out wallets that held an ID card and badge that identified them as agents of the Central Intelligence Agency. Logan was a tall, slender man with a head of receding brown hair giving him a long expanse of unlined forehead. As Jerry took off his top coat, Jack noted that he looked more like a thirty-five-year-old monk than a master spy in a brown sport coat, brown sweater, and brown tie. Giles was medium height, perhaps five ten, with premature gray hair and rimless glasses that gave him the look of a history professor—but a well-built one.

Jack pointed them to the couch. He didn't waste time with formalities. "How can I help you nail Volos?"

Both of them dropped their top coats on the bed and stepped around the coffee table in front of the couch. They sat while Jack pulled up the chair that was near the desk. Logan answered with a question. "Why are you looking for Volos?"

Jack leaned forward, putting his elbows on his knees and looking closely from one of them to the other, giving what he had to say an air of confidentially. "At the heart of this situation is the woman in the next room, Martha Mae Mathis, better known as Mattie. She works for her uncle, Congressman Max Southland. She runs his district office." As Jack talked, both men made notes in small pocket tablets.

"Southland's AA is a fellow named Benjamin Novak, and his brother Theo was a law student at the U of Texas."

As Jack continued with the story, Logan interrupted. "But where does Volos come into the picture?"

"Theo's research and additional investigating by Craig Crittenden linked—"

"Who's Craig Crittenden?" Giles asked.

"He was one of Southland's staffers. The snooping that Novak and Crittenden did exposed the fact that the companies in the lawsuit are owned or influenced in large measure by Volos."

Jack continued to explain the complicated matter while the agents listened without further interruption. "Theo and Craig's research established that several of the corporations that are plaintiffs in the lawsuit are owned by each other, and that makes an almost impenetrable morass of legal firewalls. All of these corporations are represented by the same law firm, Doty, Dodson, and Diller."

Giles spoke. "One of the office types at the agency turned up a webpage that stated a man by the name of Westfall associated with that same law firm has been nominated for appointment to the Court of Appeals for the Federal Circuit. Is he connected to Volos?"

Jack nodded. "Westfall and the other partners in that firm are big contributors to the president and several members of the Senate Judiciary Committee. Volos is a major client of that firm. Moreover, it looks like Volos is behind the Westfall appointment. He's in a position to benefit substantially through this kind of 'packing the court.' I can't imagine how the bureau missed the fact that Westfall was a partner in the firm handling the case against the BLM. I can only guess that the fact that these guys are big donors and on the short list of invitees to White House events played a part in what must have been a very cursory vetting process."

As Jack finished his recounting of the events, Logan stated grimly, "And Westfall's appointment is before the Senate Judiciary Committee for approval right now."

Jack finally voiced what had been on his mind ever since he had received the call from Logan. "This is a domestic matter. The CIA can't go nosing around in this—or can you?"

"The FBI has formal jurisdiction in this kind of a case, but even then, they'd need to be called into it." Logan paused to ask Jack, "Have you contacted them?"

"I talked off the record with a friend at the bureau, and he warned me that the fact that Volos and the partners in Doty, Dotson, and Diller are tight with the president would put the case on the back burner, even if someone there was interested in pursuing it. He went so far as to recommend that I not make a formal report to the bureau as any member of the Senate Judiciary Committee could request and receive a report on any investigation into the matter."

Logan nodded. "He's got it right. The agency wouldn't be encumbered with the handicaps that are limiting the powers of the bureau. We don't worry as much about who ranks as a close friend of the president. Our big challenge is getting Volos out of the U.S. where we can *officially* get our hands on him." Logan was quiet for a few moments before turning to Jack. "What's your official status right now?"

"I suspect that Dex told you that I'm on suspension while the IA boys investigate the second shooting."

"So you have some time on your hands." It was a statement, not a question. "How long will you be here?"

"Until Friday morning at least. Southland's office has planned a news conference Wednesday at noon, and Mattie will be handling a lot of the responses to media inquiries on Thursday."

Logan nodded at Giles. They both rose. "We'll be in touch tomorrow. We've got to clear some things with the powers that be at Langley, but we'll get back to you. Don't leave town before you hear from us."

***

When Jack and Mattie arrived at Southland's office the next morning, Ben looked harried. He was getting ready to leave. "Mattie, I'm going to pick up your aunt and uncle at the airport. I'll drop her off at the apartment in Georgetown so she can rest, and then your uncle will come back here to the office. I'm running late. And by the way, I just got a call from the director of the FBI. He wanted to speak to your uncle, but I explained that he wasn't in the office. I said I'd have him call this afternoon. He did not sound like a happy man."

When Southland and Ben returned to the office more than two hours later, the congressman took one look at Mattie, and the words were out of his mouth before he could stop them. "Mattie, what have you done to your hair? I didn't realize it was you for a minute." His tone was full of disapproval.

"Considering that someone was trying to kill me, changing my appearance seemed like a good idea." She grinned apologetically.

He was immediately conciliatory. "Of course, of course, my dear. I didn't mean to be insensitive. It's just that it really did take me off guard. Don't you think that it might be a problem at the news conference? There are so many people here in Washington that know you."

Jane stood up behind her desk. "Sir, I have a couple of wigs at home. Maybe Mattie could use one of them tomorrow. They are both kind of a honey blonde. One is short, and one is medium length."

Ben responded. "Bring them tomorrow morning. Come in early so if they won't work, we can still get her another one."

She smiled and nodded, pleased to be of help.

The first thing Southland did was return the telephone call to the director of the FBI, who wanted to know where the information on the website had been obtained.

Southland's response was as terse as the director's question. "The same place that your men would have found it if Westfall had been properly vetted. Send someone to the news conference tomorrow and you may learn more of the details your boys could have found had they done a more thorough investigation of Westfall." In his mind, all of Mattie's danger was the fault of the FBI, and his anger was evident in his tone.

The balance of the day was spent with Mattie and Ben composing and reproducing copies of the news release that would be handed to every person invited to the event the next day. Ben muttered more than once, "I wish Frank hadn't gone skiing."

***

Holst was made aware of the website by a phone call from Volos's right-hand man, Sid Glenn. When he checked it out, he found the announcement of the news conference. Ben had posted it without consulting Mattie, assuming that she would want the widest possible publicity for it. On Tuesday, while Mattie and Jack had ridden the metro to the Longworth Building, Holst had dressed like a tourist and walked about the Capitol grounds. He studied the layout of the building, seeking the most likely place for a sniper's nest. He paid close attention to the double exterior staircases that rose to the impressive west face of the building. He was looking for an open line of fire to the landing between the upper and lower stairs. He found one in the old growth of pine trees that were part of the small grove to the left of the base of the broad staircase. One tree in particular had sturdy, thick branches. In the shadows of the tree, he would be impossible to spot.

Stitz, the man who had accompanied him from Europe, had disappeared upon reaching Washington, D.C. They were to have no contact with one another unless it proved necessary. Each would report directly to Volos.

Stitz had been instructed to pass himself off as a homeless panhandler and spend some time moving around the government buildings on Capitol Hill. He decided that he would sleep on one of the grates that covered the heating exhausts, as many of the homeless did every night during the winter seasons. That way he would have acquired a knowledge of the area, if he needed it.

***

That evening, Holst donned two layers of clothing. The first layer was a tight-fitting running suit and black running shoes. The second layer was a blue uniform ordered from the same uniform supplier that furnished the Capitol Hill Police Department. He carried a leather gun case that looked like a businessman's briefcase. It contained an unassembled, custom-made Bravo 51 sniper rifle with a telescopic sight, an aerosol can of animal repellant, a flash suppressor, a bottle of water, and a tightly folded bundle that, when opened, would be a camouflage cape.

About ten fifteen that night, he made his way onto the Capitol grounds, unchallenged because of the uniform, and when the late tourists and staffers had trickled away for the night, he looked around to make sure he was not being watched. On his earlier reconnaissance, he had spotted some of the closed-circuit television cameras and had selected the most unobtrusive location for his purpose.

Standing near the great pine, he pulled a handkerchief from his pocket and let it fall to the ground, just in case he was on a security camera somewhere. Bending to pick it up, he unobtrusively sprayed the ground with the powerful animal repellent. Stuffing the handkerchief and the small can of repellent into his pocket, he turned with his back to the outside world and melted into the embrace of the pine tree, one dark shadow disappearing into another. At the trunk, he lifted his tall form and his leather case into the branches. The angle from the trees to the location of the news conference was not ideal, but it was adequate. He had a good shot at the location where he expected the gathering of politicos, media, and tourists.

He paid no attention to the scratches and gouges he received in the process of locating a perch two-thirds of the way up the tree. They were a small price to pay for the two million he had been promised for the job. He wrapped himself in the camouflage cape and sat throughout the night ignoring the cold, impossible to spot between the pine needle–covered branches. He demanded that his body comply with his will. As the sky lightened in the east, he put on latex gloves and assembled the rifle and scope. He took special pride in that scope. It had been manufactured by the European company Zeiss with O-ring seals and nitrogen fill for fog proofing, giving him an enhanced field of vision. He regretted that it would be left behind.

He pulled the picture out of the inside of the gun case and studied it again. The short, black shag haircut and the big sunglasses hid much of her face, but he was good at studying jaw lines. He had also been furnished with the older yearbook picture. It was plain to him that the face belonged to the same woman.

He waited patiently. Twice during the night, the Capitol Hill Police walked a German shepherd across the vast lawns. It sniffed at the base of nearly every tree or shrub that might hide a man—every one except where Holst was hidden. The repellent did its work.

***

On Wednesday morning, Mattie dressed in the electric blue suit she had brought for the purpose. When she arrived at the office, she spent twenty minutes in one of the ladies' rooms arranging a wig brought by Jane.

When she returned to the office, Southland gave her a great one-armed hug. "Now you look more like my Mattie."

The office staff was kept busy answering the phone that rang almost continuously throughout the morning. Four members of the Senate asked if they could be present to lend their support to Southland's efforts to halt the Westfall appointment, and another nine senators were to be represented by staffers. Each was told that he or she was welcome to join the group behind the podium.

Chapter Twenty-Three

At eleven forty, Southland stood in the outer office and asked, "Is everyone ready?"

The little group included Southland, Ben, Jane, a staffer by the name of Jordan, and Mattie, who was holding Jack's arm. The other staff members were to remain behind in the office to handle the continuing phone calls and other business. Jane and Jordan were each carrying a bundle of news releases for distribution as they walked out of the front entrance of the Longworth Building. The sun was bright, almost warming the chill in the air.

Mattie had noted that Jack was unusually tense that morning but had said little. He finally broke his silence. "Stay close to me, Mattie. I think we should have chosen a location easier to protect." His voice was tight.

"But, Jack, look at that sight." He followed her eyes to the Capitol dome where it rose against the blue sky. Mattie's heart was pounding with the thrill she always felt when she saw that great building, the center of democracy in the free world. "I know that democracy is not the most efficient form of government, but if efficiency were our primary goal, we would put our faith in a dictatorship. But we haven't. We're seeking genuine representation of the people's wishes—and that is what we usually get. Partisan logjams do happen, but that's part of our form of government."

Jack put his hand over hers where it held his arm. He appreciated her feelings but was still looking over the scene with worried eyes.

Trying to help take the edge off the situation, he stated, "I think this is as good a time as any to have faith to walk to the edge of the light and wait for Providence to light the path ahead." *But sometimes it's hard to tell the difference between faith and foolishness. I hope we haven't confused the two*, he was thinking.

Southland and Ben led the group across Independence Avenue, where they turned left and walked parallel to Southwest Drive to the entrance of the Capitol grounds where First Street NW became First Street SW at the roundabout. The landing between the two flights of stairs was a couple of hundred feet farther.

As they climbed the lower flight of stairs to the broad landing, she looked at Jack and admitted, "I'm beginning to wish Frank were here to handle this. I've got butterflies in my stomach." Trying to recharge her own courage, she smiled and added, "But there isn't a better location in this day of television news coverage than this. Surely no one would try anything in such a public setting."

Jack hoped she was right.

Ben had arranged for a podium with wireless microphones and two large speakers. The crowd had already begun to gather, and Jane and Jordan began to pass out the printed news release. It was a crowd of nearly sixty, composed of members of Congress and their staff, the media, and a sprinkling of curious tourists. Three members of the Uniform Services Bureau of the Capitol police stood nearby. Since 9-11, no news conference was held by a federal official in Washington, D.C., without their presence.

As they turned to face the crowd, Jack whispered to Mattie, "See the two guys in dark suits at the back of the crowd?" She nodded. "They look like FBI to me."

"I hope they are," she responded.

Television vans had set up their satellite feeds, and cameras were ready to roll, most of them at the back of the crowd. Other individuals were hurrying toward the group.

At noon, Ben stepped up to the podium and cleared his throat as a signal that the news conference was about to begin. "Thank you for your presence today. I'm Benjamin Novak, administrative assistant to Congressman Max Southland, whom you see standing behind me with other members and staff of Congress. I'll turn the microphone over to Congressman Southland. After he has concluded his remarks, he or his staff members will take questions." He turned and motioned with his hand. "Congressman Southland." He stepped away from the lectern as Mattie's uncle stepped up.

Mattie stood between Jack and Ben on the great marble landing, watching her uncle with pride as he began to speak. "I and several of my congressional colleagues are here today to express opposition to the appointment of George Westfall to the Court of Appeals for the Federal Circuit. A vote that will send the appointment to the floor of the Senate is expected at any time. As was pointed out in the e-mail many of you received and on the more extensive Internet site, Mr. Westfall's appointment is suspect for several reasons. The New York law firm in which he is a partner, Doty, Dodson, and Diller, represented multiple plaintiffs in a recent lawsuit against the Federal Bureau of Land Management.

"That case was decided in the lower courts for the BLM, but that decision is expected to be appealed, and the court of jurisdiction that would hear that appeal is the Court of Appeals for the Federal Circuit on which Mr. Westfall would sit if he is confirmed by the Senate. This flagrant conflict of interest is deeply troubling to many members of Congress. Should that lower court decision be overturned, the plaintiffs in the case, which include fifteen energy exploration companies, would have a near monopoly on the extraction of oil and natural gas on federal lands in large areas of several western states."

After Southland had finished reading his formal remarks, the questions from the gathered media representatives started to flow. At least six voices yelled questions. The question that was asked by the Associated Press representative was heard the most clearly. He called out, "It's well known that Arizona is not an oil or natural gas producing state. Why was it included in the law suit?"

"I can only speculate that Arizona was included because adjoining areas of New Mexico, Colorado, and Utah share some oil and natural gas resources, and it is anticipated that Arizona may also prove rich in some of these resources in the future."

Another question could be heard above the others. "Isn't much of the state of Arizona Native American reservation land?"

Southland nodded. "Much of it is, and for that reason, the Bureau of Indian Affairs and both the Navajo and Hopi Nations have been invited to file *Amicus Curiae* briefs as friends of the court in this case."

Another reporter called out, "If there are fifteen companies involved, how could a change in the court decision create a monopoly?"

Southland smiled and said with some relief, "Let me have my staff member Martha Mathis address that question." He put his arm out toward her and waved Mattie to the podium. Trying to look relaxed, she smiled at the television cameras and at the group of reporters watching her with notepads and pens held expectantly.

She spoke directly into the microphone while looking at the man who'd asked the question. "The fifteen companies involved in the lawsuit are interrelated. Three primary corporations actually own several of the others, and we have discovered that all of those which are publicly held are at least influenced—if not controlled—by one individual." She paused for effect.

***

Holst had been waiting for the best opportunity. As the congressman finished speaking and began taking questions, he raised the rifle. He suddenly experienced a moment of mild confusion. He had kept his eyes on the young woman standing behind the congressman, partially hidden by another person. She had short black hair and sunglasses like the most recent picture. He moved the scope from her to the one with the head of blonde curly hair who was now speaking. *Is that her?* He concluded that the solution to his confusion was to take them both out. The blonde behind the podium was the cleaner shot. He did a quick double-check through the scope, forgetting to make sure the sun wouldn't catch the lens. He was trying to control the excitement of carrying out such a public hit. Then he squeezed the trigger.

***

"That individual will derive millions, if not bill—" Suddenly Mattie felt herself being hurtled across the marble surface and landing on her stomach, the wind knocked out of her. Her hand came away from her forehead with blood on it. Her vision was blurred for a few seconds, but she rolled over into a sitting position to better determine what had happened.

Jack had knocked her and Southland down in a flying tackle. Her head hadn't even cleared before he was pulling her up. People were screaming and fighting to get past each other. She became aware of the crack of a high-powered rifle and the sound of a bullet ricocheting off marble. Again and again, shots rang out. Ben was trying to help Southland to his feet with the assistance of a Capitol Hill police officer when he was hit by a bullet and dropped. The men Jack had concluded were FBI were crouched with weapons drawn, firing toward the trees where the shots were apparently originating.

"Mattie, we've got to get you hidden. He's after you." Jack literally picked her up, his right arm around her waist, and with her feet hardly touching the ground, he ran toward the south edge of the marble landing, away from the source of the shots. Bullets dug trenches in the grass near them. He continued to carry her toward a cluster of trees, unwilling to put her down until they reached the cover of a wide tree trunk.

"Stay there." He leaned against the tree and tried to catch his breath.

The shots stopped, but the three police officers and the two men from the bureau were still stooped with guns pointing toward the copse of trees and the vast sheet of green lawn that stretched out from the Capitol. One of the uniformed officers was shouting orders into a radio clipped to the shoulder of his uniform.

Many of the panicked crowd had run in different directions across the broad lawn. Others had rushed up the upper flight of stairs, trying to find cover. Several had run for the same grove of trees where Mattie and Jack waited.

***

Holst cursed. As he had prepared to squeeze the trigger, one of the men standing a few feet behind the podium flew at both the congressman and the woman who was speaking. The impact of his body buckled the knees of both just as the first shot blew off her wig. *I must have got her! There's that short dark hair!* She was trying to get up with a bloody hand to her head. Holst took aim again, trying to hit the congressman, but a staffer and a uniformed police officer were shielding him. As he pulled the scope back to focus on the woman that had gone sprawling across the marble landing, the man that had knocked her down grabbed her by the waist and ran for the trees on the other side of the landing. Holst ignored the screams that filled the air as those in the crowd scattered, seeking some kind of cover.

His hands were shaking slightly in a cold rage, but he fired several more times, hitting the young man who was assisting Southland. The young man went down, and another officer ran to cover the congressman while another tried to assist the wounded. Holst dropped him. One of the bureau men stepped in to cover the rescuers, firing at the copse of trees while the injured were helped away.

The fact that his target had made it behind the tree trunk put Holst into a cold sweat. He knew he couldn't stick around any longer. He jammed the German-made rifle between two branches. All its identifying marks had been removed. He also left the latex gloves and the cape in the tree. With the trunk between him and the police officers on the stair landing, he lowered himself to the ground and stepped out between the low branches. He began to yell orders as if involved in crowd control. He yelled at the police officers arriving in black-and-whites. As they piled out of their cars, he pointed toward the entrance to the metro a half block away, yelling that a man with a rifle was seen running that direction. The officers rushed toward the station.

That gave Holst the opportunity to make it to an enormous decorative hedge against another government building, where he faked searching the shrubbery. When he was sure he was not being watched, he slid behind the hedge and removed the blue uniform. He quickly reappeared as a jogger, lopping down the sidewalk and watching emergency personnel and vehicles arrive.

He ran hard for four miles, angry with himself for the hesitation that cost him a clean kill. Why had that man thrown himself at the congressman and the woman—a glint on the scope, a movement in the branches? He'd never know. He could only hope he had given the woman a head injury that would take her life. *Volos doesn't accept failure.*

Holst was now as committed to killing the woman, her protector, and the congressman as his employer was, but he knew he needed to get out of the U.S. immediately. He hardly spoke to the flight crew of the corporate plane on the trip back to Ottawa, where he would wait at the Hyatt for the call from Volos that he dreaded.

Chapter Twenty-Four

"Are you badly hurt?" Jack's voice was harsh with alarm. He pushed Mattie against the trunk of the tree, where she was protected from the shooter.

"I hit my head on the podium, I think." She lifted her hand away from her head and looked at the blood smeared on her palm.

Jack pulled out a clean handkerchief and dabbed at her head to wipe away some of the blood and get a better look at the wound. He pressed the handkerchief into her hand. "Hold this against it. We're not taking any chances. We need to get you to a hospital."

Hearing the frightened screams and looking around at the chaos, Mattie asked, "Jack, what happened?"

"It looks like a sniper tried to kill you."

Mattie's face took on a stricken expression. She finally forced the words through a tight throat. "Did they hit anyone?"

"I'm not sure."

***

It became apparent that one of the Capitol police officers had contacted the communication office beneath the Russell Senate Office Building with the report, "Member down." The wail of sirens quickly filled the air. Within a few minutes, several members of the Contingency Emergency Response Team, referred to as CERT, had begun to arrive in black, government-issued SUVs, some wearing camouflage and all with bulletproof jackets. They poured onto the site, carrying M-249 automatic weapons capable of firing more than a thousand rounds a minute.

News of the shooting had prompted the police chief to leave his office on the seventh floor of the Capitol Building to direct the scene personally. He ordered that all individuals entering or leaving any government building on the Hill be required to show their credentials, effectively sealing out the public.

Down in the circle, patrol cars were sealing off that intersection and the five other intersections that marked the perimeter of Capitol Hill. There were thirteen hundred members of the Capitol Hill Police Department, and it looked like a large number of them were arriving.

***

Visually searching the scene for any further signs of trouble, Jack stated, "I need to get you to an ambulance. I can see one from here." They waited behind the tree for another five minutes while the chaos began to ease.

After members of CERT and the two FBI agents searched the area and could find no sign of the shooter, Jack helped Mattie up the marble stairs and around to the east parking lot where ambulances had gathered at one end of the Capitol Building. There, the EMT insisted that she lie down on the gurney, which was pushed inside. When she was settled, he lifted the handkerchief and wiped away some of the blood. Against the attendant's objections, Mattie insisted that Jack get in the ambulance and go with her.

"Jack, could you see if anyone else was hurt?" she asked as he found a place to sit.

"I saw Ben loaded into one of the other ambulances, but he seemed alert and awake. I don't think he was hurt very badly." He hoped.

"Was anyone else hurt?" she whispered.

"It looked like one of the Capitol police officers was hit."

"It all turned into a nightmare. You were right. We should have chosen a different place . . . or just not done it at all." She murmured as she drifted into unconsciousness.

***

She had recovered consciousness by the time they reached the hospital. The emergency room physician at Georgetown University Hospital diagnosed her head wound as a crease in her scalp caused by a gunshot.

She told the doctor, "I thought I just hit my head on the podium."

"I've seen a few wounds of this kind. A quarter of an inch to the left and you'd be singing with the angels."

"Evidently, God doesn't want me in the choir just yet." She whispered as she looked at Jack.

He had been allowed to stand at the foot of the examination table and was telling the doctor what had happened while he examined the wound.

When the doctor started to shave the hair around the wound, she raised her hand in an attempt to prevent it. "Hey, can't you stitch me up without shaving my head?"

He grinned at her. "Nope. It won't look too bad on you. You can comb your hair to the side to cover some of the shaved spot until it grows out."

She exhaled a long sigh of acquiescence. She looked at Jack. "What made you knock me and Uncle Max down?"

"I was on edge because of how exposed we were, so I was watching the surroundings closely. As you stepped up to the mic, I saw the glint of a rifle scope in the big pine tree. I've seen that kind of thing many times in Iraq. Admittedly, if I'd been wrong, the whole thing would've made the ten o'clock news and I'd have had some major apologies to make."

"I think it will make the ten o'clock news anyway," Mattie stated with a wan smile.

As the last stitches were put into Mattie's scalp, the doctor added, "The X-ray shows a mild concussion. I'd like to keep you overnight."

One of Mattie's eyebrows rose. The other was still numb and unresponsive from the pain killer injected into her scalp. "I'd feel like a target here. Can't I go back to my hotel room now that you've finished your needlework?"

Jack tried to put her mind to rest. "Stay here, and I'll see that there's a guard put at your door, even if I have to stay here all night myself."

Her head was beginning to throb despite the pain killer. All she wanted to do was sleep. "Okay," she said docilely. "But can you find out how Ben is—and the police officer?"

He nodded, and by the time she had been brought to an overnight room, he had returned. "I've called the Capitol PD, and they'll have a uniformed man over by six this evening. Until then, I'll get the hospital to put a security guard at the door. Ben is going into surgery. He has a broken shoulder blade where he was hit in the back, but I caught his doctor before he started to scrub up, and he said it shouldn't be complicated. He'll have his left arm in a sling for a while. The cop just received a flesh wound in one thigh,"

"Thanks for the update. I must not be hurt very badly because I'm hungry. We didn't get any lunch."

"With a concussion, I doubt that the doctor is going to okay any food for you for a few hours. You'll just have to suffer." All of Jack's relief was wrapped up in one big grin as he sat down in the only chair in the room and folded his arms. When the hospital security officer arrived, he bid her good-bye and left to return to Southland's office.

Mattie had just drifted off to sleep when the nurse came in and woke her. "You can't go to sleep with a concussion—at least not for several hours. Doctor's orders."

***

When Jack arrived back at the office, he was glad to find that two of the uniformed guards in the main lobby of the Longworth Building were acquainted with Mattie. When he produced his police ID card, they were willing to allow him inside the building while the media was kept outside.

As soon as he entered the office, he noted that the staff were all standing or sitting in the reception area. Jane was at her desk. "Jane, where's Max?" Jack asked. In the stress of the moment, he didn't bother to use Southland's title.

"In his office with detectives from the Capitol police. They told us to wait here until they could question us. They told me to turn off the phones. The media was driving us crazy."

When Southland exited the office, he motioned for Jane to step in for her turn at answering questions. Jack could see that worry had made the congressman look ten years older.

"Jack, how's Mattie. You were with her, weren't you?"

"Yes, she's okay. She has a crease in her scalp and a slight concussion. The doctor stitched up her head and is keeping her overnight. Hospital security is guarding her room now, and the Capitol PD will be there tonight."

One of the detectives looked at Jack with narrowed eyes and asked, "Were you at the news conference?" When Jack nodded, the man added, "Don't leave until we've talked to you." The man's voice was filled with authority. "Where've you been?"

Jack tried not to let his irritation and weariness reflect in his voice. "I've been with Mattie Mathis over at Georgetown University Hospital." He turned to her uncle and added, "The doctor that was preparing to operate on Ben said he expected the surgery to go well, but Ben's arm will be in a cast for a few weeks."

Southland's relief was evident, and the lines of worry on his face eased. "Thank God for that," he said fervently.

Two hours later, after the detectives had finished their questions and left, Southland concluded that no work was likely to be accomplished for the balance of the day and told the staff to go home. He wanted no unofficial or unauthorized statements coming out of the office from well-meaning staffers.

Jack stayed, and as Southland sat back wearily in the big chair behind his desk, Cecelia rushed into his office, white faced and upset.

"Max, what happened? The news said that there had been shots fired and people hurt at the news conference. They keep showing the video over and over. Is Mattie all right?" Her voice was high and frightened.

Southland rose and put his arms around her. "She and Ben were hurt, but they're going to be fine. They're both at the hospital over at Georgetown. If it will make you feel better, we can go over and see them both."

"Of course. Let's go right now." She took her husband's hand and like an impatient child started to pull him toward the door.

He called over his shoulder, "Hold down the fort, Jack."

Exhaustion began to creep over Jack. He stretched out on one of the couches in Southland's office and was almost asleep when he heard the outer office door open followed by voices in the reception area.

He rose and stepped into the outer office, where he came face to face with Logan and Giles. "I wondered when the two of you would show up." He put his hand out and shook each of theirs.

Giles stepped back and closed the door as Logan asked, "Are you alone?"

Jack nodded. "The staff has headed home, and Southland and his wife just left for the hospital to see Mattie and Ben."

As Giles turned the dead bolt in the door, Logan said, "While we can, we need to talk." He pointed at the couch. "Sit."

When they were seated facing each other, he spoke again. "Since we apparently have a similar interest in Gregorovich Volos, we're here to see if you're willing to take part in our little plan."

"What can I do?" Jack's tone made it clear that he was ready.

"As near as we can tell, Volos has been staying at his Adirondack compound ever since he made his deal with the Russian Mafia. He feels safe in this country because the bureau knows he's tight with the president, so they don't sniff around much. As long as he's in the country, he believes that the CIA won't touch him. We're going to change the whole scenario."

Giles took over the explanation. "We need you and a woman posing as Miss Mathis to get inside his residence. We want to send the two of you in through the front door and accuse him of being behind the attempt on her life at the news conference."

"You've got someone who can pass for Mattie?"

"We'll find someone. We have a plant among Volos's security people. Don Price is undercover. We've had him there for two years, waiting for a break we could use. He'll arrange for our team to breach security while you're keeping Volos busy. We'll take Volos into Canada on his own plane, where the Mounties will hold him on currency smuggling charges until we can extradite him back to the U.S. for prosecution. Are you with us?"

"A hundred percent."

"We'll be back in touch with details within the next day or two." They shook hands with Jack again before leaving.

***

The FBI investigators found the rifle in the tree. Their lab found a couple of partial fingerprints inside the latex gloves and a partial on a shell casing. When they were processed through the NCIC informational systems, nothing turned up, so the prints were sent to Interpol.

A plea went out to anyone who had been present at the news conference to make their pictures and videos from the event available to the FBI. One particular video taken by a tourist from Minnesota was the most useful. He had been standing about two hundred feet away from the cluster of trees where the gunman had hidden. The video on his cell phone showed a man in a police uniform appearing from between the branches of the largest pine and mixing with some of the panicked crowd, appearing to direct some of the police officers toward the metro station. The video was of such poor quality that identification was impossible.

***

Ben wouldn't be released from the hospital for another two days at the earliest, so Southland asked Jack to drive him and Cecelia to the hospital in the morning, where they visited Ben briefly and waited while a very relieved Mattie was formally released.

After dressing, she had stood in front of the mirror in her hospital room noting that her hair was wild and curly and that on the right side of her forehead, there was a patch missing where stitches held her scalp together. The little bandage didn't begin to cover the stitches. She carefully swept some of the curls over the spot and surveyed her look wryly.

As the nurse pushed her wheelchair toward what Mattie thought of as "freedom," her aunt and uncle followed closely. Jack had gone to get the car.

"I'm so glad to be out of here. Even with the officer guarding the door, I felt like a stationary target."

Southland responded, "There's a bunch of media types gathered at the front door, so we're taking you out the emergency exit."

But their ploy had been anticipated, and several reporters and two television cameras were waiting there. Questions were called out to the small group as they pushed their way through the crowd to the car that Jack had brought around to the door. Southland waved but did not respond to any questions.

"Well, Mattie," Southland said with a weary tone after they were seated in the car, "I think we're going to be on television again."

She was assisted into the front seat next to Jack, who was driving. Cecelia climbed into the rear seat with her husband. As they put the hospital behind them, Cecelia reached forward and patted her niece's shoulder. "I want you to come back to the Georgetown apartment and get some rest."

"Aunt Cecelia, I need to go back to the office. Without Ben or Frank, there's no one to do a follow-up news release about what happened yesterday. People need to know that Uncle Max, Ben, and I are okay and that it wasn't the act of a terrorist or a madman. They need to know that we believe the entire incident was an attempt to keep us quiet about the Westfall confirmation process and," she paused, "related matters."

"Are you sure that's a good idea, Mattie?" Southland asked.

"Yes, Uncle Max. I'm sure. Right now public interest is high, and the media is giving us attention that can't be equaled. Surely you can see that?"

"That was a tough way to gain media attention." Southland looked resigned but nodded his agreement. He leaned forward and spoke to Jack. "Cecelia and I are going back to the apartment and turning off the phone for a few hours. We're going into seclusion while Mattie stirs up the hornet's nest."

When they reached the Georgetown apartment, Max grimaced when he saw the gaggle of reporters waiting outside the front stoop. He helped his wife out of the backseat and looked at Jack. "Mattie will show you where to park when you get back to the Hill." As if to give her one more chance to change her mind, he asked, "Mattie, are you sure you're up to dealing with the onslaught of media attention another news release will bring?"

"I've got a headache, but I'll be fine. With Jane and Jordan's help, I can handle it. I want to keep stirring the pot to put on sufficient pressure to halt that appointment and trigger an in-depth investigation."

When Max and Cecelia reached the top step of the stoop, he paused and spoke to the reporters. "There will be more information available to the media tomorrow. Contact my office then."

As they maneuvered through traffic on the way back to the Longworth Building, Jack asked, "Are you going to make any references to Volos in that news release?"

"No, I think I'll keep this focused on the Westfall confirmation. I want the FBI to have time to save some face and pursue a more complete investigation of Westfall and his ties to Doty, Dotson, and Diller. Surely that will lead them to the firm's connections with Volos."

When they reached the Longworth Building, Mattie noticed that there were four uniformed guards at the entrance rather than the usual two. "There're four of you today," she commented to Riley Standish, one of the officers she knew.

As he put her purse on the conveyer belt that would take it through the X-ray machine, he said with genuine seriousness, "That's a direct result of the shooting at the news conference yesterday. The Capitol police closed down all House and Senate office buildings to the public for several hours after it happened."

After she and Jack had both stepped through the archway of the metal detector, they made their way to Southland's office. In the elevator, she said quietly, "I never dreamed our little news conference would create such a furor."

When they entered the office, she asked Jane, "Is the media calling?"

Jane nodded. "For the time being I've got the phones on record. That way you can pick and choose which messages you want to respond to."

"Thanks. I appreciate it. Uncle Max won't be in today. He's asked that all media matters be referred to me. You can open up the phone lines now."

Jane whispered conspiratorially, "Maybe you'd rather wait. There's two men waiting to see Jack. I put them in your uncle's office. I didn't know what else to do with them. It looked important. They said they were CIA."

Mattie nodded, glancing at Jack. "Thanks. You did the right thing."

When Jack opened the door to Max's private office, both men stood. He introduced them. "Mattie, this is Jeremy Logan and Curt Giles, and Jane was correct. They're with the agency."

Mattie was clearly startled. "I had expected more questions from the Capitol police or the FBI, but the CIA? That's a surprise."

Logan responded. "There will be a lot more questions about what happened yesterday, I'm sure, but right now we're very interested in talking to Mr. Summers about another matter."

His manner suggested that they wanted privacy, but she stood her ground. "Then you can talk to me too." She called to Jane, "You were right. Don't take any calls yet." She closed the office door firmly and turned. "What's going on, gentlemen?" She had an expression like a mother who had just caught her sons with hands in the cookie jar.

Logan and Giles exchanged a surprised look and then focused a look on Jack, as if to say, "Can't you handle this woman?"

Jack grinned slowly. "Sit down, *gentlemen*," deliberately using the same word Mattie had used, "and tell us the plan."

The four of them were seated with Logan and Giles on the couch behind the rosewood coffee table. Jack pulled over a wingback chair for Mattie and one for himself.

Exchanging another look with his partner—this time one of resignation—Logan pulled a handful of glossy photos and a pen from the inside breast pocket of his sport coat. "We have the location of the Volos compound along with some excellent satellite photos."

At the word *Volos*, Mattie's eyebrows went up.

He spread the pictures on the coffee table. He pointed with the pen as he spoke. "Here's the residence inside the compound wall." Both Jack and Mattie leaned in to see what he was pointing at as he talked. They could see a low-rise, fortress-like gray block structure in a picture taken from above.

"Here are the guards' quarters and the kennel." Logan moved the pen point. "Here's the runway for the Learjet outside the perimeter wall, which encloses an area of about forty acres. It's our plan to have you, Summers, and a woman posing as Miss Mathis furnish a distraction by going in the front gate at about 10 p.m. and demanding to see Volos. While you're doing that, I and my friend Giles, here," he nodded toward his partner, "will go over the wall. You've got to give us at least twenty minutes. Price will take out the security system at exactly 10:20 and insert one of his discs to hide that fact. Volos sits down to watch the ten o'clock news every night. It's a ritual with him. We'll go over the wall and into the residence, where we'll grab Volos—"

Mattie raised both hands and stopped him. "You apparently have based this plan around the idea that you're going to get someone to impersonate me and fool Volos close up."

"We have a woman at Langley who has been a field agent. We'll have her get her hair cut and dyed black today. She generally fits your description, otherwise."

Mattie's brow was wrinkled with worry. "Tell me about her. How can she be so convincing?"

Giles pulled two folded sheets of paper from an inside coat pocket. He handed them to Mattie.

She looked at the photo in one corner. The woman had a short chin and broad cheekbones. As Mattie skimmed the background information, her head flew up and her eyes challenged Logan and Giles. "She's six years older than me, five foot four . . ." She continued to read for nearly a minute. "Aside from being much shorter and thirty pounds heavier, her eyes are green, where mine are blue. She was born and raised in Brooklyn. Unless she's a linguist, she won't sound anything like a woman from the West."

Her skepticism was increasing. "This whole plan is a joke if it hangs on her passing for me—and she has a husband and two small children, so she hasn't been in the field for five years."

Logan put up his hand to calm her. Jack grinned. He was experiencing mixed feelings. He was impressed that she had recognized a serious weakness in the plan but concerned that from her criticism, it sounded like she might want to be part of it.

Logan insisted, "She doesn't have to fool him for long—we just need twenty minutes to access the compound—"

Mattie wouldn't be quieted. "Why are you endangering a wife and mother and not just using me?"

Giles tried to soothe her feelings. "We need a professional. We don't want to put you in danger—"

She stood and looked at them angrily, cutting him off. "I'll admit that I've been scared—terrified—several times during the past few days, but now I'm angry. I want you to get the man who wants me dead, and I want to help. Volos has undoubtedly been furnished with some pictures of me, and more importantly, the clip of the news conference. He's seen me and heard my voice several times by now."

She turned away from them and, in agitation, took a few steps. Her emotions were churning. She turned back. "Don't you understand? That woman has a husband and two children—a family, something that Volos cost me. Craig and I were going to be married and raise a family, and now that's all gone." Her voice faded before it caught. She balled her hands into fists and took a deep breath. Her voice was firm again. "You need this to work. You're not going to fool Volos with that woman." Her voice hardened, more than Jack had imagined it could. "I owe it to Craig . . . and to Theo." She stared from Logan to Giles. "You need me if this operation is to work."

The two men exchanged a look for a long second. Turning toward Jack, Logan said quietly, "What'd you think, Summers?"

"I'm afraid she's right. I don't want to see her put in danger, but let's face it," he shook his head, "the other woman probably wouldn't fool Volos. Mattie's going to have to be Mattie if this plan's going to work."

Both men quietly exhaled. They both had one question in mind. Could Mattie hold up her end of the plan?

"All right." Logan acquiesced. "The two of you must get into the residence no later than 10:10 and keep him occupied for at least twenty minutes. You've got to draw his attention toward you and away from his security." He smiled grimly at Mattie. "I suspect that Miss Mathis can think on her feet well enough to keep his attention. Just let him have some of what you just gave us." Mattie colored a little.

"What do we do if all this suddenly goes sideways?" Jack's eyebrows eyes were raised.

Logan exhaled. "It's basically a simple plan, but if something unexpected happens and blows our ship out of the water, you'll need to use your wits while Giles and I ride to the rescue." The response didn't put Jack's concerns to rest, but it was all he was going to get.

Giles had left the couch and walked across the office, where he picked up the phone receiver on Southland's desk. After he dialed, he said, "Skip the haircut. We're going to use the Mathis woman. Oh, you've already done it? Well, I hope you like it." He chuckled when he ended the call and returned to his seat on the couch.

Chapter Twenty-Five

LOGAN CONTINUED, "AT 10:20, PRICE will cut the power to the compound. There's a backup system, but it takes three to five seconds to come on line, giving Price time to get the CD into place. When the power comes back on, the camera monitors will be showing the disc."

"What happens if it's snowing and the disc shows a clear night?" Mattie's question was a good one.

"He's recorded several discs to make sure the weather isn't a surprise." Logan returned to the subject at hand. "There'll be four of us. We'll come in by chopper, go over the wall, and dart the dogs. Just before we enter the residence, Price will come into the room on some excuse so he can help Summers disarm Sid Glenn, who always remains with Volos. We'll grab Volos and sedate him. Then we get him, the two of you, and Price over the wall before ten forty-five, when the outside guard makes his rounds. We'll take him to one of his own planes, and Price will fly it to Canada, where the Mounties will be prepared to arrest him for the illegal transport of large sums of foreign currency. They have evidence that he's been bringing undeclared currency into the country for several years. While they hold him, we'll start the extradition process to get him back to the U.S., where he'll face similar charges, as well as anything else we can use against him." He added grimly, "If the bureau won't act, the agency will."

"Wait, wait up." Jack raised his hand. "Isn't his airstrip guarded? And how do you think you're going to get close to the compound by helicopter without being spotted?"

"Price is going to notify the night guard at the airstrip that a search and rescue is being conducted for some lost Boy Scouts on an overnight winter campout. The helicopter will drop Giles and me and two other men in the dark and then take up an apparent search pattern."

"You, Miss Mathis, will wear an earpiece so you can hear us and we'll hear you. Your hair is just long enough to cover it. And wear dark clothing and shoes that you can run in."

Both men stood. "Wheels up from the Reagan National at 2 p.m."

Stunned at the speed with which the plan was moving, Mattie involuntarily blurted, "Two this afternoon?"

Logan nodded. "Price let us know that since the failed fiasco at the news conference, our man is planning to disappear tomorrow, and he's got the means to do it. We may only have this one chance. Don't be late, and dress warm. Jack, don't take any weapons. You need to be clean when you go inside or you'll give us away.

"We'll fly into Albany, where there'll be a rental car waiting for the two of you." He handed Jack a map with the Volos compound marked in red. He added with a rueful smile, "Glad to have you aboard, Miss Mathis." As he shook her hand and then Jack's, she wondered if he meant it.

When the two men were gone, Mattie began to pace nervously. Second thoughts had begun to flood into her mind. *Am I out of my mind? Maybe I'll ruin everything.* She swallowed the bile that had risen in her throat and whispered, "I can't mess this up. For Craig, I can't mess this up." *But now I'm getting really worried.*

Jack put his hand on her shoulder and turned her around. She did not resist. He put his arms around her and pulled her to him. He could feel the silent, shuddering intake of her breath.

"You'd be crazy not to be a little scared, but you're going to do just fine," he whispered.

After a long moment, she pulled away. The intimacy of the moment made both of them suddenly self-conscious.

"I'm sorry. I didn't mean to make you uncomfortable," he said quietly.

"No, no, it's okay. I really did need someone to tell me that things are going to be all right." She gave him a weak smile.

"We'd better get back to our rooms and get those warm clothes Logan told us to wear."

"But I've got to do a news release first. Jane can distribute it in response to the media calls. Tomorrow morning, Uncle Max will need to be prepared to respond to media inquiries since I may not be here." She picked up the telephone and dialed the number for the Georgetown apartment. When the call went to the answering machine, she left a message telling her uncle that she was leaving to take care of an important issue and might not be back into the office the next morning. "You'd better be ready to respond to media inquiries." As she hung up, she said, "I hope he gets that message." She spent the next thirty minutes composing a news release before she and Jack left the office.

***

Back at the Holiday Inn, Mattie changed into black slacks, a dark sweater, and a jacket. She paused and opened her purse. After a minute of thought, she pulled out her driver's license, plastic hotel key card, and a Visa card from the wallet and slipped them into her pants pocket. Jack dressed similarly, and they made it to Reagan National on the metro by one forty-five and were pointed to the helipad by an apathetic TSA agent.

The four blades on the Bell Twin Huey were turning. Its long, sleek body was black and had stabilizers on either side of the fuselage near the tail rotor. The serial number was painted in white below the doors, but there were no other markings. Logan had been waiting and watching. He immediately waved them over. He was completely dressed in black that included a turtleneck sweater, a hooded jacket, and a knit cap.

Jack and Mattie ducked to avoid some of the blast from the blades, which were increasing in speed. Giles appeared and, taking both of Mattie's offered hands, pulled her inside before giving Jack a hand up. Two more men in black wearing earphones were seated in the rear.

Mattie was startled when Giles pulled her aside and pushed a small, pliable, flesh-colored earpiece into her left ear. He said, "Can you hear me?"

She nodded. She could hear him clearly despite the noise of the rotors. She and Jack were each given a set of earphones and motioned to sit. Giles handed Jack a map, and his voice came through the ear-phones. "Study this closely then burn it."

The pilot, also in black, lifted off as they fastened their safety harnesses.

When they were a thousand feet in the air, Logan's voice came through the earphones again. "In back are Harry Hamilton and Stan Edgley. They're good at what they do."

After that, no one spoke. Mattie wouldn't have minded if the ride had lasted twenty hours. She was in no hurry to get to their destination. Her hands were cold and clammy.

After a few hours, Logan announced, "We'll land in ten minutes."

***

When the door slid open, Mattie noted that the winter dusk had surrounded them. They were directed to National Car Rental inside the terminal, and they had hardly reached the door of the building when the big chopper lifted off again. The paperwork was complete, and the rental fee had been paid.

A detailed map of the area was in an envelope on the front seat of the new Chevy Impala. With it was another photo, apparently taken by satellite. Jack pulled out the map that Giles had given to him and compared them. He took the time to enter the destination in the GPS, but the screen read, "Location not found."

"He's insulated himself well if a GPS can't find him. The map will have to do. The satellite photo will at least give us the lay of the land."

They drove north from Albany on I-87 to State Highway 2, where they turned west. Following the directions on the back of the map, Jack proceeded past the bridge over the Branch River. Holding the map against the steering wheel, he commented, "The map shows the compound on the south slope of Boreas Mountain to our right. We have until ten, and it's only eight now. Let's go back to that little café near the turn onto Highway 2 and get something to eat."

Mattie said nothing but knew her nerves would keep her from eating much.

A waitress who looked like she might be happier at another job—any other job—took their orders. Neither had eaten since breakfast. Jack ate like a starving man, but Mattie could only manage to eat half of the salad she ordered. They studied the satellite photos and talked in low voices until eight thirty. He put some cash on the table, and they returned to the car.

Mattie had been quiet since leaving Albany. Finally, she spoke. "Jack, you don't seem nervous about this plan. Does police work give you steady nerves? Have you done this kind of thing in the past?"

"Yeah, you might say that. In Iraq I was a sniper."

She looked at him in surprise in the limited light from the dashboard instrument panel. "My cousin George served in Iraq. He had some dangerous assignments and hated it. How did you end up as a sniper?"

"After I shot two-eighty on the training range in basic, I was selected for it, whether or not I liked it. It was just one of those things I'd rather not have had to do."

It was evident from his terse words and the tightness of this jaw that he didn't want to talk about his time in the military. She led the conversation in another direction. "When we get there, how should we handle this? What approach should we take?"

"Follow your instincts. There are questions you want answered. Ask them."

But focus is a fragile thing, and Mattie was so nervous that she had trouble forming questions in her mind. All she could do was pray that her capacity to think clearly would slip into gear by the time they faced Volos. "Right now, I hardly feel coherent. I know I insisted on becoming part of this project, or whatever you want to call it, but right now I'm hardly more than a . . . a quivering lump of protoplasm." She laughed weakly.

Jack would have smiled under different circumstances. Instead he responded, "Don't let the fear win, Mattie. This is your chance to beat it, to make it bend to your will."

She swallowed and forced herself to breathe steadily and deeply.

The map pointed them up the mountainside. The only vestige of a road Jack could find at that point was a rutted, unmarked lane with a rusty chain across it and a weathered sign that read "Impassable" sitting at a neglected angle. He continued down the highway about five more miles and then made a U-turn.

"It has to be that rutted lane. There's no other street, road, lane, or path."

He returned to it and stopped. Mattie climbed out and unhooked the chain. When she climbed back in, he pointed the car into the ruts and proceeded until they were hidden from the highway by the trees. There he stopped. "See if there's a lighter in the glove box. If they want me to burn the map, there had better be."

She found one. Jack looked over the map once more and then set it on fire. When it had nearly burned his fingers, he dropped it out the window. The next half hour was spent on a twisting, rough lane that, at times, was little more than a wide gap between pine trees whose branches scraped the car. It bounced through potholes until the headlights lit a bright yellow horizontal metal bar about three inches in diameter that blocked the way. Jack got out and examined it. It was chained in place. He went to the trunk and opened it. He muttered, "Nothing to help us here."

As he closed the trunk, two men dressed in dark winter gear appeared out of the darkness with MP5 submachine guns pointed at them. They approached opposite sides of the vehicle. "Hands up!" the man on the driver's side ordered.

Jack raised his hands. The other man opened the passenger side door and motioned Mattie out of the car. With the barrel of the gun, he urged her around to the driver's side to stand near Jack. The one who had given the order swiftly ran his hands up and down Jack's body from his armpits down his legs. "Open your coat," he demanded of Mattie. She did.

He made her take the coat off and turn around. "Put it back on." To the other man he said, "They're clean." He turned to Jack. "What're you doing here? What d' ya want?"

"We're here to see Gregorovich Volos." Jack's voice sounded natural, as if they were simply there for a Sunday afternoon social visit.

"Why?"

"That's between him and us." His voice grew firmer.

"Not if you want to see him." The guard's voice was hard.

Jack turned to look at her. "Mattie, perhaps you would like to tell him why we're here."

She swallowed. An old saying of her mother's crossed her mind. *When the time to perform is here, the time to prepare is past.* She took a deep breath to steady her voice. "We believe Mr. Volos is behind the deaths of three people; one of them was the man I planned to marry. We also believe he's behind repeated attempts on my life as well. We're here to find out why."

The man didn't move for several seconds. From the set of his eyebrows, it was evident that something was going on in his mind. With a cynical, lopsided grimace, he finally spoke. "Follow me."

They were marched through the trees and up the steep side of the mountain along what must have been a path hidden in the ankle-deep snow.

After twenty minutes, they saw the wall of the compound rise in a clearing about fifty feet before them. It was silhouetted by powerful halogen lights on towers that covered the area in brightness much like a prison, throwing the shadows into stark contrast. Around the walls were old growth trees that furnished some camouflage from the air.

They could see a large, heavy metal door in the main portion of the compound, wide enough for a limousine to easily pass through, but the men with the guns halted them and pointed toward a small building to the right that was adjacent to the wall.

The man who had done the talking entered. Jack and Mattie followed him into the small structure. The sudden warmth was the only good thing that she could see about their situation. The room was about fifteen feet square with four monitors and a long desk built into one wall. Two chairs faced the monitors, which were evidently part of a large security system. The screens were divided into four quadrants; the first two screens each held exterior views of the walls and grounds. The other two reflected the interior of the residence. The scenes changed every few seconds. *How can we beat this kind of a security system?* Mattie wondered.

The man who had been sitting at the monitors rose and searched Jack again, pulling Jack's wallet from his rear pocket.

"This ID card says you're a cop. Where's your badge and gun?"

"I'm a private citizen right now." The man waited as if expecting Jack to say more. When he didn't, he handed the wallet back.

The other man moved a broad electronic wand over Mattie, both front and back. When he finished, he looked at the first man and just nodded. *Why didn't the wand pick up my earpiece?* She suddenly realized that it wasn't working. She hadn't heard anything through it since getting off the helicopter in Albany.

***

Price had seen the guards bring Mattie and Jack into the compound on the closed-circuit television system from his position in the second security office located inside the house. He removed the radio clipped to his belt and called up to the guard at the landing strip security office. "Hey, Dylan, anything happening up there?"

The man paused from pulling the plastic off the frozen dinner he had just taken out of the microwave. "Not right now. Anything happening at your end?"

"I picked up a transmission on the scanner that said there were some kids on an overnight campout that have gotten themselves lost. Evidently there's a helicopter out looking for them, so don't be surprised if you hear one in our area. You know how they pull out all the stops when a couple of kids get lost."

"Glad you called. The scanner up here isn't working."

Earlier in the day, Price had made sure it wasn't. "If there's a full-scale search party out there, we may see a chopper or two from the TV stations as well. That may get Volos bent out of shape."

"Thanks for the heads-up."

***

The black, unmarked helicopter approached the mountain where the landing strip and the compound were located. The guard had long ago finished his frozen dinner and was ten minutes into his *Mercury Rising* DVD. It starred Bruce Willis, his favorite actor, so it didn't matter that he had seen it a couple times before. He was only slightly aware of the sound of the chopper hovering deep in the adjacent valley. There, the four men in black rappelled into the darkness. Each wore night-vision goggles. The helicopter was without lights, just a dark smudge against a black sky.

They made good time as they climbed through the trees on the mountainside, and they reached the guard's quarters at the landing strip by five to ten. Logan broke out the glass with the barrel of the dart gun, and as the man turned to see what had caused the noise, the dart hit him in the neck before he had risen from his chair. The guard took two steps and dropped in a heap. Logan and Giles entered, handcuffed him behind his back, recovered the dart, and put a strip of duct tape over his mouth.

Giles patted his cheek and chuckled. "Get a good, long nap, fella. You'll have a headache in the morning."

The other two had done a fast reconnaissance of the two jets that sat in the hangar at the end of the landing strip and of the helicopter that sat nearby. One put a small radio to his mouth. "Okay, all clear." The black helicopter moved into the night before turning on its lights.

***

Both men stepped back, and the one who did all the talking walked around them, looking them over without speaking for a full minute, which increased Mattie's nervousness. "I'll see what the boss wants us to do with 'em." He moved through the small adjacent kitchenette and disappeared through a door into the compound. The other man stood looking at the two of them without speaking for the next six minutes.

"You've got quite a set up here. Have you worked for Volos long?" Jack asked, trying to draw him out.

No response.

"Volos must have some clout to keep himself off the maps and out of the GPS systems." Still no answer.

After a few more uncomfortable minutes, "Talking Man"—as Mattie had labeled him in her mind—returned.

"Follow me." It was a command.

The other man remained behind as Jack and Mattie followed "Talking Man" through the door he had used previously and into an elegant room tiled in marble the color of beach sand. A myriad of ancient sea creatures were embedded in the stone, creating a fossil museum for a floor. Four wingback chairs in pale shades of blue sat in the corners, but in the center of the long room, a dozen straight-backed chairs were arranged on either side of a long table of Louis XIV design. The ceilings were twelve feet high; large oil paintings of landscapes took up the space on the walls, giving the impression of windows looking out on scenes of nineteenth-century Tuscany.

Mattie felt like an obedient dog, trailing behind their guide. She looked at Jack questioningly. He looked straight ahead.

They moved through that room and several others, each decorated as elaborately as the first, before they reached a door at the far end of the structure. Mattie looked at her watch. It was five after ten. She jumped as a voice spoke in her ear. "Miss Mathis, this is Logan. If you're inside the residence, send us a signal. Sneeze or cough."

She gave an elaborate sneeze. The guard turned to look at her. "Excuse me. I think I've caught a chill." Her voice was apologetic.

"Mr. Volos doesn't like germs. Don't get close to him."

She simply nodded. The voice in the earpiece came again. "Good girl. You're coming in loud and clear."

Chapter Twenty-Six

As THEIR GUIDE PAUSED AT the door of the room where Volos waited, he said to them, "Remove your shoes, and remember, don't approach him unless you're told."

The lack of inflection in his voice and the narrowed eyes were quietly intimidating. Mattie looked at Jack worriedly. The thought of running through the snowy woods in stocking feet was alarming.

The man pushed the door open and spoke. "I'm sorry to interrupt your news broadcast, sir, but Mr. Summers and Miss Mathis are here to see you."

Jack and Mattie obediently stepped out of their shoes, leaving them just inside the door. The room felt much like a sauna compared to the rest of the house. Volos was sitting in a swivel recliner. He turned and looked at the two people standing just inside the doorway.

"Step in and close the door so the heat does not escape." His words were not a request. They were a command.

He sat wrapped in a quilt. The mottled scalp showed through his thinning gray hair. The veins on his hands and his feet, which were in slippers without stockings, stood out like blue ropes. The skin on his face looked like parchment. Mattie had seen a picture of him in one of the magazines when she had done her research at the law library, but this man looked fifty years older. Suddenly the story of Dorian Grey slipped into her mind. *Does evil age a person?*

Three broad windows took up three-quarters of the wall behind the television. Only the upper portion of the external security wall could be seen about thirty feet from the building. The view looked out over the wall to the pine-covered mountains. Despite her nervousness, Mattie could see that the view seemed slightly blurred, as if a film or membrane in the window glass distorted the outside world.

She quickly realized that if the outside world appeared distorted from inside, then from the outside, the same would be true. Such a thing would be a protection against assassination attempts. *This man leaves nothing to chance.*

A man stood silently behind the enormous recliner like a sentinel behind his king, his arms crossed. He looked at Jack and Mattie with unfriendly eyes but said nothing. There was a slight bulge under the left armpit of the black suit he wore.

The room was elegantly appointed with a pale blue carpet that spread like a calm sea, and Louis XIV furniture gracefully adorned the room.

Though the earpiece, Logan spoke. "We're approaching the compound. We should be over the wall within five or six minutes. Keep him occupied, but give us some guidance as to the situation."

Volos's eyes darted quickly from Jack to Mattie. He hit the mute button on the remote control irritably. "What do you want?"

Mattie realized that Jack was letting her take the lead. She clenched her fists nervously at her sides and cleared her throat. "Thank you for seeing us, Mr. Volos. I apologize for the lateness of the hour. You were a little difficult to find. We won't stay long, but it was very important for me to meet you."

"Why was it so important to meet me?" The statement was abrupt and contemptuous.

"To ask why you want me dead."

Her directness seemed to startle him. "What makes you think I want to harm you, Miss Mathis?" His voice suddenly became as oily as a drilling rig.

"You have the deaths of three innocent men on your hands—the one that concerns me the most is that of a good man named Craig Crittenden, the man I had planned to marry." She swallowed to steady her voice.

"I don't know any Craig Crittenden." He waved his hand at her as if to shoo away a fly. He wanted to return to his newscast.

Dogs outside began to bark. The voice came in her ear again. "We're over the wall. Keep him away from the windows. We'll be exposed there."

Volos leaned over and punched a button on an intercom on the table next to his chair. "Price, the dogs are barking. Find out why."

To draw his attention back to her, she took two steps farther into the room and raised her voice. "Of course you wouldn't know his name—or any of their names, for that matter. They were just obstacles to be removed so you can continue to accumulate millions more for your attempt to remake the world." Her voice was rising. Jack watched her with concern. It was vital that she keep her emotions under control.

She continued. "The names of the others were Theo Novak and Professor Jurazski, killed within minutes of each other on a Friday after-noon on the campus of the U of Texas. Craig Crittenden was killed the following night at a political event. There was a fourth man, a federal judge—a victim of a hit-and-run in December. Did you arrange that so Westfall could be appointed to the bench?"

The old man's face had grown flushed with anger as she spoke. She took another step toward him. "How many other vacancies have you created so you can pack the federal courts with your handpicked puppets?" Her voice was loud enough to be heard outside the room.

"Talking Man" opened the door. "Is everything all right, Mr. Volos?"

"I'm fine, Rolovich." He waved the security man away. Looking skeptical, the man stepped back out and closed the door.

Mattie took another step toward the old man, and he put up his hand as if to create a barrier between the two of them. The bodyguard behind the recliner stepped beside it and pointed his gun at her.

Mattie was relieved when Jack stepped forward and the attention of the two men shifted to him instead. She wasn't sure what he planned to do, but she had sufficient confidence in him to believe it was the right thing.

"You don't really need that gun. Your boss isn't in any real danger, unless he's afraid of being injured by his own conscience—or does he have a conscience?" Jack's voice was hard and cold. "Do you have a conscience, Mr. Volos?"

Jack and Mattie watched as another man entered the room from the interior door behind the recliner where Volos sat. He assessed the situation and then spoke. "Mr. Volos, the dogs were agitated by a small herd of deer outside the wall. That was what upset them."

Volos was still moving his angry eyes from Mattie to Jack, determined that these uninvited guests would not get any closer. He pointed at them and said forcefully, "I don't want them here. Price, get them out."

"Yes, sir." Price pulled his gun, but instead of moving toward Mattie and Jack, he stepped behind the bodyguard. When he brought the gun butt down on the other man's head, the thud could be heard across the room. Sid Glenn had hardly hit the floor before Price stepped over to the outside door, turned the dead bolt, and opened it. Volos pushed himself out of the recliner and looked from Price to Jack as the four men in black came through the door. The black knit caps had become ski masks.

Volos opened his mouth as if to shout for help, but Price had pulled a sealed sandwich bag from his pocket and removed a cloth. He put his arm around the old man's waist and placed the cloth over his mouth. After a brief struggle, Volos folded, and Price lowered him to the floor.

Logan pointed at the quilt in the recliner. Without saying anything, Hamilton and Edgley spread it on the floor and laid the old man in it. Giles pulled a small roll of duct tape from his pocket and put a strip over the old man's mouth; then he bound Volos's wrists together. When the blanket had been folded over the limp figure, Giles and Logan pulled off their leather belts. Logan wrapped his around the knees of the old man, and Giles wrapped his around the old man's upper arms and chest. Then Giles lifted the bundle to his shoulder.

In a loud whisper, Price told Jack and Mattie, "Get your shoes and follow us—fast." He checked his watch. "We only have six minutes until the next guard check."

They both pushed their feet into wet shoes and hurried toward the outside door. Price waited for them. As they slipped out, he turned off the television and the room light before closing the door behind them.

Jack grabbed Mattie by the arm and pulled her as fast as she could run to catch up with the others, who had moved into the shadows next to the side of the building. When they reached a spot where the moon cast the darkest shadow, Hamilton and Edgley pulled themselves to the top with the help of a rope attached to the grappling hook they had used to get over it a few minutes earlier. There, they knelt and reached down to grasp the limp body of Volos, which Giles and Logan handed up. As the two men on the wall steadied the bundle that was the old man, Giles and Logan lifted themselves to the top and then dropped to the other side. Hamilton and Edgley lowered Volos's limp form to the other men and then reached back to help Mattie scale the wall. Jack made a stirrup of his hands for her and lifted her high enough that Hamilton could pull her to the top of the wall and then help her over to the other side.

Jack pulled himself up by the rope, and Price followed, removing the grappling hook just before he dropped to the ground. The others were well into the trees, moving as fast as they could. Edgley had taken Volos and was slightly slowed by the load. When they had reached the halfway point on the road that climbed to the airstrip, they could hear voices raised in alarm behind them. Hamilton took over carrying the limp old man.

"How much farther?" Mattie struggled to ask Price when they paused briefly.

"Maybe a half mile. Can you make it?"

She nodded, not wanting to expend any unnecessary breath.

When they reached the crest of the hill, Price pointed toward the Learjet 60 parked in the hangar at the nearest end of the runway. With a wave of his hand, he urged Mattie and Jack to hurry to it.

As Price loped ahead of the group, he pressed the remote control he carried with him, and a thick slice of the fuselage opened and settled to the ground, exposing a set of stairs. While Edgley pulled the chocks away from the wheels, Price bounded up the stairs and was sitting in the cockpit before anyone else had climbed into the plane. Logan and Giles leaped up the stairs next, and Giles reached out to assist Mattie. Jack entered behind her. Hamilton had been slowed by the weight of the bound man on his shoulder and was glad to drop his load on the couch. Giles closed the hatch.

As pressed for time as they were, Price paused and removed a small GPS tracker from his pants pocket. He pulled off the cover that protected the adhesive backing and waited for the pulsing green light to tell him the locator beam was operational. Then he reached down and placed it on the underside of the pilot's seat. Giles had taken the copilot's seat and said nothing as he watched, but Price responded to the questioning look on his face. "That's in case someone turns off the manual for any reason. After we separate, you may need to know where Volos and I are."

Looking out one of the windows, Mattie could see the wide, high lights of a Hummer approaching through the trees.

Volos was an unconscious lump on the seat across from where Mattie and Jack sat. Price's voice came over the cabin speaker. "Put on your seat belts. Of necessity, this will be fast."

The engines began to scream, and the plane shuddered as Price pushed the throttle forward. When he released the brakes, the jet roared down the runway and lifted off, clawing for altitude.

***

Too late to stop the plane, Glenn and Rolovich returned to the security office at the compound. Glenn stated through a tense jaw, "Rolovich, check the transmitter signal in the plane. It's on manual. We should be able to track them if Price hasn't turned it off."

***

Mattie leaned back in a leather chair in the comfortable cabin, and despite her unsuccessful attempts at stopping her teeth from chattering, she took note of the polished mahogany and leather fixtures, the indirect lighting and glowing wall sconces. Crystal glasses suspended upside down in racks shimmered from behind the glass doors of a cabinet above a wet bar.

As soon as the plane began to level off, Logan unhooked his seat belt, rose, and began to search the cabinets and the small refrigerator. When he found bottled water, he turned and asked, "Anyone thirsty?" He held up a bottle of Perrier.

A muffled "Mmm-fff" came from the quilt bundle. Giles stepped over and folded the quilt back from the face of their hostage. He carefully pulled off the duct tape that had kept the man quiet.

Volos's first words were filled with rage, and his voice sounded like sandpaper on cement. "I demand that you untie me! How dare you touch my plane! Sit me up!"

Mattie had previously found it odd that none of the men had removed their black ski masks. Now she realized why. None wanted Volos to be able to identify them.

With ease, Giles swiveled the long bundle into a sitting position. The old man's face was a splotchy red, even the scalp that showed through his thin hair.

"How are you feeling, Mr. Volos? Can I get you something to drink?" Logan's voice was calm and confident.

"Where are you taking me? This is kidnapping! You don't know who you're dealing with! You'll never be able to hide from me!" He looked apoplectic. "Don't you realize that I have enough money to get anything I want? I have more money than God!"

It was going to take much more than the offer of something to drink to calm this man. His eyes were like red coals in a face twisted with rage. He reminded Mattie of a small, very vicious pit bull.

"I want answers!" Even though he was still trussed up like a rolled rug, his sense of authority had not wavered. "No one deals with me in such a manner!"

Leaving Volos's knees bound, Logan undid the belt around the old man's upper arms and chest. He stepped over to the bar and refrigerator and picked out a bottle of Perrier. He searched through the cabinets until he located a paper cup, poured some water, and offered it to Volos.

Despite his anger and frustration, the old man took it in two trembling, still-taped hands and downed it swiftly. Then the questions flowed. "Who are you? FBI? CIA? NSA? Where are we going?" His narrowed eyes looked at each person but focused on Jack and Mattie, the only two faces he could see. Had his eyes been lasers, he would have burned a hole through them.

"I recognized you when you came into my home. You're the woman from the press conference at the Capitol Building, aren't you?" He seemed to be getting his rage under control. "Were you their Judas goat? Were you there to distract me while they overpowered me and my guards?" A malicious smile curled the corners of his mouth. "I'll see you dead for this, missy."

Mattie had found her voice. It was strong and steady. "It seems that you have wanted me dead for some time."

"I can make that death easy, or I can make it hard, missy," he slowly stated in a near whisper.

Jack's voice cracked like a whip. "Shut up, Volos. You're in no position to make threats."

Jack's words had their effect. The old man continued to study those in the cabin with hate-filled eyes, but he said no more.

Mattie rose and walked to the aft part of the cabin, where she sat down on another white leather couch and looked out of the window. She wanted to get as far away from the angry old man as possible. There, she could see the waxing moon in the east. It was a gibbous moon, reminding her of an expectant woman seeking to modestly hide behind fragments of torn and wispy clouds. She suddenly thought of her oft-pregnant twin sister, Cora Sue, and of her three little nieces, the youngest one just learning to walk.

The tears caught her off guard. Would she ever see her sister again—or her aunt and uncle. *Surely these men know what they're doing and will get me back safely*. With that thought, she lay down and drifted off to sleep. When she woke, she had been covered with a blanket. The sound of the engines had changed.

As she sat up, Logan called to her, "Put on your seat belt. We'll soon be on the ground."

"How long was I asleep? Are we landing?" She tried to focus her tired eyes on her watch but couldn't make out the time.

Jack came back to sit by her. He spoke quietly. "You weren't asleep very long. We're going to put down on a small airstrip on the US side of the Canadian border, some little place called Massena, a little south of the St. Lawrence River. All of us except Price and Volos will get off, and Price will take the plane to a little airport called Rockcliffe in Ottawa, where he'll be met by the Royal Canadian Mounted Police."

Mattie spoke quietly enough not to be heard by the others above the engine noise. "How will Price maintain control of Volos if everyone else leaves the plane?"

"Volos will be sleeping."

"Is any of this legal?"

"Probably not any more legal than half of what the CIA does, but if they'd waited for the FBI to take Volos, both you and I and maybe a few other folks would be dead. We're lucky the agency was determined to get him out of the country so he could be arrested somewhere else and extradited back to the U.S."

Mattie noted that Logan, Giles, and the other two men were wiping down every smooth surface in the cabin. When she looked at Jack, he said simply, "They don't want any fingerprints identified when the Mounties go over the plane for evidence."

The plane touched down fifteen minutes later, and Volos was sleeping soundly, stretched out on the leather couch where he had been sitting. Jack responded to her unasked question. "Logan gave him something in his Perrier to put him to sleep. He won't wake up for a couple hours. By that time, he'll be a guest of the RCMP."

Without saying anything, Jack took the blanket that Mattie had slept under, which was embossed with the ornate logo of the Volos Investment Fund, and exchanged it for the quilt Volos had been wrapped in when he had been "extracted," as Logan referred to the kidnapping. Still holding the quilt, Jack returned to sit by Mattie and fastened his seat belt.

Chapter Twenty-Seven

Clarence Quigley had been substituting for his uncle at the tiny Massena, New York, airport that day. He'd come down to visit for a couple of weeks from his home on Prince Edward Island in Newfoundland. There hadn't been much for the nineteen-year-old to do, so his uncle had taken his wife out to dinner for their anniversary and left Clarence in charge for eight dollars an hour.

The FAA insisted that during daylight hours, someone be present at the airport with its two little-used runways and the prefab combination office, terminal, and warehouse. The only other building on the site was the hangar, which housed three small private aircraft. With no control tower, any pilot using the airport got all the information available about the wind from the wind sock that flew from a flag pole. The only real amenity the airport could boast was a runway long enough for a personal jet to land.

When the Cherokee Six landed at about four that afternoon, Clarence was downright excited. Here was something official to do. As the plane taxied up to the big fuel tank near the hangar, he ran a comb through his carrot-red, somewhat frizzy hair and hurried outside to speak to the pilot. "What can I do for you?" he said in his most official voice.

The man looked him up and down and asked, "You run this place?"

"Yes, sir, I'm in charge." He absolutely bristled with pride.

"Well, I need you to fill both wing tanks and charge it to this account." He handed Clarence a piece of paper with the account number on it. As the instructions were relayed, a big, black government-issue SUV pulled up.

"Yes, sir. Will do. Will anyone be coming to fly the plane out, or do you want me to tie 'er down tonight?" he called out to the pilot as the man climbed into the SUV. "Might be some big winds."

"Don't worry about it." He called back. "A friend will be taking her out sometime after dark." With that, the man slammed the door, and the vehicle moved away.

After filling the wing tanks with fuel, Clarence hurried back into the building to put the charge on the account and get out of the cold wind. Within less than an hour, it was time for him to close up the office. The man coming to get the Cherokee Six was on his own.

***

The Learjet touched down at the tiny airport a little before one a.m. and rolled to a stop within fifty feet of the dawn-to-dusk light near the office. There were no lights in the terminal building.

Jack handed the quilt to Mattie. To answer the look on her face, he said, "You'll need this."

The door was opened, and all but Price and Volos started down the stairs. Mattie caught her breath. The hard pellets of snow felt like a thousand pinpricks on her skin, and the twenty-degree wind was like a knife in her nose and throat. Jack put his arm around her shoulders as they leaned into the wind and followed Logan and Giles about a hundred feet to the Cherokee Six.

The plane was as cold inside as it was outside—at least Mattie thought so. By the time she had buckled her seat belt and wrapped the quilt around her legs, Giles had turned on the running lights and piloted the plane down the runway.

"Where are we going?" she called to him.

"Dulles," he responded.

"How long will it take?" She was wondering how long they would be riding in the cold.

"A whole lot longer than we'd planned if the wind doesn't let up."

***

After the confusion and name calling had calmed down in the Volos compound, Sid Glenn put a cold cloth to his head, and he and Rolf

Rolovich watched the GPS signal on the screen. The blip steadily made its way north.

They were joined by two other guards, one of whom asked, "Sid, do you think they're flying him into Canada?"

Glenn removed the cold cloth from his head and handed it to the man. "Yeah, that's what it looks like. Go get some ice for this."

When the man returned and handed him the cloth, lumpy with ice cubes, Glenn said angrily, "This has got to be a CIA op. The FBI knows better than to touch him, and if they were dumb enough, they wouldn't be taking him to Canada."

"Hey, look, they must be landing somewhere around Massena." Rolovich pointed at the blip, which had become stationary. The men were very still while they waited to see if the GPS would move again. Within a few minutes, it began to move toward the Canadian border.

There was venom in Glenn's voice. "If they take the boss into Canada, they probably plan to use the Mounties to hold him until the Feds can get an extradition order. They don't know how many friends he has up there." He barked a short laugh. He paced as he held the ice against his head, thinking out loud. "As soon as Volos gets into the hands of the Canadians, he'll demand an attorney." His head flew up, and he spoke to one of the men. "Stafinski, we'll be taking the other plane." He threw down the ice and tossed another command over his shoulder as he left the security office. "Watch that screen. Tell me if anything changes. I'm going to pack a bag."

When Sid Glenn returned to the security office, he held a suitcase. As he set it down, Stafinski said excitedly, "The GPS signal halted in Ottawa."

Glenn stood looking at the screen and rubbing his chin in hard concentration. "By now, this whole matter has undoubtedly gotten very personal with the boss. So it had better be personal with us. No one does this to him and gets away with it."

He took a deep breath. "Stafinski, you'll fly me to Ottawa. Let's get moving."

***

When he awakened, Volos found himself lying on a cot in a holding cell at RCMP headquarters in Ottawa. He rose and unsteadily made his way to the locked security door. In the dim light, he could barely make out the face of his Rolex—5:10 a.m. He walked back to the cot and sat with his head in his hands for a few minutes while his thinking cleared.

As the dizziness and the sensation of being drugged evaporated, his anger filled the void. He stalked to the door and pounded, calling out, "I demand to call my attorney."

When that received no attention, he turned and examined the room. The camera in the corner of the ceiling had a blinking red light. He walked over to stare directly into it and raised his fist. "You will call Jacob Rushen, chief of staff for the PM and tell him Gregorovich Volos is an unwilling guest of the RCMP. And you *will* allow me to contact my lawyer—now!"

For such a frail-looking man, his voice was full of authority.

Chapter Twenty-Eight

After showing his Canadian Bar membership card, Sid Glenn was ushered into a private interrogation room at RCMP headquarters where Volos sat scowling at the world. The guard closed the door behind him, leaving the two men alone.

Volos was a pasty color, a combination of the effect of his emotions and the chloroform that had been used on him. His eyes were red-rimmed with rage. "As soon as you leave here, you will telephone our contact and our man on the staff of the prime minister. You will demand that I be immediately released on my own recognizance."

"Yes, sir," Glenn responded.

"Now tell me what's been going on while I had my enforced beauty sleep." There was no humor in his words, only ice-cold hate. "From the beginning of this farce, there have been too many loose ends, too many missed opportunities. By now, we've lost the Westfall appointment, but I want you to send a message that no one—*no one*—does this to me." His words were all the more fearsome for the quiet manner in which they were delivered.

"Yes, sir. We'll find a way to handle the situation."

He was only somewhat pacified. "You'd better or there will be some new faces in my world."

Glenn knew that he was included in that potential change of personnel, and that change would be very permanent.

***

The Cherokee Six reached Dulles airport as the eastern sky was turning from cobalt-blue to violet to a rose color which brightened to yellow as the sun peeked over the horizon.

When Mattie felt the wheels touch down, she roused. She was embarrassed to find that she had been leaning against Jack's shoulder as she slept. "I'm sorry. I didn't mean to hijack your shoulder, but"—she smiled—"it made a very nice pillow."

He returned her smile. "Anytime."

When the plane had taxied into a hangar, and a man wearing a jumpsuit hurried to put chocks around the wheels, Logan turned in his seat and stated, "Listen, I'm sure that the Capitol police haven't finished with your interrogations about the shooting at the press conference. I suspect that as soon as jurisdictional matters are settled, the FBI and perhaps the Secret Service will enter the picture. Don't *volunteer* any information about the little ride we gave Volos, but . . ." here he paused for emphasis, "but if they've heard about it, go ahead and tell them what happened. Put all the blame for your involvement on Giles and me. We'll handle the questions."

Jack's response was simple. "That's fine with me. Let's keep it all straightforward." Then he added with one eyebrow raised, "How would they hear about it?"

"Who knows. In this town, even the walls have ears."

As they left the plane, Giles and Logan pointed out two black Cadillac Escalades waiting for them. The two agents climbed into one, and a man in a dark suit held the door of the other for Mattie and Jack. Without a word, they were dropped at the Holiday Inn on the Hill.

When they finally got to their rooms, both noted the blinking lights on the hotel telephones. The messages were terse and had been left the night before. Southland simply said, "Where are you? Get in touch with me ASAP. The FBI has questions about the press conference shooting, and they want answers right now."

Mattie quickly changed into a wine-colored pantsuit, and Jack put on one of Craig's business suits he brought from Arizona. They hurried to the metro station a half block from the hotel. When they arrived at the Longworth Building, it was almost seven forty-five, and the sun was peeking through a sky full of stratus clouds.

The two of them were stopped at the metal detector while four guards checked their identification, operating the X-ray machine and the metal detector all businesslike.

After Southland arrived at eight, he looked at Mattie and Jack, who were sitting in the reception area. He said nothing but hung his coat on the coat rack and nodded seriously toward his office, clearly expecting an explanation for their disappearance the previous afternoon.

When they were seated in the private office with the door closed, he said, "Mattie, what's been going on?" His expression was grim.

"Yesterday morning we had two visitors from the CIA who knew Jack. They asked for our assistance with a plan, and frankly, we—or at least, I—thought it might be better if we didn't involve you. They wanted it known to as few people as possible."

The expression on her uncle's face had not lightened. She continued, "They wanted Jack's help in a plan to kid—er, 'extract' Volos and take him into Canada where he could be arrested, and I insisted on being part of it. The woman they wanted to use—"

At this point, Southland couldn't contain his frustration any longer. "You insisted on being part of a CIA operation? Mattie, have you lost your mind?"

"No, Uncle Max. Please let me explain. They needed me to approach Volos, and the woman they planned to use wouldn't have fooled him for two seconds. To make the plan work, I had to be part of it." Max Southland suddenly looked weary. "Uncle Max, you would have worried yourself sick or tried to stop us, and the plan needed to be done. And it worked," she cheerfully continued. "They got Volos to Canada where he's been arrested and charged with money laundering and other things. That should give us some breathing room. Hopefully there won't be any more attempts on our lives."

Her eyes pleaded with him to forgive her. His anger melted. "Okay, okay, it's over and done, and you're back safe and sound. Now tell me everything that happened."

Between Mattie and Jack, they explained the details of the CIA operation, and they ended with Mattie saying brightly, "We got back this morning as the sun was rising, and here we are, as you said, safe and sound."

At that point, Jane's voice came over the intercom. "Congressman Southland, there are two FBI agents here who want to see you and all the rest of us that were at the news conference."

"Show them in."

The two men were ushered into Southland's private office. All three of them shook hands with both agents. Max invited everyone to sit down, but the two agents remained standing. They reached for their IDs in their suit coat pockets and flipped open the folders containing their badges and credentials.

The taller man with a gray suit and pewter-colored tie spoke. "I'm Special Agent William Adams, and this is my partner, Joseph Hewlett." Adams was a broad-shouldered man of about fifty with a head of thick dark hair graying slightly above the ears. He bore an expression of worry, as though the day would bring new troubles. His partner was a man of about thirty-five who would have looked at home in a wrestling ring.

"We have some questions regarding the events at the news conference and also about a certain website with information regarding a federal appointment to the bench. We would appreciate your cooperation."

At least he didn't use the word 'interrogate,' Mattie thought. "Will the bureau be taking over the investigation of the shooting?" she asked.

"We will be augmenting the efforts of the Capitol police for the time being."

It's a jurisdictional dispute, just like Logan and Giles said, she thought.

"We'll be glad to be of help in any way we can," Southland responded.

One of the agents asked, "Is there an office we can use?"

"I'm sure Ben's office is available, as he's still in the hospital."

"If both of you," he looked from Mattie to Jack, "will wait here, we'll speak with Congressman Southland first."

Chapter Twenty-Nine

SOUTHLAND LED THEM TO BEN'S small office, and after nearly an hour, Mattie was called in. She noted that her uncle had remained. Agent Adams motioned her to a seat, and he sat down behind Ben's desk. Hewlett stood in the corner near the desk as there were only three chairs in the room.

A small digital recorder sat on Ben's desk, and as he turned it on, Adams stated, "We have been instructed by the bureau director to pursue the matter of the shooting at the Southland news conference and determine if it has any bearing on the information that appeared on a certain website regarding a man by the name of George Westfall. We are recording the interrogation of Martha Mae Mathis in the presence of her uncle, Congressman Max Southerland."

There's that word, Mattie thought.

He continued. "The purpose of this interrogation is to further investigate facts surrounding the selection and proposed appointment of George Westfall to the US Court of Appeals for the Federal Circuit. Those present have agreed to answer our questions without the presence of an attorney."

Max Southland rose from his chair and lifted the telephone receiver on the desk. "Jane, please get the small recorder in my middle desk drawer and bring it into Ben's office." He said nothing more until she opened the door and handed him a recorder similar to that used by Adams. Adams and Hewlett looked at each other in silence.

Southland turned on the recorder and identified himself, adding, "I am an attorney, and I am serving as legal counsel for myself, Miss Mathis, and Sergeant Jack Summers. Until we have an agreement that no prosecution against any of us will come out of the information conveyed in this conversation, or any relevant conversation that may follow, I will be instructing both Mattie and Jack to remain silent. I realize that without a Miranda warning, anything we might say could not be used in a court of law, but I am here to see that none of us is ever required to appear in a court of law. Should any of our testimony be necessary for the prosecution of others, we will discuss that matter with future counsel when the situation arises."

Special Agent Adams pressed his lips together in a thin line before responding. It was apparent that Max's demand had caught him off guard.

He looked at Hewlett and then at Southland. "You're representing Miss Mathis and Sergeant Summers and demanding full immunity for the three of you?"

"Yes." Southland's voice was hard.

This was a side of her uncle Mattie had never seen before. She put her hand on his arm. "Uncle Max, why would we need immunity?"

"I don't think we will because I know you and Jack would never knowingly do anything prosecutable, but I'm just covering all possibilities."

Adams unconsciously rubbed his chin. He exhaled. "Agreed."

Hewlett looked at him with a thinly camouflaged look of surprise. "Yeah, agreed," he repeated. "Full immunity for all of you. Now let's get to the questions."

Southland looked at Mattie. "You can be fully open and honest in this interview. Go ahead and answer his questions."

"Just begin at the beginning, Miss Mathis. How was this matter of Westfall's appointment brought to your attention?"

She sat forward in the chair, where it was easy to fold her hands on Ben's desk. "Uncle Max's AA Benjamin Novak—this is his office—had a brother, Theo, who was attending the U of Texas School of Law. He was given an assignment . . ." The whole story took over an hour. Neither Adams nor Hewlett interrupted until she told them about two CIA agents approaching Jack in her uncle's office. She had decided to plunge into the story of the mission to "extract" Volos while the promise of immunity still applied.

Adams put up his hand. "Whoa. What were the names of these two men?"

She was hesitant to answer. "I don't want to get them in trouble."

"You don't need to be concerned. The CIA has a certain unexplainable immunity to our efforts, but I will want to have a talk with them." Adams tried to soothe her concern by adding, "Perhaps we can arrange some interagency cooperation."

She thought for a moment as if weighing the situation before answering. "Jeremy Logan and Curt Giles."

A thinly suppressed, slightly cynical grin passed between Adams and Hewlett. Adams shook his head just a little.

The questions about the CIA operation lasted for another hour. Finally, almost regretfully, Adams said, "Will you tell Sergeant Summers that we would like to speak with him?" Mattie nodded. "And Miss Mathis, we need a full copy of the paper that seems to have created this situation. Do you have one?"

She looked at her uncle.

He nodded and responded, "Yes. It's in a locked file cabinet in my office. I'll have Jane get it for you."

Hewlett stood. "Where are you staying right now, Miss Mathis, just in case we have any more questions?"

"At the Holiday Inn on the Hill."

"And Sergeant Summers?"

"The same place."

"Don't change your location without notifying one of us." Each man pulled a business card from his pocket and handed it to Mattie. "Please send Summers in. In the meantime, please get the paper."

Southland remained in Ben's office while Jack was questioned. When Jane removed the bulky brown envelope holding the research paper from the file cabinet, Mattie insisted that another copy be made. When Jack was released, Jane took the copy in to give to the agents. Southland felt no need to remain for her interrogation, so he left the small office.

Before Adams and Hewlett left, Adams spoke to Mattie and said firmly, "The bureau director has told me to tell you that, in the future, there are to be no news releases coming out of this office regarding the matter of the Westfall appointment or anything else that is presently under investigation. Refer all media inquiries to the bureau."

Mattie willingly agreed. She was relieved to turn the matter over.

After the agents took Jane into Ben's office, Mattie looked at her uncle and said with a tired smile, "It seems that the only agency that hasn't come with questions for us is the Secret Service. Should we expect them?"

Southland shook his head. "No, they won't likely be involved because I'm not in the line of succession to the presidency. If I were the Speaker of the House, they would be very much involved." At that, Mattie smiled with relief.

When Mattie and Jack left, they had to push their way through a clot of media people who had been permitted into the building and had gathered in the hallway. In response to their questions, Mattie called, "No comment. Contact the FBI for more information."

They hurried to the metro station to escape the reporters who might want to follow and caught the next train back to the station near the Holiday Inn, where they ate a late lunch.

After the waitress took their order and left them alone, Mattie said quietly, "I want to go home. I want to put this town behind me."

Jack put his hand over hers. "I think you may have a tough time convincing the bureau that we should be permitted to go."

"Just the same, I'm going to ask."

***

The judge had received a telephone call at his home that morning from one of the prime minister's closest aides. The man suggested that releasing Volos on his own recognizance would be appropriate for such a well-known financial giant. It was even suggested that the money-smuggling charges were probably "just a misunderstanding."

Sid Glenn had been foresighted enough to bring one of the Italian-made suits that he knew his boss would want for the court appearance, but that had not mollified the powerful man. Volos was obviously angry during his appearance before the white-wigged judge at ten o'clock, where he was released on his own recognizance but admonished to remain in Canada.

"I have two planes sitting at the Rockcliffe Airport. May I utilize one of them in Canada, or have they been impounded?" Volos made no effort to hide his indignation.

Trying to pacify the angry man, the judge responded, "You may have access to your planes, but as I said previously, you must remain in Canada until the hearing. For your convenience, we will expedite the matter."

"What do you mean by 'expedite' the matter?" His words were curt and bordered on contempt of court.

"We should be able to schedule the hearing within a week."

Without responding further, Volos turned on his heel and exited the courtroom, leaving Sid Glenn to offer his apologetic thanks to the judge.

Volos called his pilot from the cab that was carrying both him and Glenn to the airport. "Stafinski, file a flight plan for Banff. We're taking the Learjet. It's faster and has greater range. We'll be leaving as soon as Glenn and I get to the airport, so get on it immediately."

Stafinski ordered the smaller jet hangared and checked out the Lear, having it refueled. He was waiting in the cockpit when Volos climbed in. "You have a full tank?"

"Yes, sir."

"Can we make it to Edmonton, Alberta, without refueling?"

"No, sir. We would need to stop somewhere between here and there."

"Get this plane in the air. Make a stop at a small airport where we won't likely draw attention of Canadian authorities."

Stafinski resisted the urge to ask questions and responded by starting the engines.

Volos was still smoldering. He looked at Glenn as he fastened his seat belt and demanded, "Where do we stand? Where are they—the girl and the cop?"

"Sir, when the plane reached Rockcliffe airport, there was no one else on board. The others disembarked somewhere in the U.S., probably the Massena airport. I'm sure—"

"I am surrounded by incompetents." He spit out the words. "I must handle everything myself. I knew you would bungle it. They'll return to Phoenix soon, and we'll anticipate their actions." He stretched out on the leather couch and was immediately asleep.

***

After lunch, Mattie located her purse and pulled out the business cards Adams and Hewlett had given her. She dialed Adams's number.

When he answered, she identified herself and plunged into what she wanted to say. "I'm planning on flying back to Phoenix soon; in fact, in the next few days. I want to go home. I can be reached there at any time if there are more questions."

"If you return to Arizona, I can't promise protection for you, Miss Mathis. You would have to rely on your local police department."

"But if Volos is in Canadian custody, we don't need protection. I'm willing to take the chance."

"I'll let the director know of your plans."

***

The plane stopped to refuel at the Saskatoon International Airport. It was not particularly busy that late in the afternoon. While Stafinsky oversaw the refueling, Volos roused himself and went to the wet bar, where he opened several drawers before he located a Perrier and poured it into a glass.

Glenn was startled. He had never seen his boss serve himself. "Mr. Volos, I can do that for you." He half rose from his seat.

"Stay where you are, Sid." He reseated himself across from Glenn and twirled the mineral water in his glass. "There are a lot of things you can do for me and have done for me, Sid. You've been a useful man and usually worth your salary."

Glenn cleared his throat nervously. "I'm glad you feel that way, sir." The tone of Volos's voice increased his apprehension.

"But lately, you seem to have made some major errors in judgment." From his pocket, Volos pulled the .38 caliber revolver he kept hidden in a false back of the wet bar's drawer. "You've become careless of late." He pulled a silencer from the other pocket and began to screw it on the muzzle of the gun.

Sid Glenn's eyes widened in realization of what Volos had planned. "Please, Mr. Volos, the problems haven't been my fault. I couldn't anticipate the events. None of it has been my fault." His voice was rising in panic.

"Sorry, Sid, but I've got to break the chain. Price was a plant, and you were responsible for bringing him on to the team."

"But he checked out. It could have happened to anyone. You can trust me. You don't need to do this."

Volos sat motionless for nearly a full minute, watching the beads of sweat forming on Glenn's forehead. He inhaled and leaned back on the couch. After Glenn had been made sufficiently uncomfortable, Volos began to unscrew the silencer. He had made his point. "I'm going to give you another chance, Sid."

"Yes, sir. Whatever you want." There was desperation in his voice.

Volos dropped the gun in one pocket and the silencer in the other. "In Edmonton, you will find a decent hotel where we will wait until you locate the cop and the woman. I'm anticipating that they'll fly in to Phoenix within the next few days, expecting to go about their normal lives. When that happens, we'll fly directly to Phoenix, where we're going to address the problem." The last three words were spoken with slow deliberateness.

"What about the congressman and his wife, sir?" Glenn asked quietly.

"I can locate them anytime I want to. It's the woman and the cop that I want right now. The Westfall appointment is lost, and undoubtedly the bureau has begun looking into the other recent appointments. I expect that the president may be slow to return my phone calls now." His voice was rising. "I will have no more meddling in my affairs by these people—" his eyes narrowed, "or *anyone* else." His voice became a serpent-like hiss. "Each breath they take is an affront to me."

"Yes, sir. Yes, sir. It'll be taken care of." At that point, Glenn would have promised anything to get back into his boss's good graces. He was suddenly nearly overwhelmed with a visceral hatred for this man, one of the most unpleasant people in the world—quick to abuse people and power. Glenn had often regretted becoming involved with him, but never more than now. But like quicksand, he was in too deep to get out.

Stafinski had paid for the fuel and climbed the stairs into the cabin. He nodded at Glenn and his boss. He could, no doubt, feel the palpable tension in the air but knew not to ask any questions. After he was seated in the cockpit, Glenn closed the hatch.

Volos ordered, "Get this thing off the ground."

***

That evening, the phone in Mattie's room rang. "Are you ready for some dinner?" Jack's voice was rested and cheerful.

"Sure." Hers was subdued.

When she opened her door, her eyes were swollen and red.

"Mattie, what's the matter?" He stepped into the room.

Two large tears coursed down her cheeks, and she turned away from him in embarrassment. "I couldn't sleep, so I called Craig's parents to offer my condolences. Hearing the pain in his mother's voice was so hard."

He closed the door before he wrapped her in his arms and let her cry until the front of his shirt was wet.

After a few minutes, she pulled away and hurried to the bathroom for a tissue. As she returned, she apologized in a whisper. "I'm sorry to be so weak. I thought I had dealt with this, but obviously I haven't. Will it ever stop hurting?"

"There's no time frame for grief. Take my word for it. We each have to work our way through it in our own time. This whole episode with Volos has been stressful and has forced you to postpone your grieving. The tears are okay. They're entirely normal."

After she put a cold wash cloth on her face, they made their way to the hotel dining room and found a secluded booth where they could eat a light dinner. Mattie was quiet as they ate.

Chapter Thirty

SPECIAL AGENT WILLIAM ADAMS WAS seated in Max's private office in a wingback chair in the corner of the room. His elbows were on his knees, his shoulders hunched, and his hands folded between his legs as if he had been waiting for the arrival of the others. As they entered the room, he stood.

Jane was instructed to remain at her desk in the outer office, and the other staffers were to go about their business and make sure those in the private office weren't disturbed. With Ben and Cecelia in attendance, there were six of them.

Southland looked around the room. "As we have all been very much involved in this . . ." he paused to choose his words, "complex situation, I requested that we be given an update. Special Agent Adams was willing to join us this morning to share some of what the bureau has found in its investigation."

Mattie grinned just a little. She knew that her uncle's position as the ranking member of the International Relations Committee and second in seniority on the House Ways and Means Committee gave him the leverage to get such a request granted.

When Southland finished speaking, Adams cleared his throat. "With the approval of the bureau director and the understanding that nothing said here is to leave this room, I have been given permission to speak. Do I have the commitment of each of you that you will keep this information confidential until the case comes to court?" His eyes moved around the room. Everyone nodded.

"We have reviewed the deaths of four Federal Appellate Court justices, which we now believe to have been carefully executed murders.

Each of these deaths took place in a different part of the country, and each initially appeared to be an accident and was ruled as such. Following these deaths, the four men—including Westfall—nominated to fill the vacancies all had ties at one time or another to Doty, Dotson, and Diller." As an afterthought, he added, "Westfall's appointment has been withdrawn, by the way, in case you haven't heard."

He ran his hand through his thick hair before continuing. "We contacted the sheriff out in northern Arizona after we heard all the facts surrounding the attempts on the life of Miss Mathis. The sheriff admitted that he was out of his depth and had made no progress in the investigations of the arson at the cabin and the deaths of the two men who were found there. He overnighted everything from the two bodies, including the cell phones, to our lab. We were able to trace several phone calls from Gulletti—he's the one the dog killed—back to the law firm and to the other man. It didn't take us long to determine that Gulletti was director of security for Doty, Dodson, and Diller and had flown out to Flagstaff on the corporate jet.

"There were several other calls and text messages made from that cell that helped us connect the murders of Theo Novak, Professor Juraszski, and Craig Crittenden, validating the suspicions of Miss Mathis and Sergeant Summers."

"Could you just make it Mattie? I know I'd be more comfortable."

He nodded. "We believe that one of the text messages was to a professional assassin known as Lupo. We've been trying to locate and arrest him for several years. We believe we have identified him in the videos from the airports in both Austin and Phoenix. Another call from Gulletti went to the cell of the man who was shot by Sergeant Summers at the Jardin Hotel. He had his cell phone on him, which made our job easier."

Adams rose and paced. "Another call went to the other man Jack shot a couple of days later at the Palm Winds Motel. We have identified him as a professional hit man by the name of Harden."

"What about the sniper at the press conference?" Mattie interjected.

"The weapon we found in the pine tree was German made, and we believe that a foreign shooter was brought in for that assignment. We've checked every database we can access and have found nothing on his DNA—he left a few drops of blood on the branches—but the partial fingerprint on one of the cartridges matched one left at the scene of the attempted assassination of a Spanish diplomat two years ago."

Mattie pressed him. "And what about Volos? Have you linked him to any of the deaths? Are the Mounties keeping him until he can be extradited back to the U.S.?"

"We're working on that. At the present, we're pursuing an extensive investigation of Doty, Dotson, and Diller, including all its former partners. We've presented a warrant for the telephone records of every partner of the firm for the past six years, and we're pursuing a warrant for the telephone records of Gregorovich Volos. In the face of our actions, the White House is keeping hands off, trying to avoid a major scandal." Adams exhaled heavily. "Tying Volos to the deaths so far has proven elusive. I'm sorry to tell you, Miss Ma—Mattie, that the RCMP released him on his own recognizance." The color drained from Mattie's face. She reached unconsciously for Jack's hand. "The judge instructed him to remain in Canada for the present. The Canadian authorities released him with reluctance, but a telephone call from the prime minister's office put them under pressure."

"Do you know where he is?" Mattie was insistent.

"At the present, we believe he's still in Canada." He continued. "We know he's not at his compound in the Adirondacks, and we're sure that he didn't head for his home in Switzerland. The Swiss have no extradition treaty with the U.S., but they often cooperate in matters like this. They insist that they've seen no sign of him. If he leaves Canada, then he's most likely to head for Venezuela.

"Since Chavez took over there, he and his successor have actually welcomed wealthy criminals." He shook his head in disgust. "Just in case he comes within our reach again, we're putting together a RICO case that will put him away for a long time."

Cecelia's eyebrows were up. "What's a RICO case?"

"RICO stands for the Racketeer Influenced Corrupt Organization Act, which allows us to prosecute individuals who engage in criminal enterprises affecting foreign and interstate commerce and conduct affairs knowingly and unlawfully through a pattern of racketeering activities." He sounded as if he were quoting a legal dictionary. "The RICO case will also encompass the firm of Doty, Dotson, and Diller, as there is some collusive behavior involving Volos and the partners."

"What do you mean?" Cecelia pressed.

"Shared activities from which all involved derive benefit. We expect that will be established when our forensic accountants go over their financial records."

Cecelia smiled with satisfaction. "Well, a RICO case sounds like a perfect fit for Mr. Volos. I do hope he returns to the country."

Southland had been looking very serious. "Bill, can you give us any insight into how the candidates could have been vetted by the bureau and selected for those appointments?"

Adams cleared his throat in some embarrassment. "With the permission of the director, I looked over the bureau files on each of the candidates that were supported by or in any way tied to Doty, Dotson, and Diller—including Westfall. It was apparent that the support each one enjoyed from certain members of the Senate Judiciary Committee as well as from the president tipped the scales toward a superficial vetting process. The investigating agents focused on the obvious. They made sure that these individuals had never been part of a radical student organization, were not at Woodstock, had never been arrested. They checked to be sure there were no illegitimate children, no DUIs, no military dishonorable discharges, no unexplained debt—that kind of thing, but," here he paused, "they discounted the importance of investigating cases that were handled by Doty, Dotson, and Diller. Because these judicial nominees had not acted as legal counsel in any of the cases the firm had filed against the federal government, the matter was not pursued. To investigate every case handled by such an enormous firm would have required twice as much time and nearly double the number of investigators."

Southland shook his head. "I sincerely hope that this situation throws light on the weaknesses of the vetting process for future appointees."

Adams stood. "Now, if you'll excuse me, I need to get back to the office and complete the paperwork on this case." He added with a tired grin, "It's generated about four reams so far."

Everyone else was standing by this time. Adams stepped up to Southland to shake his hand then formally shook everyone else's hand. When he reached Mattie, he added, "You helped us break a big case, Miss Mathis, and we thank you."

"It was really Theo and Craig," she said seriously. "I'm very glad to have been useful, and I think Jack deserves many thanks, especially from me, for keeping me alive." Her voice dropped. "Special Agent Adams—"

He raised his hand as if to prevent her use of the formal title. "Just Bill."

She started again. "Bill, if I die anytime soon, no matter what the cause, I hope the bureau will look into it. I think I've made a mortal enemy, and even all the way from Venezuela, he may try to reach out to get me." The look in her eyes established her seriousness.

"We'll keep an eye on him, Mattie, and I think we can count on the CIA to help with that as well."

***

The flight across Canada was long, taking eight hours, including the stop to refuel in Saskatoon, but Volos slept through most of it. By the time they landed in Edmonton, it was nine fifteen. Glenn had reserved rooms at the Hilton Garden Inn. He knew Volos would be unhappy that it wasn't of a class equal to the Four Seasons, but they needed three adjoining suites and it was all he could find on short notice.

Glenn had also arranged for a limo to pick them up at the airport and take them to the hotel. After expressing his annoyance with the "common" quarters, Volos sat down at the telephone and called Geneva. He demanded that Glenn order a decent room service meal for him, and after it arrived, the boss spent the next six hours on the telephone.

Even through the doors were closed, Glenn heard Volos order someone on the other end, "Get a flight to Phoenix as soon as you can. Wait there for my call. Obtain a dependable weapon when you get there. I'm giving you an opportunity to redeem yourself."

***

Even though three reporters and a television van were camped outside the Southland home in Georgetown, the congressman and his family had a relatively pleasant evening. After Cecelia had put her culinary skills to work, she proudly placed a meal on the dining room table that would rival any Thanksgiving dinner.

"Aunt Cecelia, this is all magnificent, but you've gone to too much work. You'll have to let Jack and me do the cleanup." Mattie looked at Jack and raised her eyebrows, hoping to see agreement on his face.

He grinned. "I'd be glad to. I know how to do dishes." His response eased her concern. Somehow she had felt he would be congenial about the request.

As they ate a dessert of cherry pie, Mattie announced, "Uncle Max, I told Agent Adams that I want to go back to Phoenix. I'm going to get a flight in the next few days so Jack and I can go home. Aunt Cecelia, do you want to come with us?"

Southland looked at his wife.

She smiled and reached out to pat his hand. "No, I think I'd rather stay here with you, Max. We've been separated too often and for too long over the past years. I think we can trust the bureau to look after us here."

Mattie nodded. "That settles it. If Jack agrees, I'll get two tickets for the flight back to Phoenix right away."

"Count me in, Mattie. I'm ready for that milder Phoenix weather." Jack sat back, obviously satisfied after finishing his pie.

That evening Mattie used her uncle's computer to purchase two tickets on American Airlines out of Dulles. The flight would leave in two days at two in the afternoon. There were no seats any sooner than that. She flinched when she saw the price but decided that it would be worth it just to get out of Washington.

She gave both Max and Cecelia a great embrace when she and Jack took their leave that evening. "I'll call your office the minute we get into Phoenix. Don't worry about us," she admonished them both.

Her aunt's face reflected her concern. "Mattie, I want you to call me every day so I don't worry about you. Will you do that?"

"Of course, I will."

"Jack, our thanks go with you for all you've done. When I'm retired, you must come to Sunday dinner every week," Southland added.

"I'd never turn down an invitation like that." Jack laughed as he shook Southland's hand.

Chapter Thirty-One

WHEN JACK REACHED HIS ROOM at the hotel, he placed a call to Logan's cell. It went to voice mail. He simply said, "Mattie and I are headed home day after tomorrow. Thought you ought to know."

The next day Mattie showed Jack some of the sights of the city. They both stood in awe at the Lincoln Monument. They spent hours in some of the various buildings of the Smithsonian. They ate at the Watergate Hotel and sat in the galleries in the House and Senate chambers as both bodies conducted business.

When they ate dinner that evening, Jack said, "It was a wonderful day, Mattie, but now I'm more than ready to go back to Mesa."

***

At ten to five that afternoon, Giles rushed back to the office he shared with Logan waving a report in his hand. His agitation caught Logan's attention.

"Volos is headed west. I just got a report from the technical people that the GPS signal in the jet says he's just the left Saskatoon airport. Don't know why it took them so long to get the information to me. Why d'you think he's headed west?"

Logan pulled his eyebrows together. "Maybe he isn't on the plane."

"Maybe he isn't but whoever is, is going to be several hundred miles closer to Arizona. Should we tell them?" They both knew who he meant by "them."

"Let's get clearance first."

"It's the end of the day, and the director's out of the office. That may take a while."

"Can't be helped."

***

The next morning, Mattie and Jack carried their luggage out of the hotel and stood under the portico while they waited for a cab. The man who had been sitting in the large lobby pretending to read rose from the couch. He made his way to the hotel parking lot and climbed into an unobtrusive rental car. When the cab carrying Mattie and Jack pulled away from the hotel, he fell in behind them and followed, allowing one or two cars to fill the gap between them for the forty-five minutes it took to get to Dulles International.

When they left the cab at the airport curb, the man drove past them and parked at the short-term curb, ignoring the signs warning drivers not to leave cars unattended. He hurried into the terminal. It took him a few moments to spot them waiting to pass through security at the A concourse. He located one of the large screens where arrivals and departures were posted. He noted the number of the flight which was due to depart for Phoenix Sky Harbor Airport in about an hour.

He hurried back to his car and pulled away just as the airport police officer had begun posting tickets on driverless vehicles. He pulled his satellite phone from his jacket pocket and hit a button. "They're on flight 207 to Phoenix, arriving at Sky Harbor Airport at 5:45 this afternoon."

***

Following orders, Holst had arrived at Sky Harbor Airport early in the morning of the previous day. He did as he had been instructed and rented a delivery-type van. He paid the extra fee to have a GPS furnished with the vehicle. His next task was to find a store where he could buy a handgun.

While the scruffy-looking clerk waited, Holst carefully examined a dozen weapons, finally making his selection: a Colt .357 automatic. The entire process reminded him of how much he hated flying commercial. He couldn't bring his own familiar weapons.

The sales clerk pushed the federally required form to him. "Fill this out. You can pick up the gun in two days."

Holst filled it out with the fictitious name on the driver's license he carried and a social security number he knew was clean. When he slid the form back to the clerk, he included two bills—hundreds—with it. "I'm sure you can get the check done by tomorrow."

Eyeing the cash, the man cleared his throat. "Yeah, maybe I can arrange that." He slipped the bills into his pocket and added, "Come in tomorrow afternoon. I'm sure it'll be done."

It was unlikely that a federal check would be done by then, but another two hundred would probably complete the transaction anyway. Holst knew he was taking a chance, but he didn't have any other choice.

The next morning, he received the telephone call from Glenn. "Stitz says that the woman and the cop will be arriving at Sky Harbor Airport today at five forty-five. Stafinski is flying us down to Phoenix, and we expect to be there by four. We're cutting this close, but if no one screws up, it'll work. Do you have the woman's home address?"

"Yes, I've got it."

"Give it to me." After Glenn wrote the address down, Volos took the phone from him. "Get yourself out to the woman's home. Hopefully she and the cop will go there directly when they get to town. Wait for us there. Look over the neighborhood thoroughly. We'll meet you there before five."

Holst found a Goodwill store and bought some old clothing. After changing in a gas station restroom, he spent the next hour going door-to-door in the Southland neighborhood passing himself off as a gardener-for-hire. He learned what he needed to know; there was a rear wall that could easily be climbed without the likelihood of being seen.

The expected call from Glenn came at four thirty-five.

"We've arrived at Mesa Gateway airport. Stafinsky will wait with the plane. We've rented a car, and we're eighteen miles from the address you gave us. We'll see you shortly. Have you familiarized yourself with the area?"

"Yes."

"Is there access to the grounds and the residence?"

"Yes, if I go over the back wall, I can let you in the front gate when you arrive."

"Do it. We'll meet you there."

It was dark when the rented Cadillac carrying Volos and Glenn arrived at Valhalla Drive. When they recognized the address on the gate post, Glenn flashed his headlights twice. Inside the property, a figure crossed to the gate from the shadows of a large tree, and as he broke the electric eye beam, the gate rolled open.

The Cadillac drove through and followed the curving driveway around to the back, where Glenn parked it on the concrete pad behind the double garages.

Glenn finally said what he'd been thinking for the previous half hour. "Mr. Volos, I think you should leave this to me and Holst. We still have time to get you to a hotel. Holst and I can handle it."

"Shut up, Glenn. I want to see their faces." He smiled malevolently. "Tell Holst to find a place at the end of the house where he won't be seen when they arrive."

Glenn still had reservations about the plan but answered, "Yes, sir."

Glenn and Volos sat in the front seat of the Cadillac and waited. Holst stood in the shadows at the end of the house, watching the front gate. When he saw the Chrysler Town & Country arrive and the gate began to slide open, he crouched behind a large arborvitae at the rear corner of the garage and watched the car as it moved up the long drive-way. Volos insisted on remaining in the front passenger seat, but Glenn climbed out of the Cadillac and moved to the far side of the vehicle, stooping so he wouldn't be seen. He held his handgun and waited.

***

When the car turned onto Valhalla Drive, it was nearly seven thirty. Mattie gave a deep, heartfelt sigh of relief. "It's so good to finally be home. Thank goodness for Aunt Cecelia's car, though it did cost me plenty to get it out of long-term parking." She leaned back and closed her eyes for a few seconds before a thought made her sit up and open her eyes. "Oh, Jack, we should have gone to your place. I could have dropped you off there before I came home."

"Don't worry about it. I'll call a cab when we get inside."

"I'm sorry to put you to the trouble." By this time they had reached the gate. "The gate code is nine-two-two-three."

Jack punched in the code, and they both watched the gate open. The car wound up the driveway and around to the rear, where a black Cadillac sat parked behind the garages.

"Mattie, whose car in that? Does it belong to your uncle?"

"No. I have no idea how it got here."

"Someone's sitting in it." Jack was suddenly very wary.

As the headlights washed over the vehicle, Glenn stood and stepped out with his gun drawn. Jack grabbed Mattie's left arm and pushed her to the floor. He threw the minivan into reverse, looked over his shoulder, and started backing down the drive. Another man stepped onto the driveway behind them. His drawn gun made his point.

The man said nothing. He didn't have to. Jack hit the brake and raised his left arm as he put the car in park with his right. Then he raised that arm.

The unfamiliar man yanked open the passenger side door. "Get out," he hissed at Mattie as he pushed the gun in her face.

Mattie struggled out of the car with her hands raised. "What do you want? Who are you?" But she was sure she knew. "You're working for Volos, aren't you?"

The slam of the door of the Cadillac drew their attention to the figure that had climbed out. The sharp intake of Mattie's breath told everyone that she recognized Volos.

The old man stood smiling before her, but it was not a pleasant smile. "Holst, go get the van," he ordered as he walked around the car toward Mattie.

Holst stated, "I'll need the gate code to get in."

"Give him the code, or I'll have Holst shoot your friend in the knee." Volos was still smiling, and his quiet voice was more threatening that a shout would have been.

"The code is nine-two-two-three."

Holst returned the weapon to its holster under his arm.

"What do you want?" Mattie was feeling light-headed, and her heart was pumping so hard and fast she wondered if she was going to faint. "You don't need to hurt us."

Volos nodded at Holst, who sprinted across the rear lawn and vaulted to the top of the wall. Volos turned back with a venomous smile. "But you see, that is just what I plan to do, missy. Remember my promise—I can make it fast, or I can make it slow."

Mattie shivered involuntarily. Yes, she remembered. The others stood without speaking until Holst brought the van through the gate. Cecelia's minivan was partially blocking the driveway, so he drove out around it on the lawn and then parked it next to the Cadillac. When he had climbed out, he went around to the rear, opened the doors, reached in, and removed a large roll of duct tape.

He pulled a pair of handcuffs from his pants pocket and nodded at Jack. "Put your hands in back." Jack did as he was told, and Holst snapped the handcuffs on him. He tore a strip of tape off and pressed it over Jack's mouth.

He stepped over to Mattie and said simply, "Put out your hands." She did so, and he tore off a long strip of duct tape and taped her wrists together. He finished by taping her hands to her waist. He taped her mouth as well.

"Both of you will get in the back of the van and lay down with your feet toward the doors." Holst motioned for Mattie to climb in first. She sat in the open doorway, pulled her knees up and in, and rolled toward one side. Jack did the same.

Holst leaned in and taped their ankles. Stepping back, he slammed the doors. Moving around to the driver's side door, he climbed in and started the engine. He backed out onto the lawn and drove around the minivan. The Cadillac followed.

Jack was desperately wondering how he was going to protect Mattie. *What is he planning? Where are they taking us?* Both questions pounded through his mind like the adrenaline pumping through his body.

The floor of the van was hard and uncarpeted, and as Holst made a sharp left turn, Mattie rolled into Jack. She closed her eyes and fervently prayed for a solution to their situation.

***

On the way to the airport, Volos dialed Stafinski's cell. "File a VFR flight plan with the tower for Tucson. If they ask, just tell them this will be a short hop, and we'll be staying under ten thousand feet."

"Where are we really going, sir?"

"Where do you think?" Volos snapped. "We're going to Cubaqua."

When they reached the airport, Holst pulled to the side of the road and let Glenn's vehicle take the lead. He then pulled in behind the Cadillac.

Glenn pulled up to a gate that blocked unauthorized vehicles from entering the hangar area. He reached out of the car window and pressed the intercom button. After Volos identified himself as the owner of the Learjet waiting in the first hangar and the driver in the van following as his pilot, the bar was lifted, and the two vehicles moved across the tarmac and into a large but deserted hangar. Both vehicles stopped near the rear of the hangar, where they were hidden from view.

Stafinski had been watching for them. He quickly opened the hatch and lowered the stairs.

Looking around to make sure they were not seen, Holst opened the rear van doors and pulled the tape off the ankles of both his prisoners. "Get out." When Mattie wasn't quick enough, he grabbed her ankles and pulled her forcefully toward the open doors. Jack managed to stand. "Get into the plane."

Mattie and Jack were hurried up the stairs with Holst behind them, his handgun hidden by a folded newspaper.

As Holst pushed her back onto a leather couch, Mattie looked around. She recognized the interior of the plane. Holst looked at Jack and pointed at the couch. Jack sat as best he could with his hands still cuffed behind him.

"Get this plane off the ground." Volos's voice cut like a whip. He sat down in the seat Mattie had used on the earlier flight to Canada and fastened his seat belt. Glenn followed his example. He took the gun Holst handed him while Holst sat down and fastened his seat belt. Then he returned the gun to Holst.

After the plane was airborne, Volos ordered, "Take the tape off their mouths." Without concern for any discomfort caused, Holst yanked it off.

"We've got a long flight ahead of us. I suggest we all relax." Volos apparently had. He spoke as if he were commenting on the weather.

An hour after they were in the air, Mattie found herself fighting to maintain her composure. *I can't let him see how frightened I am.* Her heart was banging so hard each beat hurt. She cleared her throat. "I need to use the restroom."

Volos responded with oily courtesy. "By all means, Miss Mathis. Holst, free her hands."

She stood, and while Holst cut the tape that bound her wrists to her waist, she added, "Jack's arms must be hurting, pulled behind his back that way. We're hardly a threat to anyone several thousand feet in the air." She hoped her pounding heartbeat was not discernible in her voice.

"And I suppose you want me to make him more comfortable." His voice was full of a sneer. He sat silent for a few seconds before he finally responded. "Put his hands in front of him, Holst. He's no threat to anyone." The jibe in his voice was plain.

In the restroom, Mattie leaned against the little sink and sobbed for three or four minutes, grateful that the noise of the engines would cover the sound.

"Please, please find help for us, dear God—or give us the wisdom to figure out how to get out of this mess." The words were interspersed between her sobs. Beginning to calm somewhat, she looked in the mirror. She was alarmed at her swollen eyes and red face. A few hand towels emblazoned with the logo of the Volos Investment Fund soaked in cold water helped her color return to normal. Her eyes were still slightly swollen, but she couldn't do anything about that.

She noticed the simple enamel pin on the collar of her jacket. *It might be useful.* She labored to get it unhooked until her fingers were slick with perspiration. It was awkward with both hands still taped together, so she found an end of the tape around her wrists. Scraping it against the edge of the sink until the back of her hand was bruised, she rolled back a corner. Using her teeth, she pulled about six inches loose. She pressed the adhesive side of that piece to the edge of the sink. Rotating her wrists as much as possible, she was able to pull more of it loose. Repeating the process, she finally reached the end, freeing her hands. She rubbed her wrists to get the circulation moving and removed the pin. It was nearly the same color as the pantsuit, just a pink enamel M. It wasn't flashy. She dropped it into her pants pocket. *It might be of use somehow*, she thought, *if none of them notice that it's missing.*

When she returned and sat on the couch, Holst rose and began to pull a strip of tape from the roll. Volos stopped him. "No, Holst. She was clever enough to get it off. We'll leave her hands free for the time being." Holst returned to his seat with a look of skepticism.

Jack's hands were cuffed in front now, and he was sitting back against the couch.

"Give them both something to drink, Glenn. We should be good hosts for our guests."

Glenn moved to the wet bar and brought back two bottles of mineral water. Both Mattie and Jack were tired, hungry, and thirsty. They emptied the bottles in one long drink. Within ten minutes, both were yawning. Mattie looked at Jack. They locked eyes, and recognition arced between them like a jolt of electricity as they both realized what Volos had done.

"You've drugged us," Jack stated flatly.

She could hear Volos's laughter like sandpaper on concrete as the world grew dark around her.

Chapter Thirty-Two

WHEN MATTIE DIDN'T CALL, CECELIA became worried. As the hours passed, she tried Mattie's cell phone several times.

She and Max had gone to bed at eleven, but by eleven thirty, she was too agitated to sleep. She pulled the book he was reading out of his hands. "Max, she promised she'd call when they got there. I'm worried about her."

"Have you tried calling?"

"Yes, but her phone went to voice mail every time."

"Perhaps they caught a later flight and are still in the air."

"No, Max. Something's wrong. I can feel it. *I can feel it.*" She stressed each word. "Please do something."

"If it'll make you feel better, I'll call Chief Jepson. It isn't so late out there."

He reached Jepson at home and explained the situation. "Will you get the local police to send a car out to check on the house? See if they got there alright?" He gave Jepson the gate code and ended by asking, "You'll let me know what they find, won't you?"

"Of course."

***

The Paradise Valley patrol car entered the Southland estate, and the officer drove up the driveway slowly, looking for anything that might be amiss. At the end of the driveway, he found it. The Chrysler minivan sat blocking the way to the backyard and was covered with drops from the light rain that had fallen an hour earlier. He got out and tried the passenger side door. It opened. He could see a purse between the two front seats and two suitcases in the back. He hurried to the patio door and rang the doorbell several times. When there was no response, he climbed back into his car and ran the license plate on the minivan through the dashboard computer. It came up registered to Cecelia Southland.

"Dispatch, contact Chief Jepson of the Mesa PD and tell him there's a vehicle registered to the Congressman's wife sitting in the driveway. There're a couple suitcases in it and a woman's purse. The car's been here long enough for the rain to leave it wet, so it was parked here at least an hour ago, maybe more."

Upon getting the call, Chief Jepson responded, "Please have the officer stay there. I'm on my way." He slowly shook his head before he picked up the phone to return Southland's call.

Jepson's wife had muted the television and was listening to the conversation. "Is there something the matter, dear?"

"Yeah, in a big way. I've got to go out. You go to bed. I may be a while." He always told her that, even though she never went to bed until he returned home.

Southland picked up. "Yes?" His voice was tense.

"Congressman Southland, there's an officer at your home. Your wife's car is in the driveway with suitcases in the back, but no one's answering the doorbell. Do we have your permission to force one of the doors and check the house?"

"Yes, right away."

"I'll get back to you with what he finds."

Jepson drove his department car toward the Southland home using the lights and siren, keeping tabs on the situation through the Paradise Valley department dispatcher. He was halfway there when the information came back, "There's no one there. The house looks undisturbed."

He wasn't relieved. He knew an undisturbed house probably meant that Mattie and Jack had been grabbed before they got inside.

When he relayed the news to Southland, the congressman said firmly, "Call the local office of the bureau. This has got to be a kidnapping. Keep me posted every step of the way."

"Will do."

***

As Southland hung up, he knew what he needed to do. By now, Cecelia was in her robe and slippers. She watched him search the pockets of his suits in the closet.

"Max, where are they? What's going on?"

"We don't know, my dear. We're really just guessing right now, but I'm going on a worst-case scenario." He turned to look at her. "Did you find anything in my suit pockets when my suit was sent to the cleaners?"

She rose and went to her purse. "I've got a little plastic bag of things in your pockets when the man picked up the cleaning. What are you looking for?"

"A business card from Bill Adams. I need to call him."

"Here it is." She offered it to him.

He took the card out of the little bag and dialed Adams's cell number. "Bill, Mattie and Jack have disappeared. The police are on it out in the metro Phoenix area. I asked that the local bureau office be contacted, but I want you on it. And I want to contact Jeremy Logan at the CIA. Can you arrange it?"

Recognizing the tension in Southland's voice, Adams knew better than to debate the matter. "I'll get ahold of him, and either he or I will get back to you right away."

Max paced the floor for the next half hour. When the phone rang, it was Logan. Southland's voice reflected near panic. "Look, I'm sorry if this matter got you out of bed, but I need to know where Volos is."

"I have a team tracking down the most recent report on his location. I'm heading to my office immediately, but first tell me what you know."

Max recounted what little he knew. "If they've been taken out of the country, I want you and Giles on it."

"Yes, sir." Logan ended the conversation apologetically by saying, "I'll get back to you as soon as I know more—and Congressman Southland, I'm deeply sorry we involved the two of them in our operation."

"Yeah, me too." That was all Southland could bring himself to say.

Logan called back an hour later. When the phone rang, Southland sat in the chair by the bed before he answered it as if his legs might not support him if what he heard was bad news.

Logan's voice was all business. "I'm at my office at the CIA Special Activities Center. I have a report in front of me stating that the pilot of Volos's plane filed an IFR flight plan—"

"And that is?"

"That's an Instrument Flight Report, which means the plane was going to be above ten thousand feet altitude. He filed the plan the day before yesterday. The plane stopped to refuel in Saskatoon and halted overnight in Edmonton. About ten yesterday morning—their time, not ours—it left Edmonton and flew south, crossing into the U.S. well before noon and landing in Phoenix at about four thirty their time. Less than three hours later, the pilot filed a VFR—Visual Flight Report—for Tucson, which means they planned to stay below ten thousand feet, probably thinking that if they stayed low enough to avoid being tracked on radar, they could "get lost" and no one would be able to locate them. According to the GPS signal, the plane flew well beyond Tucson and right now is a couple of hours north of Mexico City and still moving south. I've been in contact with Special Agent Adams at the bureau, and we're coordinating our response." He added as if to offer some hope, "When we know where the plane finally lands, we'll find them and get them back." He said it as if he were pledging his life.

"Keep me posted." When the call ended, Southland put his head in his hands.

Cecelia approached her husband and put her hand on his shoulder. "They'll be all right, Max." He was the one who usually comforted her, but this time, she could see his distress. "She'll be all right, Max. If prayer can make any difference, they'll both be all right." She needed the comfort of her words as much as he did.

**

As the altitude of the plane continued to drop, the ringing in Mattie's ears lessened, and she managed to sit up. She shook her head to clear it. As she looked out the window on the opposite side of the fuselage, she could see that it was daylight and they were over water, a limitless, indifferent sea.

"Is that one of the Great Lakes?" she asked aloud as she yawned. She took several deep breaths to suppress the nausea she was feeling.

"Yes, missy, it's the greatest of the great lakes. That is the Caribbean." Volos spoke as if taking pleasure in explaining the situation to a child.

The plane continued its descent until Mattie began to wonder if they were headed for a water landing. Finally, she saw a flash of gray earth, an island that sat like a great rock surrounded by the ocean. The wheels bumped and came to a hard stop.

***

When the phone rang, Price cleared the sleep out of his head with a shake.

It was Logan's voice. "I know you planned to take the day off, but can you get yourself down here to the office? Giles and I are planning something that involves your favorite employer."

"Yeah, yeah. I can be there in thirty minutes."

He rolled over as his wife opened her eyes and asked sleepily, "Can't they do without you for a couple of days while you get some rest?"

"Evidently not." He gave her a quick kiss and hurriedly pulled on his clothes.

***

Logan looked at his watch. It was nearly six a.m. He looked as if he hadn't slept since receiving the call from Adams because he hadn't.

He grabbed the printout before it could be handed to him. His eyebrows drew together as he studied it. Pointing at the final location listing, he asked, "Where is this?"

The IT man turned to his computer keyboard and typed in the coordinates. "It looks like somewhere near the coast of Venezuela, sir."

With a terse "Thanks," Logan sprinted down the hall toward the office he shared with Giles. "It looks like Volos has them at his Venezuelan compound. I called Price and asked him to come in. He should be here right away. He may have usable information." He picked up his phone. "It's time to call the director." While he waited for the man to answer, he muttered, "If we don't get to them right away, we'll never see them again."

Finally the call connected, and Logan spoke into the phone. "Sir, we were right. It appears that Volos has the niece of Congressman

Southland and the Arizona cop who's been protecting her at his compound on that island he owns just off the coast of Venezuela. Do I have your permission to move forward with a rescue operation?"

"Yes, do it. Run your plans past me first though. I'll be in the office in forty minutes."

Giles spent the next fifty minutes demanding and finally obtaining satellite photos of the location of the Volos island compound. In the pictures, the little island looked like nothing more than a big rock about five miles long surrounded by water. The coast of Venezuela was a few miles south and Isla de Margarita a few miles to the north.

Logan turned his attention to contacting the US commander on the base of Palanquero, north of Bogotá, where the Columbian government permitted the U.S. to station fourteen hundred military troops and contractors assigned to lead the battle against the Colombian drug cartels.

As he spoke to the base commander on a scrambled telephone line, he stressed the urgency of the matter. "Speed is imperative. I need a SEAL team and a helicopter to rescue two hostages we believe are being held on the island of Cubaqua, just off the coast of Venezuela."

"I know where it is," Commander Parker responded.

"The female victim is the niece of a long-term congressman, and the man with her is a cop from Arizona."

"Who's behind it?"

"Gregorovich Volos."

"I'll put the SEAL team on standby."

Chapter Thirty-Three

WHEN THE DIRECTOR ARRIVED, HE picked up the phone and told Logan and Giles to meet him in his office.

"Sir, Price just got here. I think we need him too." It was Logan's suggestion.

"Bring him. Be prepared to tell me everything you know about the situation and your proposed plan to deal with it."

When the three men entered his office, the director instructed Price to close the door behind him. "Sit. What's your plan?"

"We need to send in a SEAL team to pull the hostages out. That's got to be done after dark. That gives us about ten hours to get it set up."

"What's the native population on that island?"

"Basically none. During the rainy season—which doesn't start until June—a few fishermen come over from Isla de Margarita. At that time of the year, there are evidently a couple of sporadic streams that have eroded a couple of gullies and formed a beach. Other than that, the island is little more than a big volcanic rock."

"How does he get his water and power?"

"He must have a generator and some kind of desalinization plant."

"How fortified is his compound?"

"There are no walls, so access is only complicated by the lack of cover and a lighthouse not far from the compound."

The telephone on his desk rang, and when the director picked up the receiver, he told his secretary, "I'll take it, just give me about ten seconds." He hit the mute button and looked at Logan. "Get the details shaped up and move on it. Close the door on your way out."

***

Logan called Commander Parker in Colombia again. He hit the speaker button so Giles and Price could hear the conversation.

"I need photos of the island." That was Parker's first request.

"Consider it done." He looked at Giles and instructed, "Get it done ASAP." Giles left the room.

Logan returned to his conversation with the base commander while he examined the photos in his hands. "Commander, you'll get the photos via e-mail right away. The team will need to go in under cover of dark—and it needs to be tonight."

"What about elevation? Will they be scaling any bluffs or cliffs?"

"Its highest point is only about 125 feet. The majority of the island is little more than sea level. The big problem will be getting men onto it without being seen. We have a man here who's worked for Volos." He looked at Price as he spoke. "He's been told that there're at least two guards with dogs and automatic weapons on the grounds at all times, and another guard on the roof. There's a security room with closed-circuit TV, an inside guard, and an armed house staff of two. Each team works a twelve-hour shift, so a similar team will be off duty in their own quarters. From the map, it looks like it's about eight hundred miles from Bogotá. How soon will your team be ready to go?"

"We can get that done in an hour."

"How long to get them there?"

"The team I'll use is stationed at the naval base near Santa Ana. That's a whole lot closer to your target. That puts the team less than four hundred miles from Cubaqua. They're waiting for orders right now."

"We'll need them on the island by dark."

"They can handle it."

When the call ended, Logan, Giles, and Price put their heads together and continued the discussion with one difficult question. "How do we get them off the island once we have them? Can the SEALs take inflatable rafts in with them?" Price asked.

"Probably, but getting that many people into international waters in a couple of inflatable rafts presents a whole new set of problems."

An idea ignited in Price's brain like a little explosion at the base of his skull. "The jet! Volos has the jet right there. Why can't we put a pilot into the rescue team?"

"If we did, could he access the plane?"

Price's enthusiasm increased. "Can you get me down there in time?"

Logan and Giles looked at each other as if their friend had lost his mind. "Why would you need to be there?"

"Because I have one of the two remote controls that opens the hatch and drops the stairs. Without it, you can't get inside. Volos was considering all possibilities when he had it outfitted that way. I don't know of any other way we can be sure to get our hands on the jet and get it off the ground." His words were coming almost as fast as his mind was working. "Look, if I can get out to Andrews Air Base and on an F-18, I can be in Columbia in less than six hours."

Giles looked at him in astonishment. "Price, you're forty years old. How're you going to handle a flight in an F-18?"

Price looked a little miffed. "I flew one in Desert Storm. I'm not so old that I can't handle it. Just get me on the plane and to Colombia in time to add me to the SEAL team. I'll get 'em off that island."

Giles and Logan locked eyes. "Go," they both responded at once. As Price bolted from the office, Logan picked up the phone. "Get me the director," he told his secretary.

***

Mattie and Jack were ordered off the plane by a wave of Holst's gun. As she reached the bottom of the stairs, she paused momentarily and looked around. Jack stepped beside her. "What a horrible place," she whispered. "It's no more than a big rock surrounded by ocean." Any hope for rescue began to melt. The knot tightened in her stomach.

"Do you want me to tape her hands again?" Holst asked Volos.

"No, what's she going to do? Where would she go?" He laughed raucously. "Maybe she could swim to the mainland." He looked over at Mattie and added, "Do you swim well, missy?"

She didn't bother to answer.

Stafinski busied himself putting the chocks behind and in front of the wheels. The plane sat on a runway that extended from southeast to northwest on a peninsula that jutted into the water to the north of the main body of the island. At the end of the peninsula about a thousand feet away, a tall red-and-white lighthouse dominated the scene.

About the same distance in the other direction was a large concrete building. A tall radio antenna and dish rose more than fifty feet above it. The structure was marked by a balcony which wrapped around the second story and had two large windows that looked out on the runway. A guard with an AK-47 watched their arrival from the flat roof. Two more uniformed guards stood on either side of the only visible entrance; each held the leash of a German shepherd that strained toward the newcomers with bared teeth.

Holst prodded Mattie and Jack toward the building. The two guards stepped aside, pulling the dogs out of reach, and saluted. Glenn stepped in front of the group and entered a six-digit code on the numbered lock embedded in the doorframe.

As the group stepped inside, the security guard sitting in front of two large TV monitors stood and saluted. Mattie noticed that the room looked much like the security room at the Adirondack compound. One screen displayed four views of the exterior and the other, four indoor scenes.

The guard spoke. "Buenos Dias, Senor Volos."

With a curt nod, Volos stood aside and waited for Glenn to push open the door into the next room. As Glenn motioned Mattie and Jack in, they noted the large window in the middle of the left-hand wall. The room behind it was dark.

Volos spoke. "Put them in there. I'll deal with them later. It's time for a hearty, if belated, breakfast. Glenn, you called ahead so the staff knew we were coming?"

"Yes, sir."

As Volos disappeared into an elevator on the far side of the room, Holst motioned Mattie and Jack through a heavy metal door near the large window. It opened with a simple push bar. When they were inside, Glenn flipped on the light, and the door slammed with what Mattie felt was the hard sound of the loss of hope. Her hands were damp with nervous perspiration, so she wiped them on her slacks.

The room was stark. The window into the other room reflected Mattie's white face as she looked around. The room had no exterior windows. The walls were made of rough blocks painted a dirty yellow. Stains and scuffs marred the walls and floor. The room smelled foul with old perspiration and other odors. The only furniture was a battered wooden chair. Remnants of tape clung to its arms. About eight inches below the ceiling and two feet parallel to the far wall, two pipes ran the length of the room. They each ended at an elbow joint, carrying hot and cold water into the rooms above.

Mattie could see that Jack's tension level was increasing. The muscles in his jaw were bunched and hard.

Glenn stood unmoving just inside the door. Holst stepped up to Jack and motioned for him to raise his hands. He pulled out the key and unlocked the handcuffs. Mattie's relief was short-lived though. He ordered Jack to stand under the first water pipe and raise his hands above his head.

"Put your hands up—higher—one on each side of the pipe." Jack did as he was told, and Holst refastened the cuffs locking Jack's arms well above his head.

Glenn and Holst withdrew without saying more.

As their captors exited the room, Mattie could see them through the window as they moved to the elevator.

Why did they leave me free to move around? she wondered. When the elevator closed behind them, she rushed to the door, but it was locked. A keypad that required a numeric code was embedded in the doorframe.

"Mattie, try to guess the code." Jack urged.

She halted and turned to him. "Jack, even if I guessed it and thought I could make it past the guard in the security room next door, I'm not leaving you here."

"I appreciate the thought, but if you get the chance to break out of here—with or without me—do it."

"Where would I go? We're on an island in the middle of an ocean. It wouldn't do either of us any good."

She turned away from the door and grabbed the chair. Placing it near his feet, she urged, "Here, stand on this. It'll give you some relief."

"Steady it for me." It twisted slightly under his weight. "Thanks. That helps." He stood on the chair for a few seconds before he grasped the pipe with both hands. He pulled away immediately. "It's hot."

After he had taken a deep breath, he grasped it again, testing the temperature. "It must be about 120 degrees." He ignored the heat that was burning his palms and twisted until the tendons in his arms and neck stood out. It didn't give.

"Are you turning it the right direction?" She was watching his efforts closely. "In some countries, plumbing threads turn opposite to what we're used to."

"Yeah, I should have remembered that. I'll try the other direction." He wiped his right palm on the back of his left hand, grabbed the pipe again, and twisted until his face was red and his jaw muscles a great lump. "No luck," he said breathlessly. He paused and then inhaled slowly several times before grasping the pipe again. The next time he let go, he said, "I think I felt it give a little."

As Jack put every ounce of his strength into it, the pipe gave a fraction of an inch. Again, he paused to catch his breath.

Mattie was dividing her attention between Jack's efforts and the other room, watching for any sign of Holst or Glenn. "How long before they come back?"

Jack was panting. "Soon. When they're done with breakfast, they'll come back and get to work."

"Get to work . . . ?" Mattie's question hung in the air. She was increasingly terrified for Jack.

He labored for another five minutes and then said weakly, "Hold on to the chair while I get down." He stepped wearily off it. "I don't want them to know what I've been trying to do. I need to save what strength I have for what's to come. Put the chair back where it was."

When she had done so, she sat in it weakly. The fear was sapping her strength and resilience.

The elevator door opened, and both of them could see Volos, Holst, and Glenn step out. Only Holst pushed through the door into the room with Jack and Mattie. He let the metal door slam behind him. Glenn positioned two comfortable armchairs on the other side of the glass and turned off the light in the other room, effectively making the window a one-way mirror.

Holst had brought another roll of duct tape with him. It was a grotesque bracelet on his left wrist. Mattie nervously stood.

"Put your arms out," he commanded. He swiftly wrapped each of her wrists tightly against an arm of the chair. "Hope you enjoyed your freedom while we were gone. It's over now." Mattie's fear became nearly suffocating.

While Holst casually pulled on a pair of heavy leather gloves, Mattie noticed a slow drip of water that had begun to drop from the elbow joint near the ceiling.

Holst moved menacingly toward Jack.

Chapter Thirty-Four

"WHAT DO YOU WANT FROM US? Why are you doing this? What do you want?" Mattie repeatedly screamed as Holst hit Jack in the solar plexus again and again. The blood from his broken nose had splattered on her a few minutes earlier. His lip was split, and his left eye socket was swelling. Holst seemed to enjoy his work.

On the other side of the glass, Volos rose and walked to the intercom on the wall. He pressed the button and said simply, "I'm getting exactly what I want from you, missy—satisfaction." The sound of his voice made Mattie's head jerk toward the window. He continued with malevolence. "This is just payback. I'm going to make him bleed and moan and cry for help. Then it will be your turn. Remember my promise? I can kill you quick, or I can kill you slow." He returned to sit in his comfortable chair.

After another hour, Volos turned to Glenn. "Holst is tiring, Sid. Roll up your sleeves and give him a break. You can take over for a while, can't you?"

Without comment, he stood and slipped off his suit coat and shoulder holster. He laid them in the chair he had been using. As he walked toward the door, he folded the cuffs of his white shirt back to his elbows. When he stepped inside the room, Holst paused to look at him. "Mr. Volos says I'm to relieve you." With some malice, he added, "He says you look tired."

"If you think you can do better, you're welcome to try."

Glenn held out his hand for the gloves. He took his time pulling them on as Holst left.

"Go get a shower and change, Holst. You smell." Volos returned to watching the action behind the big window.

"Do you want me back here?"

"Not immediately. When Glenn is tired, I'm going to take a nap, and then we'll have a late lunch. There's no hurry. We have all the time in the world. Later, I have entertainment of another sort planned."

Glenn moved around so his body camouflaged his movements. As his first blow came toward Jack, Jack grimaced and tightened his bruised and battered muscles in anticipation. He had expected the blow to be much harder. He looked into Glenn's eyes in surprise. With his back to the window, Glenn mouthed the words, "Make a good show of it."

Even though Glenn was not putting his full strength into the blows, they were still painful for Jack, whose face and body were swelling with purpling bruises. After nearly an hour, Glenn struck Jack a glancing blow on his jaw, and Jack let his head fly back. When Glenn stepped away, Jack dropped his head forward as if he were unconscious.

Volos stood and tapped on the window. When Glenn opened the door, his boss said briefly, "This is getting boring. Go and get changed for lunch. You smell like a pig."

"Yes, sir." Glenn pulled off the gloves and left the room.

***

Jack waited nearly a full five minutes before he raised his head and spoke, hoping that Volos had gone. He whispered in exhaustion, "Mattie, do you still have your watch?"

She lifted her head, and he could see tears streaking her cheeks.

"Don't cry for me. It isn't as bad as it looks." He gave her a crooked smile through a split lip. "What time is it?"

"I can't tell. My watch is under the tape." She tried to suppress the shudder that ran through her. "I've been praying for you, Jack—for both of us. I wish I could do more. When it's my turn, please say a prayer for me."

"Of course I will." He smiled at her to lift her spirits "But help will come before then. Hang tough. They've gone to eat, and Volos said he wanted a nap, so that gives us some time. Can you scoot your chair over here?"

"I'll try."

She bent forward and lifted the chair off the floor. She goose walked nearer. "Now what?"

"Turn around and put your back to me so I can stand on the back edge of the seat."

When she set the chair down, he put the toe of one shoe on the back of the seat and gingerly lifted himself up to where he could grasp the pipe again. With the toe of the other shoe also precariously on the seat edge, he returned to loosening the pipe again. "Can you push the chair back a little further so I can steady my balance?" She pushed it back about four inches. "That's good." The drip at the far end of the room increased to a steady trickle.

***

Price was introduced to the SEALs within ten minutes of climbing out of the fighter jet. They stood in the office of the base commander, who perfunctorily introduced each man.

"Just so you know who you're going to be working with, this is CB, the team commander on this mission." CB was a blond with eyebrows and eyelashes so light they looked nonexistent.

"CB? As in a CB radio?" Price said with a grin.

"No, as in Charlie Brown," the man responded without humor. He offered no further explanation.

The base commander continued. "Next to him is Stubbs, so named because he's the shortest of the group." The man named Stubbs was a bulky five ten whereas the other team members were all over six feet. "That's Nemo next to him. He's our best swimmer. The redheaded guy is, of course, Red. The tallest guy is Cowboy, and the last man is Banger. He's our primary explosives man."

The commander handed Price a wet suit and an M-16 and pointed to an adjoining room. "Get changed. You'll leave in thirty minutes, and it may take you that long to put on the wet suit." The man was not joking.

"Are we going to do some swimming?" Price asked.

"No, but these give us the best night camouflage."

The blades of the chopper were turning when the six SEALs and Price—all in identical black wet suits—climbed into the Apache helicopter. CB had looked each man over and briefly made sure that

Price's radio headset and night vision goggles were correctly positioned and working. Five of the team, including Price, carried an M-16 with a flash suppressor slung over his shoulder. Banger also had a fanny pack full of explosives. In lieu of rifles, Cowboy and Red had .45s holstered on their hips and dart guns over their shoulders.

Holding back until everyone else was on board the helicopter, Price finally had to leverage himself inside. He dreaded the long ride in the Apache. He was still queasy from the hours in the F-18. He was feeling every one of his forty years. His heart was pounding with a combination of excitement and genuine concern that he might somehow screw up the mission. He wasn't sure yet if he hoped to see Volos or to avoid him.

The helicopter rose swiftly, and the pilot spoke to the control tower. "Departing at fifteen hundred hours. Expected arrival—eighteen hundred hours. Radio silence will be observed."

The pilot took note of the cloud bank to the east, where a weather front hovered. Lightning shot through the clouds. The wind bounced the big helicopter about, and when the rain began, it combined with the noise of the rotors.

"Good grief," CB muttered as the rain hit with a burst of noise. "We didn't need this."

Price grinned as he suddenly figured out why the team commander was called Charlie Brown or CB for short. After a few minutes of being tossed around like a beach ball, Price made a silent but fervent vow to avoid both F-18s and helicopters in the future.

After a radio check, there was no conversation among the men for the remainder of the ride. They had their instructions.

***

Running lights were darkened well before they crossed into Venezuelan air space. The heavy dusk was slowly enveloping the helicopter as it swept over the little islands scattered along the Venezuelan coast. The pilot kept the altitude low enough to be well under the radar of the hostile government.

CB watched the map coordinates on the glowing screen in front of him. He finally spoke. "Twenty clicks out. Drop site in four minutes."

The chopper slowed and dropped to twenty-five feet above the water. The pilot spoke to CB. "Give 'em the signal."

"Up and ready to go in three."

Stubbs rose and slid the side door open. As they settled to the rocky surface on the south side of the island, the sound of the blades was muffled by the heavy rain as well as the two miles of low hills between the compound and the big Apache. The last man was hardly out before the chopper had risen and headed west toward friendlier air space.

After checking their compasses, the team pulled the night vision goggles over their eyes. Price followed suit. The world was suddenly a luminescent green.

Two teams of two picked up the two inflatable rafts they had brought as a backup plan. They began to move as swiftly as they could under the weight of the rafts. When the beam of the lighthouse could be seen winking in the distance, they pushed the goggles off their faces and dropped the rafts. The rain had blown over as quickly as it had come, leaving tattered remnants of clouds moving in front of the quarter moon.

"Providence has played a hand," Price whispered to the others. "The lighthouse beam is oscillating at one-eighty degrees out to sea rather than rotating." He chuckled under his breath. "Only Volos could arrange something like that to keep the light from coming into his windows and bothering him."

As they approached on their bellies, CB ordered, "Banger, you and Stubbs handle the outbuildings—especially the generator building. Include the radio tower." They moved away, crouching close to the earth to lay the C-4 charges. The generator building was easily identified by the warning posted on it in Spanish.

The remaining five men moved a hundred yards closer on their bellies. At that point, they could make out the guard on the roof. One of the guards with a dog was making his rounds, so the men hugged the ground and waited for him to come nearer.

CB muttered into the radio mouthpiece, "Take them out."

Cowboy said quietly in his Texas drawl, "I'll take out the dog, Red."

In quick succession, the dart guns each made a pronounced "Bfssst," and the dog whined briefly and dropped, followed almost immediately by his handler. While the men reloaded the guns with a second dart, the other guard and his dog came around the east end of the building. They were both quickly dropped.

CB whispered into his mouthpiece, "Price, go!" Price moved away in the darkness.

"Cowboy, you'll take out the man on the roof." CB's voice was just above a whisper. CB heard the *pfffssst* of the dart gun and saw the man drop. "You and Red will stay here to cover us when the other guards get into the fight."

Price listened as CB and Nemo worked their way to the building, pressing up against the wall as they worked around to the front entrance. "Good grief," CB muttered. "This lock requires a numbered combination."

Chapter Thirty-Five

DESPITE THE PAIN OF HIS injuries and the heat of the pipe, Jack lifted his legs and, with ankles crossed above the pipe, scooted toward the elbow joint. When he reached it, he put one foot against it and pushed until the pipe separated. His weight pulled it toward the floor with a gush of hot water soaking him as he slid off.

"Jack, what are you going to do? We can't get out of this room." Mattie's face was a map of hopelessness.

As he pulled the tape from her arms, freeing her from the chair, he instructed, "I want you to flatten yourself against the floor under the window where you can't be seen."

"What are you going to do?"

"I'll crouch in the corner behind the door. When Holst enters, I'll try to take him by surprise."

As she wiped her sweating palms on her slacks, she felt the pin in her pocket. "Wait, maybe I can undo the handcuffs." She pulled out the enamel pin. He looked blankly at her, so she motioned for him to put his hands out to her. The pointed end of the clasp proved of little use, but the decorative squiggle on the top of the M was sturdier. She worked until her hand began to shake, but finally one of the cuffs opened.

"Oh, thank God," she whispered.

***

Volos laid his napkin on the table by his plate and looked at his watch. As he pushed his chair back, he said, "Sid, Holst, it's time we had the second act of our evening's entertainment."

As the three of them walked toward the elevator, Holst asked, "Do you plan on changing your approach, sir?" He was thinking about his bruised knuckles.

"Yes, the guards are expecting a call from me. I notified them before lunch that I wanted the dogs ready—all four of them."

"The dogs, sir?" Glenn was suddenly sickened.

Volos had only done this kind of thing one other time, when he'd dealt with a guard who had stolen something from him.

"Yes. We're going to release the girl and the cop and give them about a half hour's start before we release the dogs."

The elevator doors opened, and the three men stepped inside.

***

"Banger, do you guys have the C-4 in place back there?" CB spoke into the radio mouthpiece.

The answer came back, "Yes, sir. We're just waiting for the go-ahead to detonate."

"Send Stubbs around to the front of the compound with a lump of C-4. The door here has a combination lock that we'll need to blow," CB instructed.

"Will do."

It took Stubbs two minutes in the dark to find them at the front entrance. He pressed the explosive putty over the combination lock and warned, "Get back about twenty feet," as he inserted the detonator.

"Cowboy, you and Red are going to have to handle the second shift of guards if the noise raises them." CB's voice was tight.

"Will do."

The men crouched against the wall, facing away from the explosion. As soon as the door was shattered, CB ordered over the radio in a strong voice, "Banger, it's a go. Detonate!"

***

With the pin still in her hand, Mattie looked up as the elevator pinged and the doors began to open. Jack flipped off the light switch and pushed her down to keep her out of sight. He stepped back into the corner behind the door, splashing in the water that was accumulating on the floor.

As the elevator doors opened, the sound of an explosion drew the attention of Volos, Holst, and Glenn. "Mr. Volos, get back into the elevator," Holst yelled as he literally pushed his boss back inside and reached in to hit the close button. He withdrew from the elevator and looked around the room just as the doors closed jand a louder, larger explosion rocked the compound.

**

CB and Nemo entered the security room immediately. They easily overpowered the panicked security man. Through the shattered door, the flames outside threw a flickering light into the darkened room and turned it into a scene from Dante's *Inferno*, silhouetting the second team of guards as they exited their quarters at a run. The sound of gunfire started like the timpani in a Wagnerian opera.

CB and Nemo heard Cowboy and Red yell in Spanish, "Throw down your weapons," but the order was ignored. They opened fire.

Stubbs fired at the running guards from the shattered doorway as CB and Nemo moved into the next room. Stubbs yelled above the confusion outside, "Where's the woman and the cop? Turn them over to us now, and maybe we can make a deal."

Volos was yelling from where he was trapped in the darkened elevator. "What's going on, Holst? Glenn, get me out of here! Get these doors open!"

CB returned Holst's fire, killing him.

They could see Glenn nervously waving his handgun.

"Put down the gun, and we can make a deal," CB yelled. "Otherwise, you're a dead man."

It only took Glenn a fraction of a second to grasp at the offer. "Don't shoot. I'm putting down my gun. They're in the room over there." He pointed in the general direction of the darkened room behind the window.

CB pushed the door open, and seeing Mattie crouched below the window, he grabbed her wrist and lifted her to her feet. "Miss Mathis?"

"Who are you?" In panic, she struggled to pull away.

He raised his voice to be heard above the outside gunfire. "US military. We're here to take you home. Where's the cop?"

"Behind you . . . Jack, they've come for us," she yelled above the confusion.

CB turned and yelled at Jack, "Here, put your hand on my shoulder and follow me." He took Jack's hand and laid it on his shoulder. He was holding Mattie's arm in a tight grip. "We're going out. Hang on and stay close."

Determined not to be left behind, Glenn yelled, "You're taking me with you, aren't you? I'll testify! I'll be a government witness."

CB yelled at Nemo, "Take him along."

Nemo grabbed Glenn and pulled him toward the door. "Put your hands on your head," he yelled. Glenn did so. Nemo followed them out, offering cover with his M-16.

The sound of gunfire at the rear of the compound was lessening, but CB was pulling Mattie toward the plane so fast that Jack couldn't keep up. She yelled, "He's hurt. Give him some help."

CB paused for only a second as he looked back at Jack. He didn't slacken his pace as he pulled Mattie across the rocky ground toward the jet. Price had removed the chocks around the wheels, opened the hatch, and lowered the stairs. From where he sat in the cockpit, he watched the figures running for the plane in the flickering light.

Mattie was up the stairs first. As Jack labored up, she reached out to help him. CB motioned Glenn up, his hands still raised above his head.

CB ordered into the radio mouthpiece, "Time for extraction. Get yourselves to the plane. Now!" While they waited anxiously, Nemo kept a gun trained on Glenn.

Mattie located some napkins from the wet bar and started to gently wipe some of the blood from Jack's face. A few tears trickled down her cheeks as she did so.

"Jack, I was afraid I would lose you too," she whispered. "I couldn't stand that."

He took one of her hands. "You didn't lose me, Mattie, and you never will."

***

Stubbs covered for Cowboy and Red as they crouched and darted toward the end of the compound and around to the front of the building. Then, firing a steady stream, he dashed after them. They ran for the jet with heads down.

As they climbed in, CB demanded in a voice full of tension, "Where's Banger?"

A voice came over the radio, "I'm right behind you."

A long minute later, he climbed the stairs. CB yelled, "We're all here. Raise the stairs and close the hatch."

Banger didn't immediately comply. Instead, he turned and pointed his detonator remote unit toward the compound. Then, he stepped in and did as CB had instructed. With a tense grin, he stated above the sound of the engines, "Now, we need to get out of here fast. Keep an eye out the window. You've yet to see the best of the show."

It took a very long four minutes for Price to get the Learjet turned around and prepared to taxi down the runway. It took another three before it lifted off the little island. Mattie had leaned back in the chair with closed eyes as waves of relief swept over her.

Banger called out, "Keep your eyes open. You won't want to miss this."

Mattie opened her eyes and looked out the window as the island fell behind them. The waves of expanding air from the massive explosion were felt before they were heard. The plane bounced and rocked as half the island disappeared in a cloud of flame, rock, and debris.

"Good grief," CB yelled in amazement. "Banger, what'd you do?"

The explosives man grinned. "While you guys were goofing around trying to get into the compound, I located the jet fuel storage tank. I've always heard that stuff really burns hot. I put a ten-minute, remote fuse on it. It's a good thing we didn't take any longer getting off that rock." He settled back into his seat, fully satisfied with himself.

Chapter Thirty-Six

THAT EVENING, AS THEY WAITED for their server to bring their steaks, Mattie studied her hands in her lap. She had been very quiet since they had finished repeating the details of their experience with various government agencies. The story of Volos's death had been reported in the press and on news broadcasts as an explosion caused by a leaking natural gas line at his private Venezuelan island compound. There had been no natural gas lines on the little island, but the story was no less accurate than many stories in the media.

Jack picked up her right hand and turned to look at her. He lifted her chin with his other hand until she was looking into his eyes.

"You don't need to worry anymore. I talked with Bill Adams at the FBI late this afternoon, and he told me that Wilcoxin, Westfall, and the other senior partners from Doty, Dotson, and Diller have been arrested under the RICO statutes. In the hope of minimizing his sentence, Sid Glenn is sharing everything he knows about the whole operation down to the brand of toothpaste Volos used. Now your life will gradually get back to normal." He dropped his hand, but she continued to look into his eyes.

"I hope so." After a quiet moment, she added, "I owe you my life, Jack, and you nearly lost yours. If you hadn't been there, I'd be dead. You're the best friend I ever could have had—literally, an answer to prayer." With her free hand she lightly touched the bruising around his left eye. The formerly purple swelling was beginning to turn several shades of green.

His hand still held hers. "I'm glad I was there. I hope I'll always be your best friend, especially now that things are getting back to normal."

She nodded and smiled. She had the impression that he wanted to kiss her. As she pulled away from him very slightly, the voice she hadn't heard for many days spoke again: *"Don't look back, Mattie. You have so much to look forward to. You can still have a life full of experiences, full of love, but you must look to the future not the past. Let me go. I'm part of your past. This man is part of your future and will do for you what I wanted to if you give him the chance."*

Now that the nerves, fear, and tension were fading, she realized whose voice it was. It was Craig. He had been watching out for her. Now he had fully relinquished the assignment to Jack.

She began to relax as the evening progressed. Her thoughts were churning as she tried to determine what to remember, what to forget. When the car pulled around to the Southland garages, she had a far-away look in her eyes and sat wrapped in her thoughts.

At the door to the guest quarters, when she turned to tell him good night, he leaned toward her. This time she did not pull away. She returned his gentle kiss.

He straightened and asked with a smile, "Where do we go from here? Is there a future for us?"

She responded with a tentative smile and a nod. After taking a deep breath, she spoke with increased confidence. "Yes, yes, there is. We'll just go slow and see where it takes us." She gave him a smile more relaxed and glowing than any he had ever seen before. He encircled her with his arms and pulled her close. It was a warm and reassuring place to be.

About the Author

JEAN HOLBROOK MATHEWS WAS BORN in Ogden, Utah, but spent more than half her adult life in Missouri, where she was elected to the Missouri House of Representatives for ten years and then appointed to the Missouri State Medical Licensing Board for four years, where she was elected as the first non-physician president. During more than twenty years of public service in Missouri, she traveled to Washington, D.C., several times each year, and she became well acquainted with many members of the Senate and House, testified before Senate committees, and became familiar with the inner-workings of the federal government. She presently resides in Mesa, Arizona.